“They found us ”

Caden grabbed Gw e
could hear men yelli f
the camp, shouting her name. There was no doubt
they were looking for her.

Pain shot up her calf as she rushed through the brush with Caden, but she refused to let it slow her down. Those men were armed and, from everything she knew, planned to kill her when they found her.

Caden kept his arm around her, keeping her steady on the rugged path as the voices in the camp faded.

“Where are we going?” she asked.

“There’s a shallow spot in the river nearby. We need to cross over, then head downstream on the other side.”

And then what? She knew she couldn’t keep running. Not for long. She glanced up at his profile as he tightened his arm around her. As much as she didn’t like it, Caden O’Callaghan held her life in his hands, and she was going to have to trust him.

MOUNTAIN RESCUE MISSION

LISA HARRIS

&

USA TODAY Bestselling Author

SHARON DUNN

Previously published as *Hostage Rescue*
and *Dead Ringer*

LOVE INSPIRED
INSPIRATIONAL ROMANCE

LOVE INSPIRED®
INSPIRATIONAL ROMANCE

Recycling programs
for this product may
not exist in your area.

ISBN-13: 978-1-335-60100-1

Mountain Rescue Mission

Copyright © 2021 by Harlequin Books S.A.

Hostage Rescue
First published in 2020. This edition published in 2021.
Copyright © 2020 by Lisa Harris

Dead Ringer
First published in 2010. This edition published in 2021.
Copyright © 2010 by Sharon Dunn

This edition published by arrangement with Harlequin Books S.A.

For questions and comments about the quality of this book,
please contact us at CustomerService@Harlequin.com.

Love Inspired
22 Adelaide St. West, 40th Floor
Toronto, Ontario M5H 4E3, Canada
www.Harlequin.com

Printed in U.S.A.

CONTENTS

Lisa Harris is a Christy Award winner and winner of the Best Inspirational Suspense Novel for 2011 from *RT Book Reviews*. She and her family are missionaries in southern Africa. When she's not working, she loves hanging out with her family, cooking different ethnic dishes, photography and heading into the African bush on safari. For more information about her books and life in Africa, visit her website at lisaharriswrites.com.

Books by Lisa Harris

Love Inspired Suspense

Final Deposit
Stolen Identity
Deadly Safari
Taken
Desperate Escape
Desert Secrets
Fatal Cover-Up
Deadly Exchange
No Place to Hide
Sheltered by the Soldier
Christmas Witness Pursuit
Hostage Rescue

Visit the Author Profile page
at Harlequin.com for more titles.

HOSTAGE RESCUE

Lisa Harris

He that dwelleth in the secret place
of the most High shall abide under the shadow
of the Almighty. I will say of the Lord, He is my refuge
and my fortress: my God; in him will I trust.
—*Psalm* 91:1–2

To those needing a refuge and shelter.
May you find it in Him.

ONE

Gwen Ryland held up her phone to take a panoramic photo of the breathtaking canyon spread out in front of her. Even from where she stood, halfway down the steep wall of the chasm, the view was spectacular. She took a string of photos, then turned back toward her brother, her feet slipping on the loose gravel. His hand gripped her arm.

"Hang on, sis." Aaron pulled her back a couple feet from the drop-off. "A photo isn't worth falling off the edge."

"I wasn't going to fall." She laughed away the comment, but that didn't stop her heart from pounding. And while she was still a good four feet from the edge, Aaron was right. A fall here could be deadly. Three months ago, a twenty-year-old hiker had plunged to his death, and his body had finally been recovered two days later at the base of one of the cliffs a quarter of a mile from here. No, she couldn't be too careful. And besides, in all honesty, a photo of the canyon could never do the view justice.

She slipped her phone into her pocket and decided

to simply take in the beauty of the canyon walls. The sunlight cast gray and purple shadows across the wide ravine and impressed them into her memory. Above them, on the top of the deep chasm, was a thick forest of oak trees, while below a scattering of Douglas firs and cottonwoods spread out along the river.

On the way down, they'd already seen some mule deer, bighorn sheep and an eagle soaring above them. It was definitely a world away from the hectic pace of her life in Denver. She'd been telling herself for months that she needed to take some time off and come back here. There was more to life than just working, and standing here in the middle of God's creation today had reminded her why.

"I'm glad you talked me into this," she said, breathing in the fresh mountain air.

"Rough week?" Aaron asked.

"Rough month, actually, but one of my toughest cases is finally over, and now I'm just trying to forget it."

"What happened?" he asked. "You seem… I don't know. Tenser than normal."

"There were threats made by a defendant, but it's nothing I haven't faced before."

"Why didn't you tell me?"

"Because it's over."

At least she hoped it was.

She felt a shiver run down her spine despite the warm weather as she tried to push back the vivid memories. Carter Steele had caught her gaze in the courtroom, then slowly traced his finger across his throat. The implication had been clear, and she'd tried to shake the fear for days. But giving in to it wasn't an option. Instead, she'd reported the threat and was thankful that Steele had been convicted and locked away.

She took another sip of water, then shoved the bottle into the side pocket of her backpack. Threats against her were simply a hazard of being a prosecutor, and not something she could dwell on. Which was exactly why she'd needed this weekend to get away.

"You know you can always come to me if you're in trouble," Aaron said, interrupting her thoughts. "I've got more than a little experience with people like that."

"I'll be fine, Aaron. Really."

"Then here's what I want to know. Are you going to be able to make it back up to the top once we reach the bottom of the canyon?"

"Are you kidding me?" She shot her brother a grin. The off-the-beaten-trail trip down into the canyon might have been one of the toughest hikes she'd ever attempted because of the steep slope, but while it was a welcome challenge, it was also a chance to catch up with her brother. "Not only am I going to make it to the top, I'm going to beat you there. But first we need to keep going."

She grabbed her backpack and started back down the trail, knowing she'd pay for it physically over the next few days, but that was okay. For as long as she could remember, she and Aaron had been competitive about everything they did together. And, as the oldest, she'd always had a burning desire to win. That drive had begun to mellow over recent years, and while she still enjoyed their lively debates and friendly competition, fostering their relationship after the death of their parents was what she was really interested in. That and making sure she avoided the poison ivy and didn't slip off the edge of the steep trail.

They continued chatting about his last bounty-hunting job and her next case for another forty-five minutes, then he signaled her to stop at a relatively level section. She pulled out her water bottle again and adjusted the straps on her backpack, being extra careful this time to watch her feet on the loose gravel that made up the majority of the trail.

Her heart raced as something rustled in the trees. Seconds later, a falcon soared out from its perch above them.

"You really are jumpy today," Aaron said.

"I'm fine. I just thought I heard someone—or something—coming down the trail."

She glanced behind her, but there were no other hikers for as far as she could see. Which was what she liked about this portion of the canyon. It was possible to spend all day in this isolated part of the world and not run in to anyone.

She heard another noise, this time the distinct sound of falling gravel, and looked behind her again. The two masked men ran up behind them on the trail.

The taller man immediately grabbed her, pinning her arms behind her and throwing her off balance. Aaron lunged forward to stop him, but the second man pointed his gun at Aaron's head. Gwen's mind spun. While it rarely happened, she'd heard of hikers being robbed at gunpoint, or their cars being broken into while they were on the trail, but she never expected it to happen to her. Not here.

She screamed and tried to pull away from her captor, terrified he was going to shove her over the edge.

Instead, he pinned her tighter against him. "There's nobody around to hear you, so shut up."

"What do you want?" Gwen asked.

The older man took a step forward. "I'll make it simple—"

Without waiting for an explanation, Aaron lunged forward in an effort to disarm the man, but his plan backfired as both men slammed into Gwen. The man holding her lost his grip while Gwen lost her balance and slipped off the steep slope of the canyon.

Caden O'Callaghan heard a bloodcurdling scream and immediately tried to determine the direction of the source. It seemed to be coming from right above him. As a former army ranger, he was trained to run toward trouble—never away—and this was no exception. Because what he'd just heard could only mean one thing in this isolated spot—someone was in trouble. And out here, with resources limited, the consequences could be severe. His hand automatically rested on his Glock. Spending five days alone on the trail, the extra protection was a no-brainer for him. And while he hadn't had to use it so far, he'd always rather be prepared.

Seconds later, he caught sight of three men in a standoff on a slight ledge on the trail, with two masked men holding a gun on the third man. Caden pulled his weapon out of its holster and continued up the trail.

One of the armed men shifted his aim to his hostage's head and shouted at Caden. "Back off, or I will shoot him."

"Don't do it," Caden said. "Drop your weapons now."

Caden kept the barrel of his weapon trained on them as he evaluated the situation. Their hostage looked to be in his mid-twenties and had all the telltale signs of a military service member, judging from his short haircut and stance.

"They shoved my sister over the edge," their hostage yelled. "You've got to find her—"

"Shut up." One of the men gripped his arm tighter as they started backing away, keeping him in front of them. "Stay out of this."

Caden held his weapon steady, unwilling to withdraw. "Sorry. I'm already involved, and I said drop your weapons."

"Back. Off. Now. I will shoot him."

Caden hesitated, then lowered his gun to his side, unwilling to risk the man following through with his threat.

"Don't follow us."

The two men continued to edge their way up the trail, forcing the hostage with them. Ten, fifteen…twenty feet… Caden weighed his options. He could go after the men, but if the sister really had fallen over the edge, she needed to be his priority.

He watched as the three men disappeared around the bend, then immediately moved to where there were scuff marks off the side of the trail…but no sign of the woman. He pulled out his cell, hoping to call for help, then frowned when there was no signal. He was going to have to do this on his own.

Caden pulled a pair of binoculars from his backpack, then studied the terrain below that was sprinkled with trees and brush. He followed the trajectory of where the woman would have fallen, but still couldn't see any signs of anyone. Which had him worried. Unless something had stopped her fall, there was no way to know how far she'd dropped. And on top of that, in order to find her, he was going to have to veer off the trail. Depending on where she'd landed, the chance of her surviving a fall without injury was slim.

"Hello?"

He stood still for a moment, waiting for a response, but there was nothing.

The steep, unmaintained trails leading down to the base of the canyon were known for their difficulty, and there were even warnings posted to visitors regarding the dangers. The sun wouldn't set for a few more hours, but because of the steep, narrow walls, shadows had already begun to fall across the bottom of the canyon. Even with his climbing skills, the descent was going to be difficult.

He started down the incline, careful to secure his footing with each step, while trying to avoid the poison ivy snaking across the slope. While deaths here were relatively rare, they did happen, typically from either falling off the steep walls of the canyon or rafting-related accidents in the water below. Most of the time tragedy struck because of people's unpreparedness. Sometimes, it was simply being in the wrong place at the wrong time.

His feet skidded on a patch of loose dirt, and he grabbed a branch to stop himself from sliding any farther. So much for his quiet few days of solo backpacking in God's wilderness. He continued on, moving as fast as possible while still being careful. These off-trails were marked as self-rescue, meaning if you did get hurt, you couldn't rely on the authorities to help you out. Once he reached the missing woman, he'd have to figure out how to get her the help she needed on his own.

Thirty feet down, he found a red backpack that had gotten snagged on some brush. He stared ahead of him. It had to be hers. But where was she? Another five hundred feet below him, the river roared through the narrow canyon bottom. If she'd fallen that far, there was no way she would have survived.

A flash of movement caught his attention. He zoomed in on the site with his binoculars and found her, wedged between the slope and a shrub tree. His heart raced as he scrambled down the last twenty feet to where he'd spotted the woman and tried not to push any of the loose rocks down on her in the process. He'd seen movement—which implied she was alive—but depending on how badly she was injured, he still had to figure out how to get her out of this canyon.

She was lying on her side when he got there, blood running down her forehead where she must have hit it on something. There were scratches across her arms and a long gash on her right calf. He watched her chest rise and fall and let out an audible gasp of relief. A foot or two to the right and she could easily have ended up at the bottom of the canyon.

He crouched down beside her, surprised at how familiar she looked. He searched his memory for a name, but came up with nothing.

"Ma'am…" He gently grasped her shoulder. "Ma'am, I'm here to help."

She groaned as she tried to turn toward him.

"Hold on…" he said, recognition still playing in the

back of his mind. "I need you to stay still until I can determine where you're injured."

He unzipped his backpack and pulled out a bandana and his water bottle. After soaking the cloth in the water, he started wiping the blood off her forehead. There was a cut along her temple that probably needed stiches, but it didn't look too serious.

Her eyes widened as she looked up at him. "Caden?"

He pulled back his hand and stared at her a few more seconds as the realization hit him like a punch to the gut.

"Gwen?"

Of course. Gwen Ryland. How could he forget the woman who'd accused him of breaking her best friend's heart? A flood of memories surfaced, but none of that mattered at the moment. Still, he couldn't help but wonder how he'd managed to run into the one woman in the entire state who hated him.

But what she thought about him didn't matter at the moment.

"How did you find me?" she asked.

"I was out hiking the falls today." He hesitated. She had to have seen the two men that had taken her brother, but he wasn't sure how much she knew.

She pressed her hand against her head, as if trying to remember what had happened. "Where's my brother? They grabbed him. Had a gun on him."

"They took him up the hill. There was nothing I could do to stop them, but he told me you'd slid off the trail. You became the priority."

"I need to find him." She managed to sit up.

"Slow down." Caden pressed his hands against her shoulders. "We'll figure out where he is, but you're not going anywhere right now. I need to know where you're hurt."

She frowned. "It might be easier to tell you where I'm not hurt, but my left shoulder is throbbing pretty badly."

Caden started carefully checking her over. "It doesn't look like it's fractured, though I can't be 100 percent sure until it's x-rayed. Do you think you can walk down the rest of the way if I help you?"

"Do I have a choice?" She winced as she tried to stand up.

"Does your ankle hurt? It looks a little swollen."

"It feels sprained. But only mildly. I think I can walk." She put pressure on it, winced again, then took a step. "What I need to do is find my brother, and if they took him up the trail—"

"You'll never make it back up the trail like this—"

"I have to find him."

He heard the sharpness in her voice and bit back his frustration. He might have purposely buried memories of her and Cammie all these years, but he did remember how stubborn she'd been. Clearly nothing had changed. But she was right. Her brother's life was in danger, but his wasn't the only one. Finding her had only been the first step. He had to get her out of this canyon.

"Let's take one thing at a time. Even if there were enough hours of daylight left, there's no way you can walk back up before it gets dark. But if I get you down to the bottom of the canyon, I've got a camp set up not far upstream with a first-aid kit."

"And my brother?"

"We'll search for phone service and try to get help."

She frowned, but he knew he was right. Traversing

the trail was difficult enough for a fit person, which meant it was still going to take them two or three times as long to reach the bottom of the canyon with her injuries. On top of that, even if they could get a hold of the authorities, it might take hours for help to arrive. Their best plan was to get her down to his camp and clean her up the best he could, then try to find help in the morning.

"Do you have any idea why they targeted you?" he asked.

"I don't know. It all happened so fast."

"Did you get a look at their faces?"

She shook her head. "No."

"Me, neither."

"I'm pretty sure they weren't expecting any witnesses to whatever their plan was," she said.

"What about enemies?" he asked.

"It's possible." He didn't miss the hesitation in her voice. "I'm a prosecutor, so I've faced my share of run-ins with bad guys, but this... I don't know."

He'd press for answers later. Right now, he needed to get her off the canyon wall and somewhere safer.

"Stay behind me and be careful. The actual trail is difficult enough since it's not maintained, but this is going to be even rougher until we can get back to the trail."

Caden let out a sharp huff as he stared down the steep terrain toward the trail. Gravel slid beneath her feet behind him. He reached and grabbed her hand, then immediately caught the look of irritation in her eyes. Still, he held on to her a few more seconds to ensure she was okay.

"Thanks," she said.

He would have laughed if he didn't know how serious the circumstances were. He was certain that if he was the last person on the planet and she was in trouble, she still wouldn't want to accept his help. And that was fine. In truth, he didn't blame her. She only knew one side of the story, but at the time he knew it wouldn't have mattered what he said. Maybe he'd handled the situation wrong back then, but he knew the truth, and for him that was all that had mattered. And, in the end, he'd never regretted his decision to walk away. He'd never looked back.

"You remember who I am, don't you?" she asked.

"Of course." He needed to find a way to cut the tension between them. "You haven't changed at all."

It was true. After ten years, her blue eyes were just as intense, and her hair, while a few inches shorter, had the same honey-blond highlights.

"Do you still live near here?" she said.

"I work on my father's ranch."

He paused, wanting to ignore the questions he knew were hanging between them. Questions she had to assume he was going to ask.

How is Camille? Has she gone on with her life?

But they were questions he had no desire to pose. Instead, he decided to shift the conversation back to her.

"Are you—?"

He didn't get a chance to finish as a shot rang out and a bullet slammed into the tree beside them.

TWO

There was no time to react. The realization they were being shot at had just barely registered in Gwen's mind when Caden grabbed her hand and pulled her behind the trunk of a spindly tree for cover. A second shot rang out, this time hitting the bark above them.

He signaled at her to stay down, then fired two shots in the direction of the shooter before ducking back behind the tree beside her. "We need to keep going."

She nodded, then followed him down the steep incline. Her mind spun as it tried to process everything that had happened. The men grabbing them. Slipping off the trail and tumbling down the side of the canyon. Realizing whoever had just shot at them also had her brother. It was like a nightmare she couldn't wake up from.

But he was right. With at least one shooter after them, they couldn't stop now.

Adrenaline masked most of the pain as she followed his lead. All it would take was one slight misstep, and she could slip again. And this time, there might not be anything to stop her fall.

"You can't hide out here," the man shouted from

above them, rustling through the brush as he made his way closer. "I will find you."

Caden pulled her into a small, hollowed-out depression just big enough for the two of them and signaled for her to be quiet.

Heart pounding, she listened for movement. A small avalanche of stones trickled over the lip of the hollowed-out area above them. Her mouth went dry. The shooter was there, somewhere above them. Looking. Searching. She could hear rustling in the brush. Another small shower of rocks.

Then suddenly everything was silent. She waited, holding her breath until her lungs began to burn, then slowly let out the air.

Where was he?

"Do you think he's gone?" she whispered.

"It sounded like he headed back toward the trail."

She glanced up at the sunlight drenching the top of the canyon, but where they were, shadows had already begun to move in. Before long, it would be dark, and the terrain would be too dangerous to navigate. A bird called out, echoing below them, as every unfamiliar sound around them sent her heart racing. She tried to shake off the layer of fear that had settled over her, but it was impossible.

"Do you think you can keep going?" he asked. "We can still take it slow, but I don't want to make this descent after dark, and we'll quickly run out of daylight if we don't start moving."

She nodded, determined to keep up with him despite the pain. She started down beside him in silence, ignoring the sounds around them that echoed off the canyon walls, focusing instead on each step. And she listened for any signs that the shooter was still out there. But with every minute that passed, there was nothing to indicate they were being followed.

Then where were they? Had the men given up? Were they planning to use her brother as leverage to get to her? There was no way to know the men's endgame. All she could do now was make it to the bottom of the canyon, then find a way out of here alive.

By the time they got to Caden's camp, she was exhausted and hurting. A one-man tent had been set up on the edge of a small clearing a few dozen feet from the nearby river. Canyon walls surrounded them, reaching toward the cloudy spring sky that was already chasing away the last bits of light. It was the untamed wilderness, with its scattering of scrub oak, sagebrush and aspen, that made it a favorite for people wanting to escape the modern world for a short time. And that was the reason she'd chosen to come here.

"This is a beautiful spot," she said.

"I camp here every year. Spend a few days hiking by myself. Gives me some time to reevaluate things." He helped her sit down on a sleeping mat. "I'll go grab my first-aid kit."

As she watched him head inside the tent, she struggled to pinpoint what was different about him from the last time she'd seen him. He was still quiet and serious, and he looked the same with his brown hair, blue-gray eyes and tall, muscular frame. Even she couldn't deny the appeal of his rugged stature, with his cowboy hat and the start of a beard. But that wasn't what had changed. Instead, he seemed more…calm. Focused. Not that it really mattered. She'd seen him walk out on Cammie, and while she was grateful he'd saved her life, she'd never fall for a guy she couldn't trust not to do the same to her.

He came back out with the small kit and opened it. "You're going to need some painkillers. There should also be some antiseptic wipes in here for any cuts, and I've got clean water if you're out."

"I should have some water in my backpack, as well as some food."

The last thing she wanted was to make him think she expected him to take care of her out here. She'd come prepared for anything. Well…almost anything.

"Good, then we should have plenty to last us through tomorrow." He nodded at her backpack. "Go ahead and drink some more water. We need to stay hydrated."

She followed his instructions and took a long swig, while he pulled out what they needed. The same awkwardness that had followed them down the canyon settled in between them again. They'd been silent most of the way down, and when they had spoken to each other, they'd never gotten beyond the basic small talk. Which, in all honestly, had been fine with her.

"How long were you planning to stay out here?" Caden asked.

"We were just going to hike down and back up in one day."

Caden, on the other hand, was clearly prepared for a week out in the wilderness.

"I can rig a splint for your ankle, but that and the pain medicine is really all we can do at this point, other than clean you up," he said.

"I don't think I need a splint, but I will take the pain

medicine." She grabbed the two pills he offered her and popped them into her mouth.

He pulled out an antiseptic pad and quickly cleaned up the smaller scrapes on her forehead and arms, then grabbed a second one for the larger cut on her calf.

"Do you think it needs stitches?" she asked.

"I don't think so. It will leave a scar, but you should be okay."

"Where'd you get your medical training?"

"After college I joined the army."

His answer didn't surprise her. She remembered he'd been organized and efficient when she'd known him in college, along with a number of other things she'd rather forget. But she wasn't too stubborn to recognize the fact that she needed him.

Her jaw tightened as he cleaned the gash. "Thank you. For rescuing me."

"It's not over yet, but by this time tomorrow we should be out of here, in touch with the authorities and hopefully have found your brother."

"I'm worried about him," she said.

"I know. We'll find him." Caden took another couple of minutes to finish, then stood up. "I want you to lie down and keep your foot elevated while I get some dinner going."

"Wait…there's something you need to know first," she said.

"Okay." He sat back down and caught her gaze. "What's that?"

She hesitated to bring up the matter that had been plaguing her since the attack, but he needed to know. "I don't think this was random."

"Did you know those men?"

"No, but I think I know who sent them."

"Who?"

She drew in a deep breath. "I believe it's connected with my job."

"As a prosecutor?"

She nodded. "His name is Carter Steele. He was arrested for domestic abuse, drug trafficking and child endangerment. I reported the threat he made toward me in the courtroom, but didn't think he could actually follow through. Not from prison. But this... I can't just dismiss this as a coincidence. Which also means I'm sorry for the entire situation I just roped you into."

"It wasn't your fault."

"Maybe not, but you've still been dragged into it. Threats like this have increased over the past few years, and while most won't follow through, this... I think this has to be related."

"You think he wants you dead?"

"Whoever was out there shot at us, so it seems likely. What I don't understand is why didn't they just break into my apartment or run me off the road on the highway. This whole setup was extremely dangerous."

"It was, but it also makes sense on one level," Caden said. "An accident here would be easy to cover up. A couple of hikers fall off the rim, bodies are found a few days or months later, or not at all. Everyone would simply believe it was an accident."

She felt a shudder run through her. If that had been their plan, and she was still alive...

"So they grabbed my brother...for what? To use as leverage?"

"Maybe, and then they came after you because they need to make sure you're dead."

"If that's what they want, then we have to assume they'll be back."

Caden nodded. "Which means we need to be ready."

Twenty minutes later, Caden dumped the dry pasta into the boiling water on top of his small propane stove. So much for his five days of solitude in the mountains. He worked to rein in his irritation over the entire situation. It wasn't that he minded helping out a fellow hiker—it was simply that he'd managed to run into *her*. But feeding his irritation was only going to make him even more agitated, and there was no reason to let her control how he felt.

He flicked a fly off his pant leg and frowned. Had he let Cammie's betrayal affect him so much that he'd managed to shut himself off from feeling or caring for anyone again? He loved working on the ranch, because it made him feel free. He didn't have to concern himself with anyone else. Just him and the open range. But what if he really wasn't as free as he thought he was? What if he was still running because of Cammie?

He glanced at Gwen's profile. While he hadn't known her well, they had hung out a few times with his fiancée and several of their other friends. Until the night Cammie had called off their wedding and walked out on him, blaming the break up on him.

At the time, he hadn't even seen it coming, and Cammie had caught him completely off guard. Though, looking back, all the signs had been there. Unfortunately, he'd been young, and somehow thought Cammie's devotion to their relationship had been as strong as his. That had proven to be just one of many lies Cammie had told him.

But for now, none of that mattered. He'd formulated a plan. While the distance to the top of the canyon was just over a mile, the vertical drop was so steep, experts estimated it took double or even triple the descent time when going back up. He'd noted how long it had taken them to make it to the bottom. Going up would be even slower for her, if not impossible. The only alternate route was the river, but even that came with its own set of issues. The shoreline was often narrow and bordered with slippery rocks. Rafters frequently tackled the challenge, but there were sections that should only be attempted by those with experience. More than one overconfident person had lost his life from a foolish move on the water. But Caden believed she'd be able to handle the water route better than trying to hike back up the canyon.

Gwen walked toward him across the small campsite as he was adjusting the propane bottle, then sat down on one of the logs across from him.

"How are you feeling?" Caden asked, not missing the frown on her face.

"Sore, but thankfully the pain medicine is finally starting to kick in."

"Good." He bent down and looked at her ankle. "It's still a bit swollen, but that's expected considering you just walked down the canyon on an injured ankle. You still need to keep it elevated, but it should be better by tomorrow."

"I know I should be lying down, but I just felt so restless," she said. "I was wondering if you had a plan?"

His hand automatically touched the butt of his weapon. "Until morning, we're going to have to keep our guard up. Then I'm hoping we can find a group of rafters to join so we can head downriver. That would be the easiest way out for you."

"But still dangerous."

He nodded.

"What about my brother?"

"He's another reason we need to get out of here as soon as possible, so we can let the authorities know what's going on. Even if I wasn't worried about your ankle, we can't go after your brother in the dark."

"I know, I just—I just need to do something." She picked up a small stick and snapped it in two. "Tell me what I can do to help with dinner in the meantime."

"Well, I wasn't planning on company, but pasta alfredo with salmon was on the menu for tonight." He'd already grabbed the ingredients for the meal that had been neatly packed in a plastic Ziploc in his bear-resistant canister. "I don't think it will be a stretch to feed two."

"Pasta alfredo with smoked salmon?" she asked.

He hesitated. "You don't like salmon?"

"No… I mean, yes. Salmon's fine, but is this how you always eat on the trail? That sounds like a gourmet meal."

"What did you expect?"

"I don't know—ramen noodles and a packet of tuna fish."

He chuckled. "I like to cook and realized years ago that just because I'm not standing in the middle of my kitchen doesn't mean I can't eat well on the trail. Tonight's pasta, but I can also make a mean chili from sun-dried tomatoes and dehydrated kidney beans."

She shot him an unexpected smile. "All I can say is I'm impressed."

He shoved off the compliment and started organizing the food. He'd also learned early on that an hour or two of food prep before he hit the trail translated into a much more enjoyable trip. And as long as the food was light and quick to fix—meaning no cooking, just boiled water—it wasn't that difficult to carry.

He handed her a small bunch of fresh basil from his mother's garden along with a knife. "If you'll mince this, I'll get the pasta going. Then we'll just have to add the ingredients for the sauce I already put together back at the house."

"Of course you did."

This time he wasn't sure if she was being sarcastic or complimentary, but she was smiling, so he decided to go with the latter. He dumped the pasta into the water, and for a moment, working beside her seemed oddly... normal. While he loved the solitude of the trail and a solo hike, there were times when he missed the sound of another human's voice. If only he could forget not only that someone was after them, but also who *she* was, he might actually enjoy tonight.

A noise behind them seized his attention.

He took a step back from the stove and shifted his concentration to the shadows filtering down the canyon wall. He scanned the surrounding vegetation, senses on alert, but the movement was just a squirrel. He let out a huff of air.

"What if they come back?" she asked.

"I've already thought about that."

"And?"

"While you were lying down, I rigged a trip wire around the camp."

"An alarm in case they find us?"

Caden nodded.

"How'd you do that?"

"Fishing wire and key-chain alarm. It's pretty rudimentary, but it should do the trick if they show up." He stirred the pasta, then tested it to see if it was done. "I don't usually set one, but I'd say we have reason tonight."

"I agree."

"I also don't want either of us sleeping in the tent. If they show up, that's where they're going to assume we are."

She nodded as they worked side by side for the next few minutes, mixing the dry sauce ingredients with water and letting it simmer, then combining it with the pasta, freeze-dried corn, smoked salmon and the fresh basil.

"This is delicious," she said, once they'd dished up the food.

"You look surprised."

"Most guys I know could never pull this off."

"My mother ensured all of us boys knew our way around the kitchen."

"Well, I'm impressed." She took another bite. "I remember you had brothers. Three of them, right?"

Caden nodded.

"What do they do now?" she asked.

"Reid works for the local fire department in Timber

Falls. Liam is in the army and is married with a daughter and has another one on the way."

"That's exciting. And number three?"

"Griffin is a deputy and getting married in December."

"And you—you left the military?"

"My father had a bout with cancer a couple years ago, and while he's made a full recovery, I was at a place in my career that I felt like it was time to walk away and help. I've been running the ranch with him ever since."

"I remember you talking about your ranch when we were in school. It always sounded so beautiful."

"It is."

"Do you ever regret your decision?"

He shifted in his seat, uncomfortable with all her personal questions. "There are things I miss about the military, but I love working on the land every day. I just decided if I was going to do it, I wouldn't look back."

"Still, that had to be hard."

"It was. And to be honest, it still is sometimes, but I love what I do." He stood and headed for his bear barrel, needing a distraction from her questions. "How about some chocolate cookie bars?"

"Why am I not surprised? That would top off a perfect meal."

He grabbed two, then handed her one. "You said you're a prosecutor. What kind of cases do you work on?"

"I focus primarily on family law."

"Do you like it?"

"I do, though the cases can be tough. I represent children most of the time."

"I bet you're good at it."

"It has its rewarding moments."

He took a bite of his cookie and frowned. He hadn't planned on giving her a compliment, even though he'd meant it. But smoked-salmon pasta and chocolate couldn't make him forget whom he was sitting next to.

"I guess you heard Cammie got married," she said without warning.

He set down his dessert and frowned at the news. For a moment, he could have almost imagined that they were simply old friends catching up. But now, hearing his ex-fiancée's name made him want to run.

"I did," he said finally. "Do you ever see her?"

"We used to get together several times a year, but they moved to Dallas, and I haven't seen her as much since then."

"Is she happy?"

He frowned, wondering why he'd asked the question. Why it even mattered after all this time. She was a part of his past, and he was content to leave her there.

"She seems happy. Rick's a decent guy."

The unspoken tension hung between them. He knew what Gwen was thinking. Knew she'd probably never forgiven him for what she thought he'd done. She'd made it clear that night exactly what she thought about him, and he hadn't tried to convince her otherwise. At the time, it didn't seem to matter. He'd known the truth wasn't going to change anything. Cammie would have walked away no matter what he said.

"So you never married?" he asked.

She glanced at her left hand. "I came close once, but

in the end our goals ended up being too different. I guess I was looking for something more."

He thought he'd found that something more with Cammie. He knew her friends had blamed him for the breakup the night before their wedding, but he'd decided that was fine with him. He knew the truth, and in the end, that was all that really mattered.

As far as he was concerned, he was okay with being the bad guy in the whole scenario. He'd gone on with his life, and while he still might not be able to trust his judgment when it came to picking women, at least he could live with his conscience.

He caught the fatigue in her eyes as she yawned beside him. "Why don't you try to get some sleep. I'll stay up."

"You can't stay awake all night."

"It wouldn't be the first time." He could tell she wanted to argue with him, but he didn't miss the exhaustion in her eyes. "I'll be fine."

"Wake me up in a few hours and I'll keep watch. You're going to need your rest just as much as me."

Twenty minutes later, she was asleep, and he was going through his gear, needing to be prepared to run if the men showed up. If he'd been on his own, he would have approached the situation differently, but he wasn't looking for another confrontation against armed men with Gwen's safety at stake.

He finished packing a go bag, then pulled out his Bible. He settled in on his camping chair, aware of the night noises around him as he stared up at the sliver of stars above him, and started praying that he'd be able to get her out of here before the men found them. Praying that Gwen wouldn't get under his skin. He didn't even know he'd fallen asleep until the blare of his trip wire going off jolted him awake.

THREE

Gwen heard the screech of an alarm go off, then quickly fought to dig herself out of the dream and orient herself. A couple seconds later, Caden was hovering over her.

"They found us. We have to leave. Now."

He grabbed her hand and helped her up, as everything rushed through her in one terrifying flash of memory. She could hear the men yelling at each other in the middle of the camp as they ran toward the tent, shouting her name. There was no doubt they were looking for her. No doubt Caden's plan had bought them the extra seconds they needed to escape.

She stumbled to her feet beside him, thankful not only for his suggestion to sleep in her shoes, but also for the full moon high above them. The problem was, even with the moon out, there was still barely enough light to see where they were going because of the tree cover. Pain shot up her calf as she rushed through the brush with him, but she refused to let it slow her down. She knew how this could play out if they didn't run. Those men were armed, and from everything she knew, they planned to kill her when they found her.

Caden kept his arm around her, steadying her on the rugged path as the voices in the camp faded.

"What time is it?" she whispered.

"Just past two."

"Where are we going?" she asked.

"There's a shallow spot in the river nearby. We need to cross over, then head downstream on the other side. After I set the trip wire, I left a trail of false tracks heading upstream. Hopefully they'll follow them and buy us more time."

And then what? She knew she couldn't keep running. Not for long. She glanced up at his profile as he tightened his arm around her. As much as she didn't like it, Caden O'Callaghan held her life in his hands, and she was going to have to trust him.

She struggled to catch her breath as he led her into the icy river water. She'd known that he'd planned on trying to catch a ride down the river in the morning, but there was one thing she hadn't mentioned. Her fear of water. Panic swallowed her. She gripped his hand harder but wasn't going to let him see the fear. The water was shallow here, like he'd told her, but it still rushed across her calves, almost to her knees. She took another step, and another, fear of the men behind her compelling her forward.

At the middle point of the river, she glanced back toward the camp. Beams of light hit the tree line. The men were still rummaging for clues as to where they'd gone. Confirmation they were at the right place. But it wouldn't be long before they extended the perimeter of their search. Her foot slipped on a rock—she couldn't allow herself to be dragged into the water. All it would take was one misstep, and she'd end up sucked into the current.

But Caden was there to steady her.

"Gwen?"

"I'm fine."

"How are you really feeling?"

She hesitated. "Like I was hit by a truck."

"I'm not surprised," he said as they kept walking. "What about your head?"

"Just a slight headache."

"As soon as we can stop, I'll get you some more pain medicine. Any nausea or dizziness?"

She was shaking now, as much from the cold as from fear. "I'm just sore and tired."

She knew what he was thinking. Headache, confusion, dizziness, nausea—the symptoms of a concussion. If it was a concussion, treatment meant she needed to rest, but there was no more time for that. Instead, they were looking at a long hike out of here. Her only option was to push through.

They stepped onto the other bank and started downstream, keeping to the dark shadows of the canyon to ensure they stayed hidden.

"I'll be fine."

They walked in silence along the side of the river. She tried not to think about where her brother was, or what would happen if the men found them. She just had to keep moving. Had to make sure the men didn't catch up to them. Caden stopped every twenty yards or so and listened to the night sounds. She could no longer see the flashlights or hear the people after her, but she knew they were out there.

"Did you hear something?" she asked.

"Yes, I'm just not sure if it's them."

Another few yards down the river, he steered them behind an outcropping of trees. She was barely able to distinguish his movements as Caden pulled his weapon out of his holster. Gwen shivered in the darkness. She had no idea what their plan should be, or how they were going to defend themselves if those men struck again. But clearly, they needed to be ready for anything.

"Caden..."

"Have you ever used a gun?" he asked.

"A few times at a shooting range. Why?"

"I need to go out there and figure out which way they've gone. Make sure they're not behind us, but I don't want to risk doing that with you. I also can't leave you defenseless."

She shook her head, wanting to scream at him not to leave her, but she knew he was right. They needed to know where the men were. But was leaving her alone the solution?

"You'll be fine if you stay here." He tilted back her chin and caught her gaze. "I promise I'll be back."

"I don't want the gun. You'll be defenseless."

"I have no plans to confront them. Not at this point, anyway."

He rechecked the weapon. "Leave the safety on and don't shoot unless you absolutely have to. And when I come back...don't shoot me."

She watched him walk away, then stood frozen in the shadows until she lost track of time. Five, ten...fifteen minutes... She had no idea how much time had passed, but she heard every sound around her. Her ankle throbbed and her head pounded. She didn't want to be here alone and hated the helpless feeling overtaking her. Hated that she was a liability. But there was nothing she could do to change the situation.

She studied the surrounding terrain, listening carefully for anything that sounded out of place, but every noise caused her pulse to quicken and her heart to race. What if something had happened to Caden? What if she was left alone to find her way out of the canyon? The river churned beside her, crickets chirped. If those men were out there, close by… No. She gripped the gun tighter. She wasn't going to panic. She had to be ready. Caden was counting on her to stay calm. Which made her want to laugh. As part of her job, she'd stood her ground to protect dozens of vulnerable children who had dealt with domestic violence, trauma and child abuse, but put her in the middle of a potential gunfight and her only instinct was to run.

Something rustled behind her.

She turned around and aimed the weapon in front of her. "Whoever you are, don't come any closer. I'm armed."

"Gwen…it's just me."

Her heart pounded as Caden came into view. She took a step backward and realized she'd been holding her breath. "Are you okay?"

"I'm fine."

She handed him the gun, barrel first, glad to have the weapon out of her hands. "Did you find them?"

"They're headed upstream like I hoped. Can you keep moving?"

She nodded.

"Good, because we need to put as much distance between us and them as possible. And in the meantime, pray we find someone to take us downriver once the sun comes up."

Caden glanced at her, impressed by the grit and determination in her step, knowing it had to be painful. Not that it changed anything. She'd once told him exactly what she thought about him, and he was pretty sure that even with all the time that had passed, her feelings toward him hadn't changed, either.

He'd never been able to forget her words that night. She'd caught up with him in the parking lot as he was leaving the rehearsal dinner. Twenty-four hours before he was supposed to marry Cammie. Instead, everything he'd thought was real—everything he'd believed about his fiancée—had all turned out to be a lie, and his plans for the future had suddenly come crumbling down around him.

If you don't think she's the one you want to spend the rest of your life with, then fine. Better now than after you're married. But I hope you never forget what your selfishness is about to cost you.

He'd stood in front of Gwen, lights from the barn where they'd planned the dinner twinkling in the background. He'd wanted to tell her the truth. That his actions hadn't been what broke things off between him and Cammie. But he'd seen the anger in Gwen's eyes and knew how loyal she was to her friend. No matter what he would have said at that moment, she never would have believed him. And all these years later, he was sure she still wouldn't.

Gwen let out a soft groan next to him.

He grabbed her waist to make sure she didn't fall. "Gwen…"

"Sorry, I just stepped wrong. I'm fine."

He studied her gait. Her limp was definitely more pronounced.

"You're not fine. We need to stop." He flipped on his flashlight, then reached down and checked her ankle. "It's swelling again."

"I'm fine, Caden. I can keep going."

"If you don't take care of this, you won't be able to walk out of here. We've put some distance between them and us. You need to take some pain medicine, soak your ankle in the river water and rest, at least for a few minutes."

She hesitated, then nodded. "Fine. But just for a few minutes."

"We'll leave your shoe on in case your ankle starts swelling."

He found a small inlet, where the water moved slower next to the shoreline and there was an outcropping of rocks where they could sit. He handed her the pain medicine and some water from his backpack, then kneeled down in front of her and eased her shoe into the water. It might not be an ice pack, but it was the next best thing.

"How does that feel?" he asked.

"Cold, but good."

Moonlight filtered down the canyon wall, bathing the rock's crevices in a soft glow of light before shifting across the water. While he loved exploring the canyon during the day, there had always been something captivating about the scene at night.

"You're shaking," he said, sitting down beside her. He needed to get her out of here.

"I'm just cold."

"The temperatures drop significantly down here at night." He moved closer to her and wrapped his arm around her. "On the bright side, it gets too cold for venomous snakes."

She shivered next to him. "I've tried not to think about what might be out here."

He glanced across the darkened river, knowing it was impossible. The most dangerous enemy out there wasn't the wildlife.

She needed a distraction.

"I'd like to hear more about your job," he said. "You mentioned you represent children."

"Yeah. The center I work for was started to help ensure that child victims didn't fall through the cracks. We work primarily through stopping any abuse before it starts, but we also support victims of all forms of abuse."

"Sounds like an important mission."

"It is. We end up being advocates for these families through the entire process, giving counsel and support through the criminal investigation and ensuring that the victims and their families have the resources they need."

"That's got to be a challenge."

"It is. While I love my job, I want to do more than the system allows. One of our goals is preventing abuse but there are still issues that are hard to deal with."

"Meaning?"

"I help ensure the children get placed into a safe environment and defend their rights, but most of these kids need more than that. They need help learning how to communicate and resolve conflicts. And also figuring out what they are made of. That with the right resources they can thrive."

"Any ideas on how to do that?"

"Yes, actually. I've spent the past few months researching several programs for at-risk teens that are located right here in the state. So many kids struggle navigating into adulthood, but the potential is there. If they aren't intentionally worked with, most of them will never reach that potential. And the majority of the kids I deal with don't have anyone at home to advocate for them, let alone teach them basic life skills. All they need sometimes is someone who cares. Someone who can teach them how to problem-solve and set goals. I've seen it work firsthand, but instead, we're losing too many of our young people."

"You're passionate about these kids."

"Sorry." She let out a low laugh. "I do tend to go overboard when someone asks me."

"You have nothing to be sorry about. Anyone can go to work every day and do their job, but I find so many people end up losing the passion that put them there in the first place. Sounds like you haven't done that."

"One of the things I'm actually looking at is a wilderness program where at-risk youths, in particular, can address issues and uncover their strengths in an outdoor setting."

"Maybe I'm wrong, but I don't remember you being the outdoor type."

She shook her head. "I wasn't. Not back in college, at least. I was definitely more of a bookworm."

"What changed?"

She hesitated, making him wonder if he'd asked the wrong question.

"Aaron and I… Our parents were killed in a car crash about six years ago by a drunk driver," she said, finally.

"Wow… I'm so sorry."

"It turned our world on end, but especially for my brother. He was nineteen, impulsive and anything but serious about life. I struggled reaching him for a long time, but eventually found that this was a way for us to connect. He loves the outdoors, so we plan something different every few months. We've hiked Pikes Peak, the Rio Grande Trail, Bear Creek Falls… Last year we even tried downhill mountain-biking for the first time at Crested Butte."

"He's fortunate to have you."

"It's mutual. Losing someone you love changes you. It makes you realize how fragile life is and reminds you not to take people for granted." She pulled her foot out of the water. "We should go. They know I'm injured, and more than likely assume we're still around here. It's not going to take them too long to realize they're headed in the wrong direction."

He helped her up, knowing she was right. He hoped to have them both out of the canyon by dinnertime tomorrow, but there was no way to know how this would play out. Expecting to outrun the men if they came back was foolish. Which meant they were going to have to outsmart them, and the way to do that was to get out of here as soon as possible.

But he was already questioning his decision to try to leave via the water. There were too many sections that even experts found intimidating, and he wasn't sure if she'd be able to handle it physically. He shoved aside the questions. Worrying wasn't going to help and certainly wasn't going to change the situation. Once he got a signal on his cell, he could arrange for a helicopter to pick them up downriver, but in order to do that, they had to keep moving.

FOUR

The sun's rays crept along the canyon walls as Gwen stopped to drink a few sips of water. She estimated that they'd made it a mile downstream in the predawn light, but she knew she was slowing down Caden. The cold river water—along with the medicine he'd given her—had helped block the pain in her ankle, but the remaining aches still seemed minimal compared to the danger they were in. While there hadn't been any sign of the men after them, she knew it was just a matter of time. They *were* out there. Somewhere.

Maybe she was simply being paranoid, but on the other hand, she knew they had reason to worry. She'd tried praying as she drifted off to sleep—knowing how important sleep was—but she hadn't been able to get her mind to relax. Instead, she felt as if she'd spent most of the night running from masked giants in her dreams. And the men catching them wasn't her only fear. They'd taken her brother, and as tough as he was, he'd been unarmed and outnumbered.

All because of her.

"Do you need something to eat?" Caden asked, grabbing a protein bar out of his backpack.

"Thanks, but I've got some protein snacks." She pulled a blue package out of the side pocket of her backpack.

"What is that?"

She held up the package. "Chickpeas."

"Chickpeas?"

"Want to try them?"

Caden shook his head. "Thanks, but I think I'll pass."

She just smiled. "Your loss. All-natural, roasted and taste better—in my opinion—than peanuts."

For a moment she could almost forget this was the same man who'd broken her best friend's heart. He was good-looking and charming, and on top of that had rescued her. And yet she knew the truth about who he really was.

Caden stopped in front of her and pulled out his binoculars.

"What it is?" She scanned the river upstream, then saw a white raft headed toward them through the rapids.

"I think I just found our ticket out of here."

"You're sure it's not the guys after us?"

"Definitely not. One's bearded and the other's too dark."

Caden dropped his pack, then edged closer to the river and started waving his arms.

"You guys okay?" one of them shouted as they maneuvered the raft toward the shoreline.

"We could really use a ride out of here. She fell down the side of the canyon yesterday afternoon and is pretty banged up."

The bearded man grabbed a rope, then jumped onto the shore, securing the raft. "It might be a bit crowded, but we'll make it work."

Caden pulled the raft into the shallow water, then handed one of the men his backpack.

"Bruce McCleary." The taller one with the beard shook Caden's hand. "And this is Levi Wells. We're firefighters up in Wyoming, but try to get down here and make this run every year or two."

"I'm Caden O'Callaghan and this is Gwen Ryland." Caden glanced at her for a brief moment before turning back to the men. "There is something else you need to know."

"Like why you're carrying?" Bruce asked.

"I usually do while hiking solo as a precaution, but there are two armed men who attacked Gwen and her brother up on the trail. That's when she fell. They grabbed her brother, but they're still after her. We need to get somewhere where we can call the authorities."

"That sounds pretty personal," Levi said. "We won't get phone coverage for at least three or four miles downriver. On top of that, it's going to be a rough ride, but we should be able to get you there in one piece."

"So you're in?" Caden asked.

"Are you kidding?" Levi glanced at his friend and nodded. "Trouble never scared either of us away."

"We appreciate it," Gwen said.

Still, she hesitated at the bank. It wasn't as if things could get any worse. Or could they? She swallowed hard. No, they'd get on the raft, call for help and find her brother, then all of this would be over.

"You okay?" Caden asked.

"Yeah, I'm just…" She forced herself to step into the back of the raft. "I'm just not much for boats."

"Can you swim?" Caden asked.

"I can…in a pinch. It's more an embarrassing phobia."

"You're afraid of the water?" he asked.

"Why do you think I opted to enjoy the canyon by walking down the sides, rather than going through it on the river?" She forced a grin. "But I'll be fine."

"Sounds like you better get the extra life jacket," Bruce said. "Sorry, we only have one."

"Then one will have to do," Caden said, handing it to her.

She frowned. Heading downstream in these rapids without a life jacket wasn't a smart move.

"I'll be fine," Caden said, as if reading her mind.

She nodded her thanks, then tugged on the bright orange jacket. She just wanted to get this over with. All of this.

Caden caught her gaze. "All we need to do is get through a couple miles of rapids ahead, and we can call the authorities."

Unless they capsized in the rapids.

Or the men after them had an ambush set up.

Or both.

She tried to push away the negative thoughts. Normally, she was someone who always saw the glass as half-full, never half-empty, but this situation was trying pull her into a dark place she had no desire to go.

I need courage right now, God.

The men quickly moved their equipment, giving Caden and her room on the inflatable seat.

"Up ahead is going to get pretty rough," Bruce shouted above the loud roar of the water. "We need to make sure the boat doesn't flip. Which means if we get high-sided, I'll say the word, and we're going to need to throw our weight toward the downstream tube of the raft."

Gwen clutched onto the handles on the side and made sure her feet were secured in the foot braces as the men quickly went through more instructions. How to hold the paddle properly, what to do if she got thrown out and, most of all, a reminder not to panic.

Right. Don't panic. Except she was already there.

It took all her concentration to paddle as they worked together to keep the raft upright. She drew in a deep breath. The steep rock walls of the canyon rose up on either side of them as they started down the narrow river. The churning water surged past large boulders that were scattered down the narrow waterway. She'd read the warnings about this area for its Class III rapids, and this was why. She drew in another deep breath. Ahead of them, white foam churned where there were sudden drops in the water level and narrow stretches that required navigating between the large rocks.

"You okay?" Caden asked.

She nodded, but she really wasn't. The river had them bobbing downstream in the current, leaving her feeling totally out of control. And the rapids swirling around her terrified her almost as much as the men after them, if not more.

"You've got to be in pretty good physical shape to hike these canyons." Caden maneuvered his paddle beside her.

"And you're wondering why someone who's athletic is afraid of the water?" she asked.

"It did cross my mind."

Water sprayed across her face as the river began to narrow and the white foam of the rapids increased. She braced herself for impact as the raft bumped into the side of a large boulder, shifting their trajectory downstream. She worked to stay in sync with the three men as they shoved their oars into the water to compensate, while her memories rushed through her.

She'd almost drowned that day. All it had taken was a few feet too far into the sea for it to start pulling her out instead of pushing her back onto the shore.

"Gwen…" Caden's voice yanked her to the present. "Hang on."

She grasped onto the ropes on the side of the raft and ensured her feet were secure. The back of the raft where they were sitting rose out of the water. She felt her body slide forward, but managed to hang on. She was going to be fine. They all were. They would get within cell-phone range, call for help and this would be over. Whoever was after her wasn't going to win. Just like the canyon wasn't going to win. Not today.

The raft pitched again, this time throwing her into the air. She lost hold of the raft's safety rope that wrapped around the exterior and tried to grab onto it again, but missed. A second later she felt her body hit the water. She was falling as the current pulled her down the river. Her body slammed into one of the rocks, scraping her back against something as she fought to stay above the waterline. Fought to breathe. But she was moving too fast. She could see the raft bobbing in the swirling white water just beyond her, but she couldn't reach it.

Her mind went over the instructions Bruce had given them. Don't try to swim or stand up. She turned onto her back, feet first, like he'd said, and tried not to panic as she felt herself being pulled under.

Caden watched as the raft buckled and Gwen slid into the water. A rush of panic swept through him. They wouldn't be able to slow down for another hundred feet, where the water calmed down again. Swimming after her might be their last option, but they had to try something.

He yelled at the other men. "Do you have a throw bag? We've got to get her out of there."

"Under your seat. We'll try to get you as close as we can."

He pulled out the standard rescue equipment, including a coil of rope that could be thrown into the water in a rescue scenario, while the other two men worked to steer the raft toward her while keeping it from totally flipping.

While he might not have good memories of Gwen from his past, he certainly didn't want anything bad to happen to her. And besides, it was obvious from the time they'd spent together that they were both different people from when they'd known each other all those years ago. Both of them had grown up.

All of a sudden she was gone.

He shouted at the other men. "Do you see her?"

He scanned the water in front of them, then the shoreline, as the panic began to seep in. He was surprised at the urge to protect her that rushed through him. She had a life jacket on, but even that couldn't guarantee she wouldn't be pulled under. And if she was already afraid of water and panicked…

He shoved down the fear, focused instead on simply finding her.

Where was she?

Seconds passed. The raft went down another drop into a pool of calmer water.

"There she is," Bruce shouted. "On those rocks on the shoreline."

Relief flooded through him as he caught sight of her. Somehow, she'd managed to pull herself to the edge of the water. They fought against the current to steer the raft toward the shore.

"Gwen!"

He jumped out and hurried across the rocks to where she was lying on the shoreline, half of her body still in the water.

"Gwen—Gwen, are you okay?"

He pulled her up out of the water. She sat next to him, breathing hard from the exertion.

"I just… I need to catch my breath."

"Are you hurt?"

"I don't think so, though I scraped my leg on some-thing."

He checked her out quickly and found a second large scratch running up her calf, but what worried him the most was that she was shaking from the cold. He needed to get her warm.

Bruce and Levi secured the raft, then jumped onto the shoreline next to them.

"We've got a thermos of hot coffee," Bruce said, "and a thermal blanket."

Caden took the blanket, then turned to Gwen. "I want you to take off your shirt and put on my fleece. I'll hold up the blanket while you change. You're soaking wet and you need to get dry and warm."

She nodded, still shivering.

"Thank you," she said as soon as she'd changed.

He wrapped the blanket around her shoulders, then poured a cup from the thermos and held it out for her. "Drink it slow, but drink as much as you can."

She nodded, but he could see both the alarm and fatigue in her eyes. And how could he blame her? The past twenty-four hours she'd fallen off the side of the canyon, been shot at and now this. Nothing completely prepared you for something like this.

"I can't stop shaking," she said.

"You're cold, but you're okay." He rubbed his hands against her shoulders. "Give me a second. I'll be right back."

Caden stepped a dozen feet away to where Bruce was standing.

"Levi headed upstream to see if it looked like we were being followed," Bruce said. "How is she?"

"She'll be fine, but I'd like to know what you think. You know this area as well as I do. What if we stayed here, and the two of you went ahead and called for help once you were in cell-phone range? I know she's afraid, but I'm worried about her physically, as well."

Bruce glanced out at the water rushing by in front of them. "If that's what you want, we'll do that for you, but we're only a couple miles from phone signal. If you continue with us, you'll get there a lot quicker than if you were to have someone come back here for you."

"True…"

"And on top of that," Bruce continued, "if there are men after you, and they're armed…"

"I might be in for a different kind of battle."

Caden let out a sharp sigh. The man was right. He knew that. Staying here would only give the men after Gwen a greater chance of catching up with them, and that was a risk he didn't want to take. He needed to get her out of here as soon as possible.

"Give her a few more minutes to warm up, and then we'll do everything we can to get her out of here safely."

Caden nodded. "Thank you. I appreciate it."

"Don't worry about it."

Caden went back and sat down next to her, thankful she was listening to his instructions and drinking the coffee. Right now his priority was to get her somewhere safe and warm. Then they'd be able to get the help they needed to find her brother.

"The quickest way out of here is to get back into the water and continue downstream," he said.

"I know I have to get back into that raft. I'll be fine."

He was surprised at her willingness to continue down the river after what had just happened, but on the other hand, he knew she wasn't one to simply give up.

"I'm sorry you've had to go through all of this, but a couple more miles downriver and we'll be able to get a call through. It's almost over. I promise."

She looked up at him, eyes wide and trusting. He didn't miss the irony. He was the last person she would have trusted before the past twenty-four hours, but he'd do anything he could to ensure her safety. Gwen Ryland had somehow managed to slip back into his life and turn all of his plans completely upside down.

She handed him the cup and thermos.

"Can you drink some more?" he asked.

"I think I'm ready to go."

Her cheeks were still pink, but at least she wasn't shaking as much as she had been.

Levi was making his way back down the rocks to where they sat. "I walked upstream a couple hundred feet, where you can see quite a way upriver."

"Did you see anyone?" Caden asked.

Levi shook his head. "Whoever they were, there's no sign that they're following you downriver. It's still going to be rough ahead, but we'll do everything we can to keep the raft in the river."

"Thank you," she said. "For everything."

Caden helped her to her feet, but the uneasiness wouldn't let go. Those men were out there, and he was sure they'd show up again at some point. They'd gone to all the trouble of coming after her in the night, making their intentions clear. Escaping them wasn't going to be that easy. But as a long as they kept moving, and could get the authorities involved, they'd make it.

Caden settled her into the back of the raft with the blanket still around her shoulders.

It was time to go.

FIVE

Gwen focused on breathing slowly through her nose, trying to calm her anxiety as they floated down a calm section of the river. *They* were out there. Somewhere. Waiting. Watching. She didn't know what their plan was or when they were going to strike, or even what they were planning to do with her, but she did know that the intense panic swirling through her wouldn't go away. Which meant she wasn't sure what she was more afraid of at the moment—the men after them, or the water. Either, it seemed, had the ability to win today and crush her.

She glanced at the waves slamming against the sides of the raft. On top of that, she was still so cold. The coffee and the blanket they'd given her had helped warm her insides, but it wasn't enough, and she couldn't stop shaking.

She'd read that the water temperature was about fifty degrees—far below the perfect swimming-pool temperature. She knew that water below that temperature could lead to shock, as it zapped body heat faster than cold air. And she believed it.

They let the raft coast down the river for the next few minutes in the calmer waters, just adjusting its course with the paddles to keep them away from any rocks jetting out of the water. But she could see traces of white foam ahead, where the river dropped again and started churning. It was the calm before the storm, and she wasn't sure she was ready for what was coming next.

For a moment, memories rushed through her again of that day at the ocean with her family. She could almost feel the icy sting of the water as she slipped in. The gasping for air, then the panic when she couldn't fill her lungs. It had been so cold, so terrifying. The realization that those could have been her last moments as she was sucked under. The not knowing if she was going to make it back to the surface.

"Gwen? Are you all right?"

"Sorry…" At Caden's questions, she forced her mind to come back to the present. She needed to stay focused. Needed to listen to the men, who were shouting out directions as they approached another rapid. "I'm fine."

"These river rafts are built for this kind of abuse," Caden said. "It's heavy-duty commercial grade and made for class-three rivers and up. You can't do any better out on the water."

Gwen frowned. While she appreciated his reassurance, she wasn't convinced that was going to be enough to keep them afloat in the next stretch of the river. Or enough to keep her nerves intact.

"You said you were afraid of the water," Caden said.

It was a statement more than a question. She knew he was hoping for a response, but she wasn't sure how much she wanted to tell him. And, until today, she hadn't realized how much that one incident had affected her. In the past, she'd simply avoided water. It was an easy way to not deal with memories and her fears. But today—today there was no way to escape it. She was here in the middle of everything, water churning around her like her life at the moment.

"You don't have a phobia?" she asked, putting it back on him.

"Spiders."

His answer surprised her. "You're afraid of spiders?"

"I was bit by a brown recluse when I was eight. My hand swelled up, and I was convinced it was going to be amputated. I was terrified."

"That's horrible."

"As you can see, I survived, but for an eight-year-old kid, it was a bit traumatic. And my teasing brothers didn't help."

"You know how siblings can be. Are you all close now?"

"We still have our moments, but yeah. We are."

"My brother and I are, too. Most of the time."

The raft rocked gently beneath them as they moved with the current. Another couple hundred yards and the calm of the river would be behind them. She tried to shake off the terror, but the water surrounding them reminded her too much of that day, too much of what she could have lost.

Even if this raft did get them out of here in one piece, she still had no idea where her brother was, or where the men that had seemed so intent on finding her were. Nor could she shake the fact that she'd involved Caden in all of this.

"We'd been at the ocean," she said finally. "With my parents and brother." The raft made a slight dip, spraying water across her face. She kept her focus on the tree line. "We were enjoying a few more hours of sun on our last day of vacation. The swells had been bigger than normal that day, the undercurrent stronger than I'd expected, when I walked out into the wave. It pulled me out farther instead of pushing me toward the shoreline. The more I struggled to swim toward shore, the farther away I got. I thought I was going to die that day."

"How did you get to shore?"

"My brother managed to grab me and pull me in. I remember collapsing on the sand afterward. I was cold and exhausted, and realized how close I'd come to drowning. My mother was convinced I'd drowned when she ran up to me. I was so exhausted I couldn't move."

"That had to have been terrifying."

She studied the shoreline, looking for the men who'd come after them. They could still be behind them, or, knowing how slow she'd been during the night, they could be ahead of them.

"My parents were killed a couple years after that," Gwen said. "I can't tell you how many times I asked God why I lived, and they didn't. If they'd been held up in traffic that day, or driving the other car, they probably would have lived."

"Questions like that—ones posed because of survivors' guilt—are normal."

She nodded. "I definitely learned that life is fragile. But this… I'm not sure how to deal with this, Caden. If I lose my brother, too… He's the only family I have left."

"You're not going to lose your brother."

She looked up and caught his gaze. "You can't promise me that."

She'd heard those words from well-meaning friends while her parents had been fighting for their lives in ICU. She'd learned firsthand that sometimes bad things happened no matter how hard you tried to stop them. And now, it seemed like it was happening all over again. Her brother was her one link to family, and she couldn't lose him, too.

"I know what it's like to lose someone," Caden said. "And how hard it is to move forward because you couldn't do anything to save them."

"What happened?"

"I lost my team in a helicopter crash. I was supposed to have gone out with them that day, but at the last minute I was pulled off the assignment."

"Do you ever wonder why God doesn't always intervene?"

"It's something I've thought about a lot. What you need to know is that this isn't your fault."

"It's certainly not your fault, either," she said, "and yet you're involved."

"I chose to come after you, and I'd do it all over again. Sometimes all you can do is take one thing at a time. Which means right now we only have to think about getting down this river to safety. We'll have someone pick us up and get a BOLO out on your brother and the men who came after you."

"And if they find us first?"

"Then we'll deal with them again if and when we have to."

She nodded, knowing he was right.

She let out a low laugh. "You must think I'm a drama queen."

"Hardly. I actually think you're incredibly brave."

She shook her head. "It's not as if I had a choice. Caden, I need to get out of here. I need to find my brother."

The white water started swirling around them. She stared ahead at the churning waters. Life *was* fragile. All it took was one split second, one moment, and everything could change. The truth was that no matter what they did, there was a chance she'd never see her brother again. She pushed away the thought. Ahead of them, the river narrowed, as if it was shoving all the water through a funnel into the rapids below them. She just had to hang on a little bit longer.

Movement ahead to the left caught her attention. Trees lined with poison ivy ran along the banks beside them. She couldn't make out what or who it was, but something was definitely there.

"Caden…" she said.

The men automatically pushed their oars backward, slowing down the raft, as they'd clearly seen the same thing. There was something—or someone—ahead.

Caden quickly pulled out his binoculars and zoomed in on a narrow place a few hundred yards downriver. Rocks jutted out of the water on either side, but something stood at the edges of the river.

"It could be a bear," Gwen said.

She was right. He'd seen them roaming the riverbeds more than once. But for the most part, they didn't bother hikers as long as they were left alone. He brought the binoculars into focus. No, it definitely wasn't a bear. Two armed men stood on the left bank.

"Caden...what is it?" Gwen asked, panic lacing her voice.

"They're still wearing ski masks, but I'm sure it's them. We need to cut over to the other side of the bank and get to the shore now. If we don't, we'll be sitting ducks."

Which was exactly what the men had planned.

"To the right, as hard as you can," Levi shouted.

Caden pushed against the current while automatically making a plan. Getting to the shore before they reached the spot where the men stood wasn't going to be easy with the strong currents pushing them forward, but it was the only way they might stand a chance to take them down. He was thankful, not for the first time, that he'd opted to bring his weapon while camping alone, but he wasn't sure it was going to be enough.

"I don't know if we can make it," Bruce shouted back. "The current's too strong along this section. It's pulling us too hard downriver."

Right toward the waiting ambush.

The four of them rowed harder, fighting against the current that was sweeping them into the path of the men and away from the shoreline. Caden felt the strain on his muscles. How had this happened? The men must have somehow gotten ahead of them while they'd been resting on the other side of the river during the night and planned this ambush. And they'd planned it well. Just beyond the narrow bank of the river was a drop-off, and the swirling white foam of the rapids continued on as far as he could see.

"We've got two choices," Caden shouted. "We can try and make it into the inlet ahead, giving us a chance to fight them, or fly by them down the rapids."

Both options still left them as potential sitting ducks, but if they could manage to get to shore, they might have a fighting chance. They just needed the swift currents to cooperate.

"Let's try to make it to the cove," Levi said.

They pushed harder, fighting against the swelling water to get to the small inlet, but the current wouldn't cooperate. Another seventy-five...sixty-five feet, and the men would be on top of them. Water beat against the sides of the raft, pushing them forward toward the drop-off.

There was no way they were going to make it.

One of the men fired his weapon above their heads. A second later, the other man managed to grab onto the raft's rope, then secured it around a tree stump at the edge of the river. The water continued to hammer against the raft, but they weren't going anywhere.

Caden reached for his weapon, which he hadn't been able to pull out while fighting the current, but it was too late.

"Put your hands in the air. I want to see them now!" The tallest of the two yelled against the noise of the churning rapids below them. They were jammed against the rocks—the only thing that was stopping them from going down the six-foot drop and into the swirl of water below them was the rope and two armed men.

This time he pointed the gun at Levi. "She gets out now, or I'm going to shoot you one at a time until she complies."

"Leave them out of this," Gwen said. "What do you want?"

Caden rested his hand on her leg, signaling her to be quiet. It wasn't going to take much for the situation to suddenly spiral out of control and for the man to follow through with his threat. There had to be a way to get the advantage and put an end to this.

"You heard what I said. I'll start shooting them, or you can come with us. Now."

Caden gripped her hand. Letting them take her wasn't an option.

"She's not going with you," Caden said.

"I wouldn't try calling my bluff, because I will shoot you. Toss your weapon onto the shore."

Caden hesitated, but caught the anger in the man's voice. There was a fierce determination in his eyes. Desperation, even. But what did he really want? That was what Caden needed to know if he was going to be able to negotiate out of this situation.

"Now!" the man shouted. "Toss it over here."

"Okay. I will."

Caden followed the man's instructions and tossed his gun, with the safety on, onto the shore. The taller man nodded at the shorter man—who sounded much younger—to pick up the weapon. But there was something bothering Caden. Something wasn't adding up. Why grab Gwen in front of so many witnesses? Surely they weren't planning on killing all of them. If that had been their plan, they would have already done it. Plus, killing all of them would be a huge risk, with too many things that could go wrong. No. He was missing something. What was their motivation? Their actions weren't adding up, but he couldn't put his finger on the reason.

Was this really just an act of revenge, or was there more at play? They'd left Gwen on the canyon wall, knowing that the odds of her surviving a fall were slim. But they'd taken her brother for leverage, then circled back to ensure she was taken care of. If that was true, why not just shoot her now and be done with it? Why take her? There had to be another reason.

She pulled away from him. "I have to go with them, Caden."

"Wait." He gripped her arm, then turned back to the men. "Tell me why you need her. Maybe we can work something out."

"Apparently, you're not understanding. This isn't a negotiation. You're not going to be able to talk your way out of his. Do what I say, or we will start shooting."

"I have connections," he said. "If there's something you want, money—"

"Enough!" One of the men put a bullet into Levi's leg.

The shot echoed across the water. Caden froze. He'd called his bluff, but there was no deterring the other man. And as for options... They wanted her. Alive. But why?

"Stop!" Gwen stood up. "I said I'm coming."

"Gwen, wait—"

"I have to do this."

"Listen to her," the taller man said. "And if you're smart, the rest of you won't move, because I've got enough bullets for each of you."

Blood seeped through Levi's pant leg as Gwen pulled away from Caden's grip. She stumbled slightly, caught her balance, then stepped out of the raft as Levi groaned in pain. The younger man grabbed her as Caden forced himself to sit still, heart racing and every muscle tense. He had to figure out how to rescue her. He couldn't just let them take her.

He wasn't sure how he'd become so protective of her, but she'd somehow managed to get under his skin. Gwen Ryland was the one woman, next to Cammie, that he wouldn't have minded never seeing again as long as he lived. And yet here he was, fighting for her life and willing to do everything he could to save her. The thought surprised him, but in reality this wasn't about Gwen. He'd always fight for someone in trouble. It was what he'd been trained to do. To serve and protect. But this— He had to fix this. He just wasn't sure how. Or if he was going to be able to find her in time.

She glanced at him one last time as the men cut the rope. Seconds later, the raft dropped off into the churning basin below them. Their attackers had chosen the spot well, because for the moment, there was no way to stop. And no way to go back.

SIX

Gwen glanced down at her leg as she struggled to keep up with the men. Her ankle was swollen, her head throbbed and every muscle ached from the fall—even more so today than it had yesterday. Going up-hill seemed far more brutal than going downhill had, but it wasn't as if she had any choice in the matter. All she knew to do was to keep moving forward and pray Caden would find her. Because at the moment, he was her only hope.

But even that lingering hope wasn't enough. They hadn't shot her, which meant for some reason she was worth more alive than dead, though why, she wasn't sure. And even if Caden did show up, he was no longer armed, which put them at yet another disadvantage. She could try to escape, but was that even possible? She couldn't run very fast with her injured ankle and, on top of that, where was there to go beyond the un-marked trail?

"Stop trying to slow us down. He's not coming after you."

She tried to ignore the implication of what would

happen if Caden didn't come after her, because she refused to believe he wasn't doing everything he could to get to her. He'd come after her. She knew he would, and if she could slow them down, he might be able to catch up. Even if he had to backtrack upriver, he was still faster than the three of them. At least that was what she was praying for.

She glanced back down the trail. What if he didn't come? The smart thing for him to do was probably make his way down the rapids, then call the authorities. Not try to track her down. There were a number of trails they could have taken, and while she'd left him a clue, there was no guarantee he'd see it.

But whether Caden was behind her or not didn't matter at the moment. Her body ached and she felt nauseous. She needed to stop.

"I have to rest," she said, struggling for air.

"We don't have time. Keep walking."

She stopped in her tracks, ignoring his demand. At this point, she didn't care what they did. "I said I needed to rest."

"It is hot, King…" One of the men pulled off his mask.

"Fine… I guess it doesn't matter at this point if she sees our faces." The man in charge pulled off his own mask, revealing his bleached-blond hair, then pointed his gun at her. "But we don't have time for games."

"I'm not playing games. If I'm so valuable, then let me rest."

"King…"

At least the younger of the two seemed to have a heart.

"Fine." King glared at her. "You've got three minutes and not a second more."

He glanced at his partner then handed her a bottle of water. "Since when did you become such a softy?"

She sat down on a rock, ignoring the men, and pulled off her shoe and sock, both of which were still damp. Blisters had started to form on the bottom of her left foot, but it wasn't nearly as bad as her throbbing ankle. And while they'd been hiking uphill for quite a while, they still had at least another thirty minutes to get to the top.

Which made her ask the question again. If they wanted her dead—like she'd thought—why drag her up the canyon again? It didn't make sense.

She studied the two men, who'd argued most of the way up. She'd figured out their names, and now she knew what they looked like. King, with his spiked hair, was both older and taller, and clearly in charge. Sawyer, on the other hand, had a baby face and didn't seem to want anything to do with roughing her up. But it was the dynamics between the two that interested her the most. Through her job, she'd learned to read people. Sawyer seemed almost sympathetic toward her, while King was quick to throw out threats and keep his hand on his weapon. If she could find a way to play off Sawyer's sympathy, it might give her an advantage. Or, at the very least, keep her alive. But in order to do that, she needed to figure out what they intended to do with her.

"What's your plan?" she asked.

"What do you mean?" King asked.

"I'm just trying to figure out what's going on here. I thought you wanted me dead, but instead you're dragging me up the canyon. I'd like to know what your plan is."

Sawyer took a step back. "Why would we want you dead? At the moment you're worth a whole lot more to us alive."

She tried to read between the lines, but nothing made sense. She'd assumed this entire situation was because Carter Steele wanted revenge because of her role in his conviction. How was her staying alive of any value to anyone, especially Steele? Because even if she wanted to, she couldn't do anything to change the judge's sentence. It was far too late for that. And anything he managed do to her would only get him into more trouble.

"I don't understand. I thought this was about revenge."

"What is?"

"The reason you kidnapped me. Steele threatened me in court. I thought you were his hired goons."

"I have no idea what you're talking about," Sawyer said, "but this—this is about your brother."

"My brother?" Gwen's mind scrambled to put the pieces together. "What do you mean?"

"You don't know what he did?" King asked.

"If I did I wouldn't be asking. But you had him—"

"He managed to get away," Sawyer said.

Which was why they needed her. Suddenly everything made sense. Except for one thing. She knew her brother. He would have come for her.

"What did he do?" she asked.

"He's a bounty hunter—"

"I know that."

King frowned. "He was hired by a bondsman to locate a man who had… Let's just say gotten into trouble with the law."

"What happened?"

"Your brother stole three hundred thousand dollars at the scene of the arrest. Our money."

Gwen felt a wave of nausea sweep over her as the pieces of the puzzle finally started falling into place. "And I'm your way to get it back."

King nodded.

But that wasn't possible. Aaron had always been one to take risks, but stealing three hundred thousand dollars from some crooks? He wasn't that stupid. Was he?

"My brother would never do something like that."

"Then you must not know him very well, because he did."

"Wouldn't the police confiscate any sums of money at the scene? Maybe they have it."

"Apparently he thought that we would think the police took it. Except we found out they didn't. Which left the only other person involved—your brother. And we want the money back."

At least now she knew why they wanted her alive. Three hundred thousand dollars was a lot of motivation, and they were clearly ready to do whatever it took to get it back.

King glanced at his watch. "Time's up. Let's go."

She started putting her sock and shoe back on. The bottom line was that she was on her own. She had no idea where Caden or her brother were, and once they got to the top, she was out of time.

She needed to escape.

They might need her for leverage, but once they got

the money, then what? They might let her go, but even that wasn't a guarantee. Especially since he could recognize them. No, if she planned to get out of this alive, she couldn't rely on anyone to come find her. She was going to have to bide her time and find a way out on her own.

The men were still arguing as they reached the top of the canyon. Sawyer stopped and started digging though his bag for something. She took a step back, ignoring the pain from her throbbing ankle. She was less than ten feet from the tree line. All she had to do was slip into the trees and disappear. For the moment, they weren't paying attention to her. The only thing in her favor was the element of surprise, which meant it was now or never. She took another step, then started running. Every step felt like she was being stabbed as the pain shot up her ankle, but she kept running, knowing that each step was another step closer to freedom.

Seconds later, she could hear them crashing through the brush behind her. She looked for a place to hide, knowing she wasn't going to be able to run much longer. The trees on top of the canyon were thick, as was the underbrush. It was the perfect place to hide, but would it be enough?

She crouched down behind the thick trunk of a tree, then held her breath.

"We know you're here," King shouted. "You can't run far and there's nowhere to hide."

A branch crunched behind her. They'd stopped less than twenty feet away from her, searching the trees for any movement.

"Do you really think you can outrun us?" King asked. "There's no one here to save you. No one."

"If you ask me, she's more trouble than she's worth," Sawyer said.

"Yes, but not only has she seen our faces, we still need her as leverage."

Sawyer took a step away from King. "This plan has entirely fallen apart. I agreed to going after the money, but now you've shot someone and we have a witness who can identify us. I didn't agree to murder."

"How did you think this was going to end?"

Gwen held her breath as the men continued to argue with each other. They were going to find her. Then they'd kill her.

Caden fought the current. Past the swift-flowing rapids that had almost managed to flip the raft, the river held its breath for a few hundred yards, but soon the water would drop again into another round of churning rapids. Which gave him about ten seconds to make a decision.

He glanced at the two men who had rescued them and forced back the guilt at getting them involved. But it was too late to change anything. They had to stop the bleeding in Levi's leg, and he needed proper medical attention as soon as possible. Caden glanced downriver. He also had to get off this raft and go find Gwen.

He shouted at Bruce to help him get to the shoreline, then paddled with strong, even strokes. Seconds later, they managed to guide the raft into a small alcove. The boat bobbed against the shoreline, held in place only by a jetty of land and a fallen tree.

"How much farther do you think until there's phone

service?" Caden asked, moving to where Bruce was in the center of the raft.

"I'm thinking a mile. Maybe less," Bruce said.

"Levi needs to get to a hospital, but we have to stop the bleeding."

Bruce got up and rummaged through a backpack at the front of the raft. "I've got a fleece jacket we can use."

Levi gritted his teeth and groaned.

"Hang in there," Caden said as he took the jacket.

He frowned as he put steady pressure on Levi's leg. His military training had taught him the statistics. Blood loss could kill a person within five minutes, even quicker than a gunshot wound. If the bleeding didn't stop soon, he was going to have to make a tourniquet.

"You want to go back after her, don't you?" Bruce asked.

"Yes." Caden nodded. "But I'm not sure if it's the wisest move."

"I'd want to do the same if I were you."

"What about the two of you? I'd be leaving you to make it by yourselves."

Bruce glanced downstream. "That's the last set of rapids coming up. I think I can manage getting through them on my own. After that, I can call for help."

"I packed a basic first-aid kit in my go bag," Caden said. "There should be some gauze and tape."

Levi grabbed the bag, then quickly dug around for the supplies. "I've got some bandages, but this... We weren't expecting this."

Caden nodded. None of them had been. His weeklong trek off the grid had turned into a nightmare. He glanced up at the canyon wall. The raft rocked beneath them as

Bruce's fists tightened at his sides. But the bleeding was slowing down, and Caden knew what he had to do. Gwen was out there, and he had to find her.

"Contact the authorities and let them know what's going on," Caden said, securing the gauze and tape around the gunshot wound as best as he could. "I'm guessing they took Rim Rock Trail to the top, since it's the nearest trail to where they grabbed her, and the easiest of all of them on this side of the canyon, because it's a shorter distance to the top."

"I think you should go," Bruce said.

Levi nodded. "I agree. I'll be okay."

Caden stood up. "I'm sorry we got you involved. If I'd have known what was going to happen…"

"You couldn't have known," Levi said. "Go find her."

"Please, call and speak to deputy Griffin O'Callaghan at the Timber Falls Sheriff's Department when you can. He's my brother. Tell him that two men kidnapped a woman in the canyon, and I've gone after her. Tell him I'll get ahold of him as soon as I can."

Bruce helped Levi get down to the center of the raft, where he'd be the safest going through the last set of rapids. "Will do."

"And you be careful, as well," Caden said as he climbed out of the raft. "Not only do you have an injured man, you're going to struggle just to keep the raft upright."

"I'll manage. We've wrangled worse rapids than this. We'll make it."

Caden helped push the raft back into the water, then started upstream. He figured he was at least fifteen, maybe twenty minutes behind them, but on his own he was going to move a lot faster than the three of them with an injured hiker.

All he had to do was catch up, then figure out how to take down two armed men.

Caden started up the steep trail toward the top of the canyon, certain Gwen and the men had to have come this way. There were distinct signs of recent activity along the unmarked path, where a number of hikers had made the ascent. It could be another group, or several individuals for that matter, but because of the low traffic these unmaintained trails normally received, he was convinced it was them.

He kept climbing another couple hundred feet, then stopped again and picked up a discarded piece of trash. It was the same blue plastic packaging for the chickpeas that Gwen had been carrying. She must have had some in her pocket.

No. This was no coincidence. He'd teased her about eating chickpeas on the trail, and now she'd left it as a bread crumb for him to find in case he'd come after her.

Smart woman.

He pushed aside the thought, and instead studied the area closer, certain they'd stopped here for a few minutes to rest. What he didn't know was how far he was behind them. He looked up at the steep trail toward the rim of the canyon. He knew he had to be moving faster than the party of three, but he'd lost time going down the rapids and then having to backtrack to the trail's access point. If he didn't catch up with them before they reached the top, where they could drive away, his chances of finding them were going to diminish greatly.

He tried to shove away the intense feeling of over-protection he felt toward Gwen as he forced himself to quicken his pace. While he hadn't thought about the woman for years, today he couldn't stop thinking about her. Or worrying about her for that matter.

But here he was, pushing his limits physically as he hurried up the steep mountain trail and praying he could find her in time.

His heart was pounding by the time he got to the top of the trail an hour and a half later. He checked his cell phone, even holding it up above his head, but there was still no reception. The trail at this point forked, with one branch following along the top of the canyon, and the other one heading west and eventually running into a road. Logic told him they'd headed for the road. He quickly drank from his water bottle, then reached into the side of his backpack for an energy bar. The effects of dehydration—muscle cramps, dizziness and nausea— weren't something to play with, and he couldn't afford to get sick, especially considering how the lack of sleep the night before had added to his fatigue. He studied the ground in front him at the junction. Something had happened here. One had veered off to the left while two had gone straight.

What had happened?

Had one of the captors left, or had Gwen managed to escape? He studied the footprints again. The single set of prints indicated a limp. Definitely Gwen. She'd attempted an escape. He hurried down the trail, then stopped when the three sets of footprints converged again. He squatted in the middle of the trail and studied the footprints again. Had they found her? He still wasn't sure.

While his body wanted to rest after the long, rapid hike up the canyon, he pushed himself forward, ignoring the burning in his calves and the pressure against his chest as he followed the footprints.

Noise ahead of him caught his attention.

She was running just inside the tree line. But she wasn't alone. One of the men who had grabbed her was running after her.

He had to get to her first.

SEVEN

Gwen stifled a scream as Caden pulled her behind the trunk of a thick tree. She faced him, adrenaline pumping through her, along with relief that he'd found her. He lifted a finger to his mouth, signaling for her to be quiet as he pulled her down to the ground.

"Stay down. Don't move."

She nodded, but she wanted to keep running, to scream—anything to stop the nightmare she'd been thrust into. This had become a game of cat and mouse, and she had no idea how to escape.

Instead, with her heart pounding, she followed his directions. She'd hoped Caden would come for her, but never thought he really would. And why should he? He didn't owe her anything. It would have been just as easy for him to continue downriver on the raft and simply call the authorities and let them deal with everything that had happened. Instead, he'd not only backtracked up the canyon and found her, but he'd also more than likely just saved her life.

At least, that was what she was praying.

An eerie quiet surrounded them, except for the footsteps of the men stumbling through the thick brush twenty yards to their left. Still stalking. Still searching.

"We know you're out there. There's nowhere for you to go. Nowhere for you to run."

Caden took her hand and squeezed her fingers, willing her, she knew, not to move. But she was certain they could hear her heart pounding as it pulsed in her ears. He was right. She'd tried running again once. At least if they stayed still there was no way for the men to see movement.

"Come on, Gwen. We're getting tired of the game. Come out before I lose my patience."

The muscles in her legs were cramping, but she still didn't move. The only thing keeping her alive was the fact that they needed her. Without Aaron, she was their only access to the money. But how long could this go on? They'd shot Levi, and now Caden's life was in danger, too. If someone died… No. They had to find a way to put an end to this.

With no other options, they waited in silence as the seconds ticked by and the men continued searching farther away from them in the dense trees.

"I think they're gone." Caden turned to her and brushed something off her face. "Are you okay?"

She shook her head. "They won't stop looking for me. Not until they find me."

"I need you to take a deep breath. I found you, Gwen. And you're okay. Just take it slow. In…out."

She felt ridiculous for falling apart on him. But she'd never had to run for her life. Never had someone take her at gunpoint and threaten to kill her. She drew in another breath and let it out slowly, trying to push back the panic mushrooming out of control.

"I'm usually more...composed than this," she said.

"Like all the other times you've had a couple of thugs after you."

She couldn't help but smile. "So I've never had anyone shove me off a canyon wall, shoot at me or chase me through the woods before. Not until these guys."

And she didn't want it to happen again. Ever.

He rested both of his hands on her shoulders for a few seconds, forcing her to look up at him. She caught his gaze and realized she'd never noticed the blue-gray color of his eyes, or how they seemed to change color in the light. Or how they made something stir inside her. She took a step back. She was alive because of Caden O'Callaghan, but that didn't mean she owed him anything.

Especially her heart.

She took another step. The unwelcome thoughts were ridiculous. Every time she'd seen Cammie over the past decade, she'd been reminded of the man who'd broken her best friend's heart. She'd listened to stories of how he'd betrayed her. She'd imagined him turning out to be a self-absorbed jerk. But instead, there was no hint of the man she'd created in her mind. He was the one keeping her alive. And he'd risked his life to do it.

"Did they say where they were taking you?" he asked.

"No, but they're after the money."

"What money?"

She blew out a sharp breath. "Three hundred thousand dollars."

"What?"

Her chest was heaving, her hands were shaking and she was having trouble thinking. She forced a slow breath. She had to take control of her emotions and calm down. It was the only way she was going to be able to function and get out of here.

She stared through the trees, thankful that the men were finally out of sight. "This isn't about me or one of my cases."

"Then what is it about?"

"My brother."

She waited for his reaction—clearly, he would be as surprised as she'd been. "What are you talking about?"

He listened while she told him that they hadn't been randomly targeted on the trail. That her brother had supposedly stolen money from a drug dealer during one of his arrests, and that was why the men had come after them. And it hadn't been a small sum of money, either.

"Three hundred thousand dollars?" Caden lowered his voice. "Are you kidding me?"

"I wish I were. They had him, but he managed to escape."

"And they needed leverage to get to him," he said, "so they came after you."

"Exactly." She drew in another breath, determined to get her mind focused. "What next?"

He glanced at his phone. "We need to get phone coverage so we can call for help. It looks like they're continuing to head east, but there is another dirt road to the north where we should be able to make a call and get ahold of the authorities."

"How far?"

"We should get connection on the other side of that

ridge ahead, where the terrain opens up a bit. But we'll still need to stay out of sight."

She nodded.

"Can you walk that far?"

She glanced down at her ankle. It was still swollen and sore, but she'd make it. She had to.

Something rustled behind them in the bushes. Gwen's pulse quickened. She'd always been a vigilant hiker, watching out for animals and ensuring she kept her distance. She carried bear spray in case of an encounter with a black bear or a mountain lion, even though those encounters were unlikely. This, though, was different. Every noise, every rustling in the trees, was a potential threat because there was someone out there who wanted to find her. Someone who was likely planning to kill her as soon as they got what they wanted, because she'd seen their faces and knew too much.

"Did you learn anything about the men?" Caden asked.

She forced herself to keep moving. "King's about six inches taller and definitely the one in charge. He seems far more reckless than the other one, Sawyer."

"He's young."

"And he's more sympathetic. Like he's not sure he really wants to be involved in this. King, on the other hand…" She paused. "I don't think he'll hesitate to actually pull the trigger."

"He's done it once."

Gwen nodded. "Sawyer seems to have limits to what he's willing to do to get the money. He was angry both at the fact King had shot a man, and at King's recklessness."

"All of that helps."

"Good, but I, for one, have no desire to run into them again." She checked her cell again, thankful that the terrain was comparatively level at the top of the canyon, but there was still no signal. "How much farther?"

"I'm hoping half a mile at the most."

She stopped for a moment and pressed her hands against her thighs, trying to catch her breath.

"You need to eat and drink something," Caden said, pulling his water out of his backpack.

"No. We need to keep going."

Every step forward was a step farther from the men after them.

"Drink some water, Gwen."

She nodded finally, knowing he was right. She just felt so tired. But they were almost there...

I need You to protect us, God. Please. Get us out of here alive.

And Aaron... She gave Caden back the water, then took the protein bar he handed her and ripped off the wrapper. Her brother had always been the first one to take on a challenge and never turned down a dare. His job as a bounty hunter had ended up being a perfect fit. He had just the right balance of recklessness and common sense to keep him out of trouble for that profession.

Or at least that was what she'd thought. This time he'd crossed the line. And she wasn't sure he was going to make it out alive.

"I wish I knew why he did what he did," she said, shoving the wrapper inside her pocket. "Stolen cash— did he really think he wouldn't get caught?"

"Most people either don't think it through or, yeah,

they don't believe they'll get caught. Selfishness blinds logic. He probably acted on impulse, spur of the moment, and then it was done and there was no turning back."

"Never thinking about what that effect might be on other people."

Like me.

Like Caden.

She tried to stuff down her anger, but it simmered in the background. There was no way to erase the damage his decision had caused. Instead, she finished the protein bar and stood up again.

"You've changed," she said as they started walking again.

"Meaning?"

"I'm pretty sure the old Caden wouldn't have come after me."

"I would have. You just didn't know me. Not like you think you did."

She glanced up at him, puzzled by his response. But maybe she hadn't really known him back then. Or maybe he'd just changed that much. She worked to keep up with him, determined to ignore the pain. But in the end, it really didn't matter. Their conversation had suddenly turned into something far too personal, and that was a place she didn't want to go.

Caden stayed beside her—he was worried about her ankle, while at the same time irritated at her belief that the *old* Caden wouldn't have come after her. He'd meant what he said. She didn't know him. Then or now. But the past really didn't matter at this moment. There was too much at stake to let the past come between them.

He studied her face, thankful there was a bit more color in her cheeks, but that was mostly from the sun. She needed medical care. Needed to get off her foot. But unless they wanted to risk running into the men again, they needed to try and get as far away as possible.

"I don't think we should walk along the road," he said. "We'll be too much like sitting ducks. But on the other hand, if we can get either a signal or a ride out of here, we'll be able to finally get the authorities involved."

He pulled out his phone.

"Anything?" she asked.

"I think I've got a bar." He punched in 911 and prayed that the call would go through.

Something clicked.

"Hello?"

He held up his phone and kept walking.

The call went dead.

"The signal just still isn't strong enough," he said, trying to mask the disappointment in his voice. "We need to keep going."

He bit back the sting of irritation as they continued walking along the edge of the road in silence, staying close enough for them to see any cars that might go by, and yet far enough to stay at least partially hidden. Because the longer they were out here, the longer they were going to be vulnerable.

"I'm sorry," she said.

"For what?"

"For projecting my anger toward my brother onto you. Of course you've changed. We've both changed."

He frowned. He'd been happy keeping Cammie in the past, where she belonged. "Forget it."

"You were right."

Irritation resurfaced, but he wasn't going to let Gwen pull him back to that place. The hum of a motor sounded in the distance, catching his attention. He grabbed her hand and pulled her behind him.

"Should we flag them down?" she asked.

He pulled out his binoculars, moving until he could get a clear view of the driver coming toward them. "It's a guy. In the car alone."

Gwen's fingers gripped his arm. "You're sure he's alone?"

"There's no sign of the men who took you. I think we need to risk it. You can't keep walking, and we've got to get some help."

Decision made, Caden moved out into the road and flagged down the car.

The midsized sedan came to a stop and the driver rolled down his window. "Can I help you?"

"It's a long story, but we ran into a bit of trouble and could really use a lift out of here. At least to where there are signals for our phones so we can call the police."

The man studied the two of them for another long moment. "Of course. Hop in the back. I'm headed back to my cabin, but there's a campsite a couple miles up the road. You should be able to get cell reception there."

"Thanks. We appreciate it."

He didn't blame the man for hesitating. Considering everything that had happened over the past two days, he knew they probably looked more like escaped convicts than day hikers. He opened the door and held it for Gwen to climb in, then slid in next to her.

"Thank you so much," Gwen said. "We appreciate the help."

"No problem."

"Are you from around here?" Caden asked.

"Just up for a couple days. I get tired of the city and enjoy a day or two out hiking."

"It's stunning out here."

An awkward pause followed. He'd never been good at small talk, or really interested in it for that matter. But there was something about the man that concerned him. Whatever was going on, the mountains didn't seem to have relaxed him. Plus, it seemed strange that the man wasn't curious about what kind of trouble they'd encountered.

"Are you hiking alone?" Caden asked.

"Yeah."

"I do a lot of solo hikes around here," Caden said. "At least once a year."

He studied the man's fingers gripping the steering wheel. The subtle scent of perfume lingered in the vehicle. Someone else had been in this car with him. Something was wrong.

"Like I said, we ran into some trouble this time," Caden said, deciding to feel him out. "Had a couple guys come after us with guns…"

"I'm sorry."

Caden's frown deepened. Why didn't he seem more surprised? It was as if—as if he already knew. Like he'd run into some trouble himself.

"The men are still out there." Gwen gave him a funny

look, but Caden continued, "That's why we're trying to get cell reception. We need to get ahold of the authorities."

The man still didn't say anything.

Caden decided to press on with his theory. "You saw them, didn't you?"

"I don't know what you're talking about."

"Two men. Both armed. Probably wearing masks."

"I've been out hiking and—"

"They took someone, didn't they?" Caden leaned forward. "Your girlfriend...your wife."

The man slammed on the brakes. "Stop. Please. They're going to kill her."

"Tell me what happened. We don't have a lot of time, but I might be able to help."

"Help? How can you help? They took my wife at gunpoint. Told me to find a woman matching your description," he said, nodding at Gwen. "I was supposed to bring her back to them, or they'd kill my wife. I'm sorry... I didn't... I don't know what to do."

Gwen's fingers squeezed Caden's hand.

"What's your name?" Caden asked.

The man hesitated. "Neil."

"Neil, do you have a phone?"

"No. They took my phone. Told me if I spoke with anyone they'd kill her. What am I supposed to do?"

"Exactly what they told you to," Gwen said. "Drop me off, and I'll make the exchange."

"Why would you do that?" Neil asked.

"Because I don't want anyone else getting hurt."

"I don't, either," Caden said, "but there has to be a way to keep both of you safe."

Caden stared out the window, running through every scenario he could think of. The men had pushed the line when they shot Levi. How hard would it be to cross the line to murder?

"Where are you supposed to meet them?" Caden asked.

"There's a turn off to a parking lot a hundred feet ahead of us."

"I going to try and circle around. Take them by surprise. And I need you to do something, as well," he said to Neil. "As soon as you can, call the authorities and tell them what happened. Try to send help."

"I will. I promise—"

"Caden…"

He heard the concern in Gwen's voice as he stepped out of the car, but it was too late. The two masked men he'd encountered in the canyon were approaching their vehicle, weapons pointed at them.

"Get out of the car now," King shouted.

The three of them exited the car, hands up.

"Now this is interesting. Lover boy here tried to rescue her, but it looks as if your plan didn't work."

Neil took a step forward. "I did what you said. You promised you'd let my wife go."

"You didn't do what I said. You clearly told him about your wife. I should just shoot both of you."

"Let them go," Sawyer said. "They can't identify us, and we can bring the boyfriend with us to ensure she behaves."

"Get his wife, then tie them both up—"

"You said you'd let us go," Neil said.

King stepped in front of him. "You'll be found. Eventually. But by then we'll be long gone. So forget trying to do anything heroic, or it will be the end of the line for both of you."

Sawyer returned a moment later with the woman and a fistful of twine and zip ties. She'd been crying. Mascara ran down her cheeks as she stumbled toward her husband.

"Tie them to one of the trees," King ordered. "Then we need to get out of here."

Sawyer hesitated. "I don't like this—"

"Stop worrying. This will be over soon, and then we'll be long gone before anyone can find us."

But despite the confidence in his voice, it was clear that they were working without a plan. And that things were spiraling out of control. The situation was going to come to a tipping point and there was no way to know how they would react. Or what was going to happen if Caden and Gwen pushed them too far.

EIGHT

Gwen tried to pull away from King's grip, but he simply squeezed her tighter. Pain shot up her arm. The entire situation felt oddly surreal. Part of her still hoped she'd somehow wake up and the past forty-eight hours would end up being nothing more than a bad dream. But there was also a feeling of determination fighting to surface, because she knew this was all too real. She drew in a ragged breath. She wasn't going to let these men win.

She couldn't.

She glanced at Caden as they were marched toward the van, praying that someone, somehow, would show up and intervene before they got inside. She'd been certain if Caden hadn't found her, they still would have tracked her down. But now—now it was starting all over again.

And it was the unknown that terrified her.

"Where are we going?" she asked.

"Just shut up and keep walking."

King bound her hands behind her with a zip tie, then shoved her into the back of the van. A moment later everything went dark as he pulled something over her eyes, then quickly secured her to something inside the van.

"Stay still, and if you give us any trouble, your friend here dies."

She knew he was serious about the warning. The only comfort in the situation was that she could feel the warmth of Caden's body next to her, as if he was still trying to protect her. And now his heroics might very well cost him his life.

She struggled to breathe in the darkness, and for a moment she felt as if she was drowning. Enclosed in darkness, like she had been in the river. Feeling the water pressing in around her with no idea which way was up or how to escape the nightmare.

She forced herself to take in slow, deep breaths and started praying. Her faith hadn't always been as strong as it was now. The death of her parents had felt like a stab to her soul, as she'd been forced to navigate a situation she'd had no idea how to deal with. At the beginning, most days had felt like she'd stumbled into an alternate reality, where everything she'd known and loved was gone. And she'd blamed God for not stepping in. Getting back on her feet hadn't been easy. It had been like walking blindfolded on the edge of a cliff, praying every day she didn't fall off. And while the pain wouldn't ever vanish completely from the loss, she'd clung to her faith and as the years passed, she'd begun to feel a strength she'd never thought possible.

But what happened when it suddenly felt as if her world was falling apart again? Why was it so easy to blame God for other people's actions? To hold Him responsible for not healing a loved one or stopping someone's brutal actions? Faith should never be based on circumstances, but that didn't always make the journey easy, or stop one's faith from faltering at times. She'd heard more than once how God was never taken by surprise, but she hadn't been prepared for this.

I don't know how to do this, God, but we need a way out of here.

One of the men started the engine and pulled out of the parking lot before starting down the bumpy gravel road. She could feel each bump. Each jostle of the van. She had no idea where they were going or how this would end. The only good thing was that Caden was with her, but even that just instilled guilt within her. He shouldn't be here.

She pressed her shoulder against Caden, was surprised the men were keeping them together, but escape wasn't going to be easy at this point. Not in a moving vehicle while bound and guarded by armed men.

Caden leaned closer. "Are you okay?"

His calming voice pulled her back to reality. "I think so."

Which wasn't completely true. Her heart was pounding, perspiration beaded on the back of her neck and every muscle in her body ached. But she was alive. They were both alive. Maybe that was all that mattered at this moment.

"I thought they were going to kill me," she said, barely above a whisper. "Why do you keep coming to save me?"

"I suppose I could have continued downriver. I've always loved white-water rafting and never miss an opportunity to hit the rapids."

"Very funny. I'm serious."

"So am I. I know you still probably don't like me, or

at the least would rather have just about anyone else as your knight in shining armor coming to your rescue—"

"You know you didn't exactly rescue me. I mean, I am tied up in the back of a van."

"Touché. But this is far from over. I promise."

"Can you get loose?"

"I'm trying, but it's going to take time."

"Which is something we don't have. What happens once they're done using me to get what they want?"

There was a long pause between them, as if he was trying to figure out how to respond. They were already at a huge disadvantage simply with her being injured, and on top of that, she had little experience with a weapon and didn't know the terrain well. If anything, she was a complete liability.

"So, do you have a brilliant plan?" she asked.

"I'm working on it. It makes sense now why they weren't trying to kill you like we thought at first. They need you alive if they want to get to your brother and the money."

"Yes…"

"Which buys us some time." Caden shifted next to her as they went over another bump in the road. "Do you know where the money is?"

"No. He never said anything about it to me. Actually, I don't really know if he has the money. Only that they're planning to make an exchange."

"Do you know when?"

"No."

Which meant Caden was expendable. And eventually she would be, as well. He was only someone to make her behave in the meantime, but when all of this was over, no matter how Sawyer felt about murder, she was certain neither of them was going to survive if they didn't find a way to escape.

And neither would her brother.

All for money.

"We need to get out of here," she said. They went over another bump and she hit her head on the side of the van.

"Agreed, but at the moment our options are limited. Levi and Bruce will get ahold of the authorities as soon as they can get a cell signal, and someone will find that couple eventually."

But *eventually* might not be soon enough.

"How was Levi when you left them?"

"We managed to get the bleeding to stop, but he's in a lot of pain. They were facing a rough ride down that river."

Hopefully, they'd already gotten to help, and the authorities were looking for her and Caden, but it could take days to find them. How many people's lives had been affected by her brother's actions?

The van slowed down. She could hear the tires crunching on the gravel. Metal hinges creaked like a gate was opening. She estimated they'd been in the car maybe twenty minutes. So they hadn't gone far. There were dozens of houses on the outskirts of the canyon. Most of them were isolated, which meant a perfect hideout. It would take law enforcement days to search the area.

A minute later, one of the men pulled her out of the van. "Let's go. Inside, both of you. Now."

"Where are we?" she asked.

"Your home away from home for the next few hours,

but just remember this—the more you cooperate with us, the easier this is going to be. Try to pull something and your boyfriend here is dead."

Caden's initial reaction was to try and overpower the men as they stepped out of the vehicle, but he knew it wasn't a wise move. Not at this point. Not when he'd been unable to undo his hands, and he still couldn't see. He was going to have to bide his time and wait for an opportunity. The problem was time wasn't on his side. Once Bruce and Levi called the authorities, he knew they would start a search, but narrowing down their location was going to be tedious. Which meant the men who had captured them still had the advantage.

The men left on their blindfolds as they walked toward the house, and he tried to orient himself. A bird called out and a dog barked, but there was no sound of cars or traffic. More than likely they were still somewhere fairly remote, in one of the surrounding houses. While he always camped when he came here, there were plenty of options depending on how much you were willing to spend. Anything from million-dollar houses with heated floors and spectacular mountain views costing hundreds a night, to small cottages perfect for a romantic getaway. All of them gave you a chance to retreat to a remote part of the state.

One of the men sat him down on something solid, then pulled off the blindfold before quickly rezip-tying his hands to the arms of the chair. Caden blinked at the brightness from sunlight streaming through the windows of the house, then waited for his eyes to adjust.

He glanced at Gwen, who was sitting beside him,

and caught the exhaustion in her eyes. The only positive thing about the situation—if he could even call it positive—was that she wasn't out on the trail anymore, because he wasn't sure how much longer she could have continued running. But this—this wasn't the solution he'd been looking for.

Shoving aside his frustration, he glanced around the room, needing to take in as much as possible so he could start making a plan. The dining room where they sat was part of a large open floor plan connecting to the living room and kitchen. A glance behind them showed two-story windows that led to a large wooden balcony with incredible views of the surrounding forests and mountains. Caden frowned. He wasn't sure how these guys had managed to snag this house, but he had to give them credit for finding something so isolated. And with little time to prepare, they had to have a connection to the owner. But finding them was still going to be difficult and more than likely the nearest neighbor wouldn't hear a gunshot, let alone a scream.

King stepped in front of Gwen. Caden's muscles tensed.

"I figure if anything will get your brother to respond, this will." King held up her phone. "What's the code?"

Gwen hesitated.

He turned his gun on Caden. "I said what's the code?"

"Two-two-nine-four."

"Now was that so hard? Look up at me."

King snapped a photo. "Your brother's foolishness is going to cost you your life if he doesn't follow through."

"What is your plan?" Caden asked.

"I thought that was obvious. You—*her*—for the

money. You're just motivation for her to cooperate with us, so her brother will give us what's rightfully ours. As soon as we can arrange a meeting place, we'll make the exchange, and this will all be over." King's own phone rang. He picked it out of his pocket and frowned. "I'll be back."

Sawyer stood in front of them, looking uncomfortable with the situation, something that could work for them. If Sawyer was more sympathetic, they needed to find a way to play off that and somehow gain his trust. And perhaps manipulate his guilt at the same time.

"She needs something for the swelling in her ankle," Caden said as soon as King was out of earshot.

Sawyer frowned. "I'm not a doctor. What am I supposed to do?"

"Just get her some ice. There has to be something in the freezer. Please."

Sawyer hesitated, then pulled open the door of the large freezer on the other side of the open counter. He rummaged around for a few moments, then pulled out a bag of frozen peas and held it up.

"That will work fine," Caden said.

Sawyer propped her ankle on another chair, then set the bag on her ankle.

"Thank you," Gwen said.

"Anything else?" Sawyer asked.

Caden bit back the ready comment on the tip of his tongue. He could think of a number of things he could use right now, but he needed to tread cautiously.

"No, but I appreciate your help." Caden glanced toward the entryway, where King was still talking on the phone. "Listen, while your friend's out of the room, I

have to say I don't know why you're here. You seem motivated by something different than him."

"You have no idea what motivates me."

"Maybe not, but I do know that the rap sheet you're
going to face when caught will be pretty significant."

Sawyer's frown deepened.

"I just want to help," Caden continued. "You don't
seem like the kind of person who belongs here in this
situation. Do you have a family?"

Sawyer hesitated. "Two kids and child support."

His motivation.

"So you're just looking to take care of your kids,"
Gwen said.

"Yeah."

"I get where you are," Caden continued, "but you
need to put a stop to this for their sake if nothing else.
You don't want your kids to end up with a father in
prison for the rest of his life. There are far better ways
to earn a living. Trust me."

"I tried the honest route, and there's not a lot out there
for someone like me. Minimum wage doesn't exactly
pay the bills."

"You're right, it doesn't, but—"

"Stop trying to figure me out." Sawyer held up the
gun, but his hand was shaking. "You don't know anything about my life or who I am. Nothing about why I'm
here right now. All I ever wanted was to take care of my
family, but things happen."

"You still don't have to be involved in this."

"In case you didn't notice, I already am."

Caden let silence settle between them, then chose
his words carefully. "My connections could help. My

brother's in law enforcement. All you'd have to do is call him. We'd tell him how you helped us, and I can guarantee they'd be sympathetic to you. Up to this point, no one has died, but if that changes—if you're looking at murder—it's going to be harder to fight something like that. And prison—that will become inevitable at that point. There's no turning back once you cross that line."

"We're not going there, and we won't get caught."

"Are you sure?" Caden leaned forward while Sawyer started pacing in front of him. "Have you really thought about what you are going to do when this is over? Try to disappear with your kids? Because the authorities will track you down. And, I'll be honest, there's something else that should bother you."

Sawyer stopped in front of him. "What's that?"

"Do you really think King's going to share that money with you?"

"What...? Of course he will."

"I don't know. He seems more like the kind of person who wouldn't think twice about betraying someone. And for all that cash... All I'm saying is that fifty percent won't go as far as the entire amount. It would be enough to disappear. All he'd need to do is make you disappear first, and this is the perfect setting." Caden gauged the other man's expression and decided to push harder. "It would be simple to dispose of a body so it wouldn't be found for years...perhaps never."

"Stop!" Sawyer stumbled backward. "You don't know what you're talking about, but I promise that I'm not going to be the one whose body will be found."

Caden backed off at the threat, not wanting to push

the man too far. It was clear from his body language he was already panicking.

"What's going on?" King walked back into the room, then dropped his cell phone on the kitchen counter in front of them. "What are you doing?"

"Her ankle's swollen," Sawyer said. "They asked for ice."

"So all of a sudden you're their butler."

"No, I just thought—"

"No, *that's* the problem. You didn't think. We're not here to cater to their wants and needs. We're here for one reason, and one reason only."

"We need to talk." Sawyer pulled King aside, but not far enough out of earshot that Caden couldn't follow the conversation. "This isn't what I signed up for. There are witnesses that can identify us. If the authorities find us—"

Caden glanced at Gwen. Maybe he had gotten through to the man.

"You're welcome to walk away if you don't want to take the risk. If you don't want your half of the money—"

"Of course I want it, but it was supposed to be simple. No one was supposed to get hurt. If the authorities find us now—after kidnapping them, plus, the man you shot—we're going to prison for a long time."

King's jaw tensed. "Is that what they've been telling you? Scaring you with their theories—"

"No."

"Last time I looked we're the ones with the guns, and they're the ones tied up in chairs. Stop worrying. This will be over soon, and you'll have your cut. After that, I don't care what you do."

"But—"

King held up his hand. "Enough."

King turned to Caden and kneeled down in front of him, so he was at eye level. "You're here for one reason, and one reason only, and that is to ensure she cooperates. To be honest, at this point, my patience is almost finished. So you will do exactly what you are told to do and nothing further. Do you understand?"

Caden nodded, but the seeds of dissension had already been planted. Now he just had to pray that they would come to fruition.

"And you…" he said, turning to Gwen. "You better hope your brother calls back."

NINE

Gwen glanced at the clock on the microwave. An hour had passed since King had sent the photo to her brother, and so far, there had been no response. Which had her worried. She had no idea where her brother was, or why he hadn't responded. She had no details on what had actually happened when he'd escaped, but at least he was alive. She also knew him well enough to be sure he would have come looking for her to find out if she was alive. He had to be somewhere nearby. But the message. It was possible he was still in the canyon with no cell phone reception, but if not, why hadn't he answered the message?

Right now their own escape seemed impossible. The men had tied both of them to the solid wood chairs, and trying to get loose had only managed to rub her wrists raw. Conversation between her and Caden was limited, while King and Sawyer continued to argue. She could tell they were nervous, and as far as she was concerned, they should be.

She turned to Caden, glad that for the moment, the men didn't seem to be paying attention to them.

"Do you think you can get loose?" she asked.

"Not easily. The guy knows how to secure someone."

"I was hoping your training would have given you some…secret way to escape."

"Don't worry. I'm not giving up."

But she caught the expression on his face and knew he was worried. She felt guilty, knowing he was here because of her. No matter who he'd been before, the man had integrity and courage, not to mention he wasn't bad-looking, either.

She stopped the nervous laugh from erupting, then quickly shoved aside the ridiculous thought. Knights in shining armor came in all kind of packages, but in real life—unlike in a fairy tale—it didn't mean you were obligated to a happily-ever-after ending with them.

Especially if that knight was Caden O'Callaghan.

"Why hasn't he answered?" Sawyer's raised voice broke into her thoughts.

"Be quiet." King had his back turned toward them, but his answer was still loud enough that she could hear him. "They won't find us. No one can trace us here. They have no idea which way we went and can't lead anyone to us. Without taking risks, we will have nothing."

Sawyer clearly wasn't convinced. "Except this isn't what we agreed to. We were going to follow him and take him. No one hurt. And if the brother doesn't respond, all of this will have been for nothing."

King hesitated. "Then we'll have to get rid of them, but for now, we have everything to gain."

Get rid of them.

Their voices dropped off to where she couldn't hear

them anymore, but she'd heard enough and what she'd heard chilled her.

She pulled on her hands. "Caden…"

"I heard them. We just have to wait for the right time. They'll make a mistake."

"What about a plan? I'm not sure that turning them on each other is going to be enough."

"Sawyer thinks they've already gone too far. That's to our advantage. Hopefully he'll keep King in check."

"And if he doesn't?" she asked. "Because I don't think the man is bluffing. King's definitely the one in charge. If Aaron doesn't answer soon—"

"All that matters for now is that they need you. It's the only way your brother will turn over the cash to them and they know it. We'll figure this out, Gwen. I promise. Trust me."

Trust me.

How could she trust the man who'd devastated her best friend? And yet, how could she not? He'd gone out of his way to rescue her and protect her when he could have simply waited and called the authorities. He'd risked his own life and come after her. She nodded, realizing that as crazy as it sounded in her mind, she did trust him. And at the moment, she couldn't imagine anyone else she'd rather have on her side in this situation.

"I'm assuming you've been in situations like this?" she asked.

"Tough situations, yes. Situations with my life in danger, yes. But kidnapped…no."

"What happened?"

She saw the muscles on his face flinch, and realized she'd struck a nerve. Her questions had been too personal, and yet, she needed some ray of hope that they were going to get out of here alive.

"I spent time working in military intelligence, as well as Special Forces, so there was more than one situation where I wasn't sure I'd make it out alive."

"And yet you did."

"Thankfully, yes, though I wasn't sure at the time. I decided God still needed me around for some reason."

"I'm glad."

"Me, too." He turned and caught her gaze. "I'm not going to make you any promises that this will end without anyone getting hurt. I can't do that. But I can promise that I will do everything in my power to keep you safe. Just follow my lead."

She nodded as King and Sawyer walked back into the room a moment later, both frowning. Her stomach churned as she tried to stuff down the panic. She had no doubt they would get of rid both of them, if they were no longer needed. But what would they do if her brother didn't call?

King grabbed one of the chairs, sat down across from her and leaned forward. "I'm struggling a bit, trying to imagine what's going through your brother's mind right now."

He paused, as if waiting for her to say something. But while she had the same questions, she had no desire to interact with the man.

"I'm pretty sure he wouldn't have gone to the police," he continued when she didn't respond. "That would be far too risky, because they would find out what he did, and once that happens, he'll lose everything. So knowing he's a bounty hunter, used to handling things on his own, I'm trying to figure out what he's thinking."

She pressed her lips together, still not sure where he was going with the conversation.

"I would have assumed all along," King continued, "that he would have been worried about what happened to you and come back here. He could be searching for you right now, which also means—depending on where he is—he might not have phone coverage. That would be one explanation of why he isn't responding. The other option is that I judged him wrong, and he really doesn't care what happens to you. Meaning he cares more about the money now in his possession than his sister."

He paused again, letting his horrible suggestion gain traction. Her mind started reeling with the consequences of the situation. Because like it or not, the jab struck, just like King had wanted it to. She'd been running the same scenarios through her own mind. Her brother couldn't go to the authorities for help without them finding out what he'd done, and even if he did, he had no idea where she was.

But Aaron *would* come for her, she had to believe that.

"Tell me about your brother," King said.

She hesitated, uncertain of what she was supposed to say. "What do you mean?"

"Are the two of you close?"

"Why does that matter?"

"Because I need to know if this photo I sent is going to be enough motivation for him to bring me our money."

"We're pretty close. We try to take a couple weekends

off together every year to go hiking. And we spend time together when we can."

"Did he tell you about the money?"

"No."

"If you are as close as you say you are, I find that hard to believe. You spent most of the weekend with your brother, and you're telling me he never mentioned he was suddenly three hundred thousand dollars richer. I'd imagine a secret like that would be hard to keep to yourself."

Her jaw tensed. "I don't know what you want me to say, but he never talked about the money. In fact, we didn't talk much about work. It was supposed to be a relaxing weekend."

"Something that didn't happen," Caden added.

King stood up and took a step backward. "Let's try something else then. If he can't go to the police or any of his informants that help him track down people, who would he go to for help?"

"I don't know."

"A best friend? Fellow bounty hunter that might help him?"

"I really don't know."

"We'll, that's a problem. He's not responding, and I'm running out of time." King glanced at the phone again. "I want you to leave a second message. And this time you'd better convince him you're worth saving."

Caden frowned. Even though he wasn't in a position to fight back, he'd still had enough of the man's intimidation tactics. "Maybe instead of all your threats, you just need to give Aaron some more time. He's probably trying to figure out what to do, just like you are."

King stepped in front of him. "The problem is I don't have the luxury of time. I need to put an end to this. Now."

"And then what happens?" Caden asked.

"Does that matter to you?"

"Considering the fact I'm sitting here, tied to a chair and having my life threatened, what happens next does matter to me." Caden chose his words carefully, still feeling as if his best option at the moment was to turn the two men against each other.

"A hundred and fifty thousand dollars is a significant amount of money," he continued, "but I'm not sure if you could disappear completely. That is what you're planning, isn't it? Disappearing. I've heard Colombia has nice beaches, or maybe Peru, where you can live a comfortable lifestyle for far less than here in the US. But how long will the money actually last? I don't know… eight, maybe ten years. With twice that, you'd be set for at least twenty years."

Sawyer took a step back. "King isn't going to cut me out—"

"No… I was just thinking out loud," Caden said.

But it was already too late. Caden caught the renewed panic in Sawyer's eyes. Another seed had been planted.

"Enough of this nonsense. Sawyer, don't listen to them. Because here's what is going to happen." He turned to Gwen. "I'm going to contact your brother again, and this time you need to make sure you get his attention." King pulled his weapon out of the holster and pointed it at Caden's head. "Because if you don't, I will shoot him. Do you understand?"

Gwen's lip quivered as she nodded.

"Good." King unlocked the phone. "I want you to convince him that I'm serious about my threats. And that if he goes to the authorities, you're dead. The choice is his, but he's running out of time if he wants to see you alive."

King dialed the number, then held up the phone, warning her one last time to do exactly what he'd told her.

Caden's jaw tensed. He was frustrated that there wasn't anything else he could do to stop what was happening. Instead, Gwen took in a deep breath and waited for the call to go through.

No answer.

"Leave a message," King said.

"Aaron…" Gwen's voice cracked. "I don't know where you are, but I need you to know that these men are serious. They are threatening to kill me if you don't make the exchange. Do what they say. Please. And Aaron—"

"That's enough." King ended the call.

Caden stared at the phone as if that would somehow make the return call come through faster.

"I can make something to eat," Sawyer said.

King dropped the phone onto the counter. "Fine."

Sawyer started pulling out sandwich ingredients from the fridge. A clock ticked off seconds above the stove, while the TV ran muted in the background on one of the kitchen counters. Caden could only imagine what Gwen was thinking. Fear, anxiety, even guilt. It was one of those situations you never imagine happening to you. Only to someone you read about in the news cycle. And yet, this was real and if they didn't figure out a way to stop the men, it would be their shocking deaths people would see reported on the ten o'clock news.

Tensions seemed to escalate with each passing minute. Time ticking by, frame by frame, like a horror movie where you're not sure if the good guy's going to make it out alive or not. He wanted to talk to Gwen, to reassure her that they would get out of here. Somehow. He'd figure out a way. If he couldn't undo the bindings, he'd find another opportunity. It was what he was trained for—running into trouble and figuring out a solution.

The phone rang.

King snatched up the phone. "I see you got my messages."

Caden tried to read King's reaction, wishing he could hear the conversation, but King turned away from them and kept his voice just barely above a whisper.

King muted the phone. "Your brother wants to make sure you're still alive."

Proof of life.

The entire scenario seemed so surreal. How had his weekend away ended up here?

"Tell him you're fine," King said. "Nothing more."

King unmuted the phone then held it up in front of her.

"Aaron—"

"Gwen…are you okay?"

"For now. I'm here with—"

King muted the call again, then continued the rest of

disappear for the rest of my life. Buy a little cantina south of the border and spend my days sunning on the beach…"

King pulled out his weapon.

Sawyer took a step backward. "What are you doing?"

King shifted the aim of his gun at his partner. "I'm saying that you're disposable. You've always been disposable. And without you—"

"King…don't—"

King fired a single shot at his partner.

Caden watched in horror as Sawyer dropped to the floor, his eyes staring up blankly at the ceiling.

TEN

Gwen's ears were still ringing as King quickly untied them from the chairs then bound their hands again in front of them with zip ties. He motioned her and Caden to move toward the stairs that led to the second floor, but she couldn't stop looking at the man lying on the floor. Her brain fought to process the situation. Anxiety pressed against her chest. She couldn't breathe. King had just killed his partner in cold blood, and that wasn't the only thing terrifying her at the moment. If King had killed his partner, she knew he wouldn't hesitate doing the same to them. Plus, they were witnesses to the murder, thus likely sealing their fate.

Which terrified her.

She pulled her gaze away from Sawyer and his blank stare while trying to push back the nausea. In her line of work, she'd seen plenty of abuse and devastating circumstances—things that she knew she would never be able to erase from her mind. But this… She'd seen this happen. And she had no doubt King would follow through with every one of his threats if pushed, as he got more desperate to control the situation.

Gwen's mind tried desperately to make sense of everything, but this would never make sense. Either the man was completely impulsive, or totally unhinged... or maybe both. Because something told her this wasn't a part of his original plan.

King took a step back, his weapon pointed at them. "If you ever doubted that I wasn't serious about going through with this, then I guess you know now."

"Where are we going?" Caden asked.

"You're both coming with me. Upstairs."

"Why?" Gwen didn't move.

King pointed his weapon at Caden's head. "I don't have to keep him around. You're the one who will motivate your brother to give the money back. The only reason I haven't shot your boyfriend here is because I still might be able to use him."

"We'll both come with you," Caden said.

"Good. Now go."

They walked ahead of him up the carpeted staircase to the second floor of the house, then down a hallway void of any photos or anything personal. Just like the rest of the house. Which made her wonder who owned this place and what it was really used for. It didn't exactly seem like the place where people spent their summer holidays, or winter vacations snuggling in front of the fire. It seemed more like a cold headquarters for a den of thieves.

King stopped in front of a large bookshelf at the end of the hallway and pulled one of the books off the shelf, then opened a door hidden behind the woodwork.

Gwen's jaw dropped.

You've got to be kidding.

"Since the two of you seem to have a knack for escaping, this is where you'll stay until the exchange in the morning."

Gwen felt a wave of claustrophobia press in on her as he shoved them inside the small room, then quickly closed the door behind them. The click of a metal lock added a sense of finality.

This was insane.

She looked around the room. At least there was a light bulb in the center, but beyond that, there was nothing more than the metal door with four walls that held some shelves with a few boxes and supplies on them.

"What is this room?" she asked, turning around.

"Looks like some sort of safe room. My father has one where he keeps his guns, to make sure none of the grandkids get ahold of them. They're also used sometimes as panic rooms, or even bomb shelters. It's pretty much just a reinforced room that can provide safety in case of home invasion."

"The panic-room description fits, because I'm certainly panicking." She stopped in front of the door. "So it's supposed to keep the bad guys out while you call for help."

"That's the idea."

"Then there has to be a way to communicate from in here, or at least a way out."

"In theory, yes." He started looking around the ten-by-ten space, then stepped in front of her and ran his still bound hands around the door frame. "Normally, like you said, they're built to keep people on the outside from getting in. There are also usually video cameras, communication equipment, and often food and water.

But from the looks of this door, it seems as if he's managed to manipulate it to where we're the ones locked in."

"So there's no way out."

"I didn't say that."

She glanced around the room. Concrete walls and a steel door. No obvious escape latch. They had to be missing something.

She fought for a breath.

Caden caught her gaze. "Don't tell me you're claustrophobic."

She frowned. "I never have been before, but I've experienced quite a few new things the past couple days, so who knows."

Caden kept searching the room. "Well, you have to admit it is kind of ironic."

"Like for starters, of all the people in the world, it's you and me stuck in a safe room together?"

"Think about it." He shot her a smile. "This really isn't that bad. You could be stuck in here with King."

"Or Sawyer's dead body."

She shivered at the thought. If it wasn't such a serious situation, she'd almost be tempted to laugh. A few days ago, if you'd asked her who was the last person on the planet that she'd have wanted to be stuck on a deserted island with, she had a feeling that Caden O'Callaghan's name would have come to mind. But now…now she trusted him with her life.

She took a step back and winced as a stab of pain shot through her ankle.

"Sit down over here and let me take a look at that," Caden said.

"I don't think it's any worse. It just won't stop throbbing."

He pulled up the edge of her pant leg to reveal her ankle, then pressed on the side.

"Ouch."

"It's pretty swollen. I'm not sure if it's broken, but it's definitely sprained. And there's the possibility of a torn ligament."

"Great."

She let out a sharp sigh. He was right. The swollen area was now bruising, and the pain and stiffness had increased. While she wasn't thrilled to be locked in some room, at least she wasn't having to walk on it.

"Just sit still," he said. "Hopefully there's a first-aid kit in here."

"The ice was helping. Maybe there's a cold pack."

He grabbed two blankets and propped up her leg until it was elevated a few inches. "I'll take that along with a landline or even a cell phone, though I haven't seen either so far."

"What about some kind of monitoring system?"

"There's one by the door, but it's been deactivated."

"Do you think you can fix it?"

"I can try, but let me see about a first-aid kit first." He started searching the shelves. "There's drinking water and lots of cans of beans. Plus on the bright side, there's enough military ready-to-eat meals to last us several days if King forgets us."

"Somehow I have a feeling you ate better on the trail. I wouldn't mind eating more of that salmon pasta."

"When we're out of here and this is over," he said, searching through one of the boxes, "I'll make you dinner one night. Pan-fried, garlic-and-rosemary lamb chops—"

"Stop, I didn't think I was hungry until you mentioned garlic and lamb chops."

Caden laughed. "Well, while I can't come up with lamb chops, I just struck gold. Here's an instant cold pack."

"You're pretty good at maneuvering with your hands still tied."

"That's going to be my next project." He somehow managed to squeeze the pouch, even with his hands tied in front of him, and activated the cold pack, then set it on her ankle. "How does that feel?"

"Cold."

"Funny. And here are a couple pain relievers and a bottle of water."

"Thank you." She managed to take the medicine, but a sprained ankle was the least of her worries at this point. "Caden, if he finds my brother and the money, he won't need us anymore. Plus, we just watched him kill his partner…"

"I don't think anything has gone according to his plan. He had this idea he could grab your brother and dispose of you over the side of the canyon."

"Then my brother escaped, and I survived."

"That put both men in a predicament. But let's not go there. We're still alive, and I plan to keep us that way."

"That's what I'm hoping for, but is getting out of here even possible?"

"I'm not sure about that…yet. But on the bright side, we do have water, limited food, a dozen books and here are some games." He held up the Scrabble game. "This might help pass the time if we need a distraction."

She shot him a grin. Had he always been such an optimist? "You might not want to play with me."

"Why not?"

"I'm highly competitive at games."

"Really?"

She nodded. "Really."

"Good, because so am I."

She smiled again, surprised at how much they had in common, and at how he could make her smile even in a situation like this.

"Is the ice pack helping?"

"Definitely, and I'm fine. Really."

"You're also a terrible liar."

"Okay." She pressed her lips together. "I'm trying not to fall apart on you and turn into some blubbering baby, because honestly, I'm on the verge."

What she hated the most was the feeling of having no control and no options. She spent her life looking for alternatives in order to find the best solutions for the children she represented. Finding ways to still play inside the box while making sure things went to their advantage. But right now she felt trapped.

"On top of that, I'm nervous about what we're looking at tomorrow," she said. "I spend my days fighting within the confines of the legal system, looking for options that will better my clients, but this... I don't see any way out of this, and to be honest, it's terrifying."

"What you feel is normal," Caden said, going through another box. "There's a lot riding on all of this."

She took another sip of her water. "I just still can't

believe Aaron would do something so stupid. I thought he had more sense than that."

"Just like you're not responsible for the actions of your clients, you're also not responsible for his actions."

"No, but I am stuck with the consequences. And if King gets the money, he'll kill Aaron, too."

The room began to spin. The medicine hadn't started working, but she knew what she was feeling was from fear as much as anything. Because there was still one thing they hadn't talked about.

"He killed Sawyer, Caden. I've had to work with a lot of difficult situations in my line of work, but this… I don't know how to process this." She looked up at him. "You were in the military. You had to have seen all kinds of traumatic things."

"There were a lot of things I saw that I will never be able to unsee. Incidents that sometimes suddenly start playing over and over in my head like a video."

"How did you deal with it?"

"Not always the way I should. There are resources, but sometimes it seems easier to simply deal with it on your own. Most people see me as this tough guy who fought for his country. I've always gone into a situation, dealt with it, then gone on to solve the next problem." He sat down on the ground across from her and was now working on getting his hands free. "Ignoring what you've seen isn't healthy, and it ended up numbing me."

She studied his face, surprised at his vulnerability.

"The hardest part is when you're a fixer and believe it's always the person out there who needs to be saved and not yourself," he said.

She nodded, wondering if what he was saying came

from a place of pain. "You sound like you're speaking from experience. Is that why you left the military?"

He glanced up at her. "Partly, but that's a long story."

"I'm sorry. I shouldn't have asked."

"Forget it."

"I know you're right. Trauma affects people differently and often takes you through a wide range of emotions that sometimes come in waves of shock, fear, sadness, helplessness. I'm just going to have to find a way to deal with this once it's over."

She watched him. His focus had shifted entirely to his wrists.

"What are you doing?" she asked.

"I'm listening, I promise. I have a blade in my paracord bracelet. I'm trying to cut through the zip tie…" He held out his hands. "I just got my hands loose."

Caden pulled off the zip tie, then quickly worked to get Gwen free. But with or without the bonds, they were still far from free from the confines of this room.

"What's next?" she asked, rubbing her wrists where they'd been tied. "There has to be a way to open the door."

Gwen started to get up, but he signaled for her to stay put. "There might be a time when you're going to have to run, so you need to stay off your foot and keep it elevated as long as possible. We have to get the swelling down."

"Tell me what I can do to help."

"Honestly, at the moment, I don't know." He stepped in front of the door. "From what I can see, there's no way to communicate to anyone outside this room, and no obvious way to open this door."

"There's got to be a way to open it."

"It's a vault-style door," he said. "It doesn't seem to rely on an outside power supply that could be cut off, for instance, in a home invasion. It's also built to resist a forced entry with steel-armor plating and can be manually locked and unlocked."

He'd learned a lot about safe rooms when he'd helped his father put in one, but this system hadn't simply been made to keep someone safe. Clearly, it had been built to keep someone inside. Which in itself was disturbing. There seemed to be no wired communication to the rest of the house, and no place to view the rest of the house from the room. Breaking through the wall wasn't possible, either, as there seemed to be armor plating and a steel interior finish, which probably also meant the room was soundproof.

For the next thirty minutes, they threw ideas back and forth, but none of them worked. He pressed his palms against the metal door, frustrated, as if that move would somehow open the lock. For the moment, he was out of options.

"Why don't you take a break," she said. "We can play a game of Scrabble and forget about the locked door for a few minutes. It will distract us both."

"I don't know." He wasn't ready to quit, but still... "There has to be a way out of here. These are made to keep people out, not in."

She pulled out the game and started setting it up. "It always helps to do something different if you can't solve a puzzle."

As much as he hated to admit it, she was right. How many times had he solved an issue on the ranch while out riding in an attempt to clear his mind? He was going to need to do the same thing again today.

"First word…" She laid down four tiles. "Bore."

"Bore?" His brow rose. "That's not a description of my company, is it?"

She let out a low laugh. "Not at all. Though the setting is a bit uninspiring. I would have preferred something with a view considering where we are."

"I'll have to remember that, because if you're looking for some stunning scenery, you'd love my family's ranch. It's got some of the most beautiful views in the state."

Not that this was a first date, or that there would even be a next time. Though if he did ask her out—which he never would—he could imagine taking her on a horseback ride on the ranch, showing her the pond in the canyon, or even going for a sleigh ride in winter.

She leaned back against the wall for a moment, smiling for the first time. "Tell me about your ranch."

"Scrabble isn't enough of a distraction?" He put down three tiles.

"It's going to take a lot more than a board game for me to forget where I am right now."

"True." He noticed how she scrunched her nose when she was thinking. "There are plenty of bigger ranches in the state, but I'm proud of ours. It's been in operation since the early 1920s, when my grandparents bought the land."

"I love that," she said. "Family history and heritage. It's something I missed growing up, because I never spent a lot of time with my grandparents. And then when my parents were killed a few years ago…"

"It left you feeling alone and lost."

She looked up. "You understand."

"As I've gotten older, I've learned that I haven't always appreciated what I have. I've had friends, like you, who don't have strong family support, and I've seen how hard it can be. It's something I've learned to appreciate and want for my own family one day.

"Do any of your siblings work the ranch with you?"

"It's just my father and me and some hired hands at the moment, including a woman that uses our facilities for horse therapy classes. My brothers are busy with their own careers, though they have been known to help out when we've needed them."

When he'd been given the chance to come home and work the ranch, it had initially just been something to do between leaving the military and figuring out what he was going to do next. It had kept him busy while he worked through the adjustment back to civilian life, but one day, it hit him that he was doing exactly what he loved—spending his days working the land. And while the work was never done, and the hours were long, it gave him a sense of purpose and freedom.

He shoved aside the memories. "We've got ten thousand acres nestled beneath incredible views of Pikes Peak. Hunting, hay production, grazing and raising cattle. And what I love is that it's surrounded by thousands of areas of public land, so it's private and completely peaceful no matter where you go."

"Where is it located?"

"It's about thirty minutes outside Timber Falls."

She shifted slightly in order to reposition her leg. "I love that town. I try to stop every time I drive through and buy fudge from that little chocolate shop on Main Street."

"I know the owner. She goes to my church, and yes, her chocolate is to die for."

"I can see why you came back." Gwen laid down another word on the board. "I'd like to visit one day."

He was surprised at her confession, but didn't miss the flinch in her expression. Like she wanted to take back her words as soon as she said them. Spending more time together after this was over was hard to picture. The two of them had always been like oil and water. But then again, maybe he'd never known the real Gwen. Maybe what he'd believed—like what she'd believed about him all these years—wasn't true.

"You'd love it," he said, swapping out three of his tiles. "There's a view of the mountains on every side, and if you like horseback riding, you won't find a more perfect setting."

He rested against the wall, realizing he sounded like a travel agent. While he did love the ranch, when they eventually got out of this—which they would—he had no intention of cultivating their relationship. And he was pretty sure she felt the same. All he wanted to do right now was find a way to escape. Then he would go his way, and she, sadly, would have to deal with the fallout of her brother's crimes.

"Your family sounds wonderful," she said. "I always wanted a big family with lots of kids and cousins running around."

"Me, too."

Or at least he had. Once. Years ago, with Cammie.

Now he didn't trust women—or his heart—enough to choose the right one a second time.

"And yet somehow you're still single," Gwen said.

"Reid and I are holdouts, I suppose, though I'm not sure why he hasn't been snatched up."

His brother Griffin had recently asked him about still being single. But as far as he was concerned, he was content with his life and didn't have to get married to be happy.

"You said you were doing some horse therapy. I'd like to hear more about that."

Her questions pulled him out of his thoughts, and he realized he'd missed her last move. "Wait a minute... you just scored over a hundred points."

She shot him a smile. "I always did like this game."

"And I'm realizing I need to pay more attention."

He searched for another play, wondering what it was about her that seemed to keep him constantly feeling off balance. Even...vulnerable. Something he was definitely not used to feeling. And the reason evaded him. He didn't care what she thought about him—he'd determined that a long time ago—and yet somehow that didn't seem true anymore. He owed her nothing, and yet just like he'd vowed to give his life for his country if necessary, he realized he was willing to do anything to save hers.

He switched his mind back to her interest in horse therapy. That should be a safe place to go.

"I started last year in an effort to help a single father in town and his eight-year-old boy," he said, adding an *s* tile to a word. "His physiatrist suggested therapy with a horse, but the family didn't have the money or the resources. I did a bunch of research and talked to some contacts, and in the end was able to bring the right people together. We have a woman who boards two therapy horses at the ranch and volunteers two days a week. It's ended up making an amazing difference in her clients' lives.

"Wow. I'm impressed."

"At this point, I'm not really personally involved other than offering the ranch."

Gwen studied the board and then drew new tiles. "It's interesting that you've gotten involved in that kind of therapy."

"From what I've seen so far, the results are amazing."

Gwen looked up and caught his gaze. "Have you ever thought of expanding the program?"

"At this point, I can't really call it a program. It's more of a—a test really. To see what's possible."

He studied her, wishing he didn't feel the subtle attraction between them and wondering how she'd gotten him to talk so much. Normally he was the quiet one, comfortable being with a group of people, while even more at ease alone out on the ranch.

"And yet you've already seen the results," she said. "You've got a working cattle ranch. Like with the horses, it's the perfect place to teach leadership, teamwork, life skills and accountability."

"Sounds as if you really have thought this out."

"I have."

For a moment, the game was forgotten as he focused his attention on her and wished he could ask her what was really on his mind. But maybe he was the only one feeling the unwanted tug of attraction between them.

He shifted uncomfortably on his spot on the floor. "I don't know. I've never thought beyond that one opportunity. To be honest, I don't know what all the possibilities are."

"Like I said before, I am pretty passionate about the kids I work with and tend to let my mind go a bit wild with the possibilities."

"There's nothing wrong with that. Nothing would move forward without dreams. I'm impressed with what you're doing. And I'm not just talking about the Scrabble board."

"Funny."

He matched her smile, but knew he shouldn't be flirting with her. There was simply no way to forget who she really was. He was treading far too close to the personal, a place he didn't need to go, because he shouldn't like her. Shouldn't like the way she clearly cared about other people and not only voiced her passion, but was also doing something about it.

He pushed away the memories lurking just below the surface. Maybe he'd been wrong about her, but telling her what had really happened that night with Cammie wouldn't change anything. He had no desire to go back there and dredge up the past, and trusting his heart again certainly wasn't going to happen. All that mattered right now was trying to get out of here. There had to be a way, and he just needed to figure it out.

"What are you thinking?" she asked.

"Just working on a plan to get us out of here."

"You've changed," she said, putting down another word.

"After a decade, I'd hope so."

"I meant it as a compliment. There's something about you that wasn't there before. A focus. A calmness. Besides, I never really did see you with Cammie, anyway. She's too high-strung."

"Looks like I'm not the only one who's changed," he said, realizing he was moving into risky territory. "I guess I always saw you as caught up with status and image. I've enjoyed seeing the other side of you."

"Cammie was always ready to shop, or get her nails done, or make sure she had the latest fashion. Not that I mind any of those things, but I did find that when I wasn't around her, they seemed far less important and more frivolous. I guess I was also just growing up and getting involved in a cause I feel passionate about."

"That feeling you're making a difference in your life is important. I had that when I was in the military. When I had to leave, I was lost for a long time. I was used to being a part of this larger team and mission, and when I was on my own I realized I'd lost my direction."

"What made a difference?"

"There was this old man at church. He challenged me to think about what I really wanted in life and then to not just talk about it, but write it down, and then make the necessary moves to get there. It wasn't automatic, but it worked for me."

"Can I ask you something else personal?" she asked.

He nodded, wishing she didn't both entice and terrify him at the same time.

She hesitated a moment, then said, "Do you have any regrets over not marrying Cammie?"

ELEVEN

Gwen paused again, wondering if she'd pushed too far. But what if she'd been wrong all these years about the man sitting across from her? What if he wasn't the villain in the story she'd made him out to be? She'd heard Cammie's version of what had happened that day, had sat with her friend as she'd cried for hours after the breakup. But Cammie had always tended to exaggerate *and* ensure she was the center of attention. That was part of the reason they'd ended up growing apart over the years. But Gwen's image of Caden had never changed.

Until now.

"Do I regret our not getting married?" Caden seemed to mull over the question. "At the time, I imagined spending the rest of my life with her, so it was hard, but now...honestly, I have no regrets."

She listened to him talk and realized there was another thing about their breakup that didn't make sense. For a girl with a broken heart, Cammie had recovered quickly. In less than a year, she'd become engaged again and this time had gotten married—something that had always surprised Gwen. And now, listening to Caden...

he seemed over Cammie, but she couldn't help but wonder why he hadn't found anyone else after all this time.

"I know I'm prying," she continued, "but the night you and Cammie broke up… I had a lot of choice words for you. Words that while they might have been true, probably should have been left unsaid. Or at least toned down." She glanced back down at the board. "I guess that even after all these years I owe you an apology."

"Forget it. You don't owe me anything. Like you said, we've both changed. And everything that happened back then… I'm not sure it matters anymore." Caden shifted his position on the floor. "She was your best friend. You were angry, believing I broke her heart. You also believed I deserved to hear those things. I understood."

"But something tells me you don't agree with what I said."

Caden fiddled with his tiles, but she was pretty sure his heart wasn't in the game anymore. "There were a lot of things that happened that night that no one except Cammie and I know about. Things that were said between the two of us that I put behind me a long time ago."

Something about his expression told her there were still things that he was holding on to. Maybe not grief over a broken relationship, but definitely a lack of trust. Was that why he'd never married? She wasn't sure what it was, but she was missing something.

"You're not telling me everything, are you?" she asked.

Caden let out a sigh. "I haven't talked about that night for years, and to be honest, I see no reason to dredge it up now. We went our separate ways, which in the end was fine with me."

"I understand." Gwen searched for the right response. "I guess it's just that I know her side of the story, and I'd like to know yours. It's something I never gave you a chance to do before. Instead, I made too many judgments."

Caden frowned as he laid down another word on the Scrabble board. "She's your friend. It was a long time ago, and honestly, I'd rather leave it in the past."

Gwen studied his face, trying to read between the lines. "Are you saying if I really knew what happened that night, it might change how I see her?"

"I didn't say that. What I am saying, though, is that we all made mistakes and said things we shouldn't have."

She appreciated his not wanting to speak badly of Cammie, but was he trying to protect her? Or maybe he was right, and what happened was something they needed to just let go of. The situation had been extremely stressful. She remembered that night as if it had been yesterday. She'd ended up making dozens of phone calls, while trying to evade the endless questions by friends and family. People wanted explanations, and as the maid of honor, she'd managed to simply let the guests know that there would be no wedding and leave it at that. She'd never quite understand how two people she'd believed had been in love had just canceled the wedding they'd been anticipating for months. In the days that followed, she'd helped Cammie send back the gifts, dropped off the wedding dress at a bridal shop to sell and fielded dozens of questions from curious friends. It had been frustrating, but as hard as it was, eventually people forgot. Life went on.

"Can I ask one more question?" she asked.

"You can ask."

"But that doesn't mean you'll give me an answer?"

He just shot her a smile.

"Why didn't you defend yourself back then? There are always two sides to a story, but you just walked away. No one ever knew what you were thinking."

She wasn't sure why it mattered that she heard his side of what happened that night, but for some reason—as evasive as he was being—it did.

Caden rested his elbows on his thighs, the game forgotten at the moment. "I'm not perfect, and I would never claim to be. I made mistakes in our relationship, but in the end, all I know is that I'm glad that we ended things before we got married. I believe strongly—if at all possible—marriage is for life, and I'm not sure the two of us really knew what we were getting into. I would have hated for things to have fallen apart later, especially if children had been involved."

"Is she the reason you never married?" The question was out before she had a chance to think about it.

Caden just shrugged. "I've never been opposed to marriage, but I work a lot of hours on the ranch, which makes it hard to meet new people."

"I'm just surprised."

He shot her a smile. "Because I'm such a great catch?"

"Yes, actually. You're handsome, and you can be somewhat charming when you try."

This time he laughed. "Somewhat?"

She felt her insides flip. Was he flirting with her?

"I do have to give you credit for saving my life twice. Though, to be honest, I'm still hoping for a third time. Still no brilliant ideas for getting us out of here?"

"No, and you ask too many questions."

"It's my job." She laughed, glad he seemed to finally be relaxing. "Plus, I've learned that you have to find time for relationships. If you're not proactive, it won't happen."

He caught her gaze. "Is that why you're still single?"

"Touché."

"I didn't mean it that way, but you did say you'd come close to getting married. Sometimes staying busy becomes a way to cope with that loss."

"I admit I stay too busy. It's easy to get through another day, then before you know it another week is gone. And then there's Seth. My ex. He lied to me about some pretty significant things. He left me with no desire to ever feel that vulnerable again. And now it…it's hard to take that first step again."

And from what she knew about Caden she was pretty sure she wasn't the only one.

"I was recently told by my brother," he said, "that I'm not one to give out relationship advice. I've tried dating some, but I always end up walking away for one reason or the other. Maybe my brother's right. I'm pretty sure that Cammie affected me more than I realize."

"Trust doesn't always come easy," she said, "especially after a relationship that's gone sour."

"True." He looked down at his tiles again. "I guess I'm just looking for someone who loves me as much as I love her."

"She's out there."

"I'd like to think so."

"So you are a bit of a romantic at heart."

He let out a low chuckle. "Sorry, but that's not something I'll ever admit."

"I don't know. Girls like guys who are romantics."

For a moment, she wished she could take back her words. She didn't like him. At least not in that way. Clearly, the stress of the situation was playing with her mind. She'd let the ridiculous situation they were in make him into some kind of hero. She'd meant what she'd said about not ever wanting to feel vulnerable again like she had when Seth left her. When she'd found out the truth about him.

Except Caden had been her hero. He'd already saved her life more than once and she was trusting him to once again get her out of here alive. But that didn't mean it was personal for her…or for him, for that matter. They were simply two people who had been thrown together in a terrifying life-and-death situation. When this was over, she would owe him her gratitude, but nothing more.

She focused on the board that they'd forgotten about.

"I appreciate your talking to me," she said. "I know that what really happened between you and Cammie that day is none of my business."

"You're right." He put down a new word and smiled at her. "Sappy for seven points."

"Wait a minute… I thought you weren't a romantic."

"Very funny."

She grabbed her tiles and put down another word. "Seal."

Caden glanced at the door. "That's it."

"What's it?"

"Seal."

"A cute furry animal that lives in the water?"

"No." He caught her gaze. "I think I just discovered a way out of here."

Caden walked back to the wall around the door and stood in front of it. Gwen's questions had led him to a place he'd rather forget, but he couldn't think about that right now. He'd missed something. He knew enough about these structures to know that there had to be a way out from the inside, and yet while he'd searched extensively, he still hadn't found one. At least he hadn't found anything obvious. But that didn't mean it wasn't here. Because what if this safe room had never been intended to simply keep bad guys out? What if whoever owned it had another purpose in mind?

"What are you thinking?" she said.

"I've been assuming that this is just another safe room, but what if it was actually modified for another reason?"

"What do you mean?"

"Think about it. We've already talked about how a safe room typically is a place to go in the event of a burglary when your life is at stake. People also use them as a place to go during bad weather, but you always need a way to communicate with the outside."

"And that's what's missing."

He worked through his thoughts out loud. "We know that most rooms like this have a dedicated landline or, at the least, a cell phone. There should also be a radio—some way to communicate to the outside world. But for some reason, we haven't been able to find any of those things."

"Okay."

"Clearly, King could have taken any form of communication out, but that's not the only thing missing. There should also be a way out. A way to unlock the door from the inside in case someone was accidently trapped inside."

"So how did you get all of that from a Scrabble game?"

"The word *seal* makes me think of something that's been concealed or hidden."

"And how does that get us out of here?"

"Something else is missing. If the purpose of a safe room is to keep you safe inside, there should always be a release handle that bypasses the locking mechanism—"

"So people don't get locked in."

"Exactly. And while I looked for one, and couldn't find one, that doesn't mean it isn't here. This room has been upgraded or modified recently. Don't get up, but can you see the paint here?"

He pointed to a section near the door.

"Yeah…it looks like it was sloppily done."

"The color doesn't quite match the rest of the room. There's also some spackling under this trim here."

"They were covering something."

"Exactly." He grabbed a Scrabble tile and started chipping away some of the paint.

"All of this makes me want to know who owns this house and what exactly they were planning to use this for," she said.

"It has to be connected somehow to the money your brother stole. Which means it wouldn't be surprising if this was used for a number of illegal activities." He turned around and walked to the other side of the small room. "There's a square indention on the carpet here, and I don't think this stain on the floor is rust."

"Blood?"

"More than likely, yes."

"And the indention?"

"They could have been storing something here. A gun locker, drugs…whatever made King three hundred thousand dollars."

"I think it's safe to assume that whatever he's involved in is illegal." She picked up one of the tiles. "But why are there games in here?"

"They could have been left behind by the previous owner. On the outside, if anyone was to look in, it appears to be nothing more than a safe room." He studied the wall where it had been repainted. "Have you ever done one of those escape-room parties?"

"No. Honestly, the thought of being locked in a room for an hour—even for entertainment—gives me the creeps."

"I did it with some friends in Denver a few months ago." He started chipping again at the paint. "We showed up at this house and were given a brief storyline of some far-fetched scenario where we had to stop evil spies from stealing classified information. The door locked behind us, and we were given sixty minutes to find the key before getting caught. It took us fifty-five minutes and, to be honest, I wasn't sure we were going to make it in time until the very end. Point is, we did. I'm determined to figure this out, as well."

"All I know is that after this experience, I don't think I'll have any desire to do that for fun."

"Agreed." He looked around the room, found a block of wood and started hammering. He knew she was nervous and, quite frankly, he didn't blame her. But he meant what he said. There had to be a way out of here, and he would find it.

"Is he going to be able to hear you pounding?" she asked.

"I assume it's bomb-blast-resistant, fire-resistant and soundproof."

Caden kept working on the wall, chipping away at the section someone had clearly covered up. "Do you know anything about the case your brother had been working on?"

"Only what I saw on the news, which wasn't much. Apparently there were several warrants issued connected to the case, and there were drugs involved, but really, that's all I know." She frowned. "I wonder if there's a way to trace them to this house."

"I was wondering the same thing. Problem is, even if Bruce and Levi go to the police, unless they can figure out the connection to King, it's not going to matter." A large chunk of drywall broke off, exposing a bunch of wires. "They've definitely covered this up. If I can find the electromagnetic locks…" He pulled on a lever and heard the click of the lock being released.

The door clicked open.

Caden felt his pulse quicken as he stepped out of the room with Gwen right behind him. He was grateful his idea to open the door had actually worked, but they weren't out of the woods yet. While the ice pack had probably helped numb Gwen's pain, he was also certain that every step jolted her hurt ankle. At the moment, though, their only objective was to get out of here without getting caught. They'd witnessed firsthand what King was willing to do to get the money, and as far as they knew, the man was still in the house and armed. And while they might have the element of surprise, without Caden's weapon, and with her injured, they were definitely at a disadvantage.

"Are you going to be okay walking?" he asked, keeping his voice low.

She nodded, determination marking her expression. "What's the next step?"

"Best-case scenario, we escape the house without a confrontation. But in case we don't, we need to find some kind of weapon. We also have to look for a cell phone, and a vehicle to get out of here would be far better than walking. And in the meantime, I'll try to buy us some time."

"How?"

He turned back to the door they'd just exited and pushed it shut. "I'll jam the lock. Not only will he think we're still in there, but he'll struggle to open it."

He rigged it the best he could, then glanced down both sides of the hall, hesitating for a moment before he signaled for her to follow him. While he wasn't sure exactly where they were, he knew the house was more than likely a holiday retreat. And judging from the size of the place, he could narrow it down to a handful of locations. He just had to hope that was enough and they could find help.

It was quiet in the hallway as they started down the

corridor. He paused, slowly opening each door. The house was fully furnished, and a pale light streamed through the windows, which meant it was already morning. He was surprised King hadn't come for Gwen yet, but there were clearly many variables at play. Had he even heard from her brother again? There was no way to know.

Caden heard a creak from downstairs and grabbed her hand. Voices sounded from below them, a muffled conversation he couldn't quite make out.

"Sounds like he's on the phone. We're going to need that weapon."

He opened another door that led to the bathroom, quickly pulled off two metal towel rods, then handed her one.

"Really?" she asked. "I was expecting something a bit more, I don't know... MacGyverish."

"MacGyverish?" He held up his metal rod. "Is that even a word?"

She shot him a grin and shrugged. "It is now."

"Do you trust me?"

"Completely."

He had a feeling she was as surprised at the confession as he was. A couple days ago, he'd still been on her Most-Disliked-and-Mistrusted list. But she did have a point. How were they supposed to go up against an armed man with two towel holders?

"If we do end up having to confront him, well...we'll deal with that. At least we're not against two of them anymore, but our priority needs to be finding a phone and some car keys."

He started down the stairs in front of her, praying the steps didn't creak.

He could hear King talking, but he still couldn't see where the man was. At the bottom of the staircase was expensive wood flooring. The room had high ceilings with thick wooden beams and a few pieces of artwork on the walls. To the left was a large stone fireplace. A glass wall to the right showed an incredible view of the mountains. On the other side of the windows, a wooden balcony extended the living space.

"He just stepped outside," she said. "He's probably having issues with reception like he was earlier."

Caden hurried into the kitchen, quickly pulled open a couple of drawers, then held up his find. "Here's a phone and some car keys."

Gwen frowned. "This was Sawyer's phone."

She was right. Making it a stark reminder of what they were up against.

"We need to get out of here—"

"Caden, wait…"

King's voice got louder.

"He's coming back inside."

Blocking their exit to the garage.

Caden grabbed her hand and pulled her back up the staircase. He'd counted five rooms on the second floor along with two bathrooms, plus access to another balcony, which as far as he could tell had no easy exit. But while there might be dozens of places to hide, like under beds or in closets, once King discovered they were missing, he'd come after them. They needed to get out of the house. But for the moment, they were going to have to hide.

He glanced down the hallway. He'd jammed the door to the safe room, though as far as he was concerned, going back in there wasn't an option. Instead, he led her into one of the rooms and pulled her against him behind the door. He was still holding on to the towel rod, as ready as he could be. If King realized they'd escaped, or if he'd come to get them to leave, Caden had no idea what the man's reaction would be.

He tried to hear the conversation, but whoever he was on the phone with was doing all the talking. Footsteps passed on the other side of the door. Gwen pressed in against his chest. He could feel her breath on his arm as they stood as quietly as possible beside the door. He felt her heart beating against him. His arms wrapped tighter around her. The only thing he could focus on right now was the fear he wasn't going to be able to keep her safe. He fought to reel in his emotions. Everything that had happened over the past forty-eight hours had made him question so many things about his past. While he might be attracted to her, anything beyond that was ridiculous. He had no intention of falling for her.

"I think he's in the bathroom." Caden took her hand. "We need to get out of here. Now."

Still holding her hand, they hurried back down the staircase to the garage door without running into King. Caden opened the door then clicked the key fob he was holding at the two cars.

Nothing.

"Where is it?" she asked.

"I don't know, and I didn't see any other keys. We have to go by foot for the moment. Can you make it?"

She nodded, but he could see the pain in her eyes.

They stepped outside and he held up the phone.

"So no signal?" she asked.

"Nothing." Irritation wormed its way through him. "With no car and no phone, we need to find the nearest neighbor and get help."

There was no way Gwen could hike out there for long.

"Stop worrying about me," she said. "I'll be fine. I have to be."

They started walking away from the house as fast as she could go, down the dirt driveway. Barking to their right shifted his attention as a German Shepherd lunged at them, stopped only by a chain-link fence.

Gwen grabbed onto Caden. "Where did he come from?"

"I heard a dog barking yesterday when we arrived, but I didn't see him. I definitely don't want to run into him when he's not behind that fence."

"No kidding."

He didn't want to scare Gwen, but he knew there was a good chance that Fido here had just sounded the alarm. Or, at the very least, it would get King to check and make sure no one was out here.

And that no one had escaped the house.

King had made it clear that murder was definitely on the table, which meant the next time they ran into the man, they were going to have a fight on their hands.

TWELVE

Gwen followed as closely to Caden as she could, but she knew she wouldn't be able to keep up for long. Every step sent a sharp stab through her ankle that shot up to her upper leg. The swelling had only gotten worse, and before they'd left the safe room, she'd noticed that her ankle was turning a dark blue. She wasn't sure how much longer she could walk. And yet what choice did she have? It was only a matter of time before King noticed that they were gone, and once he did, he would come after them.

Her mind automatically ran through everything that had happened over the past two days as they headed down the edge of the driveway, staying among the trees as much as possible. The entire situation had left her terrified, because she knew that without Caden, she wouldn't be alive right now. She glanced up at him, surprised at how much she trusted a man she'd despised for so long. Surprised at how everything she thought she felt about the man had changed. But that didn't really change anything in the end. She still had no desire to put her heart on the line…even for Caden. It was simply too much of a risk.

She tripped over a rock and felt her ankle twist. She let out a sharp breath and bit back the pain. Tears filled her eyes.

"Gwen?"

"I'm fine."

"No, you're not." He grabbed her arm, holding on to her until she steadied herself, then bent down and looked at her ankle. "The swelling is getting worse. If you keep walking, you're going to end up doing some permanent damage."

She sucked in a lungful of air and mentally pushed away the pain. "Really. I'll be fine."

"I'll be the judge of that."

She looked back toward the house, but she couldn't see it anymore. All around them were thick trees with dozens of hiding places. King was only one person, but Caden was right. She wasn't fine. It was all she could do not to cry from the pain.

"Maybe you should go and get help," she said. "I can find a place to hide until you come back."

Caden shook his head. "And if he finds you before I get back? You'd have no way to defend yourself."

She held up the metal towel rod he'd given her. "I've still got this weapon."

"Very funny. It might have been the best I could come up with, but against a gun…"

"I'll be fine. He's just one person. He can't look everywhere. Besides, he'll assume we both left."

"Forget it." Clearly, Caden wasn't buying her idea.

"I'm not leaving you, Gwen. We're going to have to find a way out of this together."

"Caden—"

"Just a minute…" He held up the phone in his search for signal. "Finally… I've got a signal now. If I can call 911…"

He pressed on the word *emergency* in order to by-pass the pass-code protection, then called 911 and put it on speaker.

"Nine-one-one, what's your emergency?"

"This is Caden O'Callaghan, and I—"

"Caden, can you hear me…it's Griffin. I've been running the 911 calls at the station all night hoping you'd call."

"Your brother?" Gwen asked.

Caden smiled and nodded.

"Griffin." He let out a sharp huff of air. "I've never been so glad to hear a familiar voice."

"Where are you? We've got witnesses that claim you were held up at gunpoint on the river down in the canyon."

"Let's just say I managed to get myself into a bit of trouble. The problem is I'm not sure where I am right now. You're going to have to try and trace this call."

"I'll keep trying, but I'm finding it hard to track your location."

She glanced back toward the house again, distracted by the sound of the dog barking. Certain every noise was King coming after them.

"We were told you're with someone."

"I am, and she's here with me now." He glanced at her. "Her name is Gwen Ryland, and long story short,

I found her, but so did the bad guys. We've managed to escape, but like I said, we're going to need help getting out of here."

"I keep telling you, you should carry one of those GPS trackers for hikers."

Caden frowned. "My Glock has always been enough."

"Until now. But listen, I'm running a trace. Give me any details you can of where you are in the meantime."

"We drove about fifteen, maybe twenty minutes from the top of Rim Rock Trail, but we were blindfolded. We're now outside an isolated two-story house that's probably three or four thousand square feet and has a safe room on the second floor. We're a couple hundred yards from the house near a ridge overlooking the valley, and we haven't run into any neighbors yet."

"What about the person behind this?"

"His name's King and he's somehow tied to Gwen's brother, Aaron Ryland, who's a bounty hunter who stole money from him."

"Is that what this is all about?"

"Three hundred thousand dollars. Gwen's brother took the money. At least according to King, that's what happened. He killed his partner and now he's trying to use Gwen as leverage to get it back."

"And you? How are you involved in all of this?"

"I ran into her on the trail, and somehow became the leverage to ensure she behaves."

"What's King's plan?" Griffin asked.

"I know there are plans of an exchange, but I'm not sure where he wanted to meet. And we've got another problem. Gwen is injured and walking out of here isn't an option. A possible broken ankle. At the least, torn ligaments. I can't leave her."

"Stay on the line with me a few more minutes and... someone..."

"Griffin?" Caden moved toward the clearing as the call dropped. "Griffin."

"Caden..."

He heard his brother's voice one last time before the call dropped.

"Signal's gone. I lost him."

"That might not be our only problem," Gwen said, frustration seeping through her.

"What's wrong?"

She could hear the dog's barking getting closer. But what were the odds that the dog could actually track them? King would have to know how to handle the dog and she didn't see him having any patience with animals.

But if she was wrong...

"The dog. Do you think he can track us?" she asked.

"We can't dismiss it."

"What do we do?"

"In an ideal situation, we'd keep moving, but we'll never outrun him. The only advantage we have at this point is I'm guessing King isn't a great handler." He slipped the phone into his pocket. "I'll leave the phone on. Sometimes it's harder to triangulate when there isn't strong cell-tower service, but my brother will find us, and this will all be over soon. I promise."

She nodded as he wrapped his arm around her waist. One foot in front of the other. That was all she had to do. And whatever damage she ended up doing to her ankle was nothing compared to what King might do if he found them. They moved in silence through the woods, then down a narrow trail that led, she hoped, to a main road.

He pulled her closer against him and steered her over a fallen branch. She wished his closeness didn't make her feel so...so vulnerable. But it did. Both emotionally and physically. She'd always considered herself strong. She'd gone through the death of her parents, something that had devastated her and her brother. It had also forced her to become independent and make it on her own. But this... She didn't remember ever feeling so completely out of control.

With the warmth of his arm around her, she wondered what it would be like if they hadn't been running for their lives. If they were here, enjoying the stunning beauty of this part of the country, like she'd planned to do with her brother.

Wondered what it would be like if he kissed her.

The thought completely took her off guard. She had no romantic attraction to him. He'd been engaged to her best friend, *and* he'd broken her heart. At least that was what she'd always thought. That wasn't exactly the kind of man she wanted to fall for, because she knew what it was like to have a broken heart. And yet, why was it that so many things didn't add up? The Caden she saw now was nothing like the man Cammie had told her about. She'd sat with her friend for hours while she'd poured out her heart over the man who'd broken hers. There had been no signs of compassion. Nothing heroic about him.

What was she missing? Because from her standpoint, Caden O'Callaghan was a man who'd not only risked everything for his country, but had also put his life on

the line for hers. And from her own checklist of qualities she wanted in a man, he was the first one she'd ever
met who ticked off all the boxes.

The dog's bark echoed in the distance. It was getting closer. A new wave of panic swept over her. She
needed something to distract her from both the fear and
the pain, but even Caden's towering presence beside her
wasn't enough at the moment to let her feel totally safe.

Memories flashed in Caden's mind as he tightened
his grip around Gwen's waist, trying to help keep her
weight off her foot as much as possible. She was strong.
Far stronger, he imagined, than she thought she was,
even though the situation had definitely taken a toll on
her. He'd been impressed with her clearheadedness. So
far she'd never panicked, never lost her focus, though he
knew she had to be terrified. She had every reason to be.

The situation they were in had him worried, as well.
The dog barking in the distance seemed to be getting
louder. He frowned, determined not to borrow trouble
as they kept heading away from the house, hoping to
find someone who could help them. As far as they knew,
King didn't even know they were gone. He let out a huff
of air as he helped Gwen around a log. Griffin would
find a way to track their phone and send the cavalry
after them. Then all of this would be over. For the moment all he needed to focus on was getting her out of
here and finding help.

He glanced at her profile, not missing the determination in her movements. But he needed to keep his focus
on what was happening, because underestimating King
was going to get them both killed. The man was highly

motivated and had everything to gain and, at this point, nothing to lose. The only way they were going to stay alive through all of this was to escape. Because he had no doubt that in an exchange, King wouldn't play fair.

"How are you doing?" he asked, tightening his grip around her waist.

"It doesn't matter. We can't stop."

"I know this is hard, but Griffin will pinpoint our location and send someone to find us. This will all be over soon."

She nodded, but he knew she was hurting.

"What do you like to do for fun?" he asked. "When you're not working."

"Trying to distract me again?" She kept moving beside him, clearly focused on each step she was taking.

"I thought it might help."

"You're a good distraction."

He was a distraction?

"Meaning…?" he asked.

A blush creeped up her cheeks, like she'd regretted what she'd just said. "Nothing."

"I think I'd like to know what you were thinking. The fact that you see me as a distraction intrigues me."

"I just meant I've been extremely grateful I'm not out here on my own. And Scrabble wouldn't have been nearly as fun."

He helped her over a fallen log. "I also recall you referring to me as both handsome and charming."

She laughed. "You're exasperating."

"It was just an innocent question. But you've forgotten about the pain, right?"

"I had until you reminded me."

He couldn't help but chuckle. He liked how she made him laugh even in the middle of all this. Liked flirting with her even though he didn't want her to. But she wasn't the only one distracted. Having his arm around her waist and her leaning against him—this was dangerous territory. He shouldn't be thinking about the woman who'd despised him for the past decade, and yet... Why did it seem like every time he was near her, his heart raced and his palms got sweaty?

No. That wasn't going to happen. Not with her. She didn't like him, and just because he'd managed to save her life—twice—didn't change anything. Neither did the fact that he genuinely enjoyed her company despite the mess they were in. She was funny, smart...and way, way too close.

He shoved back the ridiculous romantic feelings. He was going to get her as far from here as possible—his brother would track them down via the cell phone and all of this would be over. He just had to keep her moving as fast as possible. And what he thought he might feel toward her would have to wait.

Because that was what he wanted.

Wasn't it?

Caden pushed away the indecision he wasn't used to dealing with. He needed to ignore whatever he was feeling and focus on getting them out of here. He could still hear the dog barking in the background, and it sounded as if the animal was gaining on them. They were going as fast as he felt he could push her, but he was worried it wasn't fast enough. He glanced back again, wondering if her plan of her hiding somewhere was something they should consider, but while there were a lot of places she could hide, if King had a dog, the chances of her being discovered would increase tremendously.

No. His gut told him that separating was the wrong move. Which meant they had to keep moving…and praying.

THIRTEEN

Gwen ran as fast as she could with Caden's help, but the sound of the dog's barking was getting louder. Her lungs began to burn as he steered them off the trail and farther into the thick forest, but she knew he had no idea where they were or what direction they were taking. And even if Caden's brother did manage to track them, it would be too late. King and his dog were closing in on them, and she wasn't going to be able to continue much longer—even with Caden helping her.

Caden worked to pull her closer, trying to ensure there was no weight on her foot, but her ankle felt as if it was on fire. She worked to slow down her breathing, but if King found them, there was nothing he could do. They were both witnesses to murder and there was no way he could let them get away. Even if he didn't use them to make the exchange, their death sentence was as good as signed.

She glanced behind them and caught movement in the brush a hundred feet back. He might not have located them, but he was slowly closing in, and all she could see around them was more trees and underbrush.

"He's coming this way," she said.

Caden stopped, then pulled her toward a large outcropping of moss-covered rocks. "In here."

"He'll find us," she said.

"It's easier for him to see us if we're moving than if we're staying still."

"And the dog?"

He didn't answer as they crouched down behind the thick brush and rocks, his arm still holding her tightly. She managed to sit down on the damp ground and take pressure off her foot, while praying that the throbbing would lessen.

"This might work." Caden peered through a small break in the brush. "Looks like he's heading away from us."

"You need to go, Caden. Leave me here."

He turned back to her and caught her gaze. "I'm not leaving you."

Her heart tripped. He was far too close in the small space. It felt too…intimate. It was a feeling she hadn't expected, and like the fear she was experiencing, didn't know how to handle. All she wanted right now was for him to tell her he was feeling the same things she was. To hold her and tell her everything was going to be okay.

For a brief moment, the tension inside her eased as she explored the feeling. His strong arm still encircled her waist, while his gaze seemed to pierce through her. She knew he was formulating a plan. King might think he had the upper hand, but she knew Caden would go down fighting. He was the one thing that had kept her going. The one distraction she couldn't get out of her mind. Every time she looked at him, every time he touched her hand, or spanned her waist to help her walk, pieces of the wall around her heart had slowly begun to crumble. No matter how much she wanted to dislike him, she couldn't. Instead, she imagined what it would be like to see him again after this was all over. To visit the ranch he'd told her about and meet his family. To go on a long horseback ride with him through the mountains. He made her feel safe. Made her not want to give in to the fears no matter what was going on.

Made her want him to lean down and kiss her and never let her go.

She tried to read his expression, wondering if he was feeling the same thing she was. How, in the midst of terror, had her heart been pulled in this direction? Maybe it was nothing more than a needed distraction from the situation they were in, because she and Caden…that was never going to happen.

But if that was true, then why couldn't she shake this feeling inside her? This crazy feeling that she shouldn't just dismiss whatever was going on between them.

"Gwen, I—"

"Did you ever play hide-and-seek, Gwen?" King's voice yanked her back to reality and cut off whatever Caden was going to say. "Well, ready or not, here I come."

The dog's barks were becoming more frequent and sharper.

"He's heading our way again. We need to move," Caden said.

The tension in his voice was back as he helped her up. Whatever had passed between them was gone now.

"Stay low. We're going to try to outmaneuver him."

They headed in the opposite direction from King, but the undergrowth was getting thicker and keeping their movements quiet was impossible. She bit back a cry as her ankle twisted again, sending another stab up her leg.

I don't know how long I can do this, God.

Ahead of them, sunlight broke through the trees. With no map or knowledge of the terrain, she knew they could be going in circles. Which put them at another disadvantage. King, no doubt, knew this area. They didn't. Another few seconds later, the terrain opened up. Her foot kicked against a small rock that bounced down the slight incline, then off the edge of the canyon that spread out in front of them. Adrenaline punched through her.

"I found you," King shouted. "You lose."

She grabbed Caden's arm, looking for an escape. The canyon edge was in front of them. King and his dog were now behind them and could see them if they went left or right. Panic pressed in harder against her. There was no way out.

"I'm sorry," she said.

"This is not your fault."

If she'd been able to run. If she hadn't had to rely on him to help carry her. He'd been dragged into this situation simply because he'd decided to help her and now...

"I'd stay right there if I were the two of you. Bear will attack if I tell him to, and on top of that my gun is loaded, and I'm a very good shot. The only way out at this point—and I'm sure your minds are scrambling for an escape—would be for the two of you to jump."

King stepped out of the tree line. "Good boy. Bear is a trained search dog. This isn't the first time he's come in handy. I should have known you'd find a way out of that room, but you two just made it to the end of the line, and I wouldn't try anything. Bear might look friendly, but with one word, he's got a mean bite, which means this little game is over."

Caden took a step back with her.

"I'm not sure where you think you're going, but the two of you are more trouble than you're worth. I'm tempted to shoot you both, but fortunately for you, I still need you for a little while longer. So for starters, let's drop that phone you took on the ground."

Caden hesitated, then pulled it out of his pocket and tossed it toward King. Gwen bit the edge of her lip and tried not to cry. Even if his brother had been able to track the phone, chances were they'd never find them now.

King pulled out the battery, then stomped on the phone before throwing it over the edge. "Now, while I might be impressed with your Houdini act and escaping from the safe room, if you intend to get out of this alive, you'll do exactly what I say. Because in case you forgot, we still have an exchange taking place in the next hour. And if you want to ensure any chance of your getting out of here alive... I'd suggest you do exactly what I tell you. Let's go."

Caden's arm tightened around her waist. "She can't walk."

"Oh, I'm sorry." King frowned. "The chauffeur is running behind schedule, along with your afternoon tea."

The dog lunged forward on his leash and growled at them.

Gwen fought the panic. She knew if Caden had been on his own, this scenario would have ended differently.

She should have insisted he go on by himself and leave her. King still needed her, so she would be safe, but now, if they left the property, there would be no way for Griffin to find them, even if they had managed to trace the phone before King had destroyed it.

They were on their own from now on.

King stepped in front of her and frowned. "Walk in front of me. Try anything foolish, Gwen, and I will shoot him."

Backtracking to the house was excruciating, but stopping wasn't an option. Ten minutes later, the house loomed in front of them once again. Aaron was out there somewhere with the money waiting for them. She still couldn't believe the situation he'd gotten her into, and yet at the moment, all she wanted was for them all to be safe. But how were they supposed to end this? Her mind refused to stop replaying everything that had happened. Being shoved off the side of the canyon. Caden rescuing her. King shooting Levi, then grabbing her again. It was like a nightmare she couldn't wake up from.

And it wasn't over yet.

King finished binding their hands behind them in the back seat, then secured them with their seat belts.

"Do you have another plan?" Gwen asked Caden as King slammed the back door shut.

"I'd prefer one that works this time," Caden said.

She shot him a wry smile. "Don't give up yet."

He hadn't. Not yet.

In his work in the military, he'd seen firsthand that in situations like this, most perpetrators hadn't intended to end up in the mess they were in, which meant instead of having a formulated plan, they were simply working it out as they went. As far as he was concerned, the only option left was to leave seeds of doubt in the man's mind without making him turn on them, which meant playing on the man's impulsiveness.

Most of what King had done over the past few days had been impulsive, which could work in their favor in the end. Most people who broke the law did so believing firmly that they wouldn't get caught. But leaving a trail of dead bodies behind was taking a huge risk. Unless King somehow found a way to disappear, the authorities would find him and arrest him.

What they needed to do was find a way to keep him off balance.

"So how is this going to play out?" Caden asked as King slipped into the driver's seat. "Exchanges are always tricky with neither party trusting the other."

King's hands gripped the steering wheel. "That's my problem. I've got it all worked out."

"I'm sure you do, and I'm glad, because trust me, I just want this to go as well as you do."

The Jeep flew over a bump in the road, jarring Caden's head against the window as he continued working to loosen the bindings on his wrists, while thinking through his next move. The last thing he wanted to do was make the man angry. He could already tell King was irritated and, more than likely, nervous. And he should be. He'd killed his partner and was now having to make the exchange on his own, which automatically made things more complicated. An exchange in the best of circumstances was risky. Doing it without backup was even riskier. But his gut told him King wasn't looking at the consequences. He simply wanted out of this.

"And when it's over?" Caden asked. "I assume you're planning to leave the country with the money, which would be a good plan considering the body trail you're intending to leave behind."

The muscles in King's jaw tightened. "Sawyer was useless. I only involved him because I needed backup. I never should have let him in."

"The advantage is now you can keep all the money, but I am worried about something else."

King turned onto the main road but didn't respond. Caden decided to keep pressing.

"The problem is that the logistics of disappearing—without getting caught—aren't going to be easy."

"What do you know about disappearing?" King asked.

"I know that disappearing takes time and isn't easy. Not with the digital trails left behind, especially if you plan to stay in the country."

"My plans are none of your business."

"True. I was just thinking how this predicament of yours wasn't planned, but was pretty spur-of-the-moment, which is how you seem to work."

"You know nothing about me."

Caden glanced at Gwen and caught the worry in her eyes, but as far as he was concerned, they had nothing to lose at this point.

"I'm just wondering how much you've really thought this out," Caden said, deciding to continue. "I know you're impulsive, yet motivated. You could rent a small place under an assumed name and get lost in some big city, or you could even vanish and live off the land, but then you'd have to re-create everything about yourself. And you'll always be looking over your shoulder. So I assume you realize that Central or South America is better than staying in the US, because remember you're not just disappearing, you're a fugitive now."

"Law enforcement still doesn't know who I am."

"Maybe not, but they will, and it is true that without Sawyer in the picture, disappearing is going to be a whole lot easier."

The pause from the front seat convinced him he was on the right track.

"I'm right, aren't I?" Caden said. "You knew that this money was your one ticket out of here. It's what made you willing to take the risks you've taken—"

"You know, I've heard enough," King snapped back. "The only thing you need to know is that this exchange will go through, and after that, I'll be long gone."

Caden continued to work on getting his hands free, but he'd learned what he'd wanted to know. King wasn't simply motivated by the money. He was motivated to survive. Quiet engulfed them for the next few minutes as they headed down the main road. Several cars passed them, but there was nothing he could do to get their attention. Frustration multiplied.

"I have a friend who could get you across the border," Gwen said, breaking the silence.

Caden's brow rose at her comment. He had no idea if she was playing the man or was serious, but she'd impressed him by the gutsy move.

"You two don't give up, do you?" King said.

"I figure if I want to ensure we don't end up like

Sawyer, we need to make a deal. Unless you already have another plan."

"How does your friend do it? Make a fake passport?"

Caden smiled. The man had taken the bait.

"He's an old friend of mine, and while he hasn't told me much about his...operation, no, you wouldn't need a fake passport."

"Then how?"

"People cross into the US illegally on a daily basis. It's even easier to cross the other way. You use your own passport. He can get you and your money across for a fee. He can even get your passport stamped so you're officially in the country legally."

"And I'm supposed to believe you?"

"She's right. She has as much at stake as you do," Caden said, playing along with her. "We both do."

"It's the perfect deal," Gwen said. "We help you— you let us leave alive."

"And you expect me to trust the two of you?"

Caden's wrists felt raw, but he kept working to undo the rope. Even if King did agree to some kind of deal, there was still no way Caden was going to trust the man to keep his word. He needed to be free in order to put an end to this.

"Probably no more than we trust you," Caden said, "but you have to admit if you're going to get away with this—and whatever else you've done—you need help."

Caden caught King's frown in the rearview mirror.

"Just think about the offer," Gwen said. "You need our help."

"How much farther?" Caden asked.

"Less than an hour."

Caden glanced at Gwen. There was determination in her expression, but he could tell she was worried, too. They might have made their point that King couldn't do this alone, but trusting them…? Well, that was a long shot. Still, while Caden had no idea whether or not Gwen really had the resource she'd claimed to have, he was impressed with her quick thinking. And if all they did was leave serious doubts in King's mind, then that was enough for the moment. They needed him to hesitate over his next move and make a mistake. That was how he was going to get caught.

FOURTEEN

Dark clouds gathered above them an hour later, as King pulled off the main road and headed down a gravel road in the drizzling rain. She could tell that Caden—like herself—was still working to undo the binds behind them, but so far she, at least, hadn't made any progress. Caden had been right about King not following a plan. He was simply acting moment-by-moment and making things up as he went along. She wasn't even sure what his original intentions had been, other than to get his hands on the money and run.

While she hadn't been completely honest about her ability to help King get across the border, it wasn't exactly a lie, either. Samson just wasn't a friend. He was a convicted felon she'd helped send to prison, which was exactly where King needed to be.

A moment later, they came into a clearing where the remains of a few old buildings that had seen better days lined the road ahead of them.

"What is this place?" she asked.

"Looks like an old mining town," Caden said.

Gwen swallowed hard. The place where all of this was going to end one way or another.

She studied what was left of the abandoned log buildings and felt a shiver run through her. A hundred and fifty years ago, this had been a part of the Wild West. A thriving town filled with people convinced they were going to strike it rich. Today it just felt eerie and quiet. No doubt that was what King had wanted. The perfect meeting place for an exchange. Far enough off the main road, where there would be no witnesses, and plenty of places he could dump bodies.

And while she was sure tourists visited, the chances of them coming out in this weather were slim.

King parked about a hundred feet from the first building, then picked up his ringing phone. "Where are you?"

"Coming in from the north." Gwen could hear her brother's answer from the back seat. "I'm two minutes out."

"You better be if you want to see your sister alive. I don't have time to wait."

"Just don't hurt her. Please. I said I'd be there."

"Stop fifty feet from my car, then call me back."

King hung up the call and stepped out of the vehicle, then pulled Gwen out of the back seat. "Don't try anything stupid, unless you want your friend here to die."

She studied King's face as he checked to make sure Caden was still tied securely, but didn't have to ask if he was serious.

We need a way out of this, God, and I don't see one.

"What happens now?" Gwen asked.

King grabbed her arm again, then glanced back at Caden. "You will stay put, and don't try to be the hero, because I promise, you will regret it. I'll have a gun pointed at her the entire time." He squeezed her arm tighter. "As for you, you're going to walk, and get me the cash. You'll make sure it's there, then bring it back here."

Gwen paused. "What guarantee do I have that you won't shoot either of us in the process?"

"I don't exactly owe you any guarantees."

"And after you have the money?" she asked. "You still think you can just walk away from this and no one will find you?"

"What I do isn't any of your business."

Gwen frowned. Except it was. Especially if his business included dumping their bodies.

King pointed his gun on her. "Move now. I want to get this over with."

Ten seconds later, Aaron's car came into sight, driving toward them, and King's phone rang again. "Get out of your vehicle with the money, keeping your hands where I can see them, and walk it halfway," King said. "Drop the money then go back to your car. And don't try anything foolish, or I will shoot your sister."

"Enough with the threats," Aaron said. "I'll do it."

Gwen watched as Aaron stepped out of his car. She wanted to run up to him and ask him what in the world he'd been thinking when he'd stolen the money. How could he have put his own life on the line, as well as hers and the others he'd affected? How could he have been so foolish?

Mostly, though, she just wanted to hug him with relief and for all of this to be over.

But the game King was playing was far from over.

Her brother dropped his phone into his pocket, then

grabbed a gym bag out of the car and started slowly toward them.

"That's far enough." King held up his hand when Aaron was halfway between them, then pointed the gun at Gwen. "Walk back to your car and stand in front of it. Gwen, bring the bag back to me."

She started down the gravel road, trying to ignore the pain in her ankle while continuing to pray. She'd never wanted to be the kind of person who only called out to God when things went wrong. She'd always wanted to be the one whose faith was strong enough to believe that no matter what happened, she'd still believe. Like Daniel in the lion's den, or the three men in the fiery furnace. Her faith wouldn't waver.

It wouldn't waver if King killed them.

It wouldn't waver if she lost her brother...

She dug deeper for a thread of faith and held on tight.

"I'm sorry about all of this," Aaron said from where he stood. "Sorry we're not out hiking like we'd planned. Sorry that we're not spending our afternoons sitting at that cabin watching sci-fi marathons."

Sci-fi marathons?

She paused for a second and held her brother's gaze, trying to understand what he wanted her to do. She'd always told him that TV was a distraction when you could be outside enjoying God's creation when they were up here. They'd talked, eaten too much and hiked, but binge-watching? Never.

A distraction.

TV was a distraction.

That was what he wanted.

"Shut up and pick up the money," King shouted.

She reached down and managed to grab the bag despite her hands still zip-tied in front of her, her focus on Aaron.

"Wait…" King said. She turned around and looked back at him. "Hold up what's inside the bag."

She unzipped it slowly, then pulled out a wad of stacked bills.

"Zip it up and get back here now."

Gwen had seen the subtle look Aaron had given her, and prayed he had a plan. Both he and Caden had been trained to handle situations like this and were capable of taking care of themselves. She was the weak link.

But all she needed to give him was a distraction.

She took another step then stumbled, purposely dropping the bag in front of her. "Sorry."

She reached down to pick it back up as King rushed toward her.

"Forget it."

He shifted his attention to the bag. She glanced behind her as Aaron pulled out a handgun. She stepped back, and her brother took a shot.

"What did you just do?" King shouted, stumbling forward.

King tried to grab for Gwen as he dropped to the ground, blood quickly spreading across his shoulder. Caden ran up to her, his hands now free. He kicked away King's gun, then pinned him to the ground with his foot against the man's back.

King groaned in pain.

"Perfect distraction, Gwen," Aaron said as he headed toward them.

"Grab his gun," Caden said.

King groaned again and tried to get up, but Caden shoved the heel of his boot harder into the man's back until he quit struggling. "I said lie down."

Gwen reached for the gun, pausing as the sound of an engine shifted her attention and brought on another surge of adrenaline. A Dodge pulled up beside them, and a man emerged.

"No one move. Leave the gun on the ground." The man trained his gun on them. "I thought I'd find you here, King. And by the way, thanks for taking him down. You're going to make my job so much easier."

"Who are you?" Caden asked.

"The real owner of that bag of money." He took several steps and stood over King. "You didn't really think I was going to let you just walk away."

"I was getting the money for you," King said.

"I'm sure you were."

Aaron started walking toward them again. "You're supposed to be in prison, Anderson."

"And you never should have gotten involved in this."

Aaron kept moving their way.

"That's far enough."

"I was—"

"I said, don't move." Anderson fired a shot. The bullet ripped through the afternoon air.

"No…" She watched her brother stumble forward, a slash of red spreading across his thigh from the bullet. "Aaron?"

Gwen screamed as her brother dropped to the ground.

Caden tried to put the pieces together as Gwen shouted at the man who'd just shot her brother. A light rain had started to fall, but he barely noticed the steady drops.

"Let her go to her brother," Caden said, praying his demand wasn't met with the same result as Aaron's actions.

"Please. I need to stop the bleeding," Gwen begged the man.

Caden caught the panic in Gwen's eyes as Aaron lay motionless. Her face had paled, but he knew how he would have felt if it had been one of his brothers.

"That's all I'll do. I promise," Gwen said. "He needs help."

"Stay where you are and give me the bag."

She hesitated for a moment before grabbing the handle and tossing the bag at him.

Caden took a step back from King, his hands up. He needed to find a way to defuse the situation before someone else got shot. "Let her help him. That's all she wants to do."

The man shifted the gun toward Caden. "Drop to your knees, both of you, and put your hands behind your head."

Caden glanced at Gwen. So this was how it was going to end. Shot execution-style then buried somewhere out in this vast wilderness?

"You've got this all wrong, Anderson." King managed to sit up, still holding his shoulder where Aaron had shot him.

"I don't think so. You didn't think you were going to get away with this, did you? That I would let you take my money and disappear. You always were impulsive and didn't think things through, but betraying my trust—even I didn't think you were that rash."

"No… I thought you were still in prison. I knew the money was missing, which is why I'm here…getting your money back." King's fingers pressed into his shoulder. "You have to believe me."

"And if I hadn't managed to escape during my transport?" Anderson asked. "Am I to assume you would have simply kept the money for me?"

"Of course," King said.

"Please…just let me go to him," Gwen interrupted their conversation.

"Not yet." Anderson unzipped the bag and started digging through it. "This ridiculous charade you've been running is over, King."

"I told you—"

"I heard what you told me, but I don't believe you. I think you'd do anything for three hundred thousand dollars. Including betray me and anyone else who got in your way." He zipped up the bag. "Where is Sawyer?"

King ignored the man's stare. "I don't know."

"When I couldn't get ahold of him or you, I assumed you were here together. I'm thinking the two of you made a deal, but now I'm starting to think Sawyer got the raw end of that deal."

"Sawyer's dead," Caden said. "King shot him back at the house where he was keeping us."

"So you really have made a pretty little mess. You were at my house. Tried to take my money." Anderson leveled his weapon at King. "I should end this now—"

"Please. Don't. I'm telling the truth."

"You betrayed me and killed Sawyer. I have no reason to believe you."

"Sawyer made some bad decisions. I couldn't trust him anymore. But I wouldn't turn on you."

"I think that's exactly what you did." Anderson tossed the bag into the back seat of his car without taking his eyes off them. "Where did you think you were you planning to run to?"

"I wasn't. I was only going to—"

"You know, I really don't care what your plan was." Anderson let out a sharp huff of air, clearly done with King's explanations. He pointed the gun at the man's head. "The problem now is that you've got witnesses that have to be gotten rid of. You really didn't think, did you? You've created a huge mess that I'm going to have to find a way to clean up. Starting with you."

The rain was starting to pick up. Caden caught movement to his right. Gwen's brother was reaching for his gun. A second later he fired off a shot that clipped Anderson's leg.

Reacting automatically, Caden knocked Anderson's gun out of reach as the man stumbled to the ground. Caden grabbed the weapon off the ground and pointed it at Anderson, while Gwen grabbed for King's gun.

"Now it's your turn not to move," Caden shouted at the man. "Move and one of us will shoot you. Drop to your knees now."

Anderson groaned in pain, but obeyed.

The sound of vehicles roared behind them. Caden turned and recognized his brother's squad car. He felt a rush of relief as Griffin and two other officers jumped out of his vehicle.

"It's about time you showed up," Caden said, still holding the gun on the two men, while Gwen ran to her brother.

"Looks to me like you already have everything under control. I just might have to recommend you to my boss. He's been looking at adding another deputy to the team."

"Thanks, but I'm perfectly happy spending my days on the ranch without dealing with situations like this." Caden shot his brother a grin, but couldn't shake just how different this could have ended. "Next time, though, try not to cut it quite so close."

FIFTEEN

Gwen ran to her brother, barely feeling the pain in her ankle thanks to the adrenaline shooting through her. She was still shaking from what had just happened, but she was going to have to take time to process the situation later. No matter how angry she was at her brother for what he'd done, she didn't want anything to happen to him. At least he was alive.

At least they were all alive.

Aaron was trying to get up as she approached him. "I think I'm okay."

"You're not okay." She kneeled down beside him. "You've been shot."

"I'm sorry. All of this was my fault."

"I don't care right now whose fault it is." She pulled off the vest she'd been wearing, folded it once, then pressed it against the wound in an attempt to try to stop the bleeding.

"I never meant for this to happen," Aaron said.

"I know you didn't plan on this, but things like this don't just…happen. You made a decision to cross the line and almost got yourself killed. Almost got me and Caden killed."

"I know." Aaron closed his eyes for a moment. "I don't have any excuses."

"I'm not asking for any." She glanced back. Caden was heading toward them.

"Is he okay?"

"His pulse is a bit fast, but the bleeding seems to have almost stopped."

"Keep up the pressure and hang in there, Aaron. There's an ambulance on the way right now."

Aaron nodded.

Caden squeezed her shoulder. "Are you okay?"

"I will be."

"Stay with him, then. I'll be right back. This is almost over."

Gwen watched Caden walk away, then turned back to her brother. Aaron was in pain. She could tell by the tension radiating down his jaw, but Caden was right. This would all be over soon, but there were still questions she wanted answers to.

"How did this happen?" she asked.

"It's a long story."

She checked his pulse again. "I have a few minutes."

Aaron let out a deep sigh. "I was hired by a bondsman to locate Anderson who'd been involved in drug trafficking. I managed to track him down north of here." He hesitated. "During the arrest, I found a duffel bag in one of the rooms. There was three hundred thousand dollars in cash inside it. And I'm not sure why, but at that moment, I thought I could get away with it. I figured the police wouldn't know anything was missing, and Anderson would think the police had it."

Which unfortunately wasn't what happened. A man was dead. Aaron had been shot...

Aaron grabbed her hand. "You have to believe me when I say that I never meant to get you involved, Gwen. I didn't think anyone else would ever know. But then King and Sawyer went after the money, and Anderson managed to escape... At the very least I'm going to lose my license. I'll probably end up in prison, as well. I'm just... I'm so, so sorry."

She stuffed back her frustration.

She was sorry, too. Sorry for the entire situation he'd roped her into. Sorry she'd had to spend the past two days fighting to stay alive. But she also knew that her brother needed grace right now more than anything else.

Two ambulances pulled up behind the squad cars.

"Forget about all of that right now. We're going to get through this," she said. "The paramedics are here."

The next few minutes were a blur. Someone told her to move out of the way so they could help her brother. She nodded, then stumbled backward as a sharp pain shot through her leg. But it didn't matter. She was safe. She just had to keep reminding herself of that, because she didn't feel safe. She glanced down at her hands, which were covered with her brother's blood, and the fear and panic struck all over again.

She stepped aside while a whirl of activity continued around her, and tried to process everything. Paramedics worked on the gunshot wounds. Caden spoke to his brother and another officer. After a few minutes, one of the paramedics came with wet wipes and helped clean the blood off her hands, then started to check her ankle.

Caden walked over. "I asked him to check on your ankle."

"Thank you," she said.

"We'll do X-rays at the hospital," the man said as he finished up. "But it looks like it's just badly sprained."

"My nerves, on the other hand…" She waited for the paramedic to walk away. "Tell me this is finally over. Please."

"Anderson and King are in custody. Plus, they think they've found the house where we were held. They'll start searching for Sawyer's body there."

"It still all seems too surreal."

"I know." He pulled her into his arms and let her lean against him. "You're so cold."

He took off his jacket and wrapped it around her shoulders. "What are you thinking?"

"I'm just still trying to wrap my mind around what happened. And I'm worried about my brother. He told me briefly about what happened, but the truth is that no matter how glad I am that he's okay, I'm still angry at him."

"That's understandable. He's going to have to face the consequences."

"I know." She managed a smile. "On the bright side, you saved my life. Again."

"Your brother did help with that."

She caught his gaze and felt her heart stir at his nearness. How had this happened? They'd somehow gone from sworn enemies to her suddenly wanting to kiss him very, very badly.

* * *

Caden tried to read Gwen's expression as her lips parted, and she seemed to study his face. Something inside him shifted, pulling him to a place he wasn't sure he wanted to go. And yet he didn't know how much longer he could ignore what he was feeling toward her.

"He wasn't going to let us live," she said finally, breaking the silence between them. "Neither of them could have. I can't stop thinking of what almost happened."

"I know, but we don't have to worry about them anymore. We're safe, this is over, and like Griffin said, those men are going away for a long, long time."

She nodded, but he knew what she was thinking. For her and Aaron, this wasn't over. Not yet. The authorities were going to arrest Aaron for his part in all of this. But despite what her brother had done and the downward spiral of everything in the wake of his bad decisions, at least they were alive.

Still, the irony of the situation wasn't lost on him. He'd thought he would be perfectly content to never see the woman again, and yet they'd just spent the past forty-eight hours together proving everything he'd thought about her completely wrong.

"Caden, there's something I need to tell you. I..."

She paused as she looked up at him, but instead of finishing her sentence, she slid her arms around his neck and kissed him on the lips, taking him completely off guard. His mind spun and his heart raced as he automatically kissed her back. She felt warm against him, inviting, as he savored the discovery of the unexpected kiss. He hadn't been able to admit it to himself, but this—this was what he'd wanted.

"I'm sorry." She pulled away from him suddenly and dropped her hands to her sides. "This situation has messed with my emotions."

"It's okay." He stumbled with his words. "This *has* been emotional. For both of us."

"But I should never have kissed you. I've just been so scared, and now I'm worried about my brother… Honestly, I have no idea what came over me. You've been this rock for me the past few days, but I never should have turned it into something romantic."

His mind tried to work through his own feelings. Falling for Gwen had never been on his agenda. He'd just done what he'd known to be right.

"It's okay. We can talk about this later, but for now we need to get you to the hospital and get your foot X-rayed."

She nodded, but he couldn't ignore what had just passed between them with that kiss. Or that the past few days had twisted his heart, making him feel for the first time in a very long time that he just might want to take a chance on love again. It seemed ridiculous on the surface, and yet he also knew that Gwen wasn't the woman he'd thought she was. Instead, there was something about her he wasn't sure he was going to be able to shake.

She looked up at him, her eyes still wide. "So we're okay?"

He brushed the back of his hand against his lips, still feeling the intensity of her touch. "We are."

"I'm sorry to interrupt." Griffin came up beside him. "But we're about ready to leave."

"We're ready." Caden stepped back, even more uncomfortable, and wondered how much his brother had seen. More than likely he'd witnessed the kiss, and if he had, Caden would never hear the end of it. "Gwen, this is one of my brothers, Griffin. I think the two of you might have met back in college."

"I think we did," Griffin said. "It's nice to see you again, though these aren't exactly the conditions anyone hopes for."

The softness Gwen had in her eyes when she'd looked at him earlier was gone. "It's been a rough few days."

"I'm just glad that the two of you are okay."

"Me, too. Is there an immediate plan?" she asked.

"As soon as the doctor releases him, he'll be escorted to the courthouse for his arraignment. There's no way to know if he'll be allowed to post bail. If he cooperates, it will help. Beyond that, I really can't tell you much more at this point."

"I understand. Thank you." She glanced briefly at Caden. "What about Anderson and King?"

"From what I heard, they were pretty intent on taking each other down. What I do know is that they'll be going away for a long, long time."

Gwen took another step back. "Do you think they'll let me ride with my brother in the ambulance?"

"You can ask them, but I'm sure they'll let you."

"She does need to see a doctor, as well. Her ankle's pretty messed up."

"We'll make sure someone sees her as soon as we get back to town."

"Thank you," Gwen said.

"I'll catch up with you in a minute," Caden said to Gwen, then waited for her to leave before turning back to his brother. "Go ahead. I know you're dying to ask what's going on."

Griffin grinned at him. "I do have some catching up to do. I mean, it isn't often that you go camping on a solo weekend and come home with a beautiful woman."

"Very funny. She was just saying thank-you for saving her life."

"Really? It's just that's a pretty intimate way of saying thank-you."

"It's been an emotional few days, but I don't think anything will come of it. She'll be heading back to Denver as soon as this is over. I'll be back at the ranch…"

"You didn't exactly seem to be running in the other direction. In fact, from where I was standing it looked as if you were a willing participant."

"You're not going to let this drop, are you?"

"Nope."

"Enough. I knew her a long time ago. She was Cammie's best friend."

"Wait a minute… Your ex-fiancée, Cammie?"

Caden nodded.

"Okay, I'm definitely missing something here."

"There's nothing going on between us. Not really. Besides, even if there were, I wouldn't be too quick to judge. Who would have imagined you'd marry a girl you met while playing bodyguard for the FBI?"

"Touché, but still…once we get you home, you're going to need to catch me up on all the details."

"Like I said, there's nothing."

"You never know. Denver's not that far away—"

Caden started back toward the vehicles, with Griffin following him. "Don't even go there."

"I'll stop if you just promise me you won't close off your heart because of fear."

He dismissed his brother's advice. "I'm not afraid of falling in love again."

Griffin put his hand on his brother's shoulder and moved in front of him. "Then maybe it's finally time to give it a try."

SIXTEEN

She couldn't believe she'd kissed him.

Gwen stepped out of the exam room after seeing the doctor with a dozen things running through her mind. Gratefulness that her ankle wasn't broken. Worry about her brother's surgery. Fear over what was going to happen to him... But there was another thing she couldn't shake. What in the world had she been thinking when she kissed Caden O'Callaghan?

The confusion she felt had followed her all the way to Timber Falls, and still wouldn't leave her alone, because she had no idea what had overcome her. She was right to tell him how thankful she was to him for risking his life to save her, but that was where things should have ended. She'd acted completely out of emotion, not reality.

Reality was that her brother had committed a felony and it would take everything she had to help him get through the foreseeable future. Reality was that no matter who Caden was today, she'd watched him break her best friend's heart, something that was hard to forget.

"Gwen..."

She stopped in the middle of the hallway and turned

around. Caden was coming toward her, concern written across his expression. She let her gaze linger on him for a few seconds too long. From his cowboy hat to those piercing gray-blue eyes of his that always seemed to see right into her heart, to the stubbled beard that had grown over the past few days. She swallowed hard. No. She'd been right to stop anything before it got started. The last thing she wanted to do was lead her heart into dangerous territory, and that was exactly where she was heading if she wasn't careful.

"They told me I'd find you here," Caden said. "What did the doctor say?"

She pushed aside her tremulous thoughts and pointed to her walking boot. "I get to wear this for the next few weeks. The good news, though, is that the doctor said it isn't broken, and that it will heal completely. I just need to stay away from things like running marathons and hiking canyons the next few weeks."

"That's some pretty sound advice, I'd say."

He caught her gaze, and her stomach fluttered, while awkwardness settled between them.

All because of one kiss.

"Listen, I'm sorry about what happened earlier today." She plowed forward with her excuses, needing to clear the air between them. "I was completely out of line and have no idea what came over me. I never, ever go around kissing men unsolicited, even when they save my life. Bottom line is that I guess all of this…is just uncharted territory for me, and I'm feeling a bit lost and vulnerable."

He slipped his thumbs into the back pockets of his jeans. "What if that kiss wasn't completely unwanted?"

Her eyes widened at his response.

"I just meant... I just meant that kissing you wasn't... well, it wasn't exactly offensive," he said. "But if you'd like, we can forget it ever happened."

Oh, yeah. She really needed to forget that kiss, because she had no intentions of putting her heart on the line again.

"I think that's best," she said. "Because—"

"You don't have to explain." Caden cleared his throat. "We can just leave it at that."

"I think we should."

"Bruce and Levi are here, along with Bruce's wife, Alisha, and Levi's fiancée, Kennedy. They'd like to meet us."

"Okay." She blew out a breath, thankful for the change in subject. "Maybe we should pick up something for them at the gift shop."

"A peace offering?" Caden asked.

Gwen forced a laugh. "Something like that."

Five minutes later, they were making introductions in the middle of room 312, where Levi was lying in bed, recovering after his surgery.

Gwen held out the boxes of chocolates she and Caden had bought. "We heard you're a bit of a chocolate snob."

Bruce's eyes brightened. "You didn't."

"A friend of mine here in town makes these," Caden said. "They sell them at the gift shop. Best chocolate you'll ever taste."

"We've heard about these," Levi said. "And have always talked about picking some up. They're supposed to be amazing."

"They are," Caden said. "And while it won't make up for getting shot, we hope you enjoy them."

Levi shot them a smile. "I have a feeling these will ease the pain."

Gwen shoved her hands into her pockets. "I just want to say how sorry we are about everything. When we flagged down your raft, we had no idea just how bad everything was going to get."

Kennedy squeezed Levi's hand from the side of the bed where he was resting. "I'll admit that the initial phone call had me in a panic, but honestly, both these guys would never simply walk away from trouble. And on the plus side, according to the local news, they're heroes. Though I already knew that. I'd trust these guys with my life any day."

Trusted them with her life.

The words dug through her, as she tried to shake the conflicting emotions between wanting to give Caden a chance and running.

"Bottom line is that we owe you both our lives," Caden said.

"What about your brother?" Bruce asked. "How is he?"

"He's in surgery right now," Gwen said, "but the doctors are optimistic."

One of the nurses walked in, clearly unhappy about the crowded room and her patient who, according to her, was supposed to be resting.

"We were just heading out." Caden pressed his hand against the small of Gwen's back as they took a step back. "But thank you. All of you."

"I'm guessing you want to go see about your brother," Caden said as they left the room.

Gwen nodded. "He should be getting out of surgery soon."

"Would you like me to wait with you?"

"Do you mind?"

"Of course not."

A part of her felt relieved as they started walking down the hallway, that she wasn't going to have to wait alone. But on the other hand, she'd answered before she had time to weigh her response. Why couldn't her heart listen to her head?

Caden's phone rang, and he pulled it out of his pocket. "It's my mom."

"Talk to her. I'll be fine."

"I know, but I'll be right there."

The surgical waiting room was on the second floor of the small hospital, which was decorated in blues and grays with calming artwork on the walls. But she wasn't sure anything could calm her spirit at this point. She'd only just sat down and pulled out her phone, when a woman wearing purple scrubs and a bright smile walked up to her. "You wouldn't be Gwen Ryland by any chance, would you?"

"I am."

"I'm Tory Faraday. Caden's brother Griffin's fiancée"

"Hi. It's nice to meet you."

The woman's smile widened as she sat down next to Gwen. "I was looking for you because not only did I want to meet you, but also because I assisted with your brother's surgery and heard you were here."

Gwen's hands fisted at her sides as the anxiety struck again. "Please tell me he's okay."

"The surgeon was able to take out the bullet and repair most of the damaged tissue."

"And his recovery?"

"There will more than likely be some nerve damage, but we're optimistic he'll get back most of his shoulder movement. In the meantime, you'll be able to see him in about thirty minutes."

Gwen pressed her hand against her chest. "I'm so happy to hear that. These past few days have been pretty stressful."

Tory glanced down at Gwen's boot. "Are you okay?"

"The doctor said it just needs a few weeks to heal." The pain medicine the nurse had given her was starting to kick in, but at the moment, she'd rather forget the reminder. "When are you getting married?"

Tory held up her hand to show Gwen her engagement ring. "Four more months. I keep pinching myself to remind me it's real."

"I'm happy for you."

"Thank you, but I'm sorry about this. How are you? It's been quite a nightmare from what I've heard."

"I think a part of me still thinks I'm going to wake up. The other part is just eternally grateful that I'm still alive. Honestly, I don't think the realness has completely hit yet."

"There is something about an experience like this that will change your life forever." Tory fiddled with the ring on her finger. "You don't know my story, but someone wanting to take your life is terrifying. I can attest to that firsthand. Right now I'm just doing my best to put it all behind me. It's hard, I know, but don't be afraid to talk with someone, get some counseling or see your pastor. Or if you ever want to grab coffee sometime, I'd love to do that. I'm living here now."

Gwen nodded. "Maybe I'll get a chance to hear your story one day, but thank you. I really appreciate it." She felt her shoulders relax some, realizing there was something cathartic about talking to someone who understood. "I know you're right. And I will. At this point, though, I feel like my entire life has been ripped apart. My brother…he's really my only family, and if he goes to prison…"

"Mistakes of others can be difficult when you have to live with the consequences. I understand that. And while the pain won't necessarily completely disappear, it will get easier. Just be there for him. That's what he needs right now. And take time to care for yourself, as well."

"Thank you. I'm going to try." Gwen pushed back the tears that threatened to spill out. "So what's it like being a part of the O'Callaghan family?"

Tory laughed. "I'm learning there's never a dull minute, but I can't imagine not being a part of their lives. What about you and Caden? I heard the two of you go way back."

Gwen forced a smile, but really didn't want to go into her relationship with Caden. "I guess you could call us old friends, but *acquaintances* is probably more the right word. We haven't seen each other for years."

"Maybe not, but he sure went the extra mile for an old friend."

"He did, but there isn't anything between us. Romantically, anyway."

Then why did you kiss him?

"He's a wonderful guy," Tory said, not seeming to catch Gwen's conflicting emotions. "I'm always amazed at how good he is with the horses and running the ranch."

"I'm not surprised."

"And I think he needs a good woman in his life. I've heard enough of what happened to you to know you had to be strong to go through what you just did."

Gwen glanced at the doorway of the waiting room, suddenly feeling uncomfortable.

"I'm sorry." Tory laid her hand on Gwen's arm for a moment, then stood up. "I shouldn't have said that. When I first started getting to know the O'Callaghan family, it was pretty overwhelming because I come from a small family. But there's so much love and acceptance there. I can't imagine not having them in my life."

"I'm happy for you, but as for Caden and me... I meant what I said. There's nothing between us other than the fact that I'll always be grateful to him for rescuing me." Gwen blinked back the tears. "Congratulations again."

"Thank you. I appreciate it. And, Gwen? You already know this, but Caden is a great guy."

Gwen frowned. Maybe. But she also knew that with Caden there was too big a risk of her ending up with a broken heart.

Caden hurried toward the waiting room, trying to come up with what he was going to say to Gwen. He'd thought the past couple days had erased the years of mistrust they'd held toward each other. Thought that maybe theirs was a relationship worth pursuing. But apparently he was wrong, because she clearly didn't feel the same way.

A minute later, he paused in the doorway of the sitting room where she was sitting on one of the chairs, typing something on her phone. He hadn't wanted his heart to stir every time he saw her. And it wasn't just the connection he felt because of everything that had happened to them. She made him laugh. Made him wonder what it would be like to take a risk with his heart again. He could see them working together on his ranch, using the facilities for trauma victims and veterans...but that was never going to happen.

Maybe it was simply that Liam and Griffin, who'd managed to fall in love recently, had made him feel like he was missing something—or rather, someone—in his life. But whatever the reason, it really didn't matter. He'd tell her goodbye and never see her again. That was the reality.

"Caden..." She looked up at him and smiled. "I didn't see you. I was letting some of my friends know what was going on. Asking them to pray."

"That's good. And I'm sorry about the phone call. I hadn't been able to connect with my parents until now. As you can imagine, they've been worried sick."

"I'm sure they have. I'm glad you talked to them."

"They're on their way here now, but what about you? Any news on your brother?"

"Yes, actually." She slipped her phone into her back pocket. "I just talked to your future sister-in-law, Tory, who assisted with his surgery. The doctor is pleased and believes he'll make a full recovery. I should be able to go in and see him soon."

"That's great. I'm glad to hear that."

"Me, too, but then he'll end up in prison, and—"

"Don't think about that right now." He sat down next to her. "Just concentrate on him getting better. One thing at a time."

"I know—it's just hard."

He studied the pattern on the carpeted floor, wishing he knew what to say to help her feel better. But he also knew that this wasn't a situation he could fix.

"So you met Tory," he said, searching for something to say.

"Yeah…she seems good for your brother."

"She is."

And you—you seem so good for me.

"I know this is all hard on you," he said.

"I won't try to pretend I'm not frustrated. I thought Aaron had finally gotten to a place in his life where he was beyond doing something like this, but this choice of his…" She shook her head. "He's made such a mess of things. I had to call his boss…and his girlfriend. She's on her way here now."

"What were their reactions?"

"His boss is understandably furious. And Emma… I don't think she knew how to react. She was pretty taken aback by everything that happened. And I don't blame her. I don't know how to handle this, either."

He pressed his hands together, praying God would give him the right words that would somehow encourage her.

"I think you have to remember that while this situation with your brother probably seems insurmountable, there's a bigger picture we can't see. God can still redeem this."

"I know."

But even though she said the words, she didn't look convinced.

"I'm not trying to sound cliché—"

"You're not." She looked up at him. "It's just that while I'm praying for exactly that, I still feel so out of control."

"I've always had a hard time believing that everything happens for a reason, but I do believe God can redeem this situation. People make bad decisions. Think of King David, Moses and Jonah. And, yes, there are consequences that are going to play out, and he's going to need to take responsibility for that, but don't let this choice of his become all you see."

"I will try."

"It probably won't be easy, but the bottom line is that God designed us to be reliant on Him. Don't try to do this on your own."

"People tend to seek God when things are falling apart. I just... I've tried to be the anchor in my brother's life—"

"You've tried to handle it all on your own."

She shot him a sliver of a smile. "Most of the time, I supposed I have."

"Just remember you're not alone. In fact, my parents wanted me to ask if you'd like to come out to the ranch for a few days while you wait for him to recover. It's not that far away, and it would be quiet. I could even show you some of my favorite places. We could ride some horses...or you could use the time to be alone. Whatever you want. After all that's happened, I'd say you deserve a few days of quiet."

"I appreciate it. I really do, but I think I need to stay here in town, close to my brother. At least until they take him into custody. I called one of the local B and Bs while I was waiting for the doctor to see me, and I have a room for the next few nights."

"Okay. That's fine... I understand."

He shoved away his disappointment. At least his head understood. His heart wanted her to trust him.

"And you don't have to wait with me." She glanced at her watch and stood up. "I think they'll let me see him now."

He felt the wall back up between them, wishing now she'd never kissed him, while at the same time wishing desperately he could kiss her again.

"If you change your mind, just call," he said. "You have my number. And if you need anything—anything at all—call me."

"I will, and thank you."

"And Gwen. I just..." He searched for what to say before she walked out of the room. "After everything we went through, I don't want to leave with things sour between us."

All because of a kiss.

"I don't, either, and please know that I will forever be grateful for what you did for me."

But clearly nothing more.

He watched her walk away a moment later, wishing he didn't feel that continuous tug of his heart when he was around her. Maybe she was right, and he could never be that person in her life. Because no matter what had happened between them, she wasn't ever going to forget what had taken place all those years ago. And really, he couldn't blame her. Of course, if things had been different back then... If she'd known the truth... He shook off the thought. None of that mattered anymore. She needed to focus on getting her brother through the next few weeks, and he needed to forget her. Because while she might have trusted him with her life, she clearly wasn't going to trust him with her heart.

SEVENTEEN

Two months later

Gwen sat at one of the booths in the back of the restaurant waiting for Cammie to arrive, but her mind was struggling to focus. She'd been surprised to hear her friend was back in town. It seemed strange to be meeting for lunch with Cammie when she'd just received an invitation from Caden's parents for the Fourth of July, an invitation she'd yet to respond to, because there was still something holding her back from going.

Caden.

Which made no sense.

Didn't she want to see him?

Despite her conflicted feelings, they'd texted and called each other regularly over the past few weeks, and she'd found herself getting to know the man she'd resented so much over the past decade. And the result had been surprising. She'd found herself reaching for her phone far too often just to see how his day was going, or to get his advice on something. On top of that, she'd shared more with him about her desire to start a wilderness expedition program, while dreaming about him at night and waking up wanting to talk to him.

But the whole time they'd just skirted around the idea of a relationship between them, and she knew it was her fault. Because every time she thought about moving forward with him, she couldn't stop thinking that she was headed for inevitable heartache. Maybe Caden really was trustworthy, but Seth had broken her heart, and made her afraid to give it away again.

On the other hand, while he might not be the man she once thought he was, that didn't mean he was falling for her. He'd been honest with his input for her ideas on her wilderness trek, even to the point of considering expanding what he was doing at the ranch, but it wasn't as if that was a marriage proposal. And she wasn't looking for a business partner.

But neither could she shake the question of how the man she'd thought was so self-centered and egotistical had turned into someone who was managing to steal her heart. He might have changed, but what if what had happened to Cammie happened to her?

"Gwen?" Cammie waved at her as she approached. "There you are. So sorry I'm late."

Gwen slid out of the booth and gave her friend a hug. "I'm so glad to see you."

"You were a million miles away."

"Sorry." She shot her friend a smile. Cammie had changed little over the years, from the cute outfit she'd probably picked up at the boutique downtown, to the perfect mani and pedi, and eyelashes that were a mile long… "I was just thinking."

"I'm just glad to see you're all right." Cammie slid

into the booth. "How's your brother? When I saw the story about him on the news, I had to see you. You must be horrified."

Gwen frowned, not missing the hint of scandal in her friend's voice. "He's currently out on bail, which is ironic for a bounty hunter. His court case has just been scheduled for September. More than likely he'll end up facing some jail time."

Saying it out loud made it seem even more real, but it was what it was. He'd made bad choices and, like it or not, he was going to have to live with the consequences.

"I have to imagine it's pretty stressful," Cammie said, clearly digging for details.

"It is."

The waitress came over, and Cammie asked for a glass of ice water with lime, not lemon. "I told my mother what had happened, and she was shocked. She met your brother at least once and couldn't believe he was involved in the scandal."

Cammie waved her hands while she rambled on, leaning in for emphasis every few seconds. It was like they were back in college, but while Gwen had grown beyond the need to dig up the latest gossip, she wasn't sure Cammie ever had. Funny how it wasn't even Cammie's brother who'd been arrested, and yet her friend was still was managing to be the center of attention.

"Do you have plans for the Fourth?" Cammie asked, barely taking a breath before sipping on the water their waitress had brought her.

Gwen worked to keep her expression neutral. "I was invited somewhere for the weekend, but I don't think I'm going."

"Who's the invitation from?"

"Just some friends. A family who lives south of here on a ranch."

"I bet it's beautiful."

"It is," Gwen said, wanting to change the subject before it switched to Caden. "Tell me—"

"I'd love to tag along if I didn't have to get back to my family."

"You have a great family."

"I thought I had a great family." Cammie's smile faded. "Jeff and I are getting a divorce. That's one of the reasons I'm back in town. I needed to get away."

"What?"

"It's a long time coming, though I never thought it would really happen. Turns out we want completely different things. Have different goals."

"I'm really sorry to hear that." The confession surprised her. She'd thought—at least from the outside—that their relationship had been good. Apparently, she'd been wrong.

"Me, too."

Gwen swirled the straw in her tea and frowned. No one was perfect—she had no illusions about that—but it was still sad. She'd always looked at marriage as forever, if at all possible.

"Jeff's keeping the kids right now, but you can imagine how awkward it has been."

"I really am sorry."

"Forget about me and my drama… What about you? Are you dating anyone?"

"No."

Cammie cocked her head. "You're hiding something from me."

Gwen frowned. Even if they had been dating, Caden wasn't exactly a subject she was going to bring up.

"Don't be ridiculous."

"I'm hardly being ridiculous. You've got that dreamy, head-in-the-clouds look written all over you. Who is it?"

She signaled for the waitress. "No one."

Which was true. She wasn't in love with Caden. Just because he was handsome, charming and nothing like the man she'd believed he was didn't mean there was anything between them.

The waitress stepped up to their table to take their orders.

"I'll have the Cobb salad, please." Gwen handed the woman her menu, hoping the distraction had ended their conversation.

"Sounds delicious. I'll have the same thing." Cammie took another sip of her water, then set it down in front of her. "I was shocked to hear that Caden was somehow involved in what happened with your brother."

"He was out camping." Gwen tried to keep her voice steady. Clearly this was the real reason for the impromptu lunch. "He ended up saving my life."

"That's so crazy. How is he?"

"He's doing well."

"You must have talked with him some."

"Of course. He's—he's working his father's ranch."

Cammie's eyes widened as she put the pieces together. "Your plans for the Fourth."

So much for her plans not to talk about Caden.

"My potential plans for the Fourth."

"And why wouldn't you want to go?"

"Because…"

Because she couldn't move forward until she knew what really happened that night.

"Can I ask you a question?" Gwen asked.

"Of course."

"What really happened the night you and Caden broke things off?"

She knew she was stepping on rocky ground, but even if there was no future between her and Caden, she needed to know the truth.

"That was a long time ago, Gwen. If he's the one you're interested in and you're worried about my reaction, you don't have to be, though I certainly hope he's changed. We had issues. Both of us. And I—I admit, I had been questioning things for weeks before the wedding."

"Did he really break things off with you?"

Cammie grabbed the napkin off the table and squeezed it. "I made some mistakes. In less than twenty-four hours all the guests were going to arrive. Canceling the wedding would have ruined everything, I just… I didn't know what to do."

"So you blamed him."

"Gwen…"

"I just need to know the truth."

Friends and family had rallied around her. But if that was nothing more than a lie? She tried to shake the next thought, but it wouldn't disappear.

"Were you in love with Jeff while engaged to Caden?"

"Gwen…that was years ago. None of that matters anymore."

"It matters to me."

"Why?"

"It just...does."

"Fine. Caden was busy with school and work, and I was lonely. I never meant anything by it. Jeff and I just started going out as friends. Sometimes a movie. Sometimes dinner."

"You were engaged to Caden. He trusted you."

"I made mistakes. And now it turns out I chose the wrong man again."

"But you always told me he broke things off and broke your heart. That he was the love of your life and he'd betrayed you." A seed of frustration and anger sprouted. "I talked to him that night. Told him exactly what I thought about his behavior, and I wasn't very nice."

Cammie shrugged. "What did you expect me to do? Tell my guests that I'd cheated on my fiancé? How would that have made me look?"

Gwen couldn't believe what she was hearing. "He never told anyone, Cammie. He let everyone there that night believe that it was his fault. He took all the blame because no matter what you did, he still loved you."

"Why does any of that matter? Because you're in love with him, aren't you? He played the hero and rescued you and now you've fallen for him."

"I'm not in love with him."

Gwen stared at Cammie's necklace, then dropped her gaze. She never should have agreed to meet with her. She'd heard enough now to know that everything Caden had told her was true. And everything Cammie had told her was nothing more than lies.

"You are, aren't you?"

"I never said I was in love with him. His parents invited me to the ranch, actually. They're just being nice. They know I've been having a hard time with my brother and thought I could use a weekend away."

"It's just hard to imagine my best friend falling for my ex-fiancé. I'm not sure I can wrap my mind around that."

"He used to be good enough for you."

"That wasn't exactly what I meant. I have no interest in a relationship with Caden, and if you want my blessing, you have it. That was a long time ago and I'm certainly not the same person. I'm sure he's not, either. The two of you are probably perfect for each other, anyway. As far as I'm concerned, you can have Caden O'Callaghan and his stuffy morals."

"Cammie, I—"

The waitress stopped in front of their table and set the salads in front of them.

"You know what?" Cammie stood up and grabbed her bag. "I'm not hungry anymore."

Gwen's heart pounded as she watched Cammie stomp away. How had she been so wrong about someone? About both Cammie *and* Caden?

Caden was at the main house when he heard a car coming down the gravel road. He stepped out onto the porch, feeling the pack of nerves he'd tried to stuff down all morning shoot up again. When Gwen had accepted his parents' invitation for the Fourth of July weekend, he'd panicked at the thought of her visiting.

Which didn't make sense.

He'd enjoyed their frequent conversations over the

past few weeks, and felt like every time they spoke, he got to know her a little better. They'd spent time talking about everything from their dislikes, to quirks, to deeper things like faith and their values. And the more he'd learned about her, the more he'd realized they were on the same page. But nothing they'd said on the phone, or via texting, had crossed the line from friendship toward something more. And that was the problem. Every time he'd tried to move their relationship forward, he felt her holding back. But maybe he shouldn't be surprised. He wanted a relationship with the woman who'd despised him for over a decade.

The bottom line was he was thirty-two and had lived enough to know exactly what he wanted. And Gwen was what he wanted—but she had no feelings for him.

He met her car, opened up her door and felt a familiar stir as she slid out of the driver's seat and smiled up at him.

"I'm glad you came." He pulled her into a hug, resisting the urge to kiss her as he took in her red sundress, perfect for the patriotic weekend. "You look great."

He swallowed hard. *She* was perfect for him.

"Thanks. There was a conflict at work, and I wasn't sure I was going to be able to come for a while, but I managed to sort things out and get away."

"I'm glad." He studied those wide blue eyes of hers and wondered how he could have missed her so much. "My mother's got the guest room ready for you, so you can make yourself at home for the weekend."

She shoved her keys into her pocket. "I really could have driven back to Denver tonight. I don't want to be any trouble."

"You're no trouble. Trust me. My mom loves having the house full. The more family and friends around, the happier she is."

"I hope so." She pulled out a pink carry-on suitcase from the back seat and set it on the ground.

"Is there more in the back?" he asked.

"No. I'm a pretty light packer."

"I'm impressed. I've seen my mother take three times this much for just an overnight trip." He stopped in front of her. "Before we go in…how are you? I know that the past few weeks have been hard."

A shadow crossed her face. "It has been tough. I know Aaron will spend some time in jail and lose his bounty-hunter license, but at least he's alive. I keep telling myself that God gives second chances, and I need to be there for him."

"You're not alone in this." He glanced at her sandals. "What about your ankle?"

"It's finally healed, thankfully."

"I'm glad to hear that, as well."

She looked toward the house. "Where is everybody?"

"My mom's still here, but Mia wanted to go see the cows, so everyone took the Jeep out to the west pasture to check on them."

"Mia's Gabby and Liam's child?"

Caden nodded. "She's two and has completely stolen everyone's hearts."

"Caden?"

His mother hurried toward the car, waving at them. "I guess I'm not the only one excited to see you."

Without even hesitating, his mother stopped in front

of them and pulled Gwen into a hug. "I'm so glad you decided to come."

"I appreciate the invitation, though I was surprised."

"You shouldn't be. We've been wanting to meet you. It's become a bit of a family reunion with all my boys here, plus current and future daughters-in-law, and a grandbaby... I'm sure you'll fit right in once you meet everyone."

Gwen glanced up at him. "I still think that if I lived here all I'd do is sit on the front porch and enjoy the view."

Caden smiled at the soft blush crossing her cheeks. Maybe she felt somewhat presumptuous by her statement, but he loved the thought of the two of them spending hours on the front porch together.

"Honestly, I never get tired of the view," his mom said. "And you can sit all you want on the porch. Let me take your bag up to the house. Lunch isn't going to be ready for another hour, so Caden, why don't the two of you go for a walk before everyone gets back. The weather's perfect."

"I'd be happy to come inside and help with lunch," Gwen said.

"You didn't come here to work—"

"I would like to show you around a bit," Caden said. Knowing his family, this might be the only time he got to be alone with her.

The sound of tires on the gravel interrupted his thoughts as the Jeep pulled up in front of Gwen's car. Caden frowned. Too late.

He forced a smile as his family piled out of the Jeep and he started making introductions. "Gwen, this is my youngest brother, Liam, and his wife, Gabby, and, of course, Mia."

"I hear you're expecting another little one. Congratulations," Gwen said.

Gabby beamed. "Thank you."

"We're superexcited," Liam said. "And it's great to meet you."

"You've already met Griffin and Tory. Reid's the only one not here, besides my father, and they should both be back soon."

"Nice to meet all of you. I've been looking forward to this weekend."

He put his hand on Gwen's arm, not wanting to miss a few minutes alone with her. "Why don't you all head up to the house. I'm going to show Gwen around a bit before lunch."

Laughter and chatting faded as the group headed to the house and he turned back to her. "Sorry about that. When my entire family gets together it can be a bit overwhelming."

"No, it's fine. Really. I've been looking forward to meeting your family. They're all so nice and welcoming."

"Good, because I really am glad you're here."

They headed down a tree-lined path that led to the pond. He drew in a deep breath of fresh air, surprised at how much he'd missed her. And how glad he was that she was here with him.

"I've been talking to my father about your idea, as you know," he said as they walked. "He's really interested in bringing corporations and local businesses on board. I'd like your input, but we're thinking about implementing some of your ideas. I'd like to also have a free program for veterans."

"I love that idea."

"I thought you would. There's a lot more that we'd have to talk about, but I've definitely been doing a lot of thinking about it." *Been thinking a lot about you.* "I'd love your thoughts on making the idea a reality."

Doubts from his practical side shot through him as he tried to read her expression.

Just tell her how you really feel before you go any further.

"Gwen, I—"

"I'd love to brainstorm with you and your father, but there's something I really need to talk to you about first."

"Of course."

She turned toward him. The mountains framed her in the background, making him want to snap a photo and preserve the moment.

"I don't know how else to say it than just jumping into it," she said. "I saw Cammie a few days ago. She called me up out of the blue and wanted to go out to lunch. Apparently she'd seen a newspaper article about us and my brother, and the entire fiasco, and had to know more."

"Cammie?" His ex-fiancée wasn't exactly the topic of conversation he'd expected. "Okay...how is she?"

"Getting a divorce. I was pretty surprised to hear that, but there was something else I was even more surprised about. Why didn't you tell me the truth about her? That she cheated on you and you turned around and let her lie about you. Even when I confronted you, you never said anything. Why?"

"Back then... I suppose because I still loved her and didn't see the point in ruining her reputation."

"She didn't have any trouble trying to ruin yours."

He stuffed his hands in his pockets, not sure where this was going. "That night I was hurt, understandably. But when she started telling everyone how I'd broken up with her, I realized that I could have married her and found out later who she really was. I was simply grateful that didn't happen, even though it was painful to find out that way."

"I have to say I admire you for not trashing her reputation, because she deserved it."

How was he supposed to respond?

"Cammie had this charm about her that had me blinded. In the back of my mind, I told myself I could put up with her faults, because there was enough good in her to make up for them. But that night I realized I'd bought in to a lie, and I promised myself I would never compromise my values like that again. Instead, I would wait until I found the right person, even if that meant I stayed single the rest of my life."

He rocked back on the heels of his boots, struggling to find the right words. "Besides, I wasn't sure anyone would believe me. She painted a pretty stark picture of me. And, on top of that, what did it matter? We weren't getting married. My heart was broken, and I decided to simply walk away. But none of that matters anymore."

"It does to me." She stared out past him at the mountains. "I've held on to this grudge against you for all these years on false information."

"Honestly, I'm flattered you remembered me at all,"

he teased, trying to lighten the heaviness that had fallen between them.

"I'm serious, Caden."

"I know." He bit the edge of his tongue and started walking again. "I'm sorry."

"But that's just it. You had nothing to be sorry about. You *have* nothing to be sorry about. I just… Back then it was so hard for me to see a friend hurt, and now I know it was nothing but a bunch of lies. I still can't believe she'd do something like that to you."

"I was just as much to blame, I'm sure. She needed more than I could give her."

"But she never should have treated you that way. She lied about you."

"It's over, Gwen. I've moved on and, honestly, once I got over the shock of how I misread her, I realized I was better off without her. So can we forget about Cammie? Because I can think of a dozen things I'd much rather be talking about right now. So many things I want to show you—like this."

They stepped into the clearing. Tall grass surrounded the large mountain pond, while white clouds billowed above them. Memories surfaced of him and his brothers fishing in the summers and skating on the ice in the winter.

I want to make memories with you now, Gwen…

"Wow…this is so beautiful," she said.

Like you.

Gwen stood next to him, taking in the view of the trees reflecting in the water and the mountains in the distance. "And I agree. There are plenty of other things we can be talking about. Like you and your father's idea.

If you could come up with a solid business proposition, I have a lot of contacts—"

"I was thinking of something more…personal."

"Personal?"

He took a step toward her. Surely she was feeling what he was. "Something that has to do with you and me. Because I'm not wanting a business partner right now. I want you."

She looked up at him with those wide blue eyes that left him stumbling over his words.

"These—these last couple months of getting to know you made realize that I want you in my life as more than just a friend." He drew in a deep breath, wishing the words didn't sound so awkward. "I'm in love with you, Gwen."

"I don't know what to say."

"Say you feel the same way. That talking to me over the past few months hasn't been just about our shared experience, but because you feel the same things that I do." He tried to read her expression. "And now that you know that truth about Cammie…"

"I know I've been pushing you away because I was so afraid you'd walk out on me like you did to Cammie."

"And I was afraid to trust you. But I have no intention of walking out on you. And unless I'm totally off base about us and what's going on…"

She hesitated before reaching up and putting her arms around his neck, then she kissed him.

His mind spun, as if she was bringing light to the broken crevices of his heart for the first time. The healing they both needed.

She pulled away a few inches from him, smiling.

"Does that clear things up for you a little bit? Because I'm in love with you too, Caden O'Callaghan."

"A lot, actually, because I was so afraid of what your reaction would be."

"That could have made a very awkward weekend together, which I would hate." She sounded breathless as she looked up at him. "Do I need to prove it to you again?"

"You might have to."

"What about your family?" she asked, brushing her lips against his. "What are they going to think about me? I'm sure they've heard the story of Cammie and the things I said to you. They probably have some reservations about me."

He pulled her back against him. "For one, I never told my family all the details, but I'm not really thinking about my family right now."

Her smile widened. "Then what are you thinking about?"

"I'm thinking about the two of us starting something more…permanent together."

His pulse raced as she looked up at him.

"I think I like the sound of that, Caden O'Callaghan."

He pulled her closer. "Good. Because I've finally found the person I want to spend the rest of my life with."

* * * * *

Ever since she found the Nancy Drew books with the pink covers in her country school library, **Sharon Dunn** has loved mystery and suspense. Most of her books take place in Montana, where she lives with three nearly grown children and a hyper border collie. She lost her beloved husband of twenty-seven years to cancer in 2014. When she isn't writing, she loves to hike surrounded by God's beauty.

Books by Sharon Dunn

Love Inspired Suspense

Cold Case Justice
Mistaken Target
Fatal Vendetta
Big Sky Showdown
Hidden Away
In Too Deep
Wilderness Secrets
Mountain Captive
Undercover Threat
Alaskan Christmas Target

True Blue K-9 Unit: Brooklyn

Scene of the Crime

Visit the Author Profile page at Harlequin.com for more titles.

DEAD RINGER

Sharon Dunn

Do not fear, for I am with you; do not be dismayed,
for I am your God. I will strengthen you and help you;
I will uphold you with my righteous right hand.
—*Isaiah* 41:10

For the Ladies' Aid Society and my July brainstorming buddies. Thanks for making me laugh until my sides hurt, for supporting me in all matters personal and professional, and for praying.

ONE

Someone was in the house.

Lucy Kimbol pushed her chair back from her work-table. The noise had come from downstairs.

Tuning in the sounds around her, she held her breath. Outside, the rain tapped the roof in a muffled whisper. The view through the window was black. A fan whirred about four feet from her. She leaned forward in her chair. Downstairs, it was silent.

Yet her skin tingled. Her stomach clenched. The same physical responses she had when she was camping and a wild animal was close. Even if she couldn't see or hear the animal, she could sense it. And now she sensed…something in her house. She released a slow stream of air and remained as still as possible.

A sudden thud from downstairs caused her to jump up from her chair and dart to the edge of her loft. She gripped the wooden railing, scanning the living room and kitchen below. No sign of movement. She had definitely heard something this time, though. Her heart rate accelerated as adrenaline shot through her muscles.

Her house was not that big; most of it was visible

from the loft. That meant something or someone had to be downstairs in her bedroom.

Lucy tiptoed down the spiral staircase and crept toward the bedroom door. Another sound, like the brush of a broom or gust of wind came from within the bedroom. She froze. Her hands curled into fists. She locked her knees.

Maybe she should just call the police. No, the last thing she wanted to do was talk to anyone on the Mountain Springs police force. Past experience told her that the police did more harm than good. She could handle this herself.

She took a step forward; her bare feet brushed across polished wood. Her hand grazed the bedroom door. No light penetrated the slit between door and frame.

This could be nothing. A raccoon had probably snuck in through the open window again.

After a deep breath, she pushed hard on the door, burst into the room and flipped on the light in one smooth movement. Something was crawling out of the window, but it wasn't a wild animal.

"Hey, what are you doing?" Her words came out in a staccato burst, like gunfire.

The man in a hoodie slipped through the window and disappeared. Lucy raced to the window. Sheets of rain made the glowing circle of a flashlight murky as it bobbed across the field. He was headed toward the forest and beyond that the road. A quick survey of the room revealed open drawers and boxes pulled out of the closet. Lucy put a palm on her hammering heart. The man had been holding something as he'd escaped. She'd been robbed!

Outrage fueled by adrenaline caused her to dash out of the bedroom and into the kitchen. She yanked open the back door, covering the length of the porch in two huge steps. Focused on the light, her bare feet pounded across hard dirt and rocks. Rain soaked through her shirt and yoga pants before the pain in her feet registered.

She stopped, gasping for air. What had she been thinking? Even if she caught the thief, she couldn't subdue him. Anger over the theft had pushed her off the porch, but rationality made her quit the pursuit.

Along the edge of the forest, the bobbing light became a distant pinhole before winking out altogether.

Lucy bent over, resting her palms on her knees. Rain slashed against her skin and dripped from her long hair.

Now she was going to have to call the police whether she liked it or not. Her hand was shaking when she picked up the phone. Would this time be different from every other time she had gone to the police for help? As she changed out of her wet clothing, a sense of dread filled her. She doubted that the police would be able to find the thief, if they would even make the effort.

Detective Eli Hawkins saw only a partial view of the woman who had called in a robbery, but he liked what he saw—mainly long dark hair and a slender build. She had opened the door but left the chain lock on. Even with such a narrow view of her, heat flashed across his face. Very attractive.

"Ma'am, did you report a robbery? I'm Officer Eli Hawkins."

She lifted her chin. "I know all the cops on the force. You don't look familiar."

"I'm new." He'd only been in town for six hours. Now he wondered why all the other officers had been so eager to send him out on a call right away. None of the Mountain Springs officers had said anything directly, but the implication was that no one wanted to handle a call from Lucy Kimbol. Maybe she was one of those people who constantly called the police.

She rubbed her shirt collar. "Can I see your badge?"

Her voice had a soft melodic quality that quickened his heartbeat. He pulled his ID from his back pocket and held it up so she could look at it.

Her blue eyes narrowed. "Spokane police?"

"I'm a transfer." She didn't need to know that he was a temporary transfer for a special investigation, which had to remain under the radar. Four years ago, he had put a serial killer behind bars in Spokane. The conviction had made him the serial killer expert in the Northwest. And Mountain Springs needed that expertise.

She undid the chain lock and opened the door. "I tried to catch him myself, but he got away."

That explained her wet hair. The jeans and white shirt were dry. She must have changed after she'd called in the robbery. The lack of makeup made her pale skin seem almost translucent and her blue eyes even more noticeable. A pile of crime-scene photos flashed through his head. Lucy had the same features, dark hair and blue eyes, as the five known victims of the serial killer. Could she be a potential target for the killer? Would keeping tabs on her lead him to the murderer?

"You should leave catching thieves to the police."

Part of keeping the investigation under wraps involved him playing the small-town cop. Answering this robbery call might win points with the local police department, too, and go a long way toward them learning to work as team.

"Calling the police is always a last resort for me."

He picked up on just a tinge of bitterness in her voice. Something must have transpired between Lucy and the Mountain Springs police. "Why is that?"

The question seemed to stun her. Emotion flashed across her features before she regained composure. Was it fear or pain?

"Let's just say that it has been my experience that most cops don't always do their job," Lucy said.

He had a feeling there was way more to the story, but now was not the time to dredge it up. He'd just have to tread lightly and go by the book. Whatever her beef was, maybe being professional would be enough to convince her that all cops were not the same.

"If I'd had shoes on, I might have been able to catch him." She raised a scratched, bare foot.

"Pretty impressive." That blew his first theory of why no officer wanted to come out here. Any woman who would run after an intruder was not the type to be calling the police all the time.

"Actually, I had a moment of lucidity and realized I wouldn't know what to do once I caught the guy." She forced a laugh.

He detected the strain of fear beneath the laughter. "Why don't you tell me what happened? You think it was a man?"

"He had a man's build. I couldn't see his face." She

spoke in a firm, even tone. Only the trembling of her hands as she brushed her forehead gave away that the break-in had rattled her. "I… I was upstairs tying flies." She tilted her head toward a loft. "I teach fly fishing. I'm a river guide."

Eli knew enough not to interrupt. People usually had to back up and talk about safe things before they were able to deal with the actual crime.

Her lips pressed together. She stared at the ceiling.

He glanced around the living room, which consisted of rough pine furniture and a leather couch and matching chair. "Would you like to sit down, Mrs. Kimbol?"

"Miss, it's Miss Kimbol." She looked directly at him. "And no, thank you, I can stand."

Her voice held a little jab of aggression toward him. Her demeanor communicated that she did not trust him. It wasn't personal. He'd seen it before with people who had had a bad experience with the police. Best to back the conversation up. "I hear fly fishing is big in this part of Wyoming."

"It brings in a lot of tourists." The stiffness faded from her posture. "I know I love it."

He spoke gently. "Can you tell me what was stolen?"

She stared at him for moment as though she didn't comprehend the question. "I didn't think to look." She shook her head. "My dresser drawers were all open. He went through my closet." Her speech became rapid and clipped. "He was holding something…like a bag or pillowcase." Her hand fluttered to her mouth as her eyes rimmed with tears.

That she had managed to hold it together as long as she had impressed him. She was a strong woman. The sense of violation from a robbery usually rose to the surface slowly, not like with an assault or violent crime, when the victim acted immediately. All the same, a home invasion was still enough to upset anyone.

She collapsed into a chair and let out a heavy sigh. "I guess I do need to sit." She stared at the floor, shaking her head.

He had to do something. "How about a drink of water?" As he skirted around the back of the chair, he reached a hand out to touch her shoulder but pulled back. He desperately wanted to comfort her, but he wasn't about to feed into her ill feelings toward police. She might misinterpret his motives.

Water would have to do. Eli walked into the kitchen, found a glass and flipped on the faucet. When he glanced at her through the pass-through, she was slumped over, resting her elbows on her knees, her hair falling over her face.

Eli walked back into the living room and sat on the couch opposite her. He placed the glass of water on the coffee table between them. No need to push her. She'd start talking when she was ready.

Lucy took a sip of water and nodded a thank-you. He noticed the coffee table when she set the glass back down. Underneath the glass was a three-dimensional wooden underwater scene. Trout swam through the wooden stream complete with carved plant life.

"It's beautiful, isn't it?" She touched the Plexiglas. "My brother made it. He used to fish quite a bit. He was going to help me with the guide business." A twinge of pain threaded through her words. She crossed her arms over her body and leaned forward. "I'm not sure what was stolen. I suppose I should check the bedroom."

A department as small as Mountain Springs probably didn't have a forensics unit. He could call in for instructions, but he suspected there was a processing kit in the car, and that he would be the one doing the processing. "I need to go over the crime scene first."

The glazing over her eyes cleared. "But it must be one o'clock in the morning."

"Your house is a duplex. Is there someone next door you could stay with?"

"It's for rent. I've been running an ad, but so far, no response." She lifted her head, regaining her composure.

On his drive here, he had noticed that the houses were pretty far apart. The subdivision was on the outskirts of town. He had seen signs that indicated directions to a lake and hiking trails. Given the state she was in, it wouldn't be good for her to be alone tonight. "Is there a friend you can call?"

"Nobody I want to wake up at one in the morning." Her gaze rested on him for a moment, long enough to make him wiggle in his chair. "I appreciate your concern about me, but I can take care of myself."

Lucy Kimbol had an independent streak a mile long. "Suit yourself. I do need to process the scene." It wouldn't take any time at all to gather evidence from the crime scene, but he could stretch it out. Even though she would never admit it, he saw that she was on edge emotionally. Since he couldn't talk her into calling a friend, he'd feel better leaving her alone once she'd stabilized. "I'll get my kit out of the car." He stood up and looked at Lucy again. A chill ran down his spine. Lucy looked so much like the other victims. He had more than one reason for stretching out his time. "If you don't mind, I'll check the perimeter of your house while I'm out there. Sometimes thieves come back or maybe he dropped something."

Illumination from the porch light spilled over Lucy's backyard as Detective Hawkins circled around her house. Lucy stood at the kitchen window, gripping the glass of water he had gotten for her. She shook her head. He wasn't going to catch anyone. He was doing this to make her feel safer. The gesture touched her.

She had breathed a sigh of relief when she'd seen this stranger at her door. It had been an answer to prayer that he was compassionate and not part of the Mountain Springs Police Department she knew. Maybe *he* would actually catch the thief.

Her emotional meltdown had surprised her. She did not think of herself as someone who needed a fainting couch. She took a sip of the water and set the glass on the counter.

Outside, Detective Hawkins stepped away from the house and out of the light, where all she could discern was his silhouette. He wasn't a muscular man—more lean and tall. Probably the kind of officer who used persuasion and intelligence instead of brawn. He ambled back into the light and she caught a flash of his brown hair and a focused look on his face, a handsome face at that.

Even though he'd said he needed to process the scene first, she wanted to know what had been taken. She shrank back from the window and headed toward the bedroom. The door creaked when she pushed it open. She scanned the room. Why was her heart racing? The thief was gone. All she had to do was figure out what had been stolen. This shouldn't be that hard.

She knew enough about police work to not touch anything. She could go through the drawers and closet later to see if anything was missing. A glance at two empty hooks on the wall caused a jab to her heart. Her favorite and most expensive fly fishing rod, broken down and stored in a case, had been taken.

Lucy suddenly felt light-headed. She planted her feet. She'd pulled people out of raging rivers and hiked out of the hills with a sprained ankle. She could handle this. Her stomach tightened. She gripped the door frame.

A stranger had been in here, rifling through her things, her private things. Then she saw the redwood bowl where she kept her jewelry. Her legs turned to cooked noodles as she made her way across the floor. A lump swelled in her throat. Her jewelry was gone.

Eli's voice came from far away. "It's me and I'm just coming into the house."

Lucy's hand hovered over the empty bowl. Her grandmother's wedding ring and pearl necklace and the earrings her brother had given her had been stolen.

"Miss Kimbol? Lucy?"

Footsteps pounded on the wood floor. Eli stood in the doorway.

The warm tenor of his voice calmed her. She exhaled. She hadn't realized she'd been holding her breath.

He turned slightly sideways, indicating the outside door. "I knocked, but I was afraid that—"

She opened her mouth to speak, preparing to be all business, to let him know what was missing. Instead she bent forward, crumpling.

He rushed toward her before her knees buckled. His grip on her forearms was light but steadying. He must have seen something in her body language and facial expression, something she wasn't even aware of. No matter how hard she tried, she could not pull herself together by sheer force of will.

The heat of his touch on her forearm permeated her skin. She saw no judgment in his expression and his wide brown eyes communicated safety. "I'm… I'm so sorry. I'm not normally like this."

"Reaction to a home invasion takes a lot of people by surprise." Still anchoring her arm, he set a box with a handle on the floor.

She straightened her spine and squared her shoulders, but her stomach was still doing somersaults. "There was a bamboo fly fishing rod in a case and… my jewelry. The rod was worth thousands. It was custom-made. The jewelry wasn't worth much." But it had been priceless to her. The earrings had been a precious gift from her brother. She shuddered.

"You really need to let me process the scene first. I'll dust the area where you kept the jewelry and the windowsill and then take some photos." Leaning close, he whispered, "You might want to go in the next room."

"No, I…want to help." This was so ridiculous. Why did she keep losing it emotionally?

He bent over and flipped open the case. He spoke gently but as though he hadn't heard her protest. "To-morrow you can come back in here, but make sure a friend is with you. Look and see if there is anything else missing—make me a list with a description of each item."

She appreciated the concreteness of the assignment and the wisdom behind it. "Sorry, this is my first robbery. You've probably done thousands of them."

He lifted a camera out of the case. He rose to his feet and looked her in the eyes. "You're going to be all right, Miss Kimbol."

Detective Hawkins had been right about everything so far. She needed to trust and quit fighting him in an effort to prove to herself that this robbery wasn't upsetting her. "I'll wait in the living room."

For ten minutes, Lucy sat on the couch listening to him work, determined to stay awake. He seemed to be taking a long time for what had sounded like an easy job. She rested her cheek against a pillow as her eyelids grew heavy.

She stirred slightly when a blanket was placed on her. Relishing the comfort, she pulled the blanket up over her shoulder and drifted off again. Sometime later, the warmth of his voice surrounded her. "Miss Kimbol, you need to lock the door behind me. I'll wait outside until I hear the bolt click."

She heard his footsteps and the door swing open and then ease shut.

Still groggy, she rose to her feet, swayed slightly and trudged across the floor to flip the dead bolt. She checked the kitchen clock before falling back asleep. It was nearly 3:00 a.m.

His car started up. The rumble of the engine was loud at first but faded into the distance. Lucy pulled the blanket around her; the sense of security she'd felt while he was in the house vanished. Just as she was slipping into a deeper level of sleep, she'd wake with a start, thinking she had heard a noise. She slept fitfully until the phone rang at six.

Even though the phone was on a table by the couch, she didn't pick up until the third ring. She mumbled a hello.

Heather's chipper voice floated through the receiver. "Don't tell me you forgot."

The memory of the robbery made her shiver. "Forgot what?" She should tell Heather.

"Your second date with Greg Jackson, breakfast at Lydia's Café. You told me about it a few days ago."

Lucy winced. She had agreed to let Heather create her profile on the online dating service, but now that actual dates were involved, she wasn't so sure it was a good idea.

Heather must have sensed Lucy's hesitation. "Everything okay?"

Why was it so hard to share with her best friend? Christians were supposed to bear each other's burdens. "It's just that—"

"Do you like Greg?"

"He's seems like a nice Christian guy, but I…" Lucy gathered the blanket around her as the memory of last night invaded her thoughts.

"You only had one date. You do this every time, Lucy. You've got to give him more of a chance."

"It's not that." She had no trouble helping other people, but it was so hard to be the one who needed support.

She paced through the house. Finally, she stopped, took in a deep breath and blurted, "I was robbed last night."

"Oh, Lucy, are you okay? Were you hurt?" Heather's concern was evident even through the phone line.

"I wasn't hurt or anything." She stood in the doorway of her bedroom, looking at the dumped drawers, the empty boxes and clothes tossed from the closet. Her hand fluttered to her neck. Detective Hawkins had advised her not to do this alone.

"I'm sure Greg would understand if you need to cancel. He's probably already in town. Do you have his cell number?"

Lucy's hand gripped the frame of the door. She couldn't stay here…not alone. "Actually, I think I need to get out of this house. I'll go on the date. It'll get my mind off of things."

"Are you sure?"

"I am." Anything to get away from being reminded of the robbery. She should have taken Eli's advice and not spent the night here.

"I'll meet you right after your breakfast and then, Lucy, I'll stay with you as long as you need."

She pivoted and pressed her back against the wall, so she didn't have to look into the bedroom. "It's nice to have a friend who reads my mind."

"No, it's just that I know you. Quit trying to do everything yourself. But you've got to do something for me."

Lucy pressed the phone against her ear. "What is that?"

"I know you are not crazy about this online thing. I'm doing it because I love you and don't want you to be alone. For me, could you be a little more open-minded about Greg? You're twenty-eight—I hear a clock ticking."

Lucy's jaw tightened. Heather was well-intentioned. The little old ladies at church who kept telling her about their handsome grandsons were well-intentioned. She just couldn't picture herself in a relationship, let alone married. What man would put up with her constantly being gone on her guide trips? "I took the batteries out of that clock a long time ago."

Heather didn't laugh like Lucy had expected. Intense emotion saturated her friend's voice. "Sometimes friends see things that you can't see. I care about you, Lucy. I want good things for you."

Lucy said goodbye and got ready for her date with Greg Jackson. Because she was in a hurry, she opted to hide her hair with a baseball cap rather than take the time to fix it. The bonus of the baseball hat was that it sent Greg the message that she hadn't spent hours getting ready. For Heather, she would go on this second date, but she didn't need to knock herself out.

On the porch, Lucy pulled her house keys from her purse. She never locked her door unless she was going to be gone for days. Now she was going have to lock it all the time. Renewed fear made her hands clammy as she fumbled with the key. What if the thief came back?

TWO

Eli had caught only a few hours' sleep in his motel room when someone banged on the door. Still bleary-eyed, he pulled himself off the bed and swung the door open.

"Wake up, Susie Sunshine." Detective William Springer flashed a smile. "We got work to do."

While he leaned against the door frame of the motel, Eli shook his head, trying to clear the fog of sleep. He hadn't showered. His stomach was growling, and he couldn't stop thinking about Lucy. He hadn't met someone like her before, an intriguing mixture of strength and vulnerability. Plus, her resemblance to the other victims made him concerned for her safety. "Are you kidding me?"

"One of our suspects is in town." William rocked back and forth on his feet. He was a short man with blond hair so curly it almost looked like ringlets. "We're on surveillance in about twenty minutes."

With the exception of three undercover female officers, William Springer was the only Spokane detective Eli had been authorized to bring with him for the investigation. Right now he wished he had left him at home. "I need shut-eye." Of course, William was exuberant; he was functioning on a full night's sleep.

William tilted the paper bag he was holding in Eli's direction. "I brought breakfast."

The sticky-sweet scent of doughnuts woke Eli up a bit. "Which suspect?"

"Greg Jackson is going through town. He has a breakfast date at a place called Lydia's Café. Just got word of it. I didn't want to miss the opportunity."

They'd narrowed the suspects down to four men who fit a profile, used the same online dating service and lived in this area where the murders had taken place. A woman who was a friend of one victim and a relative of another had brought the online dating service to police attention. Local police had submitted the specifics of the two murders to the National Center for the Analysis of Violent Crime and found three similar murders within a day's drive of one another. Eli had picked Mountain Springs as a base of operation because it was central to all the other small towns where the murders had taken place.

William shoved the doughnut bag toward him again.

Eli held up a hand of protest. This time the smell made his stomach churn. "I need protein."

"Suit yourself." William strode across the motel parking lot and yelled over his shoulder. "We're taking my bug."

After brushing his teeth and splashing water on his face, Eli left the motel room and ambled toward the car.

William leaned against the driver's side door, feet crossed at the ankles. He handed Eli a manila folder.

"For your review, nothing new, other than the photos of the victims, pre-postmortem. We got them from family members."

Only William would use a term like *pre-postmortem*. The interviews of family and friends had been done by various police departments. The surveillance Eli would oversee would happen on two levels. Several female officers with undercover experience had spent a month establishing a cover in the small towns that fell within the area the murders had taken place. The officers had signed up for the service so they could get access to the suspects. Also, watching the four men for suspicious activity and to see if they favored dark-haired women might give them the break they needed.

The groundwork had been laid. They were closing in. Though much of the investigation had been handled by other departments, the ball was now in Eli's court to gather enough evidence for an arrest and to prevent another death.

Eli slipped into the passenger side of the bug, hunching slightly in the tiny car. He rubbed his eyes with the heels of his hands. The investigation could last months. The thought of living in a motel that whole time did not appeal to him, and it didn't make him look much like a small-town cop, either.

William shifted into first and pulled out of the lot. "Restaurant is about eight blocks away." He grabbed a doughnut out of the bag and munched. "We lucked out. One of the local officers recognized Greg Jackson when he was in the convenience store, struck up a conversation and got the details about this date."

As much as Eli hated going without sleep, William's call to do impromptu surveillance had been a good one. "We'll get a read on the guy, see how he operates. Then we can set the protocol for how we keep eyes on the other three guys, given the amount of manpower we have to work with." Eli's stomach growled again. "Maybe I can get a decent breakfast at this Lydia's Café."

Ten minutes later when they entered the café, Greg Jackson and his date were already seated. With the manila folder still in hand, Eli took a table so he was within earshot of Greg. He had a clear view of Greg, but could only see the back of his date, a woman with her hair all bunched up in a baseball hat. William sat opposite Eli and pulled out a notebook. Eli pretended to read a free local newspaper he'd picked up at the door and tuned in the conversation.

Lucy stared at the plate of pancakes and sausages in front of her. She lifted her head and smiled at Greg Jackson, sitting opposite her. It was a weekday morning, so the restaurant wasn't very busy. Two old-timers sat at the counter, sipping coffee. A mom with two small children, and a man occupied with his newspaper, sitting with a short man with curly blond hair, were the only other patrons.

Greg said something about one of the accounts he handled. She didn't quite understand his job. He lived in a town some distance from Mountain Springs and traveled here often for his job. He was a sales rep for a feed company or something. His work involved driving across the state and talking to farmers and agriculture supply stores. A breakfast date was a little strange, but he was in town for some sort of work thing, so they had decided to get together.

Getting out of the house had been a good idea. If nothing else, the date took her mind off the robbery.

Greg struck her as a sweet man, a stable man, but nothing went *zing* inside when she was with him.

"I was thinking, Lucy. I'm sometimes traveling through Mountain Springs on Sunday for my Monday meetings. Would you like to go to church together?" He leaned a little closer to her. "Maybe?"

She had promised Heather she wouldn't dismiss Greg so quickly. "When is the next time you're in town?" Maybe *zing* happened later.

"I have some clients to visit here in a couple of days, but that won't be a Sunday."

Going to church together felt too serious. "I don't know…maybe."

Behind her, the waitress asked the man with the newspaper what he wanted to eat. His newspaper rustled as he set it down. Lucy perked up when the man ordered pancakes and bacon. She knew that voice, the warmth of it. She removed her hat and turned toward him.

Detective Hawkins's face blanched, but then he recovered and nodded in her direction. He held up a glass container of maple syrup. "I heard this was a good place to eat breakfast."

"Best in town."

The other man, the one with the curly blond hair, cleared his throat. He shifted in his seat and lifted his chin toward Eli in some unspoken signal. As she turned back around, Lucy felt a tightening in her rib cage.

Greg shoved a large piece of French toast in his mouth. "Your pancakes okay?"

"They're great, thanks." Lucy took a bite. The sweetness of the huckleberry syrup did nothing to deter her suspicion. The knowing glance that had passed between Eli and the other man bothered her. She couldn't pinpoint it, but something about it felt strange, conspiratorial.

Greg chatted more about his work and the family ranch he had grown up on in Colorado. Lucy talked about helping a seventy-year-old widow learn how to fly fish. She angled in her chair so she saw Eli in her peripheral vision. Was he watching her?

Greg excused himself to pay the bill.

Lucy took a sip of her coffee. Any sense of trust she'd felt with Eli last night was gone. She set her coffee cup firmly on the table. Why had she thought Eli was different? A cop was a cop. People's concerns and their fears were just a big, funny joke to all of them.

Lucy rose to her feet and gave Eli a backward glance.

He looked up from the manila folder he'd been flipping through. His eyes searched hers. She couldn't quite read what she saw in his expression. Was it fear?

Greg slipped his arm through Lucy's and guided her toward the door.

When they were outside the restaurant, Greg spoke up. "Maybe I'll call you when I'm back in town in a couple of days. We can get together then."

"Sure," Lucy said absently. The look of fear on Eli's face was etched in her mind.

* * *

Eli watched Lucy pass by the restaurant window. He had nearly choked on his water when she had glanced at him. He scanned the pre-postmortem photos from the file again. His heart squeezed tight.

William doodled on his notepad. "That guy Jackson, Mr. Ordinary, huh? You know what they say. Beneath that smooth surface lurks the heart of a killer."

Eli continued to examine the photographs, taking in a deep breath to quell the rising panic. "Who exactly says that, William?"

"You know, it's always the guy who is quiet and keeps to himself who is the killer." William rested his elbows on the table and narrowed his eyes at Eli. "What is it, man? You look like you just took a left hook to the jaw."

One by one, Eli passed the photos to William. Though the women had all died in different ways— poisoning, strangulation, stabbing—their appearance and membership in the online service linked them together. "Do you see it?"

"Yeah, they all are beautiful, dark-haired women." William's tone had become more insistent. "We established that."

Eli took in a breath in an effort to slow his thudding heart. "I think I know who the next victim could be."

"You mean, the woman Jackson was with…'cause of the dark hair."

"I answered a robbery call at her house last night. I noticed the resemblance, but didn't realize how closely she matched her victims until looking at the photos." His mouth went dry. "If she is dating Jackson, she probably met him through the service." Eli hadn't failed to notice the daggers she shot toward him as she left the restaurant. Her distrust of police ran deep, and it took only the smallest irregularity to trigger it. She probably thought he was stalking her.

More than anything, when he'd seen the veil of protection fall across her eyes, he had wanted to explain why he was in the café, but he couldn't. They had put too much manpower on the case to blow it. Going public with the investigation could cause the killer to go underground, then years from now after three or four more women died, they'd have to connect the dots all over again.

Eli spread the photos across the table. He could not shake the anxiety coiling through him. He tapped his finger on one of the pictures. "Look. Same hair, same eyes. Lucy Kimbol is a dead ringer for these other victims."

The sense of justice that had led him to want to be a police officer rose up in him. They were going to get this guy. No one else was going to die on his watch. "I think we need to keep our eye on potential victims, too."

"Manpower is limited, remember." William rested his elbows on the table. "We'll be watching potential victims when they are with suspects."

Eli gathered up the photographs. "Not always. We have to rotate surveillance as it is."

William shook his head. "You have to let go of the belief that you can protect everyone all of the time. You are not supercop. None of us are."

"I just think when someone fits criteria for being a potential victim, we ought to do something about it."

Who was he kidding? Lucy wouldn't accept police protection if it came tied up in a silver bow.

He'd have to find some other way to keep her safe.

THREE

Eli's heart kicked into overdrive as he brought his car to a stop outside of Lucy's duplex. He was probably the last person Lucy wanted to see right now. If the department wasn't going to spring for the manpower to keep an eye on her, he would do it on his own time. Besides, his solution solved two problems. Two days in a motel was two days too many, and she had a duplex for rent.

In her front yard, three teenagers lined up, all holding fly rods. Lucy moved from one student to the next, adjusting their grip on the rod handle or demonstrating the casting.

Her long, dark hair cascaded down to the middle of her back. The vest with all the pockets, a T-shirt and khaki pants was probably the official uniform of fly fishers everywhere. Her cheeks were sun-tinged. Even in the bulky clothes, her narrow waist and the soft curve of her hips were evident. He liked the way the students seemed responsive to her instruction, remaining quiet and focusing on her while she talked.

Part of solid police work involved not jumping to conclusions. He could be wrong about Lucy being the next victim, but he didn't want to take a chance with her life. How many dark-haired, blue-eyed women could there be in an area that probably had more cows and sheep than people?

The three teenagers held their poles midair and stared when Eli pulled into the gravel driveway.

Part of the profile of the killer was that the dark hair and blue eyes were symbolic in some way. The other aspect of his personality was that he probably traveled for his job or had enough time and money to cover the area where the killings had taken place. On the online sign-up forms, there was an option that allowed an applicant to restrict match choices to a geographic region.

Eli and the other officers had joked as they looked at the matchmaking Web site for "investigative purposes." They all agreed that a guy would have to be pretty desperate to sign up for something like that. He noticed though that the number of single guys on the force who mentioned having dates seemed to go up quite a bit after that.

William had even signed Eli up, but he'd missed the only two dates he'd agreed to because of work. He'd been twenty-six when he had caught the Spokane killer; now at thirty, his life was his work and that was fine with him. He couldn't imagine a woman who would put up with the kind of hours he kept. He had nieces and nephews and mentored kids through the church youth group. He never sat at home, twiddling his thumbs and thinking about taking up watercolor painting.

Eli got out of his car and sauntered toward Lucy.

Her granite gaze told him all he needed to know. After a few words of instruction to the kids, she walked over to him. "The guy who called asking about the rental didn't sound like you on the phone."

"I had my partner call in and ask about it when I saw the newspaper ad." She probably would have hung up on him. "I do need a place to live."

Her chin jerked up slightly. "Wouldn't you rather get a place closer to town?"

He had counted on meeting some resistance. "It's not like there are a ton of rental choices. I like how quiet it is out here."

She studied him for a moment. Her expression softened. "That much is true." She kept her voice level, completely neutral. "It's been vacant for a couple of months, and I really do need the income."

If it was about money to her, fine. He'd stay close any way he could.

She stepped onto the wraparound porch, pulled a key from her pocket and opened the door. The house was clean and airy. Like her place, it had a loft. He would have taken it if it had been a dump.

"It's nice. I like that it's a furnished place. I didn't bring a whole lot with me from Spokane," he said. "I like being out in the country, but still minutes from town."

"I like it, too. I'm close to the river, close to my work." Lucy's voice lilted slightly when she spoke about the river.

Eli wandered through the house, opened and closed the bathroom door. He had to at least look as if he was considering. He pointed at another door.

"That leads to a half basement—sump pump and hot-water tank are down there," Lucy offered.

After a cursory glance into the bedroom, he opened the back door and stepped out on the porch.

"Be careful." Her voice grew closer. "The floor-boards on that side are old."

Eli pressed his boot against a board that bowed from his weight. Several of the planks were broken and there were some gaps where wood should have been. He lifted his head. The air smelled of pine. The breeze brushed his cheeks. A guy could get used to this. "I definitely want to take it."

Lucy came to the open door. "I'm glad to hear that." She pointed to a hole in the porch. "My friend Nelson is coming this afternoon to help me fix this. I do upkeep as I get the funds."

"The porch is not really what you notice when you step out here." He pointed to the view of the open field and the surrounding evergreens.

"It's the reason I stay." A faint smile graced her lips.

Ah, so the way to this woman's heart is to mention the beautiful landscape.

"I have rental forms for you to fill out. The lease is month-to-month." She stood, twisting the knob. "Does that sound good to you, Detective Hawkins?"

Obviously, her name choice indicated she wanted the relationship to be about business. It would be nice though if she would call him by his first name. "I did a little digging into your robbery."

"I did some work, too. I wrote out a description of what was taken. There wasn't anything else missing from the room besides the jewelry and the fishing rod." She stepped out on the porch and stood three feet from him. "What did you find out?"

"Couple down the road had a laptop and money taken a few weeks ago."

She crossed her arms. The breeze stirred the wispy hair around her face. She gazed at him with wide, round eyes—blue eyes, just like the other victims.

"I don't know if this is important or not, but I wasn't supposed to be home the night of the robbery. I delayed a fly fishing clinic because of the storm. It rains a lot in May."

"Who would have known you were gone?"

Lucy let out a gust of air. "Everyone."

He chuckled. "Oh, I forgot, small town."

She stepped away from him and stared out at the forest that surrounded her property. "What made you want to leave the city? I'm sure work in Spokane was more exciting."

He chose his answer with care, not wanting to reveal more than he had to. "Change of pace." He pressed on a weak floorboard with his foot. "So, the robber might have been surprised when you came down those stairs?"

"I hadn't told anyone other than the clients that I decided to cancel."

He hadn't seen any sign of forced entry. "Your doors were unlocked?"

"I never had a reason to lock them…until now. I'm looking into getting a security latch for the window, too."

Eli recalled the layout of Lucy's house. "The thief could have entered from either door?"

Lucy shaded her eyes from the sun as she stepped farther out on the porch. "He probably entered from this side, the back side. There is a road beyond that forest where he could have parked his car."

"So he entered by the door that led into the kitchen and left by the bedroom window." If he had come up on the front side, neighbors might have seen his car. There had been some premeditation to the whole thing. Somehow, it just didn't feel like some kid wandering the neighborhood looking for unlocked doors.

One of the teenage students, a girl with hunched shoulders and chubby cheeks, peeked around to the back side of the house. "Miss Kimbol, Tyler got his line snagged on a bush."

"I'll be there, Marnie." She turned toward Eli after jumping off the porch. "Rent is due on the first, and there is a three-hundred-dollar deposit."

She disappeared around the corner of the house.

Eli leaned against a porch post. That had gone better than he had hoped. She hadn't been warm, but she hadn't been hostile, either. He'd have to find a way to change that. It would be easier to protect her if she trusted him.

Solving her robbery and recovering the stolen items would go a long way toward rebuilding her confidence in the police. Finding out why her trust had been broken in the first place would help even more.

Shortly after a parent came for the last student, Lucy heard Nelson's truck pull up and she bounded out onto the porch. Even before she had made her way to the truck, Lucy heard Eli's tenor voice behind her.

"I could help out. I worked construction during college."

She whirled around to face him. Eli's hands hung at his sides. He squared his shoulders like a soldier waiting inspection.

Why was he being so nice? "I know I said I didn't like the police. Believe me, I have my reasons. Are you offering to do repairs to prove to me that cops are okay?" If that was why he wanted to help, he would want to hear the whole story and she had no desire to revisit that part of her past. "Don't feel like you have to be the police ambassador for Mountain Springs."

Eli's shoulders slumped. "I'm just trying to be a good neighbor." He offered her a megawatt smile. "I won't take no for an answer."

She tilted her head skyward. Partly to show exasperation and partly so she didn't have to look at him. There was something puppy-dog cute about him that she didn't want to give in to. "Don't you have moving in to do, Mr. Hawkins?"

He held his hands up, palms to the sky. "All done."

Eli had a certain charm, but something about him didn't ring true. What kind of a person gets moved into a place in less than an hour? He must have brought the stuff with him, which meant he had intended to move in regardless of what the rental looked like. Suspicion sparked in her heart. She took a step back.

As if he had read her mind, he said, "The move was kind of fast. I heard at the last minute that I had the job. So I just threw everything in my car and drove from Washington."

She hadn't thought her apprehension was noticeable. He sure was good at reading her signals. While Eli wasn't at the top of her list for renters, she had been grateful when he'd shown up. Since the robbery, she'd been jumpy, uncomfortable in her own home. Having a close neighbor might make her feel safer. Now she wasn't so sure if Eli was the right choice.

Nelson got out of the truck and ambled toward Eli and Lucy. Nelson was one of those men who showed up well groomed even for something like fixing a porch. He'd gelled his hair. His jeans and work shirt looked pressed. When they had known each other in high school, Lucy had joked that he was the kind of guy who dressed up to go to the Laundromat.

Eli held out a hand. "I'm Eli Hawkins. Lucy's new renter."

Nelson nodded. "Nelson Thane. I am an old friend of Lucy's."

Lucy placed a hand on Nelson's shoulder. "We lost touch when Nelson got a job out of state after high school graduation."

"I missed Mountain Springs and the people." Nelson lifted some boards out of the back of his truck. "So now I'm back, teaching English to high school students."

Eli lifted a can of stain from the back of the truck. "I'd love to give you a hand."

Lucy opened her mouth to protest, but before she could say anything, Nelson responded. "Jump in. The more hands, the faster it goes. Right, Lucy?"

Eli offered Lucy a victorious lift of his eyebrow in response to her scowl.

Talk about pushy. Lucy pressed her lips together, but resisted rolling her eyes. "You're probably right," she relented.

They moved the supplies to the back of the house

and started by tearing up floorboards. Eli worked at an impressive pace, stopping only when Lucy offered him a drink of water.

Sweat glistened on his forehead as he gulped from the glass.

"So would this repair work have anything to do with your date?" Nelson gathered the damaged wood and placed it in a pile.

Lucy put her hand on her hips. "You've been talking to Heather. She says I need to give Greg more of a chance. Fixing the porch isn't to impress him. We made plans to go into town."

Eli cleared his throat.

Nelson hammered on a warped board with a vicious intensity. He stopped to catch his breath, waving the hammer in the air. "I don't know if online is the best place to find true love anyway."

"I'm just doing this as a favor to Heather."

Eli handed the glass back to Lucy. "Is this the guy you were in the café with the other day?"

Lucy met Eli's gaze. A hint of anxiety lay beneath his question despite his attempt at casualness. "Yes, Eli, it is. He's a nice guy."

"I'm with Nelson. I don't think an online service is the best way to go. It's too easy for people, especially guys, to be deceptive."

Lucy's spine stiffened. What business was it of his who she dated? If anyone knew about being deceptive, it was him. He was the one who had moved into his place with almost nothing and had decided to take it before he'd even seen it. What was he up to, anyway?

She tried to keep her tone friendly. "Really, guys, I

appreciate the feedback. I can take care of myself." She was just doing this to prove to Heather that no matter how much of a chance she gave Greg, nothing would spark between them. If she went on one more date with Greg and there was still nothing but friendly feelings, maybe Heather would quit matchmaking altogether.

Besides, Greg was a sweet man, and she wanted to find a way to tell him she wasn't interested without hurting his feelings. As Lucy placed the claw end of her hammer under a nail and rocked it back and forth, her irritation grew. Why was everyone trying to run her love life?

She pulled out several nails and tossed them in the coffee can they were using for waste. Then she pounded on the rotted boards to break them up and loosen them.

When she looked up, breathless from the exertion, both men were staring at her. She readjusted the baseball hat she'd been using to hold her hair out of her eyes. "What?"

Eli grinned. "I would hate to be one of those boards."

When he smiled, his eyes sparkled. A laugh escaped her lips. She'd let herself get way too worked up. "Guess I was being a little mean to the wood."

Eli surveyed the area around her house. "Where are the tools to cut and place the new boards?"

Lucy sat up straight and massaged the small of her back. "Over in the shed. Why don't you guys go get them, since I've been doing all the hard work?" she joked.

Eli glanced back at Lucy as he and Nelson walked toward the shed. She had taken the baseball cap off to wipe her brow. The thought of her being alone with Greg terrified him. The more time she spent with him, the more danger she might be in. Was it worth blowing the secrecy of the investigation to tell her that Greg was a suspect? Given her distrust of cops, she probably wouldn't believe him anyway.

Nelson opened the shed door and clicked on the light. The shed had a concrete floor. A kayak and a variety of fishing poles lined one wall. Saws, drills and other assorted tools cluttered a table in a far corner.

Dust danced in the cylinders of light created by two small windows. Eli's eyes adjusted to the dimness. He whistled. "Lucy has some pretty nice tools."

"I think she got most of these from her brother." Nelson grabbed a piece of plywood leaning against a wall.

"Her brother?"

The scraping of wood against concrete drowned out Eli's question. Nelson pointed toward a corner of the shed. "If you want to grab the sawhorses, we can set up the tables."

Eli picked up a sawhorse in each hand. "So you don't like the idea of Lucy doing this online thing?" Maybe he could get Nelson to talk Lucy out of seeing Greg.

Nelson shrugged. "Lucy does what Lucy wants to do. I don't think we have much to worry about. After a few dates, she'll just decide she wants to be friends. That's her usual pattern. It started with me in high school."

"You dated Lucy?"

"All water under the bridge. She became a Christian a little before her mom died. We didn't share the same faith. She didn't want to date anymore."

Eli detected just a hint of hurt in Nelson's comments.

They stepped back out into the sunlight. Lucy had gathered the rotting wood into a pile and was in the process of backing Nelson's truck up to it.

They worked through the afternoon. Lucy loaded the old wood to be hauled away. Nelson cut and measured boards. Lucy brought the boards to Eli and helped put them in place so he could drive the nails in.

It was late in the day when they all stood back to admire their handiwork.

"You guys did a good job." As she stood between them, Lucy wrapped an arm around each man. "I'll just have to stain it tomorrow."

Eli's cell rang. William's voice came on the other end of the line. "Hawkins, I got a little info you might be interested in."

"Just a second." Eli stepped away so Lucy and Nelson wouldn't be able to hear the call. He ambled toward his side of the duplex. "Whatcha got?"

"The other day in the café, Greg Jackson mentioned the name of the small town where he grew up in Colorado. I remembered I had a P.I. buddy down there who owed me a favor. He tracked down a childhood friend of Jackson's."

Eli tensed. "Is the probing going to get back to Jackson? That could blow everything." The last thing they needed was for any of the suspects to know they were looking into their lives.

"Relax, this isn't my first day at camp. The friend hasn't had contact with Greg in years. They were in the same FFA club in high school. My detective friend didn't put up any flags. He just followed the guy into a bar and struck up a conversation with him. We are being very careful."

"Sorry, didn't mean to snap at you." If there was anyone he trusted to maintain the integrity of the investigation, it was William. Lucy's resistance to his advice about Greg had made him tense. "What did you find out?"

"Greg had a troubled childhood. Mom was repeatedly treated for 'injuries' until she finally divorced Dad. As we already knew, most of Greg's crimes fall into the under-eighteen sealed category, except for that one assault charge when he was nineteen. The high school friend said that after that, Greg supposedly found God and got his life straightened out."

Eli turned to watch as Lucy hugged Nelson goodbye. Nelson climbed into his truck. He waved at Eli and drove around to the other side of the house. "People do find healing in their faith, William."

"And sometimes that stuff lies just beneath the surface waiting to erupt."

He couldn't argue with that. Christ could transform lives, but religion could also mask unresolved issues. "Is there anything else?"

"While I was briefing all the small police departments who are going to help us, one of the highway patrol officers recognized Jackson's picture. Couple of weeks back, Jackson had a little bit of a run-in with this highway patrol officer for speeding."

"Who hasn't?"

"The officer was female, and he put his hands on her neck. A court date is pending."

A shiver ran down Eli's back. Lucy stopped picking up debris and tools long enough to shade her eyes and look in Eli's direction. He had to keep her away from Greg.

"Eli, are you still there?"

"Yeah, I'm still here."

Eli's pulse rate skyrocketed. He watched Lucy gather the lighter tools. He fought to maintain the objectivity required of his job, to keep his emotions at bay. Where Lucy's safety was concerned, that was hard to do.

William broke into his thoughts. "We are still trying to dig stuff up on the other three suspects. See you tonight for the surveillance in Three Dot."

"Keep me posted." Eli clicked off his phone and strode over to where Lucy was attempting to lift the heavy saw. "Let me help you with that."

She set the saw back down and faced him. "Long phone call."

She was close enough for him to smell the floral scent of her perfume. Even in a ratty T-shirt and jeans, she looked radiant. "Yeah."

"Not going to tell me more?" She picked up a bucket of nails.

"Just some police stuff." He bent over and lifted the saw. He carried the saw while she trailed behind with the bucket.

They entered the shed. He heaved the saw onto a counter. He had to try one more time.

"Listen, Lucy, I know you have the right to make your own choices, but I got a creepy vibe from Greg Jackson when we were in the restaurant the other day." She opened her mouth to protest, but he held up a hand. "I know you don't like people interfering. I grew up with two sisters, and I had like a ninety-percent success rate with predicting when a guy was bad news."

Her expression hardened, and he knew he was fighting a losing battle.

"We have to get the rest of these tools put away." She stalked toward the door. "By the way, if you are trying to succeed on your mission to convince me that cops are okay, this hyperprotective thing is not how to do it."

He darted toward her and grabbed her arm. "Please Lucy, I am just asking you to trust me. I can't explain why, but please just trust me."

She studied him for a moment. "You barely know me. I don't understand why you would even care."

"It's in my cop DNA. Though my partner says I have an overdeveloped need to protect people."

"Your partner might be right." The resolve he saw in her eyes was unwavering.

He let go of her arm. "I had a good time this afternoon helping you. I'd do it again in a heartbeat." It was the truest thing he could say to her.

Her stiff posture softened. "I had a good time, too." She patted him on the arm. "We make a good team." She checked her watch. "I have to get cleaned up for my date." She walked out of the shed.

As he followed her outside, panic spread through him. A lump swelled in his throat. He steadied his voice. "Sorry, I didn't mean to interfere. Your business is your business."

She lifted her chin. Her skin looked translucent in the early evening sun. "Thank you. I think we will get along fine if you keep that in mind."

He wanted to know if she was going to be alone

with Jackson. Would she be in a safe place, a public place? But it was obvious that probing her about the date would be fruitless.

Eli said goodbye and went back into his house. He showered, unpacked his minimal belongings and then spent some time making a list of what he needed to get in town for his new home. He flipped open his laptop and opened the investigation folder. Some surveillance photos and reports were already coming in.

He came across a photo of a woman with dark hair leaving a movie theater with suspect number two. His stomach tightened. He couldn't leave Lucy alone with Greg. He had to do something.

He checked the schedule for where he had put his surveillance team. None were assigned to keep an eye on Jackson, and he was supposed to drive out to a small town called Three Dot, where an undercover female officer had set up a date with one of the other suspects.

Even as he dialed William's cell, he kept one ear tuned to the road, waiting to hear Greg Jackson's approaching car.

"Yup." William answered on the fourth ring. "Calling back so soon?"

Eli moved the curtain back from the window, thinking he had heard something. The only vehicles in the driveway were his own and Lucy's. "Listen, I was looking at the schedule. We don't have anyone on Jackson tonight." The silence on the other end of the line told him that William was probably clenching his jaw.

"It was your idea that with the limited manpower the rotating surveillance was what would work best."

Eli pressed the phone harder against his ear. "I just found out Jackson has a date tonight."

"It didn't come up on the phone taps or through e-mail. He must have made the date in person."

"I know we can't be everywhere at once, but—" Even as he spoke, he knew that what he was suggesting was unrealistic. "I'm just concerned about Lucy."

"Lucy isn't the only potential victim. We got a undercover female officer who has made contact with two of the other suspects."

Eli closed his eyes. William was right. From an investigative standpoint, they were more likely to get information that could lead to warrants and arrests from a trained officer probing the suspect than from watching a suspect on a date. "It's just that Lucy looks so much like the others. I'm afraid for her."

"I don't want to risk another life, either."

Eli paced through the bare kitchen of his new home, his resolve growing. "O'Bannon and Peterson here in Mountain Springs don't have lots of surveillance experience. I could use this as a training exercise."

On the other end of the line papers fluttered. William must have been looking through notes. "We do have an officer in Three Dot who's been briefed and is dying to learn. I could pull him in."

"Thanks, Springer."

"If we catch this guy, we don't have to worry about anyone dying."

"Five women have lost their lives already." Eli pressed the phone a little harder against his ear. "I just don't want anyone to die on my watch."

Eli hung up the phone and stared out the window, rubbing his chin. Now he just needed to keep Lucy safe tonight.

Lucy took out her agitation on the vegetables she was chopping for salad. Eli Hawkins was nosy. What business of his was it where she was going and who she was dating? Who appointed him the goodwill ambassador for all cops?

She placed the tomatoes she had been chopping into the plastic container she planned on taking to her picnic with Greg. Heather was right. She did turn potential suitors into friends pretty quickly. At the same time, it was wrong to lead men on. If there was no chemistry, there was no chemistry.

She opened the refrigerator and pulled out a cucumber. Her hair was still wet from her shower, and she needed to put some makeup on.

There was a park in Mountain Springs that had several gazebos where they could eat their picnic. It wouldn't be too crowded this time of night. Lucy peeled the cucumber.

Maybe it was a good thing that she rented the duplex month-to-month. If Eli continued to be such a pain, she would have to tell him to find a different place.

She smiled. It had been nice of him to help with the deck repairs, she did need the money from rent and having someone next door did make her feel safer.

She brought the knife down on the cucumber and sliced through. The blade hit the cutting board with a regular rhythm.

She had no desire to explain to Eli why there was antagonism between her and the local police. He'd probably take their side anyway. Cops always stuck together, always defended each other.

As much as she appreciated Eli's help this afternoon, the best arrangement would be for him to keep his distance. There was no law that said neighbors had to be friends; they just had to be cordial.

Lucy pulled two bottled iced teas from the refrigerator, as well as the containers that held the sandwiches she had made earlier. She placed everything in a picnic basket and then went into her bedroom to change into the sundress she had picked out.

She ran a comb through her hair and put on some liner and lipstick. She glanced at herself in the mirror. The cornflower-blue sundress made her eyes look even bluer. Maybe she should change into something dowdier. If this was the date where she told Greg she just wanted to be friends, maybe she shouldn't overdo it with dressing up. She opted to keep the dress on, but toned down her makeup.

Once back in the living room, Lucy grabbed her cell phone off the counter to check the time. Ten more minutes until Greg got here. Heather had sent her a text message: *U promised.*

Lucy shook her head. What were best friends for but to turn your plans upside down? Heather was doing this because she cared. Her perceptive friend saw something lacking in Lucy's life. She would give Greg another chance.

She dug through her living-room closet in search of something that would work for a light summer cover-up. Maybe that magic electrical attraction thing happened after you'd known each other awhile. She laughed. And maybe it was just something people read about in books.

She pulled a silk wrap off a hanger. What did she know about serious relationships anyway? She and Nelson had been pretty serious in high school, but she had only been seventeen. The only other serious relationship had been with Matthew. She'd broken off her engagement with him when her brother, Dawson, had his accident and she'd had to put her energy into caring for him. After that, she had lost all interest in dating.

Lucy flung the wrap over her shoulder and peered out the window. No sign of Greg. She hadn't thought about Matthew in years. Matthew had been a sweet, supportive man. She had taken a premarriage class at church and, along with the other students, had come up with a list of character qualities they'd wanted in a mate. Matthew had fit the criteria. In retrospect, she hadn't really loved him.

Lucy stroked the smooth silk of the wrap where it rested on her arms. Somehow she didn't think that love should be as clinical as a checklist. Sure, she'd had friends act on their emotions and end up in bad marriages, but it shouldn't be like choosing a health insurance plan, either.

She wandered over to the picnic basket. She rearranged what she had packed and decided to grab some cookies out of the cookie jar. She opened a cupboard, searching for a container for the cookies.

Maybe that was the problem with this online dating thing. You gave a list of the criteria you thought you wanted in a mate, but none of that factored in attraction. Sometimes people could be attracted to someone who didn't meet any of their criteria. Sometimes, what you thought you wanted wasn't what you needed.

Lucy pulled out a container. Really, it was possible to like someone who was so obviously wrong for you. Someone like Eli Hawkins, for instance. She shook her head as she stacked the containers on top of each other. What on earth had made her think of that?

She placed the cookies in the container and slammed on the lid.

Outside, tires crunched on gravel.

Lucy walked the few steps to look out the window. Greg had just gotten out of his car. He was holding a large bouquet of tulips. How sweet. There was something poignant about the look of hopeful expectation on his face.

Lucy drew back from the window. Heather was right. She needed to open her heart up to the possibility that there could be something between them.

FOUR

Eli pulled the curtain back to check the front yard. Greg's car sat in the driveway.

If he could find out the location of their date, O'Bannon and Peterson could get set up ahead of time. Lucy certainly wasn't going to give him that information. Greg got out of the car; Eli flung the door open and stepped down the stairs.

Greg cocked his head as though surprised to see Eli. "Who are you?"

Eli held out his hand. "I'm Eli Hawkins, Lucy's new renter."

Greg's lips flattened and wrinkles appeared in his forehead as he extended his own hand. "Lucy never said anything about a renter."

"I moved in earlier today." Eli studied the man in front of him. Had he just shaken hands with a killer?

"Oh, well, that explains it." Greg crossed his arms over his chest. His stare had an unnerving intensity to it, like he was picking Eli apart with his eyes.

Eli nodded for several seconds. The guy wasn't exactly Mr. Friendly.

Greg glanced at Lucy's door and then continued with his inch-by-inch scrutiny of Eli. "So what made you decide to rent Lucy's place?"

"Just answered an ad." Certainly, Greg didn't see him as some kind of romantic competition. Maybe he was one of those guys who was so controlling, he didn't want his date even talking to any other men. "You and Lucy are going out somewhere tonight?"

Greg's head jerked up in response to the question. "Lucy picked out the place. Some little park in town."

"Sounds like fun. Which park is that?" When Greg drew his eyebrows together as though suspicious of the question, Eli added, "I'm new in town. Just trying to get to know the area."

"I don't know the name. I'm not from here. I live in Jacob's Corner, about sixty miles from here." Greg angled his head toward the sky. "I don't know if a picnic is such a good idea. Those clouds look kind of dark and foreboding."

Lucy's door opened and she appeared, holding a picnic basket. Eli's breath caught. She looked stunning in her blue sundress. Her long hair flowed freely.

Lucy's stride slowed when she saw Eli. She sauntered over to Greg's car. "So you've met Greg?"

Eli pointed to his car. "I was headed out to do some work-related things. Just thought I would introduce myself." Eli excused himself.

Even as he ambled toward his car, Eli's muscles tensed. So much pointed to Greg Jackson in terms of past behavior. His instant suspicion of Eli was just one more personality indicator. Would he be able to keep Lucy safe? Eli started his engine and shifted into Reverse. Greg and Lucy were just getting into the car as Eli pulled onto the gravel road.

When he phoned into the Mountain Springs police station, Officer O'Bannon answered. He had met O'Bannon only briefly. He was an older officer who was probably a few years from retirement. Since his arrival from Spokane, he had spent most of his time briefing all the small-town police departments and figuring out how he was going to shift manpower around to keep eyes on the suspects for the maximum amount of time.

After Eli explained the circumstances of the surveillance to O'Bannon, he added, "I don't know the name of the park."

"There are only two parks in town." O'Bannon's husky voice hinted of a longtime smoking habit. "Chances are they're headed to Memorial Park. It's got gazebos and borders the river. The other one is more of a kid park with swings and stuff."

"You can check the file to see a picture of Greg Jackson. He's driving a gold Buick LeSabre, late eighties model. First two digits of the license are 67. You go ahead and get into position. Tell Peterson I will meet him at the station. Jackson might recognize my car so I need to switch."

"And who is the lady he is with? I've lived here some twenty years. I know most everyone. Is she a local gal?"

Eli hesitated. Lucy had implied that she didn't have a lot of faith in the Mountain Springs police. "Lucy Kimbol."

Eli listened to phone static while he turned onto a paved road. So the ill feelings between Lucy and the department were mutual.

Finally O'Bannon huffed an "Oh, really."

On the night of his arrival, two of the officers had pushed hard for him to handle the call from Lucy. O'Bannon had been one of them. Officer Spitz, the other older officer, had been the other. Lucy sure wasn't going to tell him the root of the animosity. "What is it with you guys and Lucy Kimbol?"

Again, O'Bannon's response was long in coming. "Let's just say Lucy Kimbol is a troublemaker and she has been since she was in high school."

As much as he wanted to get to the bottom of the bad blood between Lucy and the department, Eli didn't press the issue. He needed O'Bannon's cooperation tonight.

Eli drove into town and pulled into the police station lot. The sky had turned a dark gray when he stepped out of his car. Officer Nigel Peterson, a young officer with red hair, was waiting for him outside.

Peterson held up a gear bag. "Camera, binoculars and two-way radios."

Normally surveillance involved scouting an area ahead of time. Doing the surveillance on the fly meant there wouldn't be time to set up audio or video equipment. An open area like a park wasn't conducive to that kind of setup anyway.

Eli slipped into the car with Peterson. The drive to the park took all of five minutes. O'Bannon was waiting there for them. Judging from the jowls and paunch, O'Bannon had to at least be in his late fifties. He had a full head of black wavy hair and a muscular build. Jackson's car wasn't in the lot when they pulled in.

A quick assessment of the layout of the park caused the tightness to return to Eli's chest. Other than a small pavilion with picnic tables and two gazebos, the ground was more forest than park. The landscape provided a thousand places where someone could disappear from view.

A quick scan of the area revealed about ten to twelve people walking dogs, sitting on benches and eating at picnic tables. A couple emerged from a clump of trees. It wasn't Jackson and Lucy. Her blue sundress would make her easy enough to keep track of.

Eli handed each of the men a radio. "This is far from the ideal, but it will be a good training exercise. Let's focus on making sure we don't lose track of the suspect and his date, and staying in communication."

"One of the rules of surveillance is that most people aren't very observant. If you don't do anything to call attention to yourself, nobody will remember you." Peterson grinned. "I remember that from the academy training. Hunting down stolen bicycles doesn't give you much of a chance to use that."

Eli patted Peterson on the shoulder. He liked his enthusiasm. "In the future, we will assign you to a different town for surveillance so there is less chance of you being recognized."

O'Bannon hung back a few feet. "So why are we doing this?"

During the briefing, even before Eli had brought up the question about Lucy's past relationship with the department, O'Bannon had not seemed excited about the added duties involved in the serial killer investigation.

Eli planted his feet. "I have concerns about Greg Jackson. Right now, he looks like our strongest suspect. I want to make sure the woman he is with stays safe tonight." He didn't use Lucy's name on purpose. "That's our job as officers—right, O'Bannon…to keep citizens safe?" Eli pulled a baseball hat out of the gear bag. "People are less likely to notice your face if you have this on."

O'Bannon drew his head back and wrinkled his nose as though he smelled something bad but took the hat Eli handed him. "I know that," O'Bannon mumbled.

"Peterson, why don't you come with me?" He handed the camera to the younger officer. "We'll be able to get a clear shot undetected if they go to that half of the park. O'Bannon, you take the bench. Alert us when they arrive. Move as needed to keep them in view."

Moments after Eli and Peterson slipped behind the trees that provided cover, O'Bannon's voice vibrated through the radio.

"They've pulled into the lot."

Crouching in the trees, Eli put the binoculars up to his eyes. Lucy and Greg made their way across the grass to the gazebo. They stopped for a moment to talk to a young woman that Lucy seemed to know. Greg's body language, all but stepping between Lucy and the girl, suggested impatience. Finally, he tugged on Lucy's arm.

Peterson clicked off several shots on the camera.

Rain had begun to sprinkle as the couple slipped under the gazebo. Lucy pulled plastic containers out of the picnic basket. Greg paced, placed his hands on his hips, looked at the sky and then threw up his arms. Though Eli could not hear the conversation, the body language suggested that Greg was upset and Lucy was placating him.

Eli handed Peterson the binoculars and took the camera. "You don't have to hear a conversation to discern personality traits. What can you conclude about our suspect from watching him?"

Greg jabbed his finger at the downpour of rain, and Lucy wrapped a hand around his wrist and pointed back at the picnic basket. Greg pulled away and crossed his arms glaring skyward.

Peterson peered through the binoculars. "The guy doesn't seem very relaxed."

Lucy relented and gathered the items back into the basket. Even at this distance, Greg's scowl was obvious as they made their way back to the car. Were they leaving because of the rain or was there some other reason? Greg had glanced toward the trees several times, but Eli doubted they had been spotted.

Lucy smiled and laughed as she made her way across the lot. At one point, she turned her head up toward the sky, taking a moment to allow the rain to sprinkle on her face.

Eli spoke through the two-way to O'Bannon. "You can get to your car faster than we can. Tail them. Keep us advised of their 10-22."

He watched as O'Bannon lumbered to his feet. Snails moved faster. Eli signaled to Peterson that they needed to get going. He pointed through the middle of the park, indicating the direction he wanted Peterson to go.

Eli followed the tree line as long as he could before cutting toward the pavilion. Greg's Buick pulled out onto the road. No sign of O'Bannon's car yet.

The road and lot slipped out of view as he moved behind the pavilion.

Eli's heart beat a little faster. Where was Greg taking

Lucy? They could have stayed dry under the gazebo. Maybe the place wasn't secluded enough for Jackson. O'Bannon was just leaving the lot when Eli came around the side of the pavilion. A little time delay with a rolling tail made sense, but O'Bannon seemed to be taking his sweet time. Peterson was already behind the wheel of his car.

Eli slipped in and peered through the windshield. O'Bannon turned left at the top of the road that led out of the park.

"Let's wait just a minute here," Eli instructed. O'Bannon's car slipped out of view. Eli clicked on the radio. "Do you have a visual on the car?"

"No," O'Bannon snapped. "I'll let you know when I do."

Eli addressed Peterson. "Our target could have gone either way. Let's take a right at the top of this road."

Their car passed a convenience store. Downtown Mountain Springs with its turn-of-the-century brick buildings came into view.

Peterson drove slowly past a drugstore and an attorney's office. "Maybe they just decided to catch a meal in town, huh?"

"Where do people take a date around here?"

Peterson snorted. "They usually take them out of town. Here, besides the fast-food places, there's Lydia's Café, and the Oasis bar serves steaks and burgers."

"Let's go there." They drove by the parking lots of both Lydia's and the Oasis. No sign of the Buick. The rising sense of panic returned. O'Bannon should have checked in by now.

Peterson pulled out of the Oasis parking lot while Eli scanned the street for Greg's car.

"What now?"

"Any other date hangouts?"

"Not sure about that. I've been married for ten years. When the weather is nice the mountains and lakes are a big draw."

That was what Eli was afraid of.

Eli's radio clicked.

"They just turned into the Hyalite Hills," O'Bannon said. "Doesn't she live up here? Looks like their date is over. You want me to keep following them?"

Eli relaxed. "Watch the road and let me know when Jackson pulls out and where he is headed."

Eli and Peterson returned to the police station so Eli could retrieve his car. After he told Peterson he had done a good job, Eli got into his car and drove to the local market to get supplies for his new place. He was in the checkout line at the grocery store when his cell phone rang.

"O'Bannon here. Jackson still hasn't pulled out. I'm off shift in thirty minutes."

Eli rolled his eyes. Heaven forbid that O'Bannon should stay longer than his shift required. He was going to have to talk to the chief about O'Bannon's attitude. "I can handle it."

Eli got in his car and drove back to the duplex. Both Lucy and Greg's cars were still here. So the date wasn't over. Tension snaked around Eli's torso.

He grabbed his groceries and walked up the stairs to the porch. While he stuck his key in the lock, he leaned back to see if he could catch any movement in Lucy's place. The curtains were drawn, allowing only a thin sliver of light to escape.

He stepped inside his own place and paced the floor. He'd rest easy if he knew she was okay. Greg wasn't likely to try anything if he knew Eli was next door. All he needed was an excuse to knock on her door.

Rain sprinkled from the sky and lightning flashed some distance away as he made his way across the wooden floorboards of the wraparound porch. He banged on the door.

He heard footsteps and then Lucy swung the door open. Behind her, he could see that a picnic had been set up on the coffee table. Greg sat cross-legged, munching on a sandwich. Soft jazzy music spilled from the CD player.

The pinched expression on Lucy's face told him she was not happy about the interruption, or maybe being with Greg was making her tense. "You're back."

"Work took less time than I thought it would."

She studied him long enough for him to become nervous. He shifted his weight from foot to foot. She'd changed out of the wet blue sundress into a silky floral dress. The heart-shaped neckline made her neck look swanlike. For a woman who spent a lot of time outdoors, her skin was like porcelain.

Greg cleared his throat and scratched the back of his head. His stiff posture and the way he kept clearing his throat indicated he resented the interruption.

Eli turned toward Lucy. "Sorry to bother you. I thought I would come over and get that written description of your stolen items."

Her lips parted slightly. "I think I left it up in the loft."

She backed away from the door, which allowed him to step inside.

"Let me go look for it." Lucy tromped up the stairs to the loft. She lifted papers and put them back on the table. Upstairs, cupboards screeched open and shut with the slapping sound of wood against wood.

Maybe he could learn something about Greg without him realizing he was being questioned. Eli rocked on his feet and shoved his hands in his pockets, gauging Greg's reaction.

Greg Jackson took a sip of iced tea. "So you like Mountain Springs so far?" Despite the friendliness of the question, his expression was harder than stone and his words could freeze water. He really didn't like having Eli around.

"You and Lucy seem pretty serious."

Greg tossed a paper napkin on the table. "Not as serious as I would like to be."

"Dating anyone else from the online service?"

Greg's chin jerked up. "Lucy told *you* we found each other on the service?"

Of course it didn't make sense to Greg that a first-day renter could know such a detail about Lucy's life, but Greg's instant suspicion seemed a little over the top.

Eli nodded. "She and Nelson were talking about it this afternoon when we were repairing the back porch."

"Oh, I see. You helped her with *that* repair." Greg set his bottle of iced tea on the table. "If you must know, I've met some real nice Christian women through the service. But they all seem kind of…desperate to be married…not an attractive quality."

Eli paced across the living room to the kitchen. "Lucy's not that way?" He did a quick survey of the food laid out on the coffee table. Probably nothing there that could be easily poisoned.

Upstairs, Lucy shuffled through her pile of papers again.

Greg shot to his feet. "Do you need some help up there, Lucy?" He cast a furtive glower toward Eli.

The longer Eli talked with Greg, the less he liked the idea of him being alone with Lucy.

Lucy leaned on the railing and peered down. "I got it under control." She disappeared from view. A moment later, she swept down the stairs. "I can't find it." It sounded as if she was demanding something, rather than making a statement.

"It would be helpful in recovering the stolen items." Eli's mind scanned through the possibilities of what he could say or do so Greg would leave. Maybe if he just stayed long enough.

She put up her hand. "It makes me crazy when I can't find something."

Now she was upset. Eli pressed his teeth together. He had firmly established himself in the role of the rude neighbor, the unintended consequence of his desire to protect Lucy. In the long run, the choice might defeat his purpose altogether. It certainly wasn't making her like or trust him any better.

She walked over to the kitchen and scanned the countertops. "I started working on it in here, then I went upstairs and then…" In a rush of energy, she opened a kitchen drawer and held up a piece of paper. "Aha."

Obviously not happy, Greg smashed a cookie into the coffee table until it was nothing but crumbs. His mouth was drawn into a tight line.

She returned to the living room and shoved the piece of paper toward him. "Told you I knew where it was."

The subtext of her words was obvious: *now you can go.*

"You were smart to have your picnic inside." Eli angled his body toward the window. "That storm is really picking up." He just couldn't leave her alone with this guy.

Lucy's glance flickered from Eli, then to Greg. She had probably picked up on the smoldering ember of antagonism between the two men. "We actually drove into town and then realized it wasn't going to work." She glanced at Greg.

Eli planted his feet. He stared at the piece of paper. She'd provided an extensive written description and drawn pictures of the jewelry pieces. "Nice drawings."

She smiled at his comment. "We can't all be van Gogh."

Eli laughed. The moment of humor sparked a connection between them.

Greg cleared his throat and spat out his words. "I should probably just be going. I still have to drive back home tonight."

"No, Greg. Please stay." Her plea sounded half-hearted.

Despite the triumph he felt at getting Greg to leave,

Eli kept his tone friendly. "Sounds like a good idea. Maybe you can beat the storm before it gets too bad."

Greg grabbed his coat. "Thanks for the nice picnic." He kissed Lucy on the cheek.

She tensed when he kissed her on the cheek. Nothing in her body language suggested Lucy had anything but friendly feelings for Greg.

Both Lucy and Eli stared at the floor while Greg's footsteps tapped on the wood, the door swung open and closed. Outside, his car started up.

"Looks like you had a pretty nice picnic."

"Things worked out okay." Her voice dropped half an octave. "Despite the interruption." She gathered plates and glasses off the coffee table.

He picked up some of the empty plastic containers and followed her into the kitchen. "He seems to like you quite a bit." If Lucy's reaction to the kiss was any indication, maybe this was going to be their last date.

Lucy yanked the plastic containers out of his hands. "Mr. Hawkins, I don't appreciate the way you are probing into my life, and I don't know why you felt the need to cut my date short."

She wasn't angry, just upset. He didn't blame her. He wondered if he wasn't driving her toward Greg with all his objections and interferences. Maybe there was a way to smooth things over. "I was thinking about your robbery. Sometimes thieves pawn things off after they steal them. Maybe tomorrow we could check some of the pawn-shops together. You know what the fishing pole and jewelry looked like."

"I really don't have time to do that. You are the

policeman. You have the detailed descriptions." She slammed a cupboard door shut.

There was nothing more he could say. "I'll get that rent and deposit check to you." He turned to go.

Her words pelted against his back as he made his way toward the door. "You can just bring it by tomorrow or, better yet, tape it to my door."

Eli trudged back to his side of the house. Rain slashed down in straight lines instead of in drops. Lightning flashed in the sky, followed almost immediately by thunder that shook the house. Eli stepped back into his side of the duplex. He had managed to keep Lucy safe for one night, but he had done nothing to win her trust. Her overt rejection of him stung in a way he hadn't expected.

Might as well concentrate on work, the part of his life that made sense. He pulled his laptop out of his briefcase and set it up on the table by the window, where he had a clear view of the storm. Eli clicked through his e-mails. Each surveillance team was required to send reports to him for review.

Officer Smith's date with one of the other suspects must have been uneventful. If anything had happened, he would have gotten a call right away. They had begun to compile photographs of the men with their dates.

What had he learned about Greg Jackson in their short interaction? Greg made a pretense of being a go-with-the-flow country boy, but he had a moodiness that he tried to cover up. An underlying irritation peeked out when plans got disrupted, and he seemed unnecessarily jealous. Not exactly what you would call hard evidence, but it did match the part of the profile that suggested their killer was controlling.

He had a gut feeling about Greg Jackson, but arrests couldn't be made based on feelings. As far as he knew, Lucy had not connected with any of the other suspects on the online service. Yet, given her appearance, she was a likely next target.

All the other victims had lived alone and been only loosely attached to family members. The victims had not been talkative about their romantic lives. When friends and family members were interviewed, they could only offer vague personality and character descriptions of the men the victims had been dating. Based on that, the killer probably dated his victims only a few times. Long enough to start to learn someone's habits, but not long enough to be introduced to friends and family members. None of the victims' computers revealed any e-mail exchanges that could have pointed to a killer. This guy was careful.

Lucy had friends, Nelson and Heather, but the only family member she had mentioned was a brother. She talked about him in such cryptic terms that Eli wondered if they had had a falling out or if something had happened to the brother.

He flipped through files, rereading the interviews done with people who had known the victims. He made a call to a local officer in a town called Cragmore where they would be doing surveillance tomorrow night. Eli sat back in his chair.

He stared at the rain falling outside. It was coming down so heavily that he could barely make out the trees that surrounded Lucy's place. He pulled a piece of paper

out of his briefcase and wrote out the names of each of
the four suspects. In list form, he scribbled everything
he knew about each suspect. All of the men were in a
profession that allowed for a level of travel. Both Greg
Jackson and another suspect, Neil Fender, had minor
police records.

Wind rattled the windows, and the thunder sounded
like it was on top of the house. Eli browned some ham-
burger he had picked up in town and tossed in tomatoes and cheese. He ate directly out of the pan while he
stood at the window, thinking.

He made a decision to keep up the surveillance for
a few more weeks and then reassess their whole ap-
proach. If they didn't see a pattern of someone who was
consistently picking dark-haired, blue-eyed women, it
would be a waste of manpower and resources to continue. What he liked about the setup was that it allowed
him to keep the potential victims safe.

The truth was they could plan until they were blue
in the face. What usually broke any investigation was
sheer luck. Sometimes, a suspect did something revealing while under surveillance, or a neighbor noticed suspicious activity. Even though investigative diligence had
to happen, it was almost always the piece of information that they accidentally stumbled on in the course of
investigation that brought things together.

Eli sauntered back into the kitchen and placed the
empty pan in the sink. He grinned. He had no dish-
washing soap. What would Lucy say if he knocked on
her door again? He settled into the chair in the living
room. Wind shook the window and the rain pattered so

intensely on the roof it sounded like pebbles bouncing around in a can.

A thudding noise caused him to jump. Lucy burst out of her side of the duplex. Through the distortion created by the storm, he could barely make out that she was pulling on a rain jacket as she raced to her van. What on earth was she doing going out in this kind of storm?

FIVE

Adrenaline surged through Lucy as she raced out of her house and jumped off the porch. The sky was already dark. The wind blew so hard, the rain came at her sideways.

When she got to her car, she fumbled in her pocket for the key.

Maybe she should get someone to help her. The call about her boat from her down-river neighbor had come in less than five minutes ago. That was five minutes of valuable time she'd already lost. She touched her cell phone in the pocket of her raincoat. She'd have to call as she was driving. Who would come out in this kind of storm anyway? Who was close enough?

Eli was right next door. She brushed the idea away. They were not off to a very good start at being neighborly. He had tried her patience, and she had been abrupt with him. The look of hurt on his face when she'd said she wasn't interested in going to the pawnshops had put a barb in her heart, but she didn't want to do anything to make him think it was okay to interfere in her life. Best keep her distance where Eli Hawkins was concerned.

I know I have a hard time asking for help, but please, Lord, send someone to give me a hand with this.

Lucy dropped her keys as she pulled them out of her pocket. With the rain pelting her coat, she groped on the muddy ground for a moment before she found them. She climbed into the cab of her van, wiping her muddy hands on her jeans.

She jammed the key in the ignition. A tap at her window caused her to turn suddenly. She rolled down the window.

Eli, rain beating hard against his face, stood there. "Where are you headed?"

"One of my drift boats broke free. I have to get it back." The kids she'd taught today must have been careless when they'd tied it to the dock.

"In this weather? That sounds dangerous."

She wasn't about to let him talk her out of this. "That boat is my livelihood." She leaned toward the steering wheel, turning the key in the ignition. She spoke above the sound of the engine. "I can't wait until the sun is shining and risk it being battered to pieces or lost."

He crossed his arms over his chest, obviously chilled from the cold. "You'll need help."

That much was true. "I got it under control." The last person she needed help from was a date destroyer like Eli Hawkins. She would rather do this herself.

Eli blinked the rain out of his eyes. "Okay."

He disappeared. Lucy shifted into Reverse. The passenger-side door opened, and he slid in. He combed his rain-slicked hair back from his forehead. "Let's go."

How nervy. She backed the van up and turned it around. "Get out of my car."

"Could you be honest with yourself for one moment?" He leaned toward her. "You can't do this alone. Every second we spend debating might cost you your boat."

She gritted her teeth and pressed the accelerator. He was right, of course. "The neighbors said they saw it lodged in a bunch of branches that have built up on a slow part of the river." She turned onto a dirt road that led into thick forest. "If it breaks free, it's going to be almost impossible to recover." They both bounced in their seats as she accelerated over the bumpy road.

Eli gripped the dashboard. "How are you going to know where to find the boat?" His voice vibrated from the jarring motion of the car.

"The pile of branches they are talking about is in an eddy just before Spanish Point." Talking about this made her even more anxious.

"Impressive, you know every bend and branch in the river."

She'd grown up on the river. Eddies, rapids and bends were like street signs to her. "River gets real rough after that. In this storm, it will be even rougher." Her voice wavered. Her business was a bootstrap operation as it was. She couldn't lose that boat.

Lucy steered the van out of the trees, and the river below came into view.

Eli craned his neck to look in the back of the vehicle, where she stored her equipment for guiding and teaching. "Are we going to need any of that stuff?"

Lucy glanced at Eli. He raised an eyebrow. Now she was impressed. "Way to think ahead." She turned her attention to the rough road in front of her. The vehicle shifted side to side in the mud. "Grab two pairs of waders. The river is going to be cold."

He unclicked his seat belt and crawled into the back. "You have everything but the kitchen sink in here."

When she looked over her shoulder, he was holding up her supply of dehydrated food. The jerking motion of the car on the rough road caused him to sway. "I'm responsible for people who may not have a lot of wilderness experience. I have to plan for every contingency."

She turned off the road. The van lumbered down the hill toward the river. She'd be able to get her vehicle within a hundred yards of the river. She bounced in her seat.

Eli let out a *whoa!*

In the rearview mirror, she watched Eli rubbing his head. She cringed. "Sorry, I can't make it any smoother."

"No problem." He flopped a life jacket over the passenger-side seat. "Will we need this?"

He sure wanted to bring a lot to rescue a boat. "Take it if you want. The river's not that deep. Those things slow you down. The big issue is the cold. Get the waders."

Lucy edged the van as close to the river as she dared, not wanting to risk getting stuck. She braked, pushed the door open and raced to the back of her vehicle. She flung the door open. Eli handed her the waders and jumped out.

The river roared in her ears. Rain poured from the sky.

"Got these for us, too." He held up two flashlights.

"Good thinking." His efficiency was admirable. She took a flashlight, flipped open a storage box in the van and pulled out a rain poncho. He was probably already chilled from the rain, but there was no time to retrieve dry clothes for him. "Put this on. It's easy to slip off when you put on your waders."

Rivulets of rain trickled down his face. "Should have remembered a coat on my way out of the house."

She patted his shoulder before grabbing a coil of rope off a hook in the car. She scrambled down the hill yelling over her shoulder. "It's slick. Walk sideways. We'll put the waders on at the bottom of the hill."

Halfway to the bank, she swept her light across the river. At this time of year, it stayed light late into the evening, but a covering of gray clouds dimmed her view. The flashlight had been a good idea. The boat was still in the pile of sticks across the river. Hard waves threatened to break it loose.

Eli came up beside her. Without a word, he slipped the rope off her shoulder.

She didn't realize how much the weight had been slowing her until he took it. "Thanks."

Raindrops, made sharp by the intense wind, jabbed at her face and hands. Lucy and Eli came to the riverbank. She kicked off her shoes and eased into her waders. Her raincoat had kept her top half pretty dry, but her jeans were already soaked, which made the process of getting in the waders even more arduous. She clicked the straps over her shoulders. Eli struggled with the drawstring around the waist of his waders. "Here." She pulled him toward her by his shoulder straps and tightened his drawstring. He stood five inches taller than she. His breath caressed her cheek. She tilted her head, and when she looked into his eyes, she completely forgot what she had intended to say.

Eli grinned, his face inches from hers. "You were probably going to bark an order at me," he offered. His tone was lighthearted.

Lucy stepped back to escape the magnetic pull of his gaze. "Why, ah...why don't you find a tree to tie that rope to?" she whispered.

Eli unrolled the rope and glanced up and down the bank. "Wouldn't it make more sense to find a bridge and pull the boat out that way, so we don't have to cross the river?"

Time was of the essence. Why was he trying to change the plan? "The bridge is five miles away on rough road. This is the best way to do it." She pointed at a tree about ten feet upriver. "That one looks strong enough."

He darted to the tree and secured the rope. She liked the way so little instruction was required for them to get this job done...once he stopped arguing with her.

He trotted back toward her. "I'll go in."

She shook her head and took the rope. "I'm the one who knows this river. I'll need your strength at the other end to pull the boat across stream."

He opened his mouth and lifted his chin as if preparing to argue, but then he bent toward her and squeezed her upper arm. "Are you sure you won't take the life jacket?"

The level of concern he showed caused her heart to swell. She wasn't used to someone caring so much about her safety. "It's all the way back up at the van. We need to get this done."

He nodded.

She lunged into the water. The waders insulated her from the cold, but the beating waves nearly knocked her over. Water chugged and surged around her. At its deepest, this part of the river only came up to her waist. The strength of the waves, though, was more than she had been prepared for. She forded the river by pressing into the water, lifting her feet as little as possible.

There was something reassuring about seeing Eli on the bank, holding the other end of the rope. He stepped a few feet into the river.

The boat, wobbling from the impact of the waves, was within ten feet. The felt bottoms of her wader boots prevented her from slipping. A final lunge put her within reach of the boat. She lifted the rope to tie it to the boat. Bending her frozen fingers took a degree of effort. She tied the rope through the metal loop on the boat's bow.

The strength of the undertow vacuumed around her legs. She grabbed the rim of the boat to steady herself. She turned and signaled with her flashlight for Eli to start pulling the boat in. She shoved her flashlight into the chest pocket of the waders. Her arm muscles strained as she gripped the rim of the boat to keep it from drifting too far downriver.

Her leg muscles tired from fighting the strength of the water. She gasped for air, leaning harder against the boat than she should have.

Eli stepped farther into the river and continued to pull on the line.

The angle of the rope indicated that she had drifted some distance downriver. The current was stronger than she had anticipated. Not taking the life jacket had been foolish. She knew better. She could be so stubborn sometimes. Maybe she hadn't taken the life jacket because she didn't want Eli to be right.

She adjusted her grip on the rim of the boat and trudged forward. The water felt like marble around her legs. Her shoe slipped between two rocks and stuck. Fighting exhaustion, she struggled to free herself. She was wedged in tightly, unable to move much at all. Waves pushed against her as she angled her upper body in an effort to twist the ankle loose.

She pivoted, swayed sideways and fell into the water. Her foot broke free, but she plunged under water.

Freezing water chilled her toes and moved up her calves. In her haste, she hadn't secured the drawstring of her waders and now they filled with icy water. All this weight would make her sink like an anchor. She took in a breath that was mostly water.

She'd lost all sense of where she was. Water covered her head, surrounded her, pushed down on her face. She flailed her arms. She had to get out of these waders or she'd drown. She pushed her head above water, gasped in a breath and went under again. Her hands were like dough as she fumbled with the zipper and straps of the waders. She was so cold, even bending her fingers took effort. She broke the surface of the water to steal another breath. Dark waves battered against her head; she could see nothing else.

Again the water overwhelmed her as its weight pushed her toward the river bottom. Air, she needed air. Lucy fought off the fog that entered her mind. She had to get out of here, had to free herself. Energy drained from her body as she pressed cold fingers against one of the click-in shoulder straps.

Like lights being clicked off in a hallway, her systems were shutting down one by one. Movement, the lifting of her arms through the water, slowed. She couldn't feel her legs. Her mind could not form a thought. She reached out for what she hoped was the boat. Nothing.

She could not move her arms or her fingers. Still underwater, she lay back, drifting toward the darkness she had resisted, growing numb.

SIX

His heart pounding, Eli lifted Lucy out of the water. Her head swayed to one side and her eyes were closed. He repeated her name several times and patted her cheek. Lucy took in a ragged breath. She opened her eyes.

"There you are," he whispered.

He placed a knife underneath one of her shoulder straps and cut. She jerked slightly when the cold metal dug into her skin. Water from his hair dripped on her face. She blinked and looked at him with glazed eyes. At least she was conscious.

He cut the other strap and tried to pull the waders off by tugging downward. The water crested around them.

She was too weak and too weighed down to make it to shore, and he couldn't get her out of the waders until she was out of the water. He had to get her into the boat, but she wouldn't be able to lift her legs to climb in by herself. She swayed slightly in his arms.

He leaned close so she would hear him above the roar of the river. His lips brushed her ear. "I'm going to let go of you just for a second, so I can lift you into the boat."

Lucy nodded. Eli slipped his hand free of her waist and then grabbed her arm and draped it over his shoulder. She grabbed the rim of the boat and tumbled in while he pushed from behind.

She lay with her back against the boat, looking up at him. With his knife, Eli cut down the side of the waders and water whooshed into the boat.

Rain sprinkled against her face. Her breathing was labored. She'd been responsive to his commands, but the unfocused look in her eyes told him she was traumatized. She was dangerously close to hypothermia.

Eli jumped back into the water and guided the boat to shore. Water had matted his hair.

"We're pretty close to shore." He shouted to be heard above the clamor of the rapids. He touched a hand to her cheek. "It won't be long now."

She mouthed the words, "Thank you."

They reached the shore. After helping Lucy out of the boat, he tugged it high up on the rocky beach, where there was no danger of the waves catching it and pulling it back into the current. Lucy hadn't brought a trailer; she must have intended to retrieve the boat later.

By the time Eli guided Lucy back up to the van, she was shivering uncontrollably and slurring her words, the early signs of hypothermia. He had all but carried her up the hill. For the fourth time, Lucy had asked about the boat.

He cupped his hands on her cheeks. "The boat is fine. We need to get you dry and warm." He leaned a little closer, a gesture that forced her to look in his eyes. "You need to get out of those wet clothes. Do you understand me?" He punctuated each word, hoping she was not beyond understanding his instructions.

She blinked several times before nodding.

He opened the back end of the van, searching through the boxes of supplies until he found a shirt and pair of pants. "This is the best equipped vehicle I ever saw."

"My clients sometimes need a change of clothes." Her voice vibrated from her shivering. "They fall in the river."

Her answers were becoming more coherent, a good sign. He handed her the clothes. "You can change in the back here. I'll close the doors." Her hands were still trembling and her lips had no color. "Or do you need me to help?"

"I can do it." She had already slipped into the back of the van.

Her response probably had less to do with modesty than her wanting to do everything without help. Even in her weakened state, Lucy was fiercely independent.

He closed the back of the van and turned away. Water drops pelted his plastic raincoat. He shook his head. Lucy had forgotten to tie her own drawstring because she had helped him with his. Why hadn't he been paying more attention? He could have prevented her waders from filling with water.

He slipped out of his waders. The rest of the gear from Lucy's vehicle had served him well. Even though his clothes underneath were damp, he was cold but not frozen. The darkness of the sky indicated that the storm was going to last for some time. Lucy was still not out of danger. He had to get her home and warmed up.

When Lucy tapped on the back window, he whirled

around and stalked back to the van. He swung the doors open. Lucy had almost no color in her face. He masked the panic he felt and steadied his voice. "How are we doing?"

"I—I—I—can't get these snapped." She held up trembling white fingers. She'd donned the pullover flannel shirt but was struggling with the snaps on the down vest he had grabbed.

Again, he swallowed hard and managed a smile that didn't give away how concerned he was about her condition. "Let me get that for you." She gazed up at him like a child getting her winter coat fastened as he worked. He pressed the final snap at her neck. His face was inches from hers. Her breathing was shallow, slow. He touched her cold cheek with the back of his hand. "Maybe we should get you to the hospital."

She shook her head. "No, no, I'm fine."

"I don't know about that." He shone the flashlight on her face. At least her pupils weren't dilated. He set the flashlight down and grabbed her hands, enveloping them in his own. "You are shaking like a leaf."

"I've dealt with this before."

"In other people, not in yourself." Her hands were like frozen stones in his.

She laughed. The out-of-place social response told him that she still wasn't beyond total hypothermia. A thermal blanket caught his eye. He grabbed it, tore open the package it was in and unfolded the covering, which looked as if it was made out of ultrathin flexible tinfoil. He wrapped it around her.

"Please, just take me home." She tilted her head. Her blue eyes filled with vulnerability.

He brushed a strand of long hair off her face and spoke gently. "Did you leave the keys in the car?"

She nodded, shivering.

Shielding her from the rain with the blanket, he helped her into the passenger side of the van.

He started the vehicle, and it lumbered up the hill. Eli kept one eye on the road and one eye on Lucy. She slumped forward slightly. The rough road caused both of them to jiggle side to side. He could monitor her condition by keeping her talking.

"So you lived in Mountain Springs your whole life?"

"Yes." She stared at the floor of the van, her voice barely above a whisper.

Not much of an answer. He pulled up onto the smoother road. He asked her several more questions. She offered only one-word answers or no answer at all.

Eli struggled against the growing tension in his shoulders and back. Her skin was still whiter than white. "Got any family here?"

She rubbed her temple. "Grandpa and Grandma and Mom are all gone."

Minutes passed as he drove. The headlights cut a swath of illumination through the twilight.

The road curved, forcing him to concentrate on his driving. Tension squeezed his rib cage. He angled the vehicle into a tight curve. In his peripheral vision, it looked as though she was slumped against the window. "So what has the fishing been like this year?" No response. He gripped the steering wheel tighter. "Lucy, I just—"

She took in a sudden breath and repositioned herself in the seat. "You just want to keep asking me questions to make sure I'm not slipping away." She lifted her head. "You know, I took first aid classes, too. I am just weak from what I went through."

Relief spread through him. Strength had returned to her voice. He reached over and squeezed her shoulder. "Back among the living."

She drew the blanket tighter around her. "Still really cold and kind of numb, but I don't feel like my brain is made of gelatin anymore."

"We'll get you warmed up." He hit the blinker and turned onto the gravel road that led to her place.

"I was stupid. I should have taken the life jacket you offered." She gathered the Mylar blanket at her neck. "I can be a little…pigheaded sometimes."

"You were just very focused on getting that boat." Mistakes had been made on both their parts. He should have insisted he be the one to go into the river. He brought the van to a stop by the duplex.

A few stars peeked out from behind the storm clouds as the rain fell. While she fumbled with her seat belt, he got out and raced to the passenger side. He opened the door, stepped up on the sideboard, reached across her and undid the seat belt. Her face brushed against his chest as he straightened his back. He held out a steadying hand. To his surprise, she didn't protest. She took his hand and jumped down from the van seat. She wobbled. He placed a supportive arm around her waist and helped her up the stairs to the porch.

He lifted the keychain he'd pulled from the car. "One of these opens your door?"

She nodded, and he placed the keys in her open palm. "I never used to have to lock my doors until the robbery." She found the right key, but fumbled when she tried to place it in the keyhole.

His hand grazed the silky surface of her palm as he took the key and twisted it in the lock.

"Guess I'm still kind of shaky. My fingers are really stiff," she said.

Was that embarrassment he heard in her voice? "You've been through a lot. You don't need to feel bad about needing help." He pushed the door open, allowing her to walk by herself.

"I'm cold." She rubbed her forearms.

"You know not to get into a hot bath or just warm your limbs." He turned a half circle in the living room.

"I had that survival training, too, remember." She collapsed on the couch. "I know I have to get my core warmed up. Internal body temp has probably dropped a couple degrees. Blah, blah, blah."

Eli chuckled. Despite the weakness of her voice, there was a little bit of that sassy, defiant Lucy in her remark, the part of her he was starting to like quite a bit.

She locked him in her gaze. "What are you smiling about?"

"Nothing. I'm glad you're feeling well enough to argue with me."

He found a space heater and a blanket and brought them back into the living room. He studied her as she wrapped the blanket around herself. She lifted her head. He shifted in the chair. "We had a little bit of a scare there, huh?"

"A little one." She peered at him with those blue eyes. Even as they spoke, he could feel the walls going up around her. Why was she so afraid to be vulnerable? "You going to be okay?"

"I'll be fine," she said curtly.

Impulsively, he breached the short distance between the couch and chair. He touched two fingers to her neck. She didn't draw back from him. Their heads touched.

"I think it is okay," she whispered.

His fingers lingered on her neck. He breathed in her sweet scent. He longed to kiss her.

He pulled his hand away from her neck. What was he doing? He scooted back to the couch. "Heart rate feels normal." He swallowed to get the lump out of his throat. He'd be lying to himself if he said his action had been purely for medical reasons. Lucy Kimbol was getting to him, which made no sense at all, since she was the most guarded woman he had ever met.

He rose to his feet and paced. Now his heart was racing. "All the same, I might give you a call a couple times tonight." He was talking a mile a minute. Stunned by the power of his attraction to her, he strode to the door.

She followed him with the blanket still around her shoulders. "Eli, thank you." She stood about two feet from him. "My friends all say I'm not very good at asking people for help. Sometimes it's nice to just have someone who gives it without being asked."

His hand twisted the doorknob. She'd called him Eli. The sound of his name on her lips caused heat to rise up in his face. "Is that what I did?"

She nodded, tilting her head, eyes clear and vulnerable again.

He couldn't bring himself to look at her. Afraid the lingering smolder of emotion might ignite. He swung the door open and stepped out onto the porch. He was just in Mountain Springs to do a job, to catch a killer, to prevent any more deaths…to keep Lucy safe. He'd be leaving when the job was done; emotional entanglements were a bad idea.

Lucy had followed him out onto the porch. Her proximity made his skin tingle.

She hugged herself for warmth. "Maybe we should go and look for my fly rod at the pawnshops. I'm sorry I dismissed the idea."

"I gotta work tomorrow." The porch light washed over her, warming her skin to a golden tone. Her parted lips and long neck enticed him. He could not bring himself to say no to her. "Maybe late in the day."

"That will work. I'll be taking some clients out on the river for a half-day workshop." She stepped toward him. "I'll knock on your door when I get back."

The energy of attraction was like warm honey underneath his skin. He reached up to touch her cheek. His fingers electrified with blue heat. "The color's returning to your skin." His reason for touching her had nothing to do with her medical condition.

She leaned into his touch. "Am I going to make it?"

He drew back. It was wrong to play these games with a woman's heart when his own emotions had taken him by surprise. He stepped away from her. "You'll be just fine," he said in the best clinical tone he could manage. He needed to be alone, to sort through things.

His boots pounded on the wood of the porch as he made his way to his door. Lucy was still standing beneath the light, looking beautiful with the silver sheath around her, when he slipped into his side of the duplex.

Eli closed the door and leaned against it. He wasn't going to be able to sleep. He did some push-ups, made himself a snack and then reviewed the files from the case. He combed through the photos of men and women holding hands, sitting with heads close together at restaurant tables, going into movie theaters. He slammed the file shut. Not what he wanted to think about right now.

He sat down in his living-room chair and kicked off his wet boots. The storm still raged outside, rattling the windows. Even the thought of Lucy made his heart rate speed up. He crossed his arms over his chest and stared at the wall. The hypnotic rhythm of the rain lulled him. Eventually, his head fell forward and he slept.

He jerked awake. His watch said it was midnight. He had promised Lucy he would call her. He doubted there was any danger of her slipping into unconsciousness. Even as he pressed the numbers on the phone, he knew it was just an excuse to hear her voice.

When she didn't pick up on the fifth ring, panic flooded through him all over again. He let it ring several more times before hanging up. He read some e-mails, paced and tried calling her again. Still no answer. The phone was right there by the couch. Even if she had fallen asleep, it would have woken her up by now.

He looked at the darkness outside. A car could have pulled up while he was sleeping and he wouldn't have heard it. Someone could park on the road just beyond the forest and walk in, just as the thief had done that night.

He swung his door open and stomped barefoot across the porch. Through the window, his could see the couch and the blanket, but no Lucy. He scanned the area around her house. Nothing.

Eli pounded hard on the door. Feeling a rising sense of danger, he thought about breaking down the door.

Just as he was about to put his shoulder full force into the door, it swung open. Lucy stood there. She touched her open palm to her heart. "You scared me half to death. I saw a flash of movement by the window from the loft. I thought the thief had come back."

Now he felt stupid for his overreaction. He tipped his head toward his shoulder and shrugged. "You didn't answer your phone."

"I couldn't sleep, so I decided to tie some flies and get some paperwork done." She held up a set of headphones. "They help me focus. When you didn't call, I thought maybe you had fallen asleep."

"I dozed off." He raised his arm to rest it against one of the porch posts but missed and stumbled forward. Since when had he become such a klutz?

When he righted himself, Lucy surveyed him head to toe. "Thanks for checking on me." She stepped back across her threshold. "Maybe I will be able to sleep now."

The door eased shut. Lucy made him feel like a bumbling seventeen-year-old. This sudden attraction had blindsided him.

Eli stood waiting for the energy of the moment to subside before he ambled back to his side of the house.

He didn't have to act on the attraction. He was headed back to Spokane when this investigation was done. A relationship would be cruel to Lucy and would make it hard for him to do his job. Lucy would just have to put him in her famous "just friends" category.

SEVEN

Lucy walked toward the pawnshop a few paces ahead of Eli. She turned, waiting for him to catch up. The navy T-shirt he wore accentuated his chest and shoulder muscles. His brown hair, with the afternoon sun creating golden highlights in it, looked soft enough to touch. Eli held the door for her, and she stepped across the threshold. A pencil-thin man with a tuft of curly brown hair and large buggy eyes stood behind the counter. He lifted his head when the bell dinged. Recognition spread across his face.

"Lucy, good to see you."

"Hey, Robert." Lucy made her way past a display of video games.

She'd had a night to think about Eli. He had nothing to do with the Mountain Springs Police Department and what had happened with her brother four years ago. She had let her past experience cloud her view of him. His willingness to help her and pull her out of the river spoke volumes about what kind of person he was.

Robert placed a trombone in its case and snapped it shut. "How has your spring been going? Fish bitin'?"

"It's not the fish I need to bite, it's the clients." Lucy lifted a fly rod off the wall where it was leaning along with an assortment of nets and poles. "I'm managing to keep the bills paid at least."

"You lookin' for some more rods for your students? Got a nice batch of them from a widow who cleaned out her garage a while ago." Robert stepped to the end of the counter.

Lucy placed the fly rod back against the wall. "No, that's not why we're here."

Creases formed on Robert's forehead as he watched Eli wander around the pawnshop. Staring at people who were not locals was the hobby of every Mountain Springs native, but Lucy worried that it would be disconcerting to Eli. "Robert, this is Officer Eli Hawkins. He's renting the other side of my duplex. He's helping me look for some items that got stolen from my place."

Robert rubbed under his chin, which drew attention to his large Adam's apple. "I heard about that." He placed the trombone case on a shelf behind him. "What got stolen?"

Lucy described each item that had been taken. Even talking about the jewelry caused her spirits to drop. "It was mostly costume jewelry. My grandmother's ring did have a small ruby in it. Maybe the thief grabbed them because they looked like they were worth something."

Eli crossed his arms and rested them on the glass of the jewelry case. "I don't see anything remotely close to what you described."

Lucy edged toward him and stared into the case. She scanned each piece of jewelry, and then stood up straight. She strained to keep the disappointment out of her voice. "It was a long shot, anyway."

Eli clamped a supportive hand on her shoulder. "Don't give up so easy. This is only the first pawnshop we've come to."

Robert leaned on the counter. "Your bamboo rod got stolen, too, huh?"

Lucy nodded.

"That was such a unique rod." Robert grabbed the glass cleaner from a shelf behind him. "A thief would be stupid to try and pawn it anyplace close to where it was stolen. I know I would recognize the engraved handle."

"I suppose you're right." Her voice broke. Maybe they would recover the fly rod, but she doubted they'd find the jewelry. It was the jewelry that mattered more to her. Those few simple pieces were her connection to the past and to the people who had loved her. "The robber probably threw the earrings and other things in a trash can when he realized they weren't worth anything."

"You never know." Robert shrugged. "Sometimes people come in here, and they think something is really valuable when it isn't or vice versa."

Maybe there was still hope. "Grandma's wedding ring was pretty simple, but it must have had some value. I wrote up a description of everything. I can get that to you."

"That would be good. I promise I'll keep a lookout for you." Robert sprayed the glass cleaner where Lucy and Eli had touched and wiped it clean with a cloth he had in his back pocket. "I know a guy who works at a pawnshop up to Wilson. I can give him a call."

Robert's kindness touched her. "Thank you. Don't put yourself out, but if you do come across anything, let me know."

Music from a nearby park streamed through an open window. The jazzy tune cheered Lucy. The arts festival must be getting underway already.

Eli ambled around the store, stopping to examine the hunting rifles. "Are there any other stores around here that sell used sporting goods?"

The festival music swelled to a crescendo. Lucy stepped toward Eli. "Sure, there are at least five towns within a couple hours' drive of here. You're not thinking about checking all of those?"

"That's how police work is done," Eli said. "So glamorous, right?"

But Eli was helping with this search on his off-duty hours. "I hate to take up so much of your free time."

He turned toward her and met her gaze. "I don't mind, really, Lucy." He tilted his head toward the window. "Where is that music coming from?"

"The arts-and-crafts festival over in the park." Robert lifted a box of DVDs off the floor, scooted out from behind the counter and slipped the movies into slots on a display shelf. "I saw Dawson setting up his booth a while ago."

"Who's Dawson?" Eli glanced toward her, eyes searching.

Lucy's back muscles pinched. Eli didn't need to know everything about her.

Robert slapped a DVD on the counter. "Lucy's brother. You haven't met him yet?" He stopped shelving the movies and directed his comment to Eli. "Dawson Kimbol is a world-class wood sculptor. He does beautiful work. Lucy, why have you been keeping your brother a secret?"

"I wasn't keeping him a secret. We have plans to go fishing while he's in town." Lucy fought to keep the emotion out of her voice. Even as she spoke, anxiety rose up in her. She was proud of her brother, of what he had accomplished, but Eli's way of gently barging into her personal life made her feel exposed. "I barely know Detective Hawkins. I'm not going to tell him my whole life story." She stepped toward a rack of leather coats and pretended to be interested in a blue one with fringe.

Why do my defenses go up so easily around him?

"A festival, huh?" Eli angled his head so Lucy would look at him. "I like celebrations." He stepped toward the rack of leather jackets.

"You guys should go on over there. Lots of good food and music," Robert offered.

"I really need to get back home." She gave Eli a steely look but felt herself weakening even as she spoke. What was it with him? He had this way of making her both afraid and excited by the prospect of spending time with him, the same heightened mixture of emotions she'd felt when she'd gone cliff gliding. "I have a lot of prep work to do."

"I don't know. I'm with Robert." Eli hooked a thumb through the belt loop of his faded Levi's. "It might be kind of fun."

"Park is only three blocks up. Get yourself a beef pasty and homemade lemonade. They're the best." Robert gave Eli a thumbs-up sign.

Lucy glared at Eli. He responded with a grin. She

hadn't noticed what an intense shade of brown his eyes were before now. No use putting up a fight. She was out-numbered. "Okay, but I only want to stay a short time. I'll introduce you to my brother and we'll go."

Lucy thanked Robert and made her way to the door. Once outside, she whirled around to face Eli. "I don't like being talked into things."

"I understand that. It's just that I'd like to meet your brother, since the way you talked about him, I thought he was dead." He looped her arm in his.

"I never said my brother was dead. My private life is my private life." Even as familiar anxiety rose to the surface, she was reminded of how safe she had felt with him last night when he had rescued her from the river. "You're kind of a buttinsky."

His eyebrows drew together. "Buttinsky? I don't think I've heard that word since seventh grade."

His lighthearted response made her feel less de-fensive. "Oh, quit." She punched him in the shoulder. "You're nosy. You're finding out all this stuff about me. I don't know anything about you."

"You haven't asked."

"I can ask you anything?"

Eli's bicep stiffened slightly where her arm was looped through his.

"Sure…okay," he said. He pulled free of her arm.

The music grew louder as they made their way up the street. The park had two clear sections divided by a road. One side consisted of craft booths. The other side featured tents that sold food and two visible per-formance areas. On one stage, the jazz band they had heard from a distance performed, and the other was a smaller stage in a grove of trees where it looked as though a Shakespeare play was going on.

Eli pointed to the row of concession tents that advertised everything from pizza slices to pulled pork. "I am starving. My treat."

"The plan was to meet my brother, remember." Lucy matched Eli's pace. The food did smell good. Maybe they would have to get something to eat. "So what about you?" They passed booths that had jewelry, hand-painted scarves and framed watercolors.

"Not much to tell. I have one older sister and one younger one. Mom is a nurse and Dad owns a car dealership."

"Sounds like you had a pretty normal childhood." Nothing like her own. Lucy had only vague memories of her father. Before the cancer diagnosis, her mother had worked so much that Lucy had been her brother's caretaker from a young age. The time she had spent with her grandfather fishing and learning the river was what had made life bearable.

Even from a distance, Lucy knew which booth was Dawson's. Carved wooden animals, everything from bears to tropical birds, populated the grassy area around the booth. Seeing the large crowd milling through, marveling at the sculpture, made Lucy's heart swell with pride. Dawson had done so well...despite...

"We'll just stay for a minute. I guess it wouldn't hurt to get something to eat, too."

Lucy made her way to the tent where Dawson sat in a wheelchair holding up an intricately carved eagle for a woman to look at. The woman took the sculpture, turning it over in her hands.

Dawson's face brightened when he saw Lucy. "Hey, big sis. Thought I wasn't going to see you until late tonight."

She leaned down and gave him a hug. "Change of plans." Memories of Dawson as a skinny teenager flashed through her mind. They'd both been so young when their world had turned upside down. It was a blessing that it was a week past her eighteenth birthday when their mother had died. With Grandpa and Grandma already gone, Dawson could have ended up in foster care.

Dawson leaned forward and held out a hand for Eli to shake. "I'm Lucy's brother." He slanted a mischievous glance toward Lucy. "My sister is not good at introductions," he teased.

Lucy made a *tsk*ing noise. "I was going to introduce him. Dawson, this is Eli Hawkins. He is my renter." She swept her hand toward the craft booths. "I thought I would show him some Mountain Springs culture."

Dawson sat up a little straighter in his chair. "New in town, huh? What brings you to our thriving metropolis?"

Eli cleared his throat. "I just joined the Mountain Springs police."

"I heard they hired a couple of new officers." He craned his neck to face his sister. "I'm surprised that Lucy rented the place to you."

Dawson had chosen his words carefully, but any reference to the police department made her tense. In so many ways, Dawson had recovered better from the accident than she had. Her brother still struggled, but the initial anger and devastation he had expressed about the radical rerouting of his life had been transformed into creative energy.

Over and over, she had told herself she had forgiven the police; she'd prayed about it, gone to counseling. If these old emotions were just beneath the surface, though, maybe she really hadn't worked through it. Maybe avoiding the police was a way of avoiding the emotions. She twisted the hem of her shirt. She really didn't want to think about the past.

"Eli is from Spokane." Lucy dug into the soft dirt with the heel of her shoe. "He is new to the force here."

Dawson's voice flooded with compassion. "I know that, sis." His hand stroked her forearm.

Eli rocked back and forth on his heels. "Oh, and I forgot to tell you about my second job. I am the self-appointed ambassador for the Mountain Springs Police Department." Eli squared his shoulders and flexed his biceps theatrically. He must have sensed the tension in the air. The tone of his comment was intended to lighten the moment.

Dawson threw back his head and laughed. "That's a good job for you."

Lucy crossed her arms and shook her head. She appreciated Eli's sense of humor, but what exactly had Dawson meant?

A woman sauntered over to Dawson, holding a carved horse. She stood a few feet away, waiting to ask him a question. Traffic in the booth had picked up.

"We should probably let you get back to business." Lucy ruffled her brother's hair. He was a grown man, but she couldn't help herself. No matter how old he got, he would always be her little brother. The only family she had left. "We're going to get something to eat. Can we get you anything?"

Dawson shook his head as more people came into the booth. "I got work to do."

Lucy leaned closer to her brother. "Are you sure you're not hungry? I can bring it over to you."

"You'll have to forgive my sister, Eli. She was eighteen when Mom died, and she had to take care of a rambunctious thirteen-year-old. She still likes to act like my mom."

"Oh, really?" Eli leaned toward Dawson, indicating that he wanted to hear more.

That settled it. Lucy tugged on Eli's shirtsleeve. "You're starving, remember." She led him over to the pasty booth.

When their order was up, Eli handed Lucy her pasty and a lemonade.

"It's a little quieter over there." She pointed toward a picnic table on the edge of the park beside a children's slide and swing set. They settled on top of the picnic table, facing the activity of the festival. Three children played on the slide while a mom watched from a bench.

"So was that your turning point...when your mom died?" Eli took a sip of his lemonade and set it on the table. "Is that when you became a Christian?"

The question was fair enough. She liked talking about her faith, but Lucy couldn't help but think it would lead to more questions. "Actually, I became a Christian a little bit before. By the time she finally went to the doctor, the cancer was stage four."

Even as she spoke, she realized she hadn't shared the whole story and all the emotions that went along with it with anyone. She had prayed all through her mother's illness. God had been so close to her during that time. She hadn't been alone. The older women from the church had been kind, bringing by casseroles and offering hugs, but she had never talked about her feelings. This was a small town; everybody knew everybody's business. She had never had a reason to tell anyone what was going on with her mom. "Before the diagnosis, she was always tired and kept saying she couldn't get a deep breath. I think we all saw it coming, but we just didn't want to say the word *cancer*."

As she shared, her throat got tight and her voice broke. All of this was such ancient history, why were these emotions coming to the surface now? Lucy angled slightly away. She tore at the paper her pasty had been wrapped in.

Eli rested a warm hand on her shoulder. She tensed. Maybe she had told him too much. With gentle pressure on her shoulder, he turned her around to face him. Compassion filled his brown eyes. "That was a lot for a kid to go through alone."

"Yeah, but I'm not a kid anymore." Her vision of him blurred. "That was ten years ago."

"Then those tears have been due for ten years."

She swiped at her eyes. "I guess they are." With anyone else she would have been apologizing and running off somewhere to cry alone, but with Eli she didn't feel the need to do that. "I didn't cry much when the whole thing was happening. I had to be strong for Dawson."

"Sometimes the emotion comes later. When you are in the middle of a firefight, you don't break down and bawl."

She hadn't thought of what she had been through as like being in a war. She sniffled. Fair was fair. He had to answer some questions, too. "So what about you? What was your turning point? I bet you came from a good Christian family—a total *Leave It to Beaver* life."

He chuckled. "I did come from a good family, but I didn't become a Christian until about four years ago."

"What happened?"

"It was a…a case we were working." Eli shook his head and stared at some unseen object in the distance. His features hardened, and he spoke in a low voice. "I looked evil in the face and knew I couldn't handle it alone."

The shift in mood was dramatic. All the levity of his personality had vaporized.

She leaned a little closer to him and whispered, "What was the case about?"

He lifted his head and grinned, but the smile didn't quite make it to his eyes. "You ordinary mortals don't need to know about those police things."

"Us ordinary mortals?"

Eli scooted away from her. "As a cop, you see so much…ugliness. Other cops understand. We share with each other." He slipped off the picnic table, scooped up the paper containers from their lunch and headed toward the trash can.

Lucy stared at the view of Eli's back. His reaction seemed almost nervous. What was that about? She'd shared her heart with him, and he'd closed up like a clam. Even Eli had secrets.

EIGHT

Eli wasn't surprised when he heard Dawson's van pull up to the house. Lucy had said he was going to stay with her and that they were going out on the river after he was done with the festival tomorrow. The knock on his door, though, made him jump.

He walked the short distance from the kitchen where he had been making a snack and swung the door open.

Dawson was on the porch. When Eli had moved in, he had noticed the ramp at one end of the porch and not thought anything about it until now. Though his hair was dark brown, Dawson had the same light skin and blue eyes as his sister. The arch of his eyebrows and his sunny mood gave him an almost elfin quality. Eli had a hard time picturing Dawson ever being sullen.

"Did you forget which side your sister lives on?"

Dawson laughed. "Nah, man, I just wanted to invite you to come fishing with us tomorrow."

"I don't think Lucy would like that." She'd been so transparent with him when they'd talked at the festival. He hadn't seen what dangerous ground he was treading on until Lucy had probed about his work. He could talk about his personal life and childhood all day long, but talking about the circumstances of the serial killer case in Spokane could have led to more questions about his work and a breach of secrecy on the case.

Dawson offered Eli a smile. "Lucy is not inviting you. I'm the one inviting you because you win the prize."

"What prize is that?" Eli rested a shoulder against the door frame.

"So far, you are the only cop to get within twenty feet of Lucy."

Now he realized he was going to have to increase that distance. He would be lying to himself if he said he wasn't attracted to Lucy. The gravitational pull toward her hadn't been entirely about keeping her safe.

Whatever his feelings, it wouldn't be fair to her to keep being evasive.

He was paid up until the end of the month. After that, if the investigation was still going on, he'd move out and find some other way to provide protection.

Still, it bothered him that she thought cops couldn't be trusted, and Dawson seemed to think he could fix that. Officer O'Bannon had been vague about the reason for the mutual animosity. He couldn't picture Lucy saying negative things about the department without good reason. If he knew the whole story, maybe there was some way he could smooth things over.

Eli pushed his shoulder off the door frame and stepped outside onto the porch. "I don't suppose you being in that chair has anything to do with why Lucy doesn't trust the Mountain Springs police?"

Dawson tapped the heel of his hand on the wheelchair arm. "Lucy is kind of a private person. I'm not going to violate her trust. She'll tell you when she's ready."

"I really don't think Lucy would want to hang out with me tomorrow." He'd seen the look on her face when he'd refused to answer her question about the serial killer case that had made him see a need for God in his life. She probably felt played after she'd been so vulnerable.

"Being in this chair isn't easy." Dawson pulled on a Velcro tab on his fingerless glove and pressed it back into place. "Every day when I wake up, I wish I had my legs back, and I think about the life I might have had. Lucy and I were going to run the guide business together. It's not easy, but I'm getting through it."

"And Lucy?"

"Lucy has had to be a grown-up since I was born. She's lost all the people she loved and nearly lost me. She's a little overprotective of me. I had to move to a different town so she would quit hovering." Dawson rolled back in his chair and touched his thigh with a fist. "The damage that was done to me is obvious. With Lucy it's deeper, more hidden."

Eli traced the pattern of the wood in the door trim. "I don't know. I think it might be better if I just stay Lucy's renter."

Dawson motioned with his hand for Eli to bend closer. "I heartily disagree, my friend." He scooted back in his chair. "We're going to meet at the river, Spanish Creek exit about a mile up, around 5:00 p.m. after the booths close up at the festival." Dawson lifted his front wheels and swung in a half circle. He turned his head and spoke over his shoulder. "I expect to see you there. I'll bring extra gear."

Eli spent the next day running surveillance on suspect number two, Neil Fender, who lived in Wilson, a town about fifty miles from Mountain Springs. His thoughts kept wandering back to Dawson and his invitation. All afternoon he had debated about going. He found himself thinking about Lucy all the time.

William sat opposite Eli at a restaurant, reviewing the case. Two tables down, Neil Fender had just wrapped up another successful date and left the restaurant.

William poured sugar into his coffee and stirred. "You notice how Neil Fender is somebody different to every woman he dates." He set the spoon on the table. "But does that make him a killer?"

In the time they had watched Neil, he had pretended to be a hunting guide and a millionaire, and had told one woman about his tragic childhood in an orphanage. None of his stories were remotely true, but all of them made the women he dated want a second date.

"Isn't dating all about deception?" Eli flipped through a written report. "Only showing the best side of yourself?" Yet another reason he had chosen career over marriage. Courtship was so filled with land mines. The bad guys were easier to identify in his job.

"Neil Fender isn't showing the best side of himself." William took a sip of his coffee and slammed the cup on the table. "He's showing a false side."

"He's really good at reading women and saying what they want to hear. I'll give him that." Eli flipped through the photos on his laptop of Neil that showed him with his various dates. Some were blond. Some brunette. In fact, none of the suspects so far were consistently picking dark-haired, blue-eyed women, which made him wonder if they were on the wrong track. "I really don't think Neil Fender is anything more than a sleazebag. I feel like we are wasting time and manpower."

"Could you use some good news?" William rested his elbows on the table and leaned closer to Eli. "Officer Smith has managed to snag a date with Greg Jackson."

"Good. I still think Jackson is our strongest suspect." Jillian Smith had proven herself to be quite adept at undercover work. At least that part of the case was moving forward. "She has been well-prepped. Hopefully, her line of questioning will push Jackson to reveal something that will allow us to obtain search warrants, maybe even bring him in for questioning. If we can get a search warrant, we might find something in his place that links him to the deaths." If. If. If. Eli clenched his teeth. The longer they were stalled, the less likely they would find anything.

William doodled on a cover page of one of the reports. "We have been focused on means and opportunity with this guy—what about motive?"

Eli enjoyed the feeling of the late-afternoon sun streaming through the window. He should be outside, maybe on a river with a beautiful woman. He smiled at the thought and refocused his attention on William. "We might not know that until we make the arrest."

"Maybe he was hurt by a dark-haired and blue-eyed woman. Maybe his mother had dark hair and blue eyes and she was horrible to him."

"It's not usually that straightforward. All the same." Eli clicked through files on his laptop; he turned the screen so William could see the photograph of Greg Jackson's mother. A large man in coveralls stood behind her, his hand resting possessively on her shoulder. His scrunched eyebrows and cold eyes communicated inflexibility. It wasn't a great picture, but the woman with a weary expression had dark hair. A grainy enlargement of the photograph showed that her eyes were blue.

William shook his head. "Jackson has a lot of key personality indicators. You said he seems pretty tightly wound. Do you think we should watch him closer?"

It was a tough choice. What if they pulled the attention away from the other three suspects and another woman died? At the same time, they didn't have the funds to spend months and months watching men take women to the movies. With the case in Spokane, the killer had messed up while under surveillance. He'd had a victim's shoe in his car, and it had fallen out while he was being watched. They needed that kind of break in this case. Eli rubbed the stubble on his face. "There has to be something we're not seeing here."

Eli examined a hard copy of the file. The murders had taken place over a year and a half. The first murder had been Easter weekend in April of the previous year. Murders had occurred on different days of the week in August, October and December. The final murder had been in February. Time of death was always set between dinner and evening, date time for most people. Eli studied the map of where the murders had taken place. The varied methods of murder suggested that although there was planning in waiting for a time when he was alone with the victim, the killer tended to use whatever weapon was available. The two poisonings had been with materials found in the victims' homes. One woman had been stabbed with her own kitchen knife, and the other two strangled with a curtain cord and a dog leash.

Eli rubbed his eyes. He was so buried in the details of the case he couldn't see the big picture anymore.

He studied the place mat on the table, a picture of a man holding a large fish with the mountains and river in the background. He checked his watch. Four o'clock.

"You got some place you need to be?"

"I had a fishing invitation." The drive from Wilson to Mountain Springs was less than an hour. He could still make it to the dock by five. He wanted to see Lucy one more time. Maybe he could get the ball rolling on fixing things between her and the police. He could at least do that for her, without getting tangled up in her life.

William sat back in his chair. "I don't suppose this has anything to do with a pretty, dark-haired lady?"

"She is beautiful, and I am still concerned for her safety. Don't worry, I'm not going to let it get personal."

William crossed his arms and raised an eyebrow. "Too bad the circumstances of your meeting weren't a little different, huh?"

William had voiced a thought that had run through Eli's mind a thousand times. "There is just something I need to resolve for her."

"You are not required to work 24/7." William tossed a sugar packet at him. "Why don't you go have some fun? Make it look like you're becoming more a part of the community."

As he rose to his feet, Eli clarified the plan of action. "Let's prep Officer Smith even more before her big date. Maybe we can bring in a forensic psychologist to fine-tune the line of questioning that might get Jackson to reveal things."

"Sounds good." William stood up and stretched. "Smith has picked the date location, so we can get A/V in place ahead of time."

The drive from Wilson to Mountain Springs went by quickly on the straight road. As he pulled into the flat gravel area that served as a parking lot by the fishing access, he'd come to a clear conclusion. Lucy had been hurt enough by his need for secrecy. If he couldn't share fully with her who he was, he needed to keep his distance.

Even as he made his way toward the dock, he noticed Lucy's spine straighten. No surprise there.

A woman he assumed was her friend Heather sat cross-legged on the dock, staring at a laptop screen. Nelson positioned himself beside her, holding an open tackle box. The gel on Nelson's wavy hair caused it to take on a bright sheen in the late-afternoon sun. His clothes looked almost too new for the river. Dawson and Lucy huddled on the shore, untangling fishing line.

As he watched Lucy from a distance, his resolve weakened. Being with her felt so right.

When Eli got within earshot of the group, he heard Dawson say, "I invited him." The look of hopeful expectation on Dawson's face cut right through Eli. The guy just wanted his sister to find some healing for all the pain of the past.

Lucy shot her brother a stern look, but managed a

smile for Eli. She rose to her feet and placed a hand on her hip. "Extra gear is right there."

Eli picked up a fly rod.

"Have you ever been fly fishing, Eli?" Lucy grabbed a pair of hip waders and slipped into them.

"My dad took me when I was a kid. We used a spinning thing that made noise."

"You used a lure." Lucy pulled flies from a tiny box and stuck them in her hat. "That's a different kind of fishing."

"Spin casting is for Neanderthals." Dawson raised his arms theatrically. "Fly fishing is an art form, and Lucy is the painter of masterpieces."

Heather pointed to a picture on her laptop. "What about this guy? He just lives in Wilson."

Lucy came up on the dock to look at what Heather had found. "There is no Internet connection out here. Did you save these files or something?"

When Heather nodded, her ponytail bobbed up and down. "Just trying to get the ball rolling on your future."

Eli positioned himself so he could see the screen, which revealed a picture of the charming and deceptive Neil Fender.

"It says he's a Christian and he likes the outdoors," Heather offered.

"I don't want to do that online stuff anymore. There has to be chemistry between a man and a woman. You can't find chemistry with e-mail exchanges and reading profiles."

Heather sighed and tilted her head toward the sky. "How are you going to know if there is chemistry unless you meet this guy?"

"I gave Greg three dates...nothing."

"Lucy's running out of space in her life to put the guys who are just friends, Heather," Nelson teased as he rose to his feet.

Lucy tossed her hat on the dock. "Would you two stop?"

Eli picked up Lucy's hat and handed it to her. "I agree with Lucy." He'd do anything to keep her away from Neil Fender.

"Thank you, Eli." Lucy's glowing expression as she took the hat communicated that she appreciated his support.

"I think she has a full life." He pointed to the picture on the laptop. "Besides, this Neil guy looks like a real deceiver."

"What makes you say that?" The defensiveness had crept back into her voice.

Once again, he had pushed it too far. Of course, the comment had made it seem like he was trying to run her life. She had seemed willing to let go of his weirdness in his interference with Greg. He didn't need to add fuel to that fire and rev up her suspicions again.

Eli leaned a little closer to the computer and scanned the profile. "Do you really want to date someone who sounds that perfect? Makes you wonder what he is hiding." He spoke out of the side of his mouth in a tough-guy conspiratorial tone. "He's probably unemployed and lives in his mom's basement."

I'm only trying to protect you, Lucy.

Lucy's blue eyes twinkled when she smiled. "I agree. Everyone tries to say the best things about themselves. That's why I don't think it is a good way to meet people." Lucy put her hat on and picked up a cylindrical canister that must have contained a fishing rod.

"Maybe you should give up dating altogether." Nelson wandered toward the river. "Just hang out with your friends."

"Fine, we don't have to do the online thing." Heather closed her laptop and rose to her feet. She walked past Eli, sizing him up. She was a short woman. Her eyes had a clearness to them that could be disconcerting. "I think Dawson and I should go out in the boat."

Dawson slapped his leg. "That's a great idea, Heather."

"But I thought…" Lucy glanced from Heather to Eli. Her stare sent a charge of heat through him.

"Eli has never fly fished." Dawson lined his wheelchair up with the boat.

Lucy crossed her arms. "Why don't *you* give him a basic lesson?"

"It's a lot easier for me to cast from the boat. I don't get that much of a chance to go fishing anymore. You are the best teacher."

"Looks like it has already been decided then." Eli hadn't failed to notice the conspiratorial signals that passed between Dawson and Heather.

Heather held the boat steady so Dawson could transfer from wheelchair to boat. Without a word, Lucy raced over to her brother and helped him position his legs in the boat first. Then she slipped her arms under his armpits to move his upper body.

Eli stepped forward. "I'll help you push off." His shoulder brushed against Lucy's.

Heather grabbed Lucy's cell phone from its case

on her belt and held it up. "Smile for the camera, you two." She clicked, handed the camera back to Lucy and winked at her.

Lucy and Eli exchanged a what-was-that-about look.

Heather placed the gear in the bottom of the boat and hopped in as soon as it began to drift. She waved at the two of them as the boat traveled downriver. "Have fun."

Eli shook his head. Someone was doing a little matchmaking. "They seem like good friends."

"They are. I got to know Heather when she was Dawson's physical therapist." Lucy shaded her eyes. Nelson had worked his way downriver about a hundred yards. She turned to face Eli. "Ready for your first lesson?"

"I am ready to learn from a master."

The smile gracing her lips warmed his heart. "Okay, then." She picked up a rod and handed it to him. "Your first lesson is establishing a comfortable grip." She angled the handle of the rod toward him.

He wrapped his hands around the spongy handle.

"Are you a golfer?"

"No, why?" It shouldn't matter whether she was cold to him or not, but it did. If something as small as her smile could elevate his spirits, he was acutely tuned in to her mood changes.

"There are three basic grips." She stepped toward him. "The way you naturally held the handle is called the golf grip. Lift the rod. Does the grip feel comfortable?"

"Not really. What are my other options?"

She repositioned his fingers so his index finger rested across the top of the handle of the pole. "That's point grip."

"No, that doesn't feel right." He had a hard time focusing on what she was saying about his thumb and third finger when her smooth, cool hand brushed over his.

"Eli, are you listening?"

"What?"

Her shoulder touched his as she gripped his hand and readjusted his finger. "Rest your thumb on the top of the rod."

He bounced the pole up and down. "Guess I can live with that." The sun warming his neck and back relaxed him. "Now do I get to go in the water? There aren't many fish out here on the beach."

His joke produced another smile. "You earn the privilege of getting in the river by showing me you can get your cast right consistently."

Eli's mouth dropped open. "You are a tough teacher."

"Fish really aren't going to be bitin' strong for another hour or so. You have time to practice. What you want to do when you cast is imitate a fly coming to feed on the water. We'll start you out with a dry fly, one that skirts the top of the water. Let me see what your cast looks like."

Eli lifted his arm and flung the line out. He turned toward her for feedback.

The sun brought out the dark brown highlights in Lucy's black hair. Her eyes looked like they were made of crystal. She pursed her lips, then tapped her finger on her chin. "That fly was dead when it hit the water. You would have had too much drag on your line. No fish would be interested."

"Are you this mean to all your students?"

"Only the ones that talk my brother into inviting them." Her tone was playful.

"I assure you, it was entirely his idea. He likes my second job as ambassador for the Mountain Springs Police Department."

As though a cloud had passed overhead, her expression darkened. "That job probably doesn't pay very well." She stared at the water.

"I get to be with you on the river—payment enough." If this was going to be the last time he would be this close to her, he might as well enjoy it.

She lifted her head. "Why don't we work on your cast?" She edged toward him, standing close enough for him to smell the floral scent of her perfume. "There are two parts to a cast, back cast and forward cast. You control your line based on what you do with your rod. Strip out some of your line with your free hand. Lift your pole until it almost passes your ear." She pressed her fingers into his forearm. "Elbow down."

His tricep muscle strained from holding it in one place. "How long do I have to stay like this?"

She pressed a little harder on his forearm. "I just want you to be aware of where your line is before you do your forward cast. You're not focused."

It was hard to pay attention when all he could think about was how nice she smelled. "The fish are getting away."

"Eli," she reprimanded before she let off the pressure on his arm. "Now, start over. If twelve o'clock is right above you, stop your back cast at ten o'clock. Stop your forward cast at two o'clock, just past your shoulder. Keep your wrist tight the whole time."

He let the line go as she had instructed. "How was that?"

She placed her hands on her hips. "Not bad. Practice on shore a few more times." She waded out into the water. "When you are ready to come into the water, put those hip waders on." She cast a couple of times, describing what she was doing. Her line zinged through the air. The murmuring hum of the river had a calming effect on him.

Being with Lucy didn't hurt, either. Was he going to be able to disconnect from her? She hadn't brought up questions about his work. Still, it was only a matter of time.

Lucy pointed out the best places to catch fish. "Look for smooth water areas around rocks and logs." She cast again. Her line looped through the air with the grace of a ballet dancer and landed delicately on the water. The corners of her mouth curved up and her expression was the serenest he had ever seen. She was a woman in her element, as if the river was merely an extension of her.

After slipping into hip waders, Eli stepped into the river. The water was so clear he could see the rocks. He worked his way toward her in water that was just above his knees. The river took on a silver sheen where the tiny waves crested.

He could see Nelson a ways downriver, but the boat with Heather and Dawson had drifted around a bend. He stood beside her. "It's nice here, isn't it?"

"I think it's pretty special," she whispered. "I love worship on Sunday morning in church, but some of my best conversations with God happen out here."

"I can see that. God's creation makes us understand

him better, like it says in Romans." He turned to face her. She tilted her head. The sunlight backlit her hair. Her cheeks flushed with color. Her lips were full and inviting.

I could just kiss her now.

He took a step back and lifted his fly rod. What was he thinking? Kissing her would be cruel, misleading.

"I wasn't thrilled when you showed up, but now I'm glad that my brother invited you. What exactly did he say?"

"He didn't tell me what went on between him and the police. He said you would tell me when you were ready."

Lucy cast her line in the water. She pressed her lips together and angled slightly away from him. "What happened four years ago between the police and my brother has nothing to do with you, Eli. Besides, the whole thing is complicated. It goes further back than Dawson's accident. Back to high school." She drew her fishing line in. "I don't dislike all cops. You have nothing to do with what happened. I know you are a good cop."

The revelation warmed him. He still had to believe he could make things better between her and the rest of the department. "Wish you felt that way about the other guys on the force."

She still didn't face him when she spoke. "I thought they would be there to help me more than once, and each time I was disappointed. The last time, my brother ended up in a chair." Her voice had an edge to it. While a soft breeze rustled through the cottonwoods along the shore, she cast her line several more times.

He dropped his hand to his side, awed by how she cast so beautifully. "How do you get your line to curve like that?" Her emotion was still so raw; somehow, the smart move seemed to be to change the subject.

She laughed. "Practice. Which is what you should be doing."

"Yes, ma'am," Eli saluted. He waded upstream. The water rushing and whooshing around him had a hypnotic effect. Now he understood the appeal of being out on the river. No wonder Lucy loved it so much. Imitating what he had seen Lucy do, he attempted to cast. The fly splatted on the water. Behind him, Lucy giggled.

He turned back to face her. "Is that how you motivate? By laughing at your students?" He pushed through the rippling water so he was closer to her.

She reeled in her line and cast several more times.

He swallowed and chose his words carefully. "Tell me what happened, Lucy. What went on between your brother and the police?"

Her arms went limp as her line dragged in the water. She bit her lower lip. "Four years ago, Dawson was helping a youth pastor at our church. He was thinking about becoming a pastor himself." Her voice broke. She waded back through the water to the shore, where she flipped open the tackle box.

Eli followed her to the rocky beach. It was up to her how much she wanted to tell him. If she shared, he might be able to help her, but if she chose not to, he'd let it go.

She reached up toward him. "Hand me your rod. I want to change your fly to something a little heavier."

He sat down beside her while she removed the fly he'd been using. While she selected a different fly and attached it, she continued. "One of the kids Dawson was mentoring stopped coming to the youth group. The boy listed his address as a house just outside of town." She took in a breath. "I don't think Dawson quite understood what he was getting himself into. He didn't know it was a meth house…nobody did."

Eli placed a supportive hand on her back.

Lucy shook her head. "He went out to the house thinking he would just check on the kid. But when he got out there, something didn't feel right. There was no one around, but the door was open and water was boiling on the stove, like people had run and hidden somewhere." Lucy squeezed her eyes shut. "So he called me and said if I didn't hear from him in twenty minutes, I should call the police." Lucy exhaled a shuddering breath. "Dawson didn't want to panic unnecessarily. I had a feeling, though. I called the police right away." .

Eli leaned closer to her. This was probably the first time she had shared the whole story.

"He was on the way back to his car. One of the drug dealers jumped him. Dawson got away. He ran into the trees, the guy went after him." She shook her fist at the sky. "Dawson dodged the guy long enough for the cops to have gotten there, but they didn't believe me that he was in danger. They didn't show up until after the dealer shot Dawson."

She sat with her knees pulled toward her chest, eyes closed, head bent. A tear slipped out from beneath her lid. Eli reached up and brushed the moisture away from her temple.

She folded into his arms and buried her face in his chest. Though she was silent, her quivering shoulders indicated that she was crying. His heart ached for her.

She'd lived a lifetime of pain and had to go through so much of it alone.

After a few minutes, she pulled away and wiped her eyes. "Of course, they tried to cover it up, said that they went out there right away. But I knew better. They were ignoring me on purpose to punish me for something that happened a long time ago. I was really angry. I wrote some letters to the editor, made some phone calls. We filed a lawsuit to get Dawson's medical expenses covered. The chief of police was fired, but the other cops just kept working there. They agreed to seek funding to step up the fight against meth. None of that gets my brother out of that chair."

Eli lifted Lucy's chin. He wanted to delve further but knew this was not the time. "What they did was not right. A good cop would have responded immediately." Anger burned inside him for what she had endured. No wonder she didn't trust them. He still wondered why they didn't trust her.

Her eyes searched his. "Thank you."

"Catch anything?" A voice boomed behind them.

Eli pulled away. He'd been so tuned in to Lucy, he hadn't heard Nelson come up to them.

Nelson held up a fish in his net. Though obviously losing strength, the fish flipped side to side, causing the mesh of the net to wiggle. "I caught a good-size one."

Lucy scooted away from Eli. Color rose up in her cheeks as she bent her head and covered her face with her hair. Being caught in a moment of vulnerability had embarrassed her.

Lucy stood up, brushing sand off her back and legs. "At least somebody caught something."

Nelson pulled the fish from the net by looping his finger through its gills. He sat down beside Eli. The expansion and compression of the gills lessened and then they ceased moving altogether. "I'm going to have a nice dinner tonight."

Lucy came up behind the two men and rested a hand on Eli's shoulder.

Even as he welcomed her touch, Eli knew he could not hope for more. He had broken through her walls for one beautiful moment, but he could give her nothing in return. With his heart aching for her and for what couldn't be, he slipped free of her hand.

NINE

Lucy flipped the light switch in her living room, but the room remained dark. She worked the switch up and down. "Something is wrong with the light." She turned a half circle at the entrance of her house.

Eli came up behind her. "Electricity out?"

"I'm not sure, it might just be the bulb." Having Eli close calmed her. They had had a good day together.

After they'd finished fishing, the four of them had decided to go out to eat, all except Nelson, who had caught his dinner. As they had wandered through downtown Mountain Springs and into the park where a final festival concert was taking place, Lucy had vacillated between feeling as though she had told Eli too much and knowing that it was the right thing to do. This was all so new to her, feeling safe enough with someone to share.

Eli brushed past her and leaned into her living room. "It's darker than a cave in there. Do you want me to go get a flashlight? I know right where one is."

"That would be good. I think all my flashlights are in the van." It was nice to have Eli next door. Dawson had already made plans to drive back to his home.

Eli's footsteps pounded on the porch floorboards, fading slowly.

Lucy stepped into her place. The light over the stove, which she always kept on, was not working, either. That meant it wasn't a bulb. Her heartbeat quickened in response to the darkness. She'd been jittery since the break-in, and the lack of light didn't do anything to calm her nerves.

She had candles and a lighter in a kitchen drawer. Those would be easy enough to find. She made her way across the living room. Her feet bumped against a laundry basket. She'd forgotten about leaving that there. Her hand brushed over the sleek wall between kitchen and living room. She entered the kitchen, counting drawers by touching the metal handles.

As she slid the third drawer open, she heard a muffled click on the other side of the room. "Eli?"

Lucy held her breath and listened. Even though her eyes had begun to adjust to the darkness, she could make out almost nothing in the room, only vague outlines of furniture. A little light from the moon filtered through the windows. Out of habit, she had closed the door when she'd stepped inside.

She turned slowly, brushing her fingers over the items in the kitchen drawer. She recognized the waxy texture of the candles right away, but nothing felt like a lighter. Her hand touched several hard square objects, chargers for something she either no longer owned or couldn't find.

Had she left the lighter by the fireplace or outside by the barbecue? Gripping the candles, she opened another drawer and felt around, lifting objects and tossing them back in. Again, she thought she heard a noise coming from the living room.

As she walked back into the living room, her soft-soled shoes were nearly silent on the wood floor. She could make out the outline of the coat tree by the door. A lump swelled in her throat. "Eli," she whispered, knowing even then that he wasn't in the room.

She stood frozen for a moment waiting for another sound, anything to verify that she wasn't imagining things. The last time she'd had a soak in the tub after a long cold day on the river, she had lit the lavender candles. She'd probably left the lighter in the bathroom.

Lucy shook off the feeling that there was someone else in the room. Darkness had a tendency to accelerate the imagination. She placed a hand on the textured wall and inched toward the bathroom. She patted her hands over objects in the medicine cabinet until she found the lighter. As she struggled to produce a flame with the lighter, she heard a thud in the living room and something scraping across the floor. Her head shot up. Her heart hammered in her chest. That was not her imagination.

The last home invasion was still fresh in her mind. She had to get out.

She flicked the lighter one more time. The candle wick caught the flame. She slipped out of the bathroom and edged back toward the living room, toward the door, toward where Eli was. In the small circle of illumination, she could see nothing out of place.

She darted the final yard across the living-room floor. Her hand wrapped around the knob; it didn't budge. Someone had thrown the dead bolt. She adjusted the candle so she could see the lock.

Something tightened around her neck. An unseen force pulled her back, dragged her across the floor. The candle slipped from her hand. She choked and gasped for air.

She swung side to side, trying to break free. Her fingers clawed at her neck. She recognized the silky fabric of one of her own scarves. She wheezed in air, growing light-headed. Orange pops of light filled her vision.

She had only seconds before she passed out. In her thrashing, she angled herself toward her assailant, barreling into where she thought his torso would be. He groaned. Her hand reached up. Something covered his face—a knit cap.

The suctioning around her neck let up as they both fell to the floor. Before she had her bearings, he yanked on her hair.

She screamed. Pain seared through her scalp.

She'd lost all sense of where she was in space. He pulled harder on her hair. She flailed her arms, trying to grab hold of something, anything to anchor herself. Her hand brushed the mantel of the fireplace. Framed photos spilled to the floor. Glass shattered.

Then her head slammed against the hard rock of the fireplace. More winking golden circles filled her vision. Temporary paralysis from having the wind knocked out of her invaded her limbs.

A cold hand stroked her cheek. Fingers slithered down her face to where her pulse throbbed in her neck.

Eli fumbled through the dark of his half of the duplex. He'd tried two light switches, enough to tell him that his electricity was out, as well. He'd managed to crash into a box and a chair on his way to the duffel he kept in his bedroom. It wouldn't hurt for him to keep the place a little tidier, considering how little he had accumulated. He owned half a dozen flashlights, but he knew for sure one was in the duffel.

As he felt around the bed, he remembered the way Lucy had looked at him at dinner and while they'd watched the concert. He'd seen affection in her eyes and the realization made his stomach tighten. He did not want to hurt her. All night, he had wanted to leave, but the smallest insistence from Lucy had made the word *no* impossible to say.

Heather's words to him only confirmed that he needed to tell Lucy he was moving into town even before the end of the month.

Heather had pulled him aside at the concert. "I don't think I have seen Lucy so relaxed in ages."

"She seems to be enjoying herself," Eli had said.

"I'm very protective of my friend." He towered over her by nearly a foot, yet her posture and the look of resolve on her face had made him feel as if he was the short one. "She has lost everyone she depended on. I was with her after Dawson's accident, and we thought we might lose him, too."

Heather's eyes had fixed on him with a steel-like gaze. "I want more than anything for Lucy to find someone special. It's obvious she likes you. If you are not the guy who can stay in her life and be good to her, don't be in her life at all. I don't think her heart can take any more loss."

Eli found the flashlight in his duffel with little effort. He wasn't about to cause Lucy more pain. He needed to back off, but he could still help her from a distance. Now that he knew what had happened to Dawson, he was going to have to talk to officers who had been around four years ago. He needed to find out too what O'Bannon and Lucy had meant by their references to high school.

Eli clicked on the flashlight and left the bedroom. He had no idea where the breaker box was. Lucy would know. Most duplexes had separate breaker boxes for each house. It wouldn't hurt to look in a few obvious places for the breaker box. Lucy had probably already found some kind of light of her own.

There hadn't been any storms all day, and all the other houses had had lights on as they'd driven back to the duplex. No reason to think the loss of current was anything but a fluke. He headed toward the half basement, thinking the breaker box might be there.

He stopped gripping the handrail. His heart froze. Realization entered his mind.

Eli raced up the stairs. There was no reason for the electricity to be out. Someone had thrown the breakers on purpose. Someone had been waiting for Lucy to come home and had assumed that he would be busy in his own place trying to get the lights on. He flung his door open and ran across the porch. The knob on Lucy's door turned, but the door didn't open. Dead-bolted. He placed the flashlight in his mouth and tried the door one more time with both hands. It would be futile to try to kick it in. When he peered in the window between the slit in the curtains, he couldn't see anything.

Eli ran around to the back of the house and tried the door that led directly into the kitchen. Dead-bolted, as well. This time when he peered in the window, he saw rising smoke and flames.

"Lucy!" he shouted. He slammed his weight against the door and then kicked it. Brute force was not going to get him inside. Eli whirled around, assessing what he had to work with. Maybe there was something in the tool shed.

Once inside the shed, his flashlight shone on several handsaws and a sledgehammer before he noticed the ladder. The night he had met Lucy, the intruder had slipped out of a window. He grabbed a hammer in case the window wasn't open and dragged the ladder across the yard.

When he leaned the ladder against the wall, it was higher than the window. His hand curled into a fist. Panic had muddled his thoughts. If the thief had gotten in and out without a ladder, he could, too. He pushed the ladder to one side, angry that he had lost so much time.

The thief must have boosted himself up by standing on the rock beneath the window.

Still holding the hammer, he climbed up, relieved to see that the window was open. The screen had been set to one side just like before. This time though it looked like Lucy had installed some kind of lock over the window. Battered trim indicated that the thief had beat on the window with something to get it open. He dropped the hammer on the ground.

As he crawled through the window, Eli was aware that the intruder may still be inside. In his haste, he had left his gun at his duplex. His feet landed on the carpet in Lucy's bedroom. He shone the light around the room, probing dark corners as adrenaline surged through his body. Once again, the place had been torn to pieces. Same guy as before. It had to be.

He raced into the living room. A throw blanket had fallen to the floor and caught on fire. Judging from the toxic smell in the air, the blanket wasn't made of natural fabric.

Lucy had risen to her feet. A spark of recognition crossed her features. Relief coursed through him. She swayed.

Eli lunged forward, gathering her in his arms before she fell. He kicked a chair aside. Still propping Lucy up, he clicked back the dead bolt on the front door. She was like a rag doll in his arms. The night sky twinkled with stars as he laid her on the front porch, taking a moment to touch his palm to her cheek. Though she didn't speak, gratitude flashed in her eyes.

They both coughed from inhaling the toxic fumes.

Cupping his hand over his mouth, he ran back inside and opened all the living room windows. The fire was not raging but had produced significant smoke. He ran to Lucy's bedroom and grabbed a wool blanket he'd remembered seeing. He placed the blanket on the flames and smoke. He spotted Lucy's cell phone on the counter, picked it up and dialed 911 for the fire department. Then he phoned William's cell number.

Eli grabbed another blanket from the bedroom and walked out to the porch, where Lucy rested against a supporting post. He shone his flashlight in her direction.

The look on her face told him everything he needed to know. This was not the time to ask questions, not the time to be a cop. She needed a friend.

He wrapped her in the blanket and pulled her close.

"Fire department will be here in a minute. It's going to be all right."

She tried to speak but only managed a horrible cough. When she touched her neck, he saw the dark red marks and scratches. He drew Lucy to his chest and held her. She trembled in his arms.

Rage over what had been done to her filled him. The crime had some similarity to the first robbery. Since Lucy had probably locked the doors this time, the assailant had entered and exited through the bedroom window, but this wasn't a simple robbery anymore.

This guy had been waiting for Lucy. There was premeditation in shutting off the electricity to make it harder for Lucy to escape and to keep Eli busy trying to get the electricity on in his place. Who would do this?

Lucy tilted her head. "If you hadn't been here..." Her voice was hoarse.

His jaw clenched. He should have gotten here faster. He should never have left her alone. "Lucy, this is my fault, I—"

Lucy gripped his collar. "Please don't. I am so glad you were here."

He touched her forehead where there was a bump. "That's going to hurt."

She winced. "I think I lost consciousness, just for a moment." She cleared her throat and then her hand fluttered to her neck. "Eli, he could have killed me, but he didn't."

"I might have scared him off." The assailant had to have escaped by the window—both doors were still dead-bolted. Eli hadn't seen anyone in the field or by the shed when he'd crawled in.

Lucy shook her head. "No, he left before I heard you shouting and knocking."

"But he—" Eli touched the red marks on Lucy's neck. The guy had had opportunity to kill Lucy and had chosen not to. Was the assault intended as some kind of warning?

"I heard you pounding on the door...and then I saw the fire. I wasn't thinking clearly." She attempted to laugh, but it sounded more like a cough. "I actually had it in my head that I needed to get water to pour on the fire."

Up the road, two sets of headlights shone through the darkness. A single car followed by a fire truck came into view. "I want you to call Heather and stay with her. The fire damage isn't bad, but it smells in there, and I don't want to take a chance that—" He caught himself, not wanting to alarm her anymore. She'd been through enough for one night.

"—that he will come back." Lucy pressed the heel of her hand against her forehead. "For a third time. It was the same guy, wasn't it?" Lucy sat up a little straighter. "I'll call Heather."

The Volkswagen came to a stop, and William got out.

Lucy scooted away from Eli so he could get up. He leaned close and rested a hand on her cheek. "I must have left your cell in your house. It'll take a minute for those fumes to clear out. My place is open—go in there and use the phone." He studied her for a moment. She hadn't cried, hadn't fallen apart. That concerned him. It would be better for the emotions to come out than for her to deaden inside and pretend like the assault didn't bother her. "Are you sure you're okay?"

She nodded in short, jerking motions.

"Are you telling me a lie?"

She nodded again, and this time her eyes rimmed with tears. She stood up and fell into his arms. He held her and spoke softly into her ear. "You don't always have to be the strong one, Lucy."

She let out a gasp. "I want to believe that." When he pulled back to look at her, she wasn't sobbing, only a few tears trailed down her cheeks. He brushed one away with his finger.

She pulled back and lifted her chin in a show of feigned composure. Eli gripped Lucy's arm at the elbow and helped her up the stairs.

He waited on the porch until Lucy disappeared inside before going over to William, who instructed the firefighters to not disturb anything in the house that might be evidence.

"Why did you phone me directly?" William asked.

"I have some doubts about this police department when it comes to dealing with Lucy." Eli turned back toward the open door of Lucy's place. "Do we have a line on Greg Jackson's whereabouts?"

William's expression was grim. "He was in Mountain Springs earlier. Some kind of agriculture banquet. He took a woman he'd met from the service."

"And what time did the banquet end?"

"I know what you're thinking. This is not our guy's M.O. If it had been, you know and I know, Lucy would be dead."

The thought made Eli shudder. William had a point. Their guy didn't build up to a murder with robbery and assaults. He planned and he carried out his plan.

"This guy had time to kill her and he chose not to. All the same, I would like to know exactly where Greg Jackson was about an hour ago."

William nodded and pulled his phone from his pocket.

Eli paced while William made the call. Lucy would want to move back into her place within a few days. He couldn't blame her for that. She needed to be close to the river, close to her work. He was grateful she hadn't argued with him about not staying here tonight.

William hung up the phone. "Greg Jackson took his date home around nine and went back to a hotel."

"So we can't account for his whereabouts after that?"

William nodded.

Eli aimed the flashlight at his watch. Eleven o'clock. "Could he have gotten out here in that time?"

William shook his head. "It's possible."

Eli combed his fingers through his hair. Up to this point, he had treated Lucy's robbery as a separate crime and had thought of it as just a robbery, but now the crime was directed at Lucy.

Lucy stepped out onto the porch, crossing her arms over her chest. The color had returned to her cheeks. "Heather is on her way."

Eli moved toward her. "I want to go over your place."

Lucy took in a deep breath. "I don't think you'll find anything."

"It still might be worth it. I'll make sure we dust the breaker boxes." If he had the time and money, he could get a full forensics team out here. But without any clear link to the serial murders, he doubted he would get the okay on such an expenditure. He spoke gently.

"Your room was messed up again. He may have taken something."

Even in the scant illumination provided by the flashlight, Eli read fear in Lucy's reaction.

"I'll need some things to take to Heather's, at least a toothbrush and my cosmetic bag. The fumes shouldn't be as bad now. I won't touch anything that might give you evidence."

Eli squared his shoulders. "I don't know if that's such a good idea."

"I can't survive without a toothbrush," she offered. "I'll just go in quickly and grab it."

"Okay," Eli said.

Lucy trudged up the stairs and disappeared inside.

William had already retrieved the forensics kit out of the car and taken out the camera.

"Let's just wait until she comes back out." Having Lucy watch them turn her home into a crime scene could trigger emotions unnecessarily.

Eli glanced toward the door. Maybe it wasn't such a good idea for her to go in there alone. He leapt up to the porch and followed her in. The firefighters with masks on were gathering the charred remains of the blanket and had set up a fan. Eli wrinkled his nose. The fumes were still evident, but not as strong. A breeze billowed the curtains. The lights were on again. Someone must have thrown the breaker box—so much for good fingerprints on Lucy's side.

She emerged from the hallway, holding a small floral bag. The glaze in her unfocused eyes told him what had happened.

"You looked in the bedroom, didn't you?"

She nodded. "Like picking a scab. What is my problem?" She shook her head. "I just had to peek. He took several of my favorite books. There was a gap on the shelf." Again, she touched her neck. "He must have taken that scarf, too, and some others are missing from the rack where I hang them."

Now the thief was taking personal items that were worth nothing monetarily. Their serial killer had never taken anything from his victims. The only reason Eli wanted to link the crimes was because Lucy was such a dead ringer for the other victims. He had to let go of the idea. "Lucy, do you have any idea who might want to do this?"

Her chin jerked up. She glanced at the photos and broken glass that surrounded the fireplace. "Those photos got knocked down in the struggle." Her gaze dropped, and she rubbed her bare arm. She placed a hand over her mouth when she coughed.

Was there something she wasn't telling him? Now was not the time to press her, but he had seen a flash of something when he'd asked the question. He edged closer to Lucy and glanced down at the destroyed photos. There was a recent picture of Lucy and Dawson. And one of a younger Lucy in a basketball uniform, surrounded by her teammates.

"This assault reminds me of something that happened in high school with my high school coach, but he left years ago," Lucy said.

"Lucy." Heather stood in the doorway. "I got here as fast as I could." She rushed over to her friend and escorted her out while putting a supportive arm around her shoulder.

Eli followed the two women out onto the porch. Heather led Lucy to the car. The backward glance she gave him, an expression filled with trust, crushed him.

I can't give you what you need, Lucy.

Whoever was doing this, one thing was clear. Lucy was in ongoing danger. Even if he could talk the chief into watching Lucy's home, she wouldn't accept the help. He couldn't move out.

Lucy glanced back at Eli standing on the porch. For a second time, he'd saved her life.

She got into the car. Heather clicked the key in the ignition, turned on the headlights and pressed on the gas. "You can stay in the guest room. It's full of my sewing and craft stuff, but the bed is really comfortable."

Lucy appreciated that her friend was trying to keep things light with chitchat. But Heather's clipped, nervous tone betrayed that she was upset.

Lucy laced her fingers together and rested them on her lap. "Thanks for coming out to get me." She coughed. Her throat felt gritty from breathing in the fumes.

"Thanks for calling me."

"Big step for me, huh? Asking for help." Lucy glanced out the window at the darkness.

"That's what friends do for each other."

"I'm not the big wreck I could have been. Having Eli here made it so much easier."

Heather pulled out onto the road that led into town. "It is nice to have a friend who is a cop."

Lucy cleared her throat.

"He is a friend, right?"

Warmth pooled in Lucy's chest as she took in a deep breath. "I never thought I would be saying this, but Eli is different."

"Dawson and I were talking about that. I saw you two out there on the river. The way you were with him."

"I know I put up walls, but he has a way of breaking through them."

"So what are you going to do about it?"

"This is all new for me." Lucy stared out at the dark road as the yellow lines clicked by. They had encountered no other cars so far. What would she do about Eli? She did hope their friendship would become something more. She glanced down at her hands, which were white from clenching them so tightly. "I really can't think about Eli until this whole robbery thing is resolved."

"Two robberies in less than a month," Heather said. "What do you think is going on?"

"I don't think this is about money like we first thought. The guy keeps taking personal stuff." Lucy rubbed her bare forearms. "This whole thing feels like what happened in high school when I was being stalked. When I saw the photo of me with the basketball team, I remembered Coach Whitmore."

"Who was Coach Whitmore?"

"He was the girl's basketball coach in high school. Someone kept leaving explicit pictures in my gym and school locker. Sometimes after practice, a car followed me home." Lucy's rib cage tightened. "Then some personal things were taken from my locker…and then from my bedroom. I was pretty sure it was the coach, but when I went to the police, they didn't believe me. They investigated but said there was no evidence to support my claim." She closed her eyes and pressed her head against the back of the seat. Her history with this police department had started long before Dawson's accident. "Some of them were Coach Whitmore's drinking buddies. I think the reason the police didn't respond quickly when Dawson was shot was because of what I said about Coach Whitmore years before. They thought I was making it up."

Compassion permeated Heather's voice. "You never told me."

She'd never told anyone. The other girls on the team had known some of the details. Their nickname for Coach Whitmore had been *the creep*. They were memories she would prefer to not revisit. At the time, her mom had been fighting for her life. "I could never prove that it was Coach Whitmore. He left town after my senior year, and the stalking stopped." She shuddered. "I had heard rumors that he was back in town. I didn't think anything of it until now."

"Lucy, this is serious. You need to find out if he has moved back here."

Lucy pressed her back against the car seat as familiar anxiety returned. "Even if he is living in Mountain Springs, the police probably won't do anything this time, either."

TEN

A tight knot formed at the base of Lucy's neck as she parked her car outside the Mountain Springs police station. She hadn't been in there since Dawson's accident. In the two days since she had gotten home from Heather's, she had hardly seen Eli at the duplex.

She jumped down from the high seat of the van and shut the door. If she couldn't catch Eli at home, she'd have to find him at work.

It had only taken a few phone calls to old high school teachers to find out that Coach Whitmore was back in town. Information Eli needed to know.

Lucy treaded up the stone walkway. A struggling hedge surrounded the squat brick building. The rest of the grounds consisted of brown grass with a few splotches of green and a flagpole.

The door flew open and two men in uniform stepped out. Officers Spitz and O'Bannon stuttered in their stride when they saw her. Chills trailed down her spine. Spitz ran a hand over his bald head as he passed her. The weight of their stares pressed on her back. She opened the door of the station.

Anxiety corseted Lucy's rib cage by the time she stepped inside a small room with a high counter. Usually the receptionist stood behind the counter, but today it was empty. Ten years ago, she'd walked through these doors as a scared teenager. Both Spitz and O'Bannon had been on the force back then, along with the chief who would later be fired, after Dawson's accident. Lucy had pushed for all of the officers to be fired.

"Yes, can I help you?" A male voice echoed in the silence.

Lucy leaned around the counter to peer inside the main office, which consisted of four desks, all empty. Where had the voice come from?

"Ah… I was looking for Eli Hawkins." She massaged the back of her neck where the knot had formed.

A uniformed officer Lucy knew as Nigel Peterson came out from behind a carrel, holding a cup of coffee. Lucy clutched her purse a little tighter to her chest. Peterson had been one of the officers on the force when Dawson had had his accident.

Peterson placed his coffee cup on the top of a file cabinet. "He's out on a call. What can I help you with?" He crossed his arms over his chest.

Peterson had been fresh out of the academy and only a couple of years older than Dawson when the shooting had taken place. He hadn't aged much in four years. His red hair looked a little thinner, and he had put on a few pounds.

"He's been working on my robberies. I have an idea who it might be." She only felt comfortable talking to Eli about this. "I can just come back later."

"No, wait." He took a few steps in her direction.

"He's going to be gone most of the day. Why don't you tell me what is going on?"

"If you could just give him a message. He asked if I knew of anyone who might have a reason to...break into my place." Nigel was from somewhere in Montana. He hadn't been around when she was in high school. Ten years ago, she had walked through the same doors, thinking she would find help. The condescending voices of the officers, their knowing glances at each other, floated back into her memory.

"We've all been briefed on the circumstances of your robberies. I can help you," he coaxed.

Would he even believe her? Her hands sweated as she readjusted her purse. He seemed sincere enough, but maybe he would act different once he was around the other officers. "His name is... George Whitmore. He used to be a coach at the high school. Years ago, I think he might have... I'm not here to point fingers. That's not my intention. It's just that Eli asked."

Nigel picked up a pad of paper and wrote down the name. He stood, pencil poised to write more.

Lucy shifted her weight from one foot to the other as the muscles in her neck turned rock hard. "There were some incidents in high school that made me think that maybe..."

Nigel put his pen and paper on the desk. His eyes searched hers. "It would be easier if I gave the information to Eli, wouldn't it?"

She nodded.

He placed his hands on his hips, let out a heavy sigh and shook his head. "Four years is a long time, isn't it, Lucy?" Sadness, not anger, colored his comment.

Nigel's freckles made him look younger than he really was. She had spent all this time blaming the whole department. He had just been a green rookie. "I'm sorry for the horrible things I said publicly about this police department. My hurt and my anger over what happened to Dawson made it hard for me to control my tongue."

"Some of what you said was well deserved. The chief needed to be fired. He's the one who allowed for that kind of do-nothing atmosphere. Dawson's accident was a wake-up call for all of us."

"Not all the officers feel the way you do."

He shrugged. "I can't help what Spitz and O'Bannon think."

"Maybe I'll just come back when Eli is here."

"No, wait." Nigel took a step toward her. "Eli had a talk with all of us a few days ago. We need to get past this."

Her breath caught. "Eli did that?"

"Why don't you let me see if I can close the file on these robberies? I can't accuse this Whitmore guy of anything, but I can do a little discreet digging."

There was nothing in Nigel's demeanor to confirm her suspicions, yet the old familiar fear that her needs would be dismissed snaked through her. "Eli will know about this?"

"Eli is pretty busy with…another investigation." He turned to face her. "Please trust that I will look into this for you."

She couldn't help the fear that happened almost automatically any time she even had to think about dealing with this police department. Lucy stopped fidgeting with her purse and adjusted the strap on her shoulder.

Sometimes forgiveness required action, even if the emotions weren't cooperating. "Okay, Nigel...that sounds good."

A sparkle filled his green eyes, and the corners of his mouth curved slightly. "All right then."

"I'm headed out for a weekend fishing trip later this afternoon," Lucy said. "So I'll be hard to reach, but you can leave a message on my machine if you find out anything."

Nigel picked his coffee cup off the file cabinet. "I'll keep Eli in the loop as much as I can."

Lucy walked with a lighter step as she made her way back to her van. Would Nigel do what he said? She had no way of knowing. She did know that it had felt good to voice her apology and to hear Nigel's willingness to try to make things right. Officer Peterson was just one cop out of the three that had been on the force four years ago, but it was a start.

When she arrived at the duplex, Lucy shaded her eyes and stared at Eli's closed door. Was Eli avoiding her or was he just busy with work like Nigel had said? Over the past two days, she had heard him come and go. The one time she'd caught him on his way out the door, he had seemed distracted. He was pretty short on conversation. Yet he was coming home in the middle of the day as if to check on her.

She walked around to the back of her van, opened the back door and scanned the gear she had put together for the Memorial Day weekend fishing trip. Lucy took in a deep breath. Eli's actions didn't make any sense—trying to figure him out was making her head hurt.

She scanned the equipment she had packed. Heather would be going with her to help, along with ten paying clients. She had hoped for a few more clients to sign up. These months before the weather was consistently warm could be kind of lean financially.

Being out on the river would be a good way to get her mind off of everything that had happened, and it would help her stop thinking about Eli. She flipped open the first-aid kit, running through a checklist in her head to see what she needed to replenish.

She had to let thoughts of Eli go. No harm, no foul. She and Eli hadn't even been on an official date. Maybe she had just been reading him wrong, assuming he had feelings for her. She slipped the earbuds of her iPod into her ears and turned the music to full blast.

Lucy shook the fishing poles in their racks to make sure they were secure. Most of the people would be bringing their own gear and sleeping bags, but it never hurt to be prepared.

She closed her eyes and stood back, taking in a powerful song chorus. As the music moved toward a climax, the words reminded her that there was no fear for those who loved God. She had heard that truth a hundred times, but had she ever really lived it? She opened her eyes and stared again at all the equipment she had packed in the van. It was one thing to be prepared, and it was another thing to think that all this stuff would prevent bad things from happening.

Lucy shook her head, pulled some of the extra equipment out of the van and tossed it on the ground. She stopped for a moment, closing her eyes again, to listen to the song that played in her ears.

A shadow crossed her path as if a blanket had been thrown on her. She looked up, expecting to see a bird or an airplane. Except for a few drifting clouds, the blue sky was empty.

She sensed someone was standing behind her. Eli? She turned. Her spirit deflated when she saw that it was Greg Jackson. Her music had been so loud, she hadn't heard his car pull up.

She slipped the earbuds out.

"I saw Heather in town a while ago." Greg lifted the straw cowboy hat he was wearing off his head and bent the brim. "She said you were taking some people on an overnight fishing trip."

"Yes, we're going to camp Friday and Saturday night."

"I want to go with you." He must have detected her hesitation because he added, "As a paying client. I'd like to work on my fishing skills."

"Sure, Greg, I've got room."

"I can give you a check right now." There was something pained and desperate in his expression. "Can I ride out with you? My car is not really made for driving up in the mountains."

"What do you have in the way of gear?" She suspected this was a last-minute decision on Greg's part. "I supply the tents if needed, and I can rustle up almost anything else, too."

"I always have my fly rod with me." He chuckled. "I drive so much. Every once in a while I see a beautiful river and just have to stop and fish it."

Greg had never mentioned before that he liked to fish. Given that she fished for a living, it ought to have come up in conversation. She was touched that he was trying to make some kind of connection with her. In her effort to keep her word to Heather, she had probably sent Greg some really ambiguous signals. She would tread lightly around his feelings, but if he was coming with her on this trip, she needed to make sure they were on the same page with their relationship. "Greg, I've decided not to do the online dating thing anymore."

His face brightened as he leaned toward her. "Oh, really. Have you met someone special?"

She had met someone special, but he wasn't around anymore. Greg had totally misunderstood her comment. "You are more than welcome to come on this trip. I enjoy your company, but I really think we should just be friends."

Greg's mouth drooped. "Okay." The tone of his voice implied that he didn't quite believe her. "I don't have a sleeping bag with me."

"Just so we understand each other. We're just friends, right?"

He nodded.

"Good then, load up whatever you have with you. I am sure I can find another sleeping bag. I'll just go inside and grab one." She picked up the things she'd pulled out of the van and darted up the stairs without waiting for a reaction from him. She hadn't wanted to hurt him, but it had felt good to clarify their relationship.

Lucy turned the knob on her door and left it open while she darted up to her loft, where she kept extra camping and fishing supplies. She rifled through several cupboards before she found a sleeping bag appropriate for the season and the right size for a tall man like Greg.

She scampered down the stairs. Greg stood in the doorway.

"You find one?" His voice had taken on a low, husky quality.

She held up the bag. "We should get going. Memorial Day weekend is a great time to be out on the river."

Greg still didn't budge. He was tall enough that he blocked out most of the light streaming through the open door.

As he moved toward her, his footsteps echoed on the wooden floor. "I'm looking forward to being with you." His Adam's apple moved up and down. He lifted his chin. His eyes narrowed. Something about his expression, maybe it was the hardness of his features and the slant of his eyebrows, struck her as unpleasant and brooding.

Lucy took a step back. This house reminded her too much of the assault that had just happened. Maybe that was why her heart was racing.

Lucy handed Greg the sleeping bag. "Load up whatever you have and get in the van."

She did a quick walk through her house, making sure the window, now repaired, was latched. She clicked the dead bolt on the kitchen door. As she locked the front door, a feeling of unease permeated her emotions.

She wiggled the doorknob, double-checking to make sure it was locked. Would her stalker be back to steal something else? Hopefully, Eli would be around more so he could keep an eye on things. She hadn't had a chance to tell him about her trip.

She bounded down the stairs with one backward glance at Eli's closed door. Lucy slipped into the driver's side of the van and clicked on her seat belt. Even as she offered Greg a faint smile, a heaviness she recognized as heartache settled on her. She had begun to open her heart to Eli and that was where it would end.

"You have kind of a faraway look in your eyes." Greg leaned toward her.

Lucy shifted into Reverse and turned the car around. "It's nothing…just thinking." *About things that might have been.*

"Catching some trout should be fun," Greg offered.

Greg's unwavering gaze made her wiggle in her seat as she turned out onto the gravel road and headed toward the river.

"Yes, we should be able to catch something." She needed to get away from this house and out on the water, where she always found peace and the world made sense.

"I'm looking forward to this drive with you." Greg's voice slipped into a hoarse whisper.

A sense of uneasiness rose up in Eli as he pulled into the gravel drive by the duplex and recognized Greg Jackson's car. He'd just gotten word from Officer Smith that Greg Jackson had canceled his date with her tonight. What was Jackson up to?

Eli squeezed the steering wheel a little tighter. Lucy's van was gone.

He got out of his car, grabbed his briefcase and headed toward Lucy's door. Even as he knocked and called her name, he knew it was futile to hope that she was home safe. She and Greg had gone somewhere in her vehicle. He needed to find out where…and quickly.

He traversed the distance to his own side of the house and unlocked his door. He said a prayer for Lucy's safety as his door swung open. Lucy had a cell phone, but he had no idea what the number was. Mentally, he kicked himself for not thinking to ask for it. She had been on his mind in other ways.

When he was home working, he was always aware if she came and went. Every noise she made seemed to be on a higher volume than the rest of the world. Her footsteps on the floorboards of the porch and the sound of her vehicle starting up always caught his attention. He was tuned in to her as if some invisible cord tied them together.

Keeping his emotional distance from her was the hardest thing he had ever done.

He placed his briefcase on the table by the window. He could probably get her number from one of her friends. He hadn't ever been told Heather's last name, but Nelson might know where Lucy was.

Eli rooted through a cupboard to find the phone book he'd gotten the day before. Fear pulsed in his veins as he flipped it open to find Nelson's number. He'd done everything he could to make sure she was okay. He had been coming home for lunch to check on her. On the days he had to do surveillance out of town, he'd requested a patrol car go out in this direction. Realistically, he couldn't keep an eye on her 24/7. Still, knowing that she was alone with Jackson felt like a blunder on his part.

His finger trailed down the list of phone numbers.

It had to be here. He exhaled when his finger landed on Thane, Nelson. Eli dialed the number and paced through his living room. He stood at the window, staring at the pine trees and cottonwoods that surrounded Lucy's property.

Nelson picked up on the fourth ring.

"Nelson, it's Eli. Lucy's…" What was he to her? "Lucy's renter."

"Yeah."

"Listen, I just got home, and a strange car is in Lucy's drive. There's no sign of Lucy, but her car is gone. I don't suppose you know where she might be."

"Is she okay?"

He didn't want to trigger any alarm bells or give away too much by identifying Greg Jackson by name. "I'm just concerned about this car and Lucy being gone."

There was a pause on the other end of the line as if Nelson were formulating an answer or deciding if he should answer at all. "Lucy didn't say anything to you about where she would be?"

It was understandable that he wanted to protect Lucy's privacy. "She's had those two break-ins. Guess I am just kind of worried."

"Oh, right." He relented. "She usually takes clients for an extended fishing trip on Memorial Day weekend."

"Are you going with her?"

"I'm a teacher, remember. I have some workshops I have to attend out of town. I think Heather said something about going with her."

"Do you know where they went?"

"You don't think somebody has…taken… Lucy."

"No, there is nothing to indicate that. But given the break-ins, it makes sense to check on her. It kind of comes with my job description. Do you know her cell number?"

Nelson gave him the number and then added, "A lot of times she doesn't take it with her. A ringing cell phone messes with the serenity of the weekend. The signal drops out a lot once you get up in the mountains, so it's not of much use, safety-wise."

"Do you know where she was planning on camping?"

"There are a hundred campgrounds she could pick. I know she favors the Beartrap campgrounds by the lake. There is a fishing supply place out that way where Lucy usually fuels up. The owners know her."

"That's enough to go on, thanks."

Eli hung up and grabbed his coat. Before he started his car, he tried Lucy's cell phone. No answer. It had been worth a try.

He struggled to stay under the speed limit as he drove toward the main road. He stopped at the first gas station he saw and got directions to the Beartrap store. Eli barely noticed a landscape of rocks and evergreens clipping by as he sped along the mountain road. To keep his mind from shifting into hyper-worry mode, he prayed.

A psalm floated into his head. "I lift my eyes up to the mountains. Where does my help come from? My help comes from the Lord, the maker of heaven and earth." He glanced up at the high mountain that the curving road had been cut through.

He couldn't control outcomes; he couldn't protect everyone all the time, but whatever the circumstances, God would be there for him.

A sign indicated that the turnoff for the Beartrap campgrounds was a mile away. Eli slowed the car and hit his turn signal. The store was not hard to spot. With the exception of a few cabins off in the distance, it was the only structure around. The dusty sign outside advertised that they sold gas, bait and groceries. RV hookups were also available. Two struggling cottonwoods stood on either side of the low-roofed building.

Eli parked his car off to one side. Four motor homes along with several tents were parked behind the store. The river had slipped in and out of view while he was driving. Now he could hear the distant roar of rushing water but not see it.

He raced into the store, where a teenager with pink hair and a nose ring stood behind the counter. The rich brown of her skin suggested she spent more time outside than in the dim store.

"I am wondering if a woman with long, dark hair came in here earlier. She's a fly fishing guide, and she is taking a bunch of people to the lake."

"You're talking about Lucy Kimbol."

Hope fluttered through him as he stepped around a stack of boxes. "Yes, do you know where she is camping?"

"She reserved several spots up by Madison Point. People who said they were with her have gone through here today, but I haven't seen Lucy yet."

He swallowed to produce some moisture in his mouth. He didn't know anything for sure yet. No need to panic. "Could you have missed her? Or maybe she didn't stop here this time."

The girl shook her head. "I've been behind this counter since ten o'clock. And even if people don't stop, I see them go by. Lucy's van is pretty distinctive. She must have been delayed."

His shoulders slumped. This meant she might be driving around with Greg Jackson...or worse.

The myriad metal bracelets on the teenager's wrist jingled when she lifted her arm and grabbed a map from a rack. "I can give you directions to the camp if you like. I'm sure she'll show up sooner or later."

Eli massaged his chest where it felt tight. "I guess that is the best option."

The young woman gave directions that included things like turning right at the rock with the tree growing out of it. When she finished, she said, "You can keep the map, no charge."

He thanked her and headed out the door. Maybe Lucy had just stopped somewhere for supplies or had a flat tire. He shouldn't think worst-case scenario.

Eli hopped in his car and headed up the road until he found the marked turnoff the teenager had told him about. The road followed the river. He half expected and hoped that he would see Lucy's van before he even got to the camp.

He came to a crossroads and took a right. Several cars, none of them Lucy's van, came into view. The road ended where the land sloped gently down. The silver shimmer of a lake was visible through the trees. When he got out of his car, Eli saw several tents set up in a circle around a fire pit.

He counted five people milling around the camp and three lined up against the edge of the lake, fishing. He trotted down the hill toward the camp.

An older woman in a lime-green T-shirt with large flowers on it noticed him. "Are you one of Lucy's clients? We've all just been getting acquainted and waiting for her."

"She's not here yet?"

The woman shook her head. "I'm sure she'll be along. I'm Betty Daniels, by the way. Lucy taught me how to fly fish just last year." Betty lifted her chin proudly. "I hold the record for being her oldest client."

Eli glanced around the camp. There seemed to be an equal number of men and women. He recognized one of Lucy's high school students from the day he'd rented her duplex, a chubby-cheeked teenager named Marnie. The girl waved at Eli when he made eye contact.

"I hope Lucy gets here soon." The older woman swatted at a mosquito on her arm. "Some of us brought our own tents, but she supplies the others, and she's bringing all the cooking equipment. What did you say your name was?"

"Eli Hawkins."

"Why don't you go down to the lake and enjoy the beauty of God's creation. Lucy will be along anytime now."

He hoped that was true. Maybe he should retrace his steps back into town to see if he could find her. Doing nothing never felt right to him, but he could at least wait a few minutes. Eli tromped down to the edge of the lake. He sat on a flat stump and listened to the sound of the water lapping against the shore while he tapped his foot on the soft dirt. Ten minutes passed. Where was she?

Though there was no dock, several boats and a canoe were arranged upside down not far from the water's edge, along with some float tubes. Lucy must have hauled those up earlier. Behind him, he could hear the sound of people laughing and chatting.

The sky was a clear blue now, but it would start to get dark in a couple of hours. The sun slipped a little lower on the horizon. Eli allowed the soothing murmur of the water to relax him. The memory of the afternoon he and Lucy had spent on the river flashed through his mind.

A shout rose up from the camp and Eli turned. Lucy's van came into view at the top of the hill. Doors slammed, and he saw Heather's blond ponytail and then Greg Jackson gripping a fishing pole. The hat Jackson wore covered his face, but Eli recognized the hunch in his shoulders. Lucy appeared a moment later from the back of the van, holding a cooler.

Eli let out a sigh of relief.

He remained on the edge of camp while the others circled around Lucy. She was wearing a hot pink shirt that made her stand out from the group. Several people ran up to the van and pulled out supplies. With Greg here, it made sense to hang around for as long as he could.

He stalked up the hill and asked a middle-aged man who stood by the van if there was anything he could take down to the camp. The man stacked several tents in storage bags in Eli's arms.

"I'm sure we'll be needing these," said the man.

The hard metal of the tent poles pressed against Eli's

forearm through the nylon fabric. He made his way down the hill and sought out Lucy. Her pink shirt was easy enough to spot. Her back was turned toward him as she kneeled beside an open cooler.

"Where should I put these?"

She jerked around and rose to her feet. Her distressed expression chilled him.

The last thing I wanted to do was cause you pain, Lucy.

"What are you doing here?" She took a step back.

"I came for some fishing lessons from a great teacher."

His compliment did nothing to diminish the coolness in her eyes. Lucy pulled a package of hot dogs out of the ice chest. "You need to go."

"Look, I know I have been making myself scarce." Even when she was upset with him, he relished being close to her.

Heather came up behind Lucy. "Hey, Eli. I didn't know you were coming this weekend."

"He's not staying," Lucy said flatly.

"He's not?" Heather cut a glance toward Lucy and then looked at Eli. "Oh, well, at least join us for dinner." She took the package of hot dogs. "We should be eating in about twenty minutes."

Lucy turned away and stalked down toward the lake. She lifted her hand to her face, obviously wiping her eyes. Eli stepped toward her, but Heather caught him.

"Give her a moment. I don't know what's happened between you two, but maybe you can get things smoothed out over dinner."

"That's all right." He could watch out for her without having to talk to her. Greg probably wouldn't try anything with all these people around. He punched his fist against the palm of his right hand. Still, it bothered him that she was hurting.

During the meal, Lucy kept her distance, then disappeared altogether. Eli visited with the other clients, looking for any excuse to stay longer. While he talked to Betty, he scanned the campground. His heart lurched. Lucy stood at the shore with Greg, pushing a canoe into the water.

"What is Lucy doing?" He watched as Greg wandered back up the hill.

Betty crossed her arms. "Some of the clients paid extra for individual instruction. Lucy is probably taking that fellow out on the water. The rest of us are thinking about a sing-along. We've got a couple of guitar players among us. Want to join?"

"I need to take care of something first." Eli strode down to where Lucy was loading gear into the canoe.

"Haven't you left yet?" she asked. She clicked herself into her life jacket.

"I don't think it is a good idea for you to go out on the water alone with that man." He labored to keep his voice calm, to not reveal the hurricane of anxiety brewing inside.

Greg was already on his way back down the hill.

Lucy straightened her back. "He is a client and a friend. He paid for private instruction, and I am taking him out on the lake. You have to stop this…behavior, Eli. It's crazy."

He searched her eyes, desperate to keep her safe on shore. "Please, don't go."

"You can't tell me what to do." Her reprimand was soft, and he could discern the distress beneath her words. Pain he had caused. Nothing he could say would stop her.

Greg yelled across the camp, holding his fly rod. "I'm ready to go."

Eli stepped away. "Be careful, Lucy."

Lucy and Greg pushed the canoe off the shore and jumped in. As they drifted, Lucy mimed a casting motion while Greg watched her and dragged the paddle through the water.

Maybe he could still keep an eye on her. He was a strong swimmer. If he heard sounds of a struggle, he could jump in the water. Someone had already taken the other boats, but he'd seen the extra fishing rods and waders that Lucy had laid out for anyone to grab.

His shoulders tensed when Lucy's boat slipped behind a peninsula populated with trees.

He worked his way quickly down the shoreline, scanning the water for signs of Lucy's canoe. This part of the lake was narrow enough that he could see the other side of the shore, where several fishermen were visible. Four other boats drifted on the water, as well. Lucy's boat was not overly distinctive, but he recognized her pink shirt. He stepped into the water.

He cast several times. At this distance, Lucy probably wouldn't even be able to discern that it was him on the shore.

He heard the swishing noise of someone moving through water behind him.

"Mind if you have some company?" Betty smiled

and squared her shoulders. "Couldn't quite put the sing-along together, so I decided to get in some practice."

He still had a clear view of the boat, but it was drifting farther away. "I'm just working my way down the river."

Betty drew back her rod. "Getting any hits?"

He squinted. Lucy's pink shirt had become a dot. "No, not really."

"It helps if you actually put your line in the water." Betty drew back her own fly rod and cast. "'Course, you are probably distracted keeping an eye on Lucy while she is with that other guy."

"No, that's not why I'm…um." Betty thought he was watching Lucy because he was jealous of Greg. Was that the impression he was giving?

"You don't need to worry about that guy in the boat with her. You can tell she doesn't like him." Betty reeled in her line. "Nope, I would say the field is wide-open for you."

"I rent half of a duplex from her. We're just friends." He didn't sound convincing even to himself. Even if there could be nothing romantic between them, he cared deeply for Lucy. More so than he had about any other woman.

Betty laughed. "I watched the two of you back at camp. Only people who like each other fight like that. I saw how you changed when her van showed up. I don't know what is stopping the two of you, but I'm sure you can work through it."

Eli sighed. "I wish it were that easy."

"Love is always that easy." The line clicked on Betty's reel. "Just move whatever is standing in the way out of the way."

He scanned the lake, panic rising in his chest. No sign of Lucy's boat. This lake was huge. There were a dozen eddies she could have slipped into. If he watched long enough, she would glide back into view. "I do have feelings for Lucy." Saying the truth out loud intensified the emotion he'd been pushing down.

"I thought so." Betty nodded. "This is a lovely time of night to be out here. Fish are always biting right before the sun goes down." Water whooshed around her as she stepped away from Eli. "Won't catch anything if we keep jabbering."

They cast silently for several minutes as the distance between them increased. Waves lapped against his waders, and the sky turned from blue to gray. Over and over, he scanned the lake in the waning light. Maybe there was enough traffic on the water to prevent Greg from trying anything.

He saw a flash of pink. He had worked his way to a wider part of the lake; the opposite shore was no longer visible.

As the sun slipped behind the horizon, Betty waved at him. She was far enough away that he couldn't hear her even if she shouted. The older woman worked her way to shore and disappeared into the trees.

Slowly the population on the river diminished as fishermen returned to their camps to cook their catch or, more likely, the beans and burgers they had brought with them.

Eli stepped as far into the water as he could in order

to get a maximum view of the lake. Even though there were fewer boats, none of them were Lucy's.

He'd lost her.

ELEVEN

Tension pinched the muscles in Lucy's neck. The farther they got away from the camp, the more agitated Greg grew. He cursed when his line caught on something in the water. After they got his line free, Lucy made a suggestion about holding the rod at a different angle.

He tossed his rod into the boat. "I don't want to fish." He crossed his arms and glowered.

"Sorry, I didn't mean to sound bossy."

Eli's words of caution floated back into her head. Why had he been so determined not to let her go out on the water with Greg? As their boat had edged away from the shore, Eli had stood on the beach, watching them. At the time, his actions had confirmed her fear that, despite his kindness, Eli was controlling.

Now as she and Greg drifted farther out, she wondered if Eli's cautions hadn't been valid all along. When Eli had shown up, all she had wanted to do was get away from him and the strong emotions his presence evoked. His hot-cold behavior toward her was too much to take.

Greg stared at the water. Lucy paddled the canoe into a quiet spot where they were likely to catch something.

"Tell you what. I'll cast for a while." She picked up her rod. "You just enjoy the quiet."

Greg unfolded his arms and rubbed them on his thighs. "So what is between you and that Hawkins guy anyway?"

Was that what his pouting was about? "Nothing. We're friends, that's all." Even as she said it, she knew it wasn't true. She wasn't about to get into a relationship with someone whose signals were so inconsistent, but she had to be honest about how much she cared about him.

"You're friends with everyone, every guy." His tone held an undercurrent of irritation.

On the ride up, the thought of having to be alone in the van with Greg was more than she wanted to handle. He kept pressing the conversation toward the personal, as if he hadn't heard that she was only interested in him as a friend. She'd taken a detour and picked up Heather, despite having made plans to meet at the lake, so the conversation would remain light. "Heather keeps telling me I turn every guy into a friend." She laughed. "Actually, it's what everyone keeps saying."

Her comment seemed to break the tension. Greg chortled and picked up his fly rod. They cast for some time. Greg offered to paddle, and Lucy indicated a place she thought the fish might be biting.

The blue sky of midday faded into a shroud of gray. The gentle plopping sound of the fish rising to the water's surface to feed in the evening increased. Lucy attached a different fly to her tippet. Thinking about Eli, trying to make sense out of everything he had done, made her head hurt. He was a hard man to figure out.

"Lots of fish out here. I don't know why nothing's taking the fly." Greg's words broke through the tumult of her thoughts.

She angled around in the boat, assessing where they were in the fading light. She'd been so lost in thought, she hadn't been paying attention to where Greg was paddling. She'd been out on this lake a thousand times. All she needed was a familiar landmark to know where she was.

"It's almost dark, Greg. We really should be headed back."

She scanned the shoreline, looking for a grove of trees or an outcropping of rock that was distinct. They were in the wide part of the lake; only one shoreline was visible, and it was distant and dark.

"Is everything okay?" he asked.

She pulled her compass out of one of her pockets. "We're fine, I just need to get a stronger sense of where we are." Lucy held the compass closer to her face, trying to decipher the numbers and letters.

"Lucy, I didn't sign up for your clinic and ask you out here so I could improve my casting technique."

Still gripping the compass, Lucy looked at Greg. His expression wasn't readable in this light, but his tone had warmed.

"What do you mean?" She had a feeling where this was going.

He cleared his throat. "I know that you said you just wanted to be friends."

She couldn't see her compass. She slipped out of

her life jacket so she could dig deeper into her vest to find her flashlight. "We can talk about this later, Greg. Right now, we need to focus on getting back to camp."

"I don't want to talk about it later." Greg readjusted himself on the seat with such energy that it shook the canoe.

Lucy dug through her pockets. She zipped and unzipped. She always had her flashlight with her. It had to be here somewhere. Her stomach tensed in anticipation of what she was pretty sure Greg was going to say.

"I've been wanting to say this for some time, but you always set things up so we are never alone."

Where was that flashlight? Lucy struggled to keep her voice calm. "Greg, I thought you understood that we were just friends." Now she was mad at herself for being in such a hurry to get away from Eli that she hadn't thought about the consequences of being alone with Greg. She had seen this coming when they were in the van, but Eli showing up had thrown clear thinking out the window.

"Not every man in your life wants to just be your best buddy. When are you going to see that?" Greg shouted, standing halfway up in the canoe and then plopping back down with force.

Water sloshed against the side of the boat. She gripped the rim. "Careful, canoes aren't like boats—they tip easily."

Leaning closer to her, he grabbed her hands. "I have stopped dating all the other women I was paired up with. It's you, Lucy. You're the one for me. I've been praying about it."

"Greg, you are a nice guy, but—"

He stood up, looming over her. "God told me you were the one." The boat rocked.

"Greg, please sit down." She raised her voice. He didn't comply. She spoke in a monotone, enunciating every word. "I think you are projecting things onto God because it's what you want."

"I've been patient. I've been nice." He lunged toward her, and she fell backward.

The boat tipped dangerously to one side. He reached for her, and she scrambled to get away from him. Water cascaded into the boat.

"Greg, please sit down."

Greg shot up onto his feet, unsteady as the boat rocked. "When, Lucy, when are you going to see how much I like you?" He wobbled.

He reached for her, yanking her to her feet. "Please, stop," she begged.

The canoe angled dangerously to one side. Greg stumbled, grabbing Lucy to steady himself. Instead, he pulled her into the water with him. The lake engulfed her. She thrashed around, unable to orient in the depths of the cold water.

Something anchored her in place, a weight on her shoulder, like hands holding her down. Lucy kicked her legs, trying to break free, but the weight on her shoulder made it impossible to move.

She needed to breathe. She flailed her arms, then angled downward trying to escape the force clamped on her shoulders. The weight lifted. With a final burst of energy, she scissor-kicked her legs and reached upward.

Lucy swam to the surface, breaking through the

water into the dim of evening. She gasped. Breath wheezed through her nose.

She could make out the fuzzy silhouette of the shore. She waited for her eyes to adjust. Slowly the outline of the boat came into view. A soaking wet Greg crawled into the canoe.

"Over here." She swam toward it, her strokes sluggish and uneven. When she stopped to see how close she was, Greg was paddling the boat…away from her. She shouted one more time. The stroke of the paddle stuttered and then he seemed to glide across the water even faster. Stunned, she treaded water as he disappeared around a bend. Had he left her here to drown? She wondered, too, if it hadn't been his hands holding her under.

Lucy turned a slow circle in the lake. Lakes were warmer than rivers, but the cold could be a factor if she stayed in the water too long.

Though distant, the shoreline was visible. It was on the opposite side of the lake from where camp was, but it was dry land. There were campers all around the lake. She'd likely find help.

Lucy shivered. Her arms cut through the water. She focused on the shoreline, careful to pace herself, so she didn't run out of energy.

She stopped to tread water and catch her breath. Her muscles were heavy, on fire with pain. Water lapped around her.

Her calf muscles contracted. The chill of the water had soaked through to her muscles. Her vest with all its filled pockets was weighing her down. Much as she regretted the loss, she was going to have to let it go.

Lucy slipped free of the vest and flipped over on her back. With the night sky as her canopy, she backstroked through the water.

A few stars had already come out. With renewed vigor, she turned over on her stomach and stroked toward the shore. The outlines and shadows of the forest grew closer.

Lucy swam the final yards to shallow water. She didn't have an ounce of energy left. Her feet brushed over the rocky bottom of the lake. She pulled herself the rest of the way out of the water, collapsing on the muddy shore. Her lungs felt as if they'd been scraped with a utility knife, and her arms and legs burned from exertion.

She pressed her face against the earth, waiting to get her breathing under control. Every part of her felt heavy, numb and cold. Her head seemed as if it was stuffed full of marbles. She closed her eyes, listening to her own raspy, rapid breathing, waiting for it to slow down.

She rolled over on her back and stared at the night sky. Stars twinkled back at her. Could Eli have been right about Greg? Had he tried to hold her under water? She closed her eyes. Eli had tried to warn her from the beginning. She'd been too stubborn to listen at first and then, tonight, too blinded by hurt.

She sat up, pulling her knees to her chest. The night was chilly, but not freezing. Her wet clothes clung to her body. First things first—she needed to get warm and dry. She placed a palm on her shoulder expecting to feel the pocket of her vest. Her heart sank. The waterproof matches were in the vest she had peeled off in the water.

Lucy shivered and stared up at the dark sky.

* * *

"Are you sure you'll be all right going alone?" Heather asked as she opened the back of Lucy's van. "They always say it's better to work in pairs."

Eli loaded his pack with everything he thought he might need for a night search. He ignored the panic that had invaded his thoughts ever since Lucy had slipped out of view in the boat. He stuffed a flashlight in his pack. "At this point, I think we need to divide our efforts. If I'm not back in camp by daylight, you can send a search party out for me."

Heather nodded. "I'm going to take the road around the lake one more time to see if I can spot their boat, and then I'll head back to camp to wait for news from the others."

Eli clamped a supportive hand on Heather's shoulder. "We'll find them." It wasn't the thought of Lucy being out in the elements or the possibility that something had gone wrong with the boat that worried him. Lucy was experienced enough to deal with the wilderness. The problem was that she was with Greg Jackson.

When it had grown dark and Lucy and Greg hadn't shown up, two people from the camp had gone down the mountain to notify the police and search and rescue. Campers all along the shoreline had taken their boats out to search the water. Others had gone out to check the trails.

After saying goodbye to Heather, Eli turned onto the trail. The waxing gibbous moon provided some light as he trudged on the hard ground. He'd kept thoughts of Lucy and what might have happened to her at bay by focusing on organizing the search. Now that he was alone, hundreds of crime-scene pictures flashed through his head.

If something happened to Lucy, he would never forgive himself. Greg had been the last person she'd been seen with. Certainly he wouldn't try anything.

That rationality did nothing to make him less anxious. The forest grew thicker, blocking out the moon. Eli switched on his flashlight.

Lucy had become such an important part of his life. She mattered to him more than any woman he'd known. His throat tightened. What would he do without her?

He couldn't keep his distance. He didn't want to. He loved her.

The trail beneath his feet had gotten narrower until it had disappeared all together. Eli took a few steps through the dense forest, hoping to find the trail again. His flashlight flickered. Great, the batteries were going dead.

As he banged the flashlight against his palm to get it to work, he refused to believe that anything had happened to her. He would find her.

Lucy's teeth chattered as she crossed her arms over her body. She had been walking for close to an hour. She'd stayed close to the lake, yet she hadn't come across a single camper.

The night sounds of the forest, branches creaking and waves lapping against the shore, surrounded her. The scent of pine and mountain cleanness hung in the air. From the time Grandpa had first taken her backpacking, the forest had never been a scary place. Being this close to God's creation comforted her even now, though she was cold and tired.

With her strength renewed, she vowed to get home and apologize to Eli. He had been right about Greg.

Lucy stepped into a clearing.

The glow from lanterns and fires should make it easy to find campers. The people from her party must have been alarmed by now. Greg's behavior had been so strange. Would he go back to camp? She doubted it. What kind of believable story could he tell about her whereabouts?

A branch cracked. Lucy's breath caught. She glanced around, looking for something to use as a weapon. A deer emerged from the trees, followed by a second doe. They sauntered across the clearing. Lucy stood still, not wanting to alarm them or destroy the sacredness of the moment. The deer came down to the water and dipped its head to drink. Lucy held her breath and willed herself to be a statue. Moonlight washed over them. Their heads shot up. White tails flickered.

They suddenly bolted back into the trees, opposite the direction they had come from. Something had scared them. Every ambient sound fell away as she focused on the forest. A breaking branch crackled.

Lucy tensed. A shadow emerged from the trees. Could be a man. Could be an animal. Something was definitely over there. It was too far to run to the trees where the deer had fled. She edged toward the water.

The shadow separated, and she saw that it was a man. Greg maybe? Had he come looking for her to finish the job he had started on the lake?

She eased into a crouch by the water, hoping to blend

into her surroundings. Her heart hammered. Kneeling made her keenly aware of how much her tired muscles ached.

The man, still shrouded in shadow, moved across the clearing, stopped, cupped his hands over his mouth and yelled, "Lucy!"

She knew that voice. "Eli." She sprang to her feet, closing the distance between them.

Eli enveloped her, wrapping his arms around her, repeating her name over and over. "I am so glad to see you." He stroked her hair. "We were looking for you everywhere."

She rested her face against his chest. "Eli, you were right…about Greg."

"Lucy, I…" He kissed the top of her head. "When I thought something…"

She pulled back and looked up at him. Something about him had changed. The intensity of his gaze drew her in.

His fingertips brushed her temple and trailed down her cheek. He leaned toward her and pressed his lips against hers. She touched the roughness of his face as he deepened the kiss. Her skin tingled. His hand rested on her back, pulling her even closer.

He released her from the kiss. His smile faded. "I had some time to think about you, about us." He rested his fingers beneath her jaw, lifting her chin slightly. "I know you fear losing people you love. Don't let that fear control you. I'm here. You don't have to be afraid anymore. I am not going anywhere."

"I want that to be true." Lucy closed her eyes, and he kissed each lid.

"Almost losing you made me realize what I have to do," he whispered. He nestled his face against her neck. His lips grazed her skin.

She melted against him. This was where she had longed to be, safe in Eli's arms. Why had she fought his kindness, his need to protect her, for so long? Was fear really ruling her choices?

He pulled free, still resting his palm on her back. He touched her wet hair with his other hand. "We need to build a fire and get you dry and warm. I have something to tell you." He pulled his jacket off and draped it over her shoulders.

"A fire? I ditched my vest in the lake because it was weighing me down. My matches were in there."

He placed a warm finger on her lips. He reached into the pocket of the jacket he had just given her and pulled out a tiny box. "Waterproof matches. I grabbed them out of your van."

He slipped his hand in hers and guided her across the clearing toward a flat rock. "You sit here. I'll get some wood together."

"I can help."

"No, Lucy." He tucked a strand of hair behind her ear, tracing the outline of her ear with his finger. "You have been through so much. You don't have to do everything."

"Okay." Lucy sat down on a large rock. The warmth of Eli's touch lingered on her skin. Her limbs, which a few minutes before had felt heavy from exertion, now were light like helium.

Eli sauntered toward the forest, leaning over to gather logs and twigs. She was shivering by the time he got back with wood. He stacked the sticks into a tee-pee shape and placed the kindling inside the structure.

"After we get you warmed up, we'll hike out," he said.

"How far are we from camp?"

"Heather dropped me off at the trailhead. I walked for about an hour." With the fire going, he sat on the rock beside her. Eli poked at the burning logs with a stick.

Lucy held her hands out closer to the fire. Eli's leg pressed against hers. She breathed in his clean soap smell. Explanations could come later. For now, she just wanted to savor this moment. Eli had promised not to leave her and that was all that mattered.

Feeling even more protective of Lucy, Eli wrapped an arm around her shoulder. Betty's advice echoed through his head. Love was easy, you just needed to move whatever was in the way out of the way. What was in the way was this investigation. "There is a reason why I was concerned about you being with Greg."

"I even had an inkling about him when I was driving up here." Lucy crossed her arms over her chest and stared at the fire. "I wasn't thinking straight. I wanted to get away from you. My emotions were so mixed up."

"I understand. I know I sent you really mixed signals." His pulse rate increased. Would telling her the truth drive them apart? The kiss had melted his feet in his shoes. He'd wanted to do that for a long time. He turned his head and kissed her cheek, basking in the warmth of being so close to her.

She tugged the coat up around her shoulders. "I

think Greg tried to drown me." She shuddered, and he squeezed her tighter. "What if he was the one who was in my place those two times?"

He still viewed the robberies as a separate crime. Lucy's assumption was logical since she didn't know anything about the investigation.

Eli cleared his throat. He had done everything he could, and Lucy was safe. He had to let go of feeling like he hadn't done enough to protect her. "What makes you say he tried to hurt you?"

"He pulled us both out of the boat…and I… I thought he held me under water."

He rubbed her arm. "But you're not sure?"

"It all happened so fast. I think falling in the water was an accident, but then…" She stiffened. "Did they find Greg?"

"No. He never came back to the camp. We have a ton of people looking for both of you all around the lake."

"He took off in the boat. I know he heard me shouting. Why did he leave me there?"

Greg's behavior did sound suspicious. "You're still shivering. Why don't we sit a little closer?"

She slipped off the rock and used it as a backrest. He tossed another log onto the blazing fire and sat down beside her.

After a moment, she rested her head against him. Her breathing deepened as she fell asleep. He held her, watching the flames in the fire and enjoying her closeness.

She stirred. He wrapped an arm around her, and she nestled closer. He touched her soft hair.

Eli stared out into the darkness and listened to the

soft rhythm of Lucy's breathing. She had stopped shivering. He'd missed his opportunity to tell her about the investigation. Maybe it was better this way. He'd clear it with the chief first. Lucy needed to know. He was tired of the deception.

He'd have to wake her in a few minutes. He tilted his head to stare at the twinkling stars and prayed for more chances to hold Lucy. There was still so much in the way.

One thing was clear. If Greg had tried to drown Lucy and then left her, they had a reason for bringing him in. Then maybe this investigation would be wrapped up and out of their lives.

Ten minutes later, Lucy opened her eyes and sat up.

"Hey, sleepyhead. Let's go see if we can find some help."

They hiked for hours toward the trailhead in the rose light of predawn until they found a camper who was willing to take them back to their camp. Heather and Betty were the only ones still there when they showed up. Betty greeted them with a hug and returned to taking down tents.

Heather wrapped an arm around her friend. "I'll get the word out that we found you." She squeezed Lucy's shoulder. "You look tired and beat-up. I can wait here to notify the others. Why don't you ride back in with Eli? I'll bring the van in later."

Eli slipped his hand into Lucy's. "Has Greg Jackson been found?"

Heather shook her head. "They found the boat pulled ashore, but no sign of him. Go home and get some rest. Betty and I can do any cleanup that needs to be done."

They drove down the mountain in Eli's car with the sun brimming on the horizon. As they neared the duplex, Eli checked his phone. His signal was back, and he had twelve messages.

Lucy leaned toward him. "Something wrong?"

He paged through the messages as ice froze in his veins. All the calls were from William's cell or the police station. He dialed William's number.

William picked up before the first ring ended. "Where have you been? We've had another murder over in Cragmore."

TWELVE

Eli's stomach churned as he stepped under the crime scene tape. William emerged from a tight circle of people. He handed a framed photo to his partner. Outside, two police cars were parked beside William's car.

"Jessica Mason, age twenty-six." William turned slightly. "Most of the crime scene work is done. When I couldn't get hold of you, I opted to have the body taken in for autopsy. I figured we have to move fast on this."

A chill ran down Eli's back. He stared at the photo of the dark-haired, blue-eyed woman. "This shouldn't have happened on my watch."

"It shouldn't happen on anybody's watch. Don't beat yourself up."

"Thanks for the reminder." Eli glanced around the simply furnished living room. "What about our suspects? Did any of them have contact with our victim?"

"Far as we know, none of the three came near here. We've only done preliminary questioning. Something might turn up later. Is Jackson still unaccounted for?"

Eli nodded. He had already explained the reason he couldn't answer his phone to William. When he had pulled up to Lucy's duplex, Greg's car was still parked there. Lucy had promised she would go to a neighbor's house until Heather showed up with the van.

"Thought you might want to do a walk-through before we go to the morgue." William gestured for Eli to follow him. "The prelim exam suggests it might have been strangulation."

"That fits the M.O. of the other victims." Eli's footsteps seemed to echo in the cold, still house. "Who found her?"

"Paper boy. She's always sitting on her porch with her cup of coffee, waiting for him. She wasn't there this morning."

A hot sear of pain jabbed through Eli. Jessica would never sit on her porch again. "So she could have died last night?"

"We're trying to track down who may have seen her last and find out what she did yesterday." William's voice trailed off. This was hitting them both harder than they wanted to admit.

"We should probably keep the crime scene tape up, just in case we need to go through again in light of what the autopsy reveals." Time of death was paramount. Cragmore wasn't that far from Mountain Springs. If the TOD had been early Friday or before, Jackson could have been here before he headed up the mountain with Lucy.

Eli came into the kitchen, which was painted a fresh shade of yellow. Nothing in the kitchen indicated that someone had started to make coffee or begun a morning routine.

Two clean plates and wineglasses rested in the drying rack, signs of a dinner date.

"I've got an officer working the neighborhood to see if they saw anyone coming or going," William offered.

A calendar with pictures of wildflowers hung on the wall. There were three cat stickers on the Saturday, Sunday and Monday of Memorial Day weekend. He lifted the calendar to June. She'd put a cat sticker on Father's Day, as well. That small detail about Jessica, that she marked all the holidays ahead of time with cute stickers, intensified the ache he felt in his chest.

Eli jerked back. Something about the calendar haunted him. He touched the picture of daisies in a field that represented the month of May.

William patted his shoulder. "Why are you looking at the calendar?"

Eli shook his head. His finger trailed over one of the cat stickers. "She didn't have dates with any of the other three suspects. What about with Jackson?"

"That's just it. Her picture never came up on any of the surveillance. We took her laptop in for evidence."

Eli's throat went dry. "That throws a wrench in it." But Jessica did have dark hair and blue eyes.

"I still think it's the same guy. This is too rural an area to think we are dealing with two killers. Nothing in the media ties the deaths together, so it can't be a copycat."

"I agree. We have to figure out what the link is between her and the others." Eli moved toward the hallway and stepped back out on the porch. The street was quiet. In the distance, children laughed and played. A woman on the other side of the street sauntered by with a dog on a leash. Eli's mind whirred a mile a minute. "Do we know where she worked?"

"The paper boy didn't know. The landlord is absentee. She didn't have any family close by as far as we know. Her mom is flying in to identify the body."

Eli trotted down the stairs with William close behind him. He felt a sense of urgency in his stride as he made his way to the car. Now the clock was ticking. They had to find this guy before his path crossed another dark-haired, blue-eyed woman.

The Mountain Springs police station buzzed with activity, most of which centered around all the information-gathering taking place to catch Jessica's killer. Eli rubbed the stubble that had formed on his face. His eyes were blurry from reading the reports over and over. What was he missing?

Officer Nigel Peterson made his way toward Eli's desk. He ran his fingers through his thinning red hair. "I know you're really focused on the big case, but I promised Lucy I would keep you up to speed on her robberies."

Eli sat up a little straighter. Even though O'Bannon and Spitz hadn't let go of their grudge toward Lucy, Officer Peterson had made a concerted effort at attitude change. "What did you find?"

"I told you about her suspicions concerning her high school coach, George Whitmore."

Eli nodded. The thought of anyone harassing Lucy when she was a vulnerable high school student made his blood boil.

"He has never had any charges against him. But

when I talked to some people at the school where he taught after leaving here, they hinted of inappropriate behavior toward the girls he coached." Nigel placed a photograph on Eli's desk. "From the high school yearbook."

Eli stared at the photo of a lean man with dark hair. His grin took up most of his face. "I took fingerprint samples from after Lucy's first robbery, but if he doesn't have a record, he won't be in any databases."

"I can see if I can find a way to get his prints. Maybe he was in the military."

As much as he wanted to resolve Lucy's robberies, he needed to focus on Jessica Mason's murder. "Thank you for doing that, Nigel."

Eli returned to reading the compiled reports for what felt like the hundredth time. He spread the hard copies of the photographs out on his desk. Jessica just looked too much like the others to dismiss her outright, even though she wasn't connected to the dating service.

He tapped a pencil on his desk. If he pulled out the dating service as a factor, what linked the women together besides looks? Maybe Jessica's death was a crime of opportunity.

Eli stroked the stubble on his cheek. He hadn't been home for more than a few hours for the last two days. He had called Lucy at least twice a day. The sound of her voice revived him. The chief had not given him permission to disclose the details of the investigation to Lucy. His gut told him he was close to an arrest. After that, he and Lucy could be together.

Greg Jackson was still unaccounted for. His car had been taken to the impound yard. Authorities had combed the whole area around the lake, and all the local departments in nearby towns were told to notify him right away if they spotted Greg or if an unidentified body was found anywhere.

Eli returned to his notes. Jessica Mason had worked as a manager at a sandwich shop. She had lived in Cragmore for five months and everyone had liked her. Neither coworkers, friends or neighbors said Jessica had ever mentioned being signed up for a dating service. Nothing in her apartment or on her laptop indicated any connection to the online service.

One neighbor had seen a car she hadn't recognized parked Friday night on the block where Jessica lived.

Eli rose to his feet and paced through the station. His stopped at the watercooler, his back to his desk. He filled his cup with water.

William came up behind him. "The officer watching Greg Jackson's place said a taxi just dropped him off at his home. The deputy in Jacob's Corner is picking him up now. Thought you might want to be there for the questioning."

Finally, a break. This could be it. He bent his neck side to side and blinked in an effort to find more energy.

An odd hush permeated the police station. When Eli turned around, Lucy was standing by his desk; a picnic basket rested on the floor beside her. She held one of the victims' photos in her hand. The stiff backs and stares of Officers O'Bannon and Spitz added to the tension of the moment.

The look of devastation on Lucy's face made his knees buckle. He squeezed the paper cup he was holding. "Lucy, what are you doing here?"

She pointed to the picnic basket. "I wanted to surprise you with lunch." Lucy waved the photograph in the air. "What is all this?"

He wasn't going to lie to her. "It's the investigation I was brought in to lead." Eli tossed his paper cup and gathered up the photographs and reports.

"Those women look like me. What is going on?" Her breath caught. "Did Greg Jackson hurt them?"

"I don't know if he did or not. But we are getting close to finding out." He reached out to touch her arm, but she pulled away.

William hovered close by. "We got to go, boss."

Eli held up his hand. "Just a second." He stepped toward Lucy. A punch in the gut would hurt less than the expression on her face. "I wanted to tell you, but we couldn't risk having this guy go underground and start killing again years from now."

"Is that the only reason you spent time with me?" Her eyes glazed. "Because it helped you find your killer?"

"No." His voice broke. What had he done?

"So if you were brought in for the investigation that means you're leaving after it's done. Soon as this guy is caught, you're going back to Spokane, right?"

"That was the original plan." But so much had changed.

"Hawkins, we need to get going," William pressed.

She shook her head. "I trusted you. Was everything you told me a lie?"

"I meant every word I said. Please believe me." He longed to gather her in his arms. "I have to go do this interview. I want to talk later. I can explain."

"I have to go to my brother's murderball tournament

later." Her voice took on the wavering tone of a person trying to hold back tears. "You don't have to explain anything."

Eli watched her stalk out of the police station as a sense of overwhelming despair invaded every part of his being.

THIRTEEN

Eli stared at Greg Jackson hunched over a table in the police station. The station was too small to have an interrogation room, so one of the officers had set up a table and chairs in a quiet corner.

He struggled to clear his mind of thoughts about Lucy. He had wanted to tell her that he would quit his job in Spokane in a heartbeat. That while she had started out as a lead in his case, she had become so much more to him. He'd be a small-town cop if it allowed him to be close to her, but the look on her face had rendered him nearly speechless.

Maybe it would be better if he stayed out of her life. The last thing in the world he wanted to do was hurt her, and yet he had managed to do it over and over.

William patted Eli on the back. "Let's get this done, huh?" He held the envelope that contained the photos of the other victims.

Eli stopped at the water fountain and filled a paper cup.

Greg Jackson's face paled as they advanced toward

him. Eli placed the cup of water on the table. "Thought you might be thirsty."

"Thank you," Jackson whimpered. He crossed his arms and rested his chin on his chest.

Eli slipped into the chair opposite Jackson while William remained standing. "Do you know why you are here?"

"'Cause you think I tried to hurt Lucy."

Eli had assumed that Jackson would be fixated on Lucy's accident. That line of questioning served as a warm-up to asking him about the other women. He leaned forward, hoping the action would force Jackson to make eye contact. "Did you?"

Greg's glance flickered up, but then he stared at the table. "Not on purpose. It's just that…" He ran a claw-like hand through his hair. "I wanted her to have feelings for me."

"You say you care about her." Eli rested his hands on the table. "Why did you take the canoe and leave her in the lake?"

"I know I have an anger problem. I was afraid of getting out of control." The cup shook in his hand as he took a sip of water. "I knew she was a good swimmer. I thought she would be okay."

Eli shifted in his chair. He could still only see Greg's profile, making it hard to read his facial expression. "Did you try to drown her, hold her under?"

Greg swung around in his chair. "She just made me so upset. I saw how out of control I was, so I left." He licked his lips.

"You tried to drown her," Eli pressed.

Jackson stared at the ceiling. "I might have pushed her down."

"You held her under?"

Greg blinked and then closed his eyes. "Yes, but I stopped. I left."

William moved in closer. The envelope he held crinkled in his hand. "Why didn't you go back to the camp?"

"Because I was ashamed." Greg scooted his chair back and bent his chin toward his chest. "I didn't want to see Lucy. I didn't want to face the others."

William stood behind Eli. "Where did you go?"

"I rowed to shore. I wandered through the forest until I found a camper to take me into town."

"A camper. What was his name?" Eli asked.

For the first time, Greg looked directly at Eli. "Why do you want to know? Lucy did make it to shore okay, didn't she?" Jackson's concern seemed genuine.

"She's fine. What was the name of the camper?"

"He said his name was Joe. I don't remember his last name. I think it started with a *T.* He drove a jeep, and he said he worked as a carpenter in Mountain Springs."

The details of his answer were too specific to be lies. "Why didn't you come back for your car?"

"I didn't want to have to face Lucy, don't you understand?" His fist hit the table with a halfhearted thump. "I was ashamed of the way I acted. I just thought if I could get her alone and talk to her, she would see how much I liked her."

"Where have you been for the last two days?"

"I went to a hotel. I needed to think things through." Greg's breathing had become labored enough for the rise and fall of his chest to be noticeable.

Eli stared at Greg, hoping it might unhinge him. Greg scooted his chair forward and then back again. He was capable of violence, but was he capable of murder? Eli lifted his chin as a signal to William.

William pulled photographs of the victims from the envelope and laid them on the table. "Do you know any of these women?"

Greg studied each photograph. "They all look like Lucy, but not as pretty." He placed a finger on one of the photographs. "I had a date with her. All she did was talk about her ex-husband." He lifted the picture of Jessica Mason. His cheeks turned tomato-red. "This is about the thing that was in the paper, isn't it? The woman who died in Cragmore. You don't think I would ever…" Greg shook his head in disbelief. "I know that it is wrong to get angry at women, but I wouldn't kill anyone."

William's cell phone rang; he stepped away from the table to answer it.

"Where were you on Friday before you met up with Lucy at her house?"

"Now, that is just too much." Greg pushed the chair back and stood up.

"Sit down," Eli soothed. He was well versed on the games that psychotic killers played when questioned. It was entirely possible that Greg had assumed the role of victim to detract from his guilt.

Greg collapsed back into the chair and rested his face in his hands. "I don't want to be like my dad was with my mom." He rocked back and forth.

Jackson's voice was mournful, filled with agony. Yes, killers like the one they were chasing were adept at mask wearing, but something in Eli's gut told him that Greg was sincere.

William snapped his phone shut, walked over to Eli and whispered, "Can I talk to you for a minute?"

Eli stood up and stepped away from Greg. He huddled with William.

William spoke in a hushed whisper. "Got the finals on the autopsy. The M.E. puts the time of death for Jessica somewhere between late Friday afternoon and early Friday night."

Eli turned back around to look at Greg, whose face was buried in his hands. That would be the time when Greg was with Lucy and then the other campers. "If we can locate the camper who gave Greg a ride into town, it would be impossible for him to have been at Jessica's house."

"Let's assume he has an alibi." William nodded. "Are we back to square one?"

Eli thoughts whirled a mile a minute. Something Greg had said floated back into his mind. "Not quite square one."

William tilted his head toward Greg. "What should we do with him?"

"He admits to holding Lucy under water. We can charge him for that. He's guilty of a lot of things, but I don't think murder is one of them. We need to get back to the station."

After giving instructions about Greg to the local officer, Eli and William left the small station and headed to the car. Eli got into the passenger side of the Volkswagen after removing the papers he had stacked there. Talking to Lucy had flustered him so much, he'd brought the picture of George Whitmore with him. He glanced at the picture of Lucy's high school coach. The image of Jessica's calendar on her wall materialized in his mind. His heartbeat quickened. Everything suddenly clicked into place.

William started up his car. "What is it?"

"You tracked down Jessica's employer, right?"

William nodded. "I have her name in my notes."

"You need to find out exactly what Jessica was doing, where she was Friday afternoon. Why don't you go back to the station and get me the info as quickly as you can."

William eased the car out of the parking lot. "What are you going to do?"

"I have to call Lucy." As Eli dialed Lucy's cell-phone number, an overwhelming concern for her safety invaded his thoughts.

The noise in the high school gym was oppressive. Fans stomped their feet and the wheelchair rugby players rolled out onto the court. Lucy sat between Nelson and Heather. Dawson waved as he glided by on the court. What a ham. Her little brother's smile could brighten an overcast sky.

Heather wrapped her arms through Lucy's. "Your brother is doing so well."

"I was just thinking that myself." Something Eli had said to her floated back into her head. Fear did rule her decisions. She couldn't live in fear of something else bad happening to Dawson or think that she could keep him safe by playing the mother role. When Dawson had had his accident, she'd broken an engagement and put her life on hold. Dawson had recovered fine; she was out of excuses.

She sighed. As upset as she was with him, she had to admit, Eli had been right about a lot of things. She pulled out her cell phone and stared at the photo of her and Eli. She should just delete the picture. He had been deceptive in a big way, too. Why couldn't she let him go?

Nelson passed Lucy some nachos and leaned in to see what she was looking at. "That guy, huh?"

"What, you don't like him?"

"He seems all right, I guess."

Nelson shrugged. On the court, the referee blew the whistle and tossed the ball in the air.

She brushed her finger over the photograph. "I don't know what to think about him."

Nelson took a bite of corn chip and wrapped an arm around Lucy. "I think you should just hang out with your friends and forget about him."

Heather leaned against Lucy. She had to speak directly into Lucy's ear to be heard above the thunder of the game and roar of the crowd. "I disagree. I think you should give him a chance to explain."

"You guys are like having the good angel on one shoulder and the bad angel on the other." She flipped her phone shut. "I just can't figure out who is who."

Though she couldn't hear the ring, her phone vibrated in her hand. She checked the number; Eli was calling her. Her arm muscles tensed as it rang two and then three times. All the anger and hurt she had felt earlier returned. She couldn't talk to him now. The wound was still too new. She clicked off her phone and snapped it shut again.

Best to focus on the game. Dawson stole the ball from an opponent and passed it to a team member. Lucy jumped up and cheered along with the rest of the crowd, but her heart wasn't in it. Thoughts of Eli danced around the edges of her mind. Memories of the warmth of his voice and the way his kiss made her head spin rose to the surface. Why couldn't he just have told her about the investigation? At least now she understood why he had been so protective of her. Had his need to keep her safe turned into something more or had it all been lies? She gritted her teeth. For sure, she wouldn't have let herself fall for him if she'd known he wasn't going to be around long.

An opponent crashed into Dawson's wheelchair, causing one wheel to catch air. Lucy gasped. Heather squeezed her shoulder. "He's all right. You can't control what happens on the court by being afraid and worrying about him from your seat."

Lucy smiled. So many of her reactions were because of fear. Maybe she was afraid of loving Eli because that would mean she risked losing someone again. Lucy sat up a little straighter. She had used the news about the investigation as an excuse to pull away from him. "Thanks, Heather, you gave me my answer. You are the good angel."

She stood up and edged past Nelson in his seat.

Nelson drew his legs up. "Where are you going?" He grimaced.

She leaned over to shout into Nelson's ear to be heard

above the noise of the game. "I have to make an important phone call."

Lucy took the steps up through the bleachers two at a time. The area around the concession stands was a little quieter. She had instantly assumed that if they lived in different cities, the relationship would be impossible. There were rivers in Spokane, too. Maybe she could move to Spokane. Maybe they could make this work long distance. It didn't matter. They would figure it out together.

A small cluster of people swarmed over to the concession window. Lucy walked through the hallways of the school, trying to find a quieter spot. She turned down a corridor.

Most of the high school classrooms were filled with kids. When she peeked inside one of them, it was obvious that a speech and debate competition was going on.

She leaned against the wall and stared at her phone. Her hair fell in front of her face as her finger hovered over the buttons. Sometimes you just had to do things even if you were afraid.

"Lucy Kimbol, it's been a long time."

Lucy looked up. "Coach Whitmore." His big-toothed smile oozed false charm. "What are you doing here?"

"I'm doing some volunteer coaching." He reached up and touched her hair. She jerked back. He leaned toward her. "I'd recognize that dark mane anywhere." One side of his lips curled. "You still playing ball?"

Lucy took two steps back and planted her feet. Even though her heart raced and her legs were shaking, she injected strength into her voice. "I have outgrown playing basketball." And she had outgrown being intimidated by him. "If you'll excuse me, I have things to do."

She whirled around and strode down the slanted ramp. Even though she didn't glance back, she could sense him staring at her.

She turned down another hallway, releasing a heavy breath as she braced her hand against the wall. How easy it was to feel like a defenseless teenager again. Lucy lifted her chin and pushed off the wall. She wasn't defenseless, and she wasn't alone in this world. So much had changed since high school.

She glanced down two diverging hallways. When she had gone to school here, the kids had called this section of the building the labyrinth. Most of it was underground, with no windows and widely spaced lights on the ceiling, half of which were burned out.

One way led to the band room. Judging from the number of people coming up that hallway, the band room was probably being used for speech presentations. The noise up the hallway increased, and kids spilled out of the classrooms. The other hallway would be quieter for talking to Eli.

The end of the hallway led to an open door. Clicking on a light revealed a weight room with wrestling mats. The single light hanging from the center of the ceiling did little to illuminate the dark corners. She had never been in here before, but at least it was quiet.

Lucy sat on a weight bench and dialed Eli's number. The phone rang four times then went to voice mail. Her shoulders slumped. Just when she had worked up the courage to talk to him.

She took in a deep breath to loosen the tension in her

rib cage. She stared again at the picture of her and Eli, heads together, the river glistening in the background.

Her phone rang.

"Did you just try to call me?" Eli's voice sounded frantic.

"Yes, Eli, I—"

"Where are you right now? Who are you with?"

"Eli I have something to say to you, and if I don't say it now, I might lose my courage."

"Where are you at?"

Was he even hearing her? "I told you earlier. I'm at Dawson's tournament."

"Who is there with you?"

The room went dark. Lucy tilted her head. "Just a second, the light just burned out."

She stood up to make her way to the door toward the light that spilled in from the hallway. The door whooshed shut, blocking out all illumination. Lucy's foot caught on the corner of a mat; she stumbled, managing to catch herself before she fell. Her phone flew out of her hand and skittered out in front of her someplace in the darkness.

She dropped down on her knees, sweeping her hand in wide arcs as she felt for her phone. She worked her fingers along the hard, cold vinyl of a mat.

Her shoulder brushed against a piece of exercise equipment, and then her head rammed into another part of the machine. She winced as the pain radiated through her scalp. She sat up, rubbing the sore spot on her forehead.

The silence enveloped her. Her throat went dry. Lucy fought to make out even outlines in the dim room. She blinked. If she just gave it a minute, her eyes would adjust. A thought nagged her just below the surface of awareness, but she refused to give in to it.

Again on her hands and knees, she swept the area around her. No phone. No matter how hard she tried not to think about it, the sequence of events streamed through her head. Her pulse drummed in her ears. It was normal for a lightbulb to suddenly burn out. But as she replayed what had just happened, she knew that doors did not close by themselves in a place where there was no wind.

Lucy felt the object in front of her. The cold metal of a weight bench. With her heart racing, she slipped onto the bench. She tapped her feet on the wooden floor, willing objects to be discernible in the blackness. Was there someone else in the room with her?

This part of the school was far away from the activity that was going on. She stopped tapping her feet. Despite her effort at not allowing the thoughts to fully blossom, memories of being attacked in her own home came back. That assailant had used darkness as a weapon, too.

"Coach Whitmore?" she whispered.

Lucy scanned from right to left. She listened. She squeezed her eyes shut. Her body trembled with fear.

Come on, Lucy, pull it together.

In an effort to slow her racing heart, she took in two deep, slow breaths. There had to be an explanation. Could someone have seen the light on, switched it off and closed the door without noticing that she was in here? That had to be it. Seeing Coach Whitmore had just spooked her.

The tightness between her shoulders let up. She just

needed to get to the door, open it and turn on the light. She rose to her feet and moved in the direction where the door and light switch would most likely be.

Even though she swung her hands out in front of her, she ran into pieces of equipment. A metal bar grazed the side of her head. Her foot rammed against a stack of free weights.

She reached out. The door had to be around here somewhere. Her hand touched the bumpy surface of the wall, and she felt along it. She continued to pat the wall. Her finger touched the sleek paper of a poster. She hadn't been in the room long enough to note where things were. The wall came to an end, and she followed along the second wall. There were only four walls. Sooner or later, she would find the door.

The sound of metal tinkling against metal caused every muscle in her body to contract. Her breath caught. Someone was moving through the room and must have bumped against the exercise equipment. Lucy turned in the direction she'd heard the noise. Her heart raced.

Frantic, she felt up and down the wall. She patted quickly across the surface until she found a hinge. She reached across the expanse of metal at the height where the doorknob should be. She breathed in a shallow, quick breath.

Her finger wrapped around the metal of the door-knob. She angled her wrist and turned.

A sound that was almost like rush of wind surrounded her, and then a hard mass bashed into her. Lucy fell, hitting the floor on her back. Shock waves of pain burst out from her spine. She couldn't breathe.

The wind had been knocked out of her. She wheezed in air that felt like it was filled with pebbles.

Her body shuddered from the impact as she lay in the darkness.

Even before she could catch her breath, a cold grip like iron wrapped around her wrist. She struggled to break free, clawing at his arm with her free hand. Her attacker grabbed her at the collar and pulled her close. His hot breath stained her face. She angled away so she was on her stomach. He clamped onto her arm and twisted it behind her back, pushing upward.

Her muscles flared from the pain. Why was this man doing this to her?

"Please," she cried.

Her stomach pressed against the hardwood floor. Did he mean to kill her or just torment her?

"Whhyyyyyy?" she sputtered.

A foot jabbed into her back. He grabbed her wrists and slipped something around them. When she wiggled to get away, he smashed his boot harder against her spine.

She moaned in protest as the shock of pain immobilized her.

"What…what…are you going to do?"

Her cheek pressed against the cool floor. She waited for her breathing to even out. Her shoulder and arm muscles strained.

Her assailant finished tying her hands with a final jerk to tighten the knot. The weight lifted off her back. She angled to one side to try to get up. The coolness of metal grazed her neck. He had a gun.

There was no way she could get away from this man.

FOURTEEN

Eli gripped the steering wheel and pressed the accelerator even harder. He tried Lucy's cell one more time. It went straight to message. He didn't know Dawson's number.

Mountain Springs wasn't that big. How many places could they hold a tournament anyway? He slowed as he drove past a workout place that he knew had a basketball court. There were only a few cars in the lot.

Eli hit his blinker and pulled into a parking lot. He had no idea where the high school was in this town, but it seemed like the most likely place for a tournament.

He phoned the police station. He recognized Officer Spitz's gravelly voice. William must have gone somewhere to track down the information he needed. Eli alerted Spitz to the situation and got directions to the high school.

"Who did you say might be in some kind of trouble?" Spitz cleared his throat.

"Lucy Kimbol."

Eli counted four seconds of silence on the other end of the line.

"I am really concerned. We got cut off from a phone conversation. I heard a scream." Eli kept his voice in a monotone to subdue his ire. He had spoken to all the men about this. It didn't matter what the department thought of Lucy. An officer was sworn to keep everyone safe regardless of their feelings about that person.

"I'll send some…some men over," Officer Spitz stuttered.

Eli stared at the ceiling of his car. Could the guy sound any more reluctant? "This is your chance to prove to Lucy that help comes when it is needed, and that you learned something from the incident four years ago." He turned the key in the ignition.

"You don't know the whole history of this thing."

"History doesn't matter." Eli fought to keep his voice level.

"I said we'll get some men out there."

Eli hung up the phone. He pressed the accelerator and pulled out onto the street.

Please, God, let her be all right.

He steadied his own breathing. The five-block drive to the high school felt like a million miles. He parked his car and jumped out. The first door he tried was locked. He circled the building to the side that faced a football field and tried another door. He stepped into a long hallway.

The boom of a cheering crowd filtering down the hallway told him he was in the right place. He stepped into the gym. He scanned the crowd, not honing in on anyone who looked familiar.

The wheelchairs sailed down the court. Eli picked out Dawson in a red jersey just as the ball was passed to him. He walked to one side of the bleachers and searched the crowd on the opposite side. He held only a glimmer of hope that his panic had been unfounded and that he would see Lucy's beautiful face at any moment.

Someone tapped him on the shoulder.

He swung around to face a teenage girl with fat red cheeks and round glasses. "You're Lucy's renter. I'm one of her students, Marnie. I come out to her house for lessons."

"Yes, do you know where she is?"

The girl angled her head around Eli so she would have a clearer view of the court and stands. "I saw her in the hallway earlier. I was waiting for my turn to do my speech, and she walked by. I don't think she noticed me, though."

His heart skipped a beat. "Where at? Which way?"

"I can show you." The girl pivoted and headed toward the door. She led him down a series of hallways and then stopped in front of a closed door. "I was in this room. The door was open. We hadn't started yet."

"You saw her pass by?"

"She had her phone in her hand. She looked really happy about something, like glowing." Marnie sighed. "Miss Kimbol is nice, but she always seems like a person who worries about things. It was cool to see her so happy."

"Which way was she going?"

Marnie pointed. "That hallway branches off and you either end up in the band room or the wrestling room."

Eli raced down the ramp. A check of the band room revealed lots of teenagers, but no Lucy and no one who had seen her. He jogged back up the hallway to where it split off, and headed down the second hallway.

He turned the knob on the door, leaned in and flicked on a light. Exercise equipment, discarded T-shirts and wrestling mats filled his field of view.

The room was empty.

Lucy sat in the darkness with the smell of her own perfume heavy in the air. She'd been tied up and blindfolded with the scarves that had been stolen from her place; the aroma of her perfume was still evident on them. Her wrists hurt from being bound so tightly. How much time had passed since he had brought her here? An hour maybe. Her kidnapper moved around the room. She picked out some distinct noises: the sear of something hitting a hot frying pan, a faucet running, feet stomping on wood.

He'd dragged her out a back door of the school and across a nearly empty parking lot. He hadn't blindfolded her until he'd thrown her in the back of the car and told her to be quiet.

Even though she hadn't been able to see, she had tried to pay attention to when the car had turned and what noises she'd heard. They had driven maybe twenty minutes. When he'd pulled her from the car, the scent of pine was heavy in the air and the ground was mushy beneath her feet. She was probably in a cabin not far from Mountain Springs. What were the chances of anyone finding her? There must be a dozen cabins that close to town. Lucy curled her bound hands into fists, refusing to give in to despair. There had to be a way to escape.

She bent her elbows in an effort to loosen her bindings, which only made her shoulders hurt. With her fingers, she scraped the area around her and felt fabric, probably a quilt. She had heard the creak of springs when he had tossed her here.

Judging from the loudness of the noises, the cabin must have had an open layout. The salty scent of ham cooking filled the air, and she heard more footsteps. Things were being mixed and stirred. Even before he had spoken, she had known who her kidnapper was. All the pieces had fallen into place. He had been the one stalking her in high school, and he had started again when he'd returned to Mountain Springs.

"Are you hungry?" A cupboard door slammed.

A chill crept over her body when he spoke. "I could use some water." Her words were strained.

She heard running water, and a moment later, he stomped across the floor. His touch on her neck made her recoil. The rim of a glass pressed against her lips and she drank. Her throat felt like it had been clawed by a cat.

He pulled the glass away.

"Why are you doing this?"

"Because I love you. I've always loved you."

His voice made her skin crawl. "I wish I could at least see."

"All right, my love." His rough fingers grazed her temples as he slipped the scarf off the top of her head. "Better?"

She nodded and looked into the face of her stalker, Nelson Thane. He had hidden his obsession beneath a veneer of friendliness and concern. As a high school student, she had sensed on some instinctual level that she didn't want to continue a romantic relationship with him, and now she knew why. All this time she had assumed Coach Whitmore, who was so blatant in his advances, had been harassing her in high school. The coach was probably more posturing than action. Instead her stalker had been quiet and polite, a perfect gentleman.

Nelson's lips curled. He glanced around the cabin. "You like it."

All the windows had thick curtains on them. The cabin was sparse in furnishings but she recognized her things, taken from her house, spread out on a dresser: her book, her jewelry and her fly rod. She craned her neck, trying to see what else he had taken. She recognized a picture frame that she thought she had just misplaced. He must have been in her place more times than when she had caught him. All the items were arranged in a tidy pattern. In the kitchen, the distance between the chairs at the table looked like it had been measured to make sure they were spaced at equal distance. She'd be hard-pressed to find a crumb or speck of dust on the floor.

He planted a chair about four feet from her, grabbed a plateful of food from the kitchen counter and sat down to face her. "Are you sure you're not hungry?"

She shook her head.

"You know what I love most about you, Lucy?" He took a bite of ham, making smacking sounds as he chewed. "Your face, so beautiful. And your purity, so untouched, so clean." He reached out and brushed a hand over her cheek. "That is the way you should stay." His teeth showed when he spoke.

Lucy jerked away from his touch as her heartbeat quickened.

He stabbed another piece of ham with his fork. "Sometimes my desire for you was so strong, I had to find…a substitute."

Her throat constricted. What was he talking about? Her memory flashed on the photographs that had been spread out on Eli's desk.

She could not form the words in her head. Nelson continued to chew, careful to dab his mouth with a napkin after almost every bite. She let out a moan that was almost a scream. Who was this monster in front of her?

Nelson chattered, oblivious to her increasing terror. "I was okay with being your friend. The online dating thing only bothered me a little. I could tell you didn't like those guys." His voice dropped half an octave. "But then he came along, and I saw the two of you at the river."

Lucy couldn't get a deep breath. Nelson's jealousy of Eli had led to the attack in her place. "Eli is a good detective. He'll find me."

Nelson grinned. "I'm counting on that. He's a smart man, and I think I left enough clues. My landlady has a big mouth. The gun I brought isn't for you." Nelson stopped eating and studied Lucy, his eyes cutting through her. "It's for him."

Lucy's stomach roiled. She tasted bile and her eyes watered. "Why?"

He jumped to his feet, threw his plate against the wall and shouted, "Because you are supposed to love me!"

She leaned away from him as the shattering of glass echoed in her ear.

Nelson crumpled at her feet, gripping her legs and peering up at her. "Why can't you look at me like you looked at him?"

His fingers dug into her knees, and she steeled herself, trying not to pull back and reveal her repulsion.

"Nelson, this isn't right—you have to stop." How long did she have before Eli found the cabin and ran straight into his death?

He reached up and ran the back of his hand over her cheek. She pressed her feet harder into the floor and closed her eyes.

Stop touching me.

"Please, Nelson," she whispered. "Don't do this to him."

He rose to his feet and sauntered over to the window, pulling back the dark curtain. "I'm sure he'll be here any minute."

Lucy took in a shallow, sharp breath. It felt like a weight was on her chest. She had to do something. Her feet were still free. She could run, try to knock Nelson over and escape to warn Eli.

Nelson strutted back to the counter, where his hands brushed over the gun, a reminder to her of who held all the power. He glanced in her direction. His eyes became narrow slits.

He stepped away from the counter, leaving the gun. She leaned forward to get more comfortable. He sprang across the room.

He made a *tsk*ing sound and shook his head. "Lucy, always planning and scheming. You think I don't know what you were trying to do." He waggled his finger.

Maybe running right now wasn't such a good idea.

Still, she could watch and wait. Sooner or later, he would have a moment of inattention when she could knock him over and get to the door. He might turn his back or even leave the room. All she needed was a few seconds.

"I'm thinking it would be better if you remained in the dark." He lifted the blindfold off the bedpost.

"No, please." How could she hope to help Eli if she couldn't see?

Lucy shook her head and angled away as Nelson tried to slip the scarf back over her eyes. She turned sideways on the bed. He clamped her forearm and yanked her up. His fingers found her neck and suctioned around it. His face was inches from hers.

"Don't. You. Dare." His fingers pressed hard against her throat. She flinched as his spit splattered on her cheeks.

She gurgled. Even as she fought for air, she narrowed her eyes at him. Whatever it took, she would keep Eli alive.

He increased the pressure on her neck. "Don't be so defiant. You are not as strong as you think you are."

He let go of her neck. She gasped. He slipped the blindfold over her eyes. Darkness augmented the thrumming of her heartbeat in her ears. She scooted away from him. She rocked back and forth, praying for strength, praying she would not give up hope, praying for a miracle.

The hours ticked by. Lucy could hear Nelson walking around, turning the pages of a book, opening and closing the refrigerator.

Fog filled her brain, and she nodded off. She lay on

the bed and pulled her feet up, sleeping fitfully. When she awoke, she heard the sound of a radio as he flipped through stations, maybe searching for some news about the kidnapping. Radio voices surrounded by static faded in and out.

She wiggled on the bed causing the springs to squeak. Her shoulders ached from having her hands pulled back behind her. The heaviness of sleep crept into her limbs, and she drowsed off again. Images of Eli being shot invaded her dreams.

When she turned slightly on the bed to get more comfortable, she felt something warm on her arm. A moment later, she realized her arm was bleeding. Pushing with her feet, she wiggled around on the bed until she felt something hard; a piece of the broken plate Nelson had thrown against the wall. If it was sharp enough to cut skin, it might be sharp enough to cut through the scarf.

She repositioned herself and angled the piece of porcelain until she felt the tension of it pressing against her bindings.

Nelson paced the floor. At one point, she thought she heard a door open. She sliced at the fabric, not even sure if she was making progress. The bindings seemed to be getting looser. The shard dug into her fingers, and she shuddered as fresh blood oozed from a cut.

She heard the steady creak of a rocking chair for what seemed like hours and then it slowed. Nelson's heavy breathing told her he had fallen asleep.

Lucy pulled at her wrists and moved them up and down. The restraints still felt tight; her shoulder muscles burned. She continued to tear through the fabric.

Sometime in the night, Nelson rose from the chair, walked across the floor and touched her hair. She lay on her side, so her wrists were not visible. Nelson kissed her forehead.

Lucy held her breath and waited for the sounds of his fading footsteps. He hovered over her. His clothes rustled.

Just go away. Get away from me.

Finally, he walked away, and she heard the creak of the rocking chair again. She sawed the jagged porcelain across the fabric. The listlessness of sleep permeated her mind and then her muscles. Her cutting slowed and she drowsed.

Eli parked the SUV he was driving on the side of the mountain road. He spoke into the two-way radio. "We stop here and hike in the rest of the way. We don't want to risk him hearing us coming."

William clicked on his night-vision goggles and pushed open the passenger-side door. A female officer got out of the backseat.

It had taken precious time to get the warrant to search Nelson Thane's place, to locate the cabin and to track Jessica's movements the day she died. On her last day alive, Jessica had delivered sandwiches to a teacher's workshop in Cragmore that Nelson had been attending.

Eli put on his night-vision goggles, too. Staging this in the dark had its advantages. Nelson would be tired by now, maybe even sleeping. There was less chance of detection.

A second vehicle pulled up. Officers O'Bannon, Spitz and Peterson got out.

Officers Spitz and O'Bannon had been cooperative. Another officer named Clark had been pulled from a town ten miles from Mountain Springs. Peterson had insisted on being part of the team. "To make things right," he had said.

"When we get within a hundred yards of the house, get off the road. O'Bannon and Spitz to the back of the house. Peterson and Clark cover the sides. Springer and I will go in by the front. I don't know how many exit points we are dealing with. He may try to run." He swallowed to clear the lump in his throat. "He may try to harm Lucy."

William slapped Eli's back. "We'll get her out."

Eli squared his shoulders. "Yeah, we will." His heart hammered at a frantic rate. He pushed from consciousness images of harm coming to Lucy and focused on the road in front of him. Whatever it took, he was not going to lose Lucy.

His hand brushed over his pistol in its holster. Up ahead, the murky glow of a barely discernible light caused the men and woman to slip into the darkness of the forest.

Lucy jerked awake. How much time had passed? Ten minutes or five hours? She had no way of knowing. Nelson wasn't making any noise. The drip-drip-drip of water hitting the stainless steel sink pressed on her ears.

The skin on her fingers stung from where she had cut it. Where was Eli? Despair threatened to overtake her. What were Nelson's plans for her? He had spared her once, but he had killed all those other women.

Lucy shivered as she propped herself up to a sitting position. "Nelson?"

No reply.

She jerked forward and rose to her feet, wobbling slightly. She swept her feet in half circles in front of her to detect where the furniture was. A door creaked open. Footsteps echoed across the floor.

The scent of cologne and hair gel surrounded her. "Trying to escape again, huh?"

All the air left her lungs.

Nelson was breathing heavily as though he had run a great distance.

He pulled the blindfold off, digging his fingernails into her forehead. "I've been watching the forest. They're on their way. I'm sure he'll be the first one through the door. Do you want to watch him die?"

Blood trickled past her temple. He pushed her into the kitchen, yanked open a drawer and pulled out some duct tape. She pressed the heels of her hands together hoping he wouldn't notice that the fabric was frayed where she had been cutting it.

He put the gun in a holster around his waist. Sweat glistened on his forehead as he forced her back to the bed, pushed her down and placed a knee on her stomach.

When she angled to get away, he increased the pressure on her chest. He tore off a length of duct tape and used his teeth to make a small tear in it.

He smashed the duct tape against her mouth. "You'll be able to watch, but you won't be able to warn."

Grabbing her by the collar, he pulled her to a sitting position. Lucy's heart pounded as tears and blood trailed down her face.

Nelson cranked open a window. "I'll be able to hear them coming," he explained. He kicked the door shut with his foot and pulled the gun from its holster. He positioned himself behind the door so that when it was flung open he would have a clear shot at the man's back—Eli's back. "I know that Mr. Hero will be the first one in. I just know it."

While she worked her wrists up and down to break free of the tightly tied scarves, she memorized the layout of the cabin. The door that led to the road and one window lined the south-facing wall. On the other side was a door that probably led to the bathroom. There might be a small window in there, but the kitchen had no windows or back door.

Nelson adjusted his hand on the gun and pressed his back against the wall.

The silence was oppressive. Eli must be moving in on foot. Who had come with him? Could she even hope that the Mountain Springs Police Department would help when they found out she was the kidnap victim?

Lucy's breathing became labored. She fought to keep her shoulders still while she worked her hands loose. If she could free herself in time, she could get the duct tape off and scream a warning to Eli. She had no way of knowing if Nelson would shoot her or not. It was a chance she had to take. She'd do anything to save Eli. With her fingers she felt a weakness in the fabric. As she increased the size of the tear, the bindings loosened.

Nelson pushed away from the wall. He had taken off his shoes at the door, his stocking feet barely making noise as he tiptoed to the window. Using the barrel of the gun, he pulled the curtain back and peered outside.

Lucy leaned forward to see out the window. She caught only a flash of darkness.

"What do you suppose is taking him so long?" A subtext of panic girded his words.

Her throat was raw from crying, and the duct tape made it hard to breathe.

Nelson whirled around and glared at her with the coldest eyes she had ever seen. She froze, fearing that he would notice that she had been working at getting her hands free. Sweat stung her eyes as her heart pounded with an insane intensity. She steeled her gaze and looked right at him. She was not about to let him see her fear.

Nelson turned. This time when he looked out the window, his shoulder spasmed. She detected a twitch in his cheek when he glanced at her. He'd seen something. He took long strides across the floor and slammed his back against the wall behind the door. He adjusted the grip on the gun as he raised it.

Lucy's leg muscles tensed. She leaned forward, not daring to take in a breath. Nelson's gaze darted to the window and then back to Lucy.

The door burst open. A man ran in. The blast of a gun enveloped Lucy. Glass shattered.

FIFTEEN

Eli kicked open the door and pressed his back against the south-facing wall. His heart lurched when he saw Lucy bound and gagged on the bed.

In the same instant that Nelson stepped from behind the door, William burst through the window. Nelson averted his gaze toward William, causing the gun to jerk up. The glass lamp beside Eli shattered into a thousand pieces.

Eli lunged toward Nelson, circling his waist and knocking him to the floor. The gun fell out of Nelson's hand and skittered across the floor. The footsteps of the other officers coming in thundered on the floorboards. William scrambled to his feet to help subdue Nelson.

Eli raced across the room to Lucy.

He cupped her face in his hands. "Are you all right? Did he hurt you?"

Her face was bloody and tearstained. She pulled her hands from behind her back and tossed a shredded scarf to the floor. She wrapped her arms around him.

Eli's throat tightened from the strength of the emotions he felt. He buried his face in her hair, drowning in her sweet honey scent. "I'll do whatever it takes to stay here with you. I meant it when I said I wouldn't leave you."

She pulled back and gazed at him with those blue eyes. She reached up to peel the duct tape off her mouth.

He brushed her hand away. "Let me." Slowly, gently he removed the tape.

"Nelson was going to kill you." She touched shaking fingers to her lips.

"But he didn't." He went to grab her hand and then noticed the cuts. The rage over what Nelson had done returned. "I thought you said he didn't hurt you."

"I did that. To cut myself loose."

"Wait here." Eli rummaged through cupboards, looking for a first-aid kit.

The other men took a handcuffed Nelson out of the cabin.

Eli returned to Lucy and sat on the bed beside her. "Give me your hand."

Her skin felt like silk against his calloused hand. She leaned toward him as he placed a Band-Aid on the cut. The look of warmth and affection on her face drew him in.

Lucy shook her head. "All these years, I thought it was somebody else. I have to tell the coach I'm sorry. I need to apologize to O'Bannon and Spitz, too, for pointing the finger at their friend."

"You were just a scared kid looking for help." Eli held her hand, brushing his thumb over each of her knuckles.

"Still, I need to own my part in what caused this mess. It should go a long way toward mending things between us." Lucy leaned closer to Eli. "Why didn't I see what Nelson was doing?"

"Nobody could have seen it. He hid it well. The key was the calendar in Jessica's house. All the women died on school holidays. We found Nelson's laptop. He was signed up with the dating service under a different name. He lied about where he lived so he fell outside the parameters of the profile. Nelson killed Jessica on impulse because she looked so much like you."

Lucy shuddered and instinctually Eli tightened his embrace.

"Something Greg said made me realize the robberies were connected to the killing. When we showed him the pictures of the other women he said, 'They all look like Lucy, only not as pretty.' Nelson's obsession with you was the reason for his crimes. You weren't just one more potential victim. You were the whole focus of the crimes."

Lucy gasped and her hand fluttered to her neck. "Those poor women."

"You're safe now," Eli said. "Something must have triggered the escalation to him kidnapping you."

"I fell in love, and he saw it when I was at Dawson's game. That's why he attacked me in my place after we went fishing. That's why he wanted…he wanted to hurt you." Her fingers touched his lips.

"You fell in love?" he asked.

"Yes." She tilted her head, put her hand on the back of his neck and pulled him toward her. "With you," she said as their lips met.

EPILOGUE

The drive out to the river where Eli knew he would find Lucy went by in a flash. Several of her students lined up on the rocky beach. The trees had just begun to turn gold and red. Lucy pushed a boat away from the shore. She stepped into the boat and lifted the oar. She set the oar down when she saw Eli coming toward her.

Four months had passed since Nelson had been arrested. Eli had testified at his trial less than a week ago and Thane soon would be sentenced and locked away. It was over. Lucy was safe. The investigation no longer stood between him and the woman he loved. Today, the things Nelson had taken out of Lucy's place had been released from the evidence room.

Eli splashed through the river, oblivious to the autumn chill of the water. He grabbed the boat.

Lucy laughed. "What is all this about? Did the chief say they would hire you so you can be a small-town cop?"

In the months they had waited for the trial, Eli had been back and forth to Spokane. Even though she was open to the idea, he couldn't take Lucy away from this river and people who loved her. Eli shook his head. "I got a better idea." He pulled the boat toward him, savoring the delight he felt at being close to her.

She placed a warm palm on his cheek. "So you didn't get the job, but you are still excited."

"I don't know why I didn't think of it sooner."

A mystified expression crossed her beautiful features. "What are you talking about?"

"You said that originally this business was supposed to be run by you and your brother."

"It would be a lot easier, sure. With extra help, I could grow the business. Dawson was supposed to be my partner, but…"

"Not Dawson. Me."

"But you're a cop. It's what you do."

"I have not only fallen in love with you, I've fallen in love with this river." His heart raced in anticipation of what he was about to say. "Lucy?"

A sudden breath escaped her lips. "Yes." She sat up straighter.

He pulled a small envelope out of his pocket. The envelope he had gotten out of the evidence room this morning. "I want to be your business partner." He opened the bag and pulled out Lucy's grandmother's ring. "And I would love it if we could do it as man and wife."

Lucy gazed at him; her blue eyes sparkled. "Oh, Eli."

He slid the ring on her finger. "I thought we could get married here at the river. The place where I first knew I loved you."

Lucy's eyes grew wide and round. She nodded then lunged toward Eli, wrapping her arms around him. She knocked him backward. They fell into the knee-deep water, laughing. The sun hinged on the towering mountains above them. The river, glistening like silver, rippled and swirled around them.

* * * * *

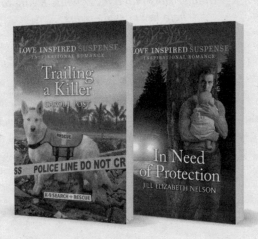

Alaska K-9 state trooper Helena Maddox headed up the grassy embankment within Denali National Park, looking for any sign indicating her estranged twin, Zoe, had been in the area recently. Upon reaching the crest, she knelt beside her K-9, Luna, a Norwegian elkhound. She ran her fingers through the animal's fluffy silver-gray fur before opening the evidence bag and offering it to her partner.

"This is Zoe. Seek Zoe. Seek!"

Luna buried her dark face in the bag, taking in the scent of a scarf Zoe had left behind well over a year ago, then lifted her nose to the air, sniffing as the gentle July breeze washed over them.

"Seek Zoe," she repeated as she released the K-9 from her leash, giving her room to roam.

Gazing upward, Helena caught a glimpse of the tallest peak in America. Denali never failed to steal her breath. Today she couldn't see as much of the mountain as she would have liked, thanks to the low clouds hinting at an upcoming storm. But this wasn't a leisurely visit.

She'd driven straight from Anchorage after receiving the uncharacteristic call from her fraternal twin sister.

Helena? I'm in big trouble— The connection had abruptly ended, and each time Helena had tried to call the number back, the phone went straight to voice mail. Zoe's full mailbox was not accepting messages.

Why would Zoe be out here? Was she working at one of the hotels? That made more sense than the thought of her communing with nature.

She glanced around again, searching for Luna. The dog's zigzag pattern indicated she was still searching for Zoe's scent, her hunt drawing her several yards away.

Helena was headed toward Luna when the sharp crack of a rifle rang out. At that exact moment, she was hit hard from behind and sent face-first to the ground in a bone-jarring thud.

Don't miss
Tracking Stolen Secrets *by Laura Scott,*
available August 2021 wherever Love Inspired Suspense books and ebooks are sold.

LoveInspired.com

LOVE INSPIRED
INSPIRATIONAL ROMANCE

UPLIFTING STORIES OF FAITH, FORGIVENESS AND HOPE.

Join our social communities to connect with other readers who share your love!

Sign up for the Love Inspired newsletter at **LoveInspired.com** to be the first to find out about upcoming titles, special promotions and exclusive content.

CONNECT WITH US AT:

Facebook.com/LoveInspiredBooks

Twitter.com/LoveInspiredBks

Facebook.com/groups/HarlequinConnection